"A child stands on a stepladder beneath a tree in his mother's garden; he is an evacuee, home for a day. Pressing his lips to each ripe fruit in turn he whispers, 'Don't fall, pomegranate, till I come back again!' A minute later he is dead, killed by the blast from the new American bomb; it is August 6, 1945. . . . We do not know whether Ibuse imagined this or whether it is true; or rather, we know that it is true in the sense that Ibuse convinces us in every word he writes that this is how it was and this is how people endured it."
—*Observer*

"Immensely effective. . . . This is a book which *must* be read."—*Books and Bookmen*

"One of the finest postwar novels we have seen in this country."—*Times Literary Supplement*

"Warm understanding, a keen sense of humor and a great compassion that lifts the story above the mere documentary level into the realm of true literature."
—*Japan Times*

"I would recommend *Black Rain* to every reader, even the squeamish."—*Spectator*

"Its subtle ironies and noble, unsentimental pity are a reminder of the strengths of Japanese fiction."
—*New Statesman*

"Excellent translation of an important novel."
—*Library Journal*

BLACK RAIN

MASUJI IBUSE

Translated by
JOHN BESTER

KODANSHA INTERNATIONAL
Tokyo • New York • London

Black Rain first appeared in installment form in the *Japan Quarterly.*

Distributed in the United States by Kodansha America, Inc., 114 Fifth Avenue, New York, N.Y. 10011, and in the United Kingdom and continental Europe by Kodansha Europe Ltd., 95 Aldwych, London WC2B 4JF. Published by Kodansha International Ltd., 17-14 Otowa 1-chome, Bunkyo-ku, Tokyo 112, and Kodansha America, Inc. Copyright © 1969 by Kodansha International Ltd. All rights reserved. Printed in Japan.

LCC 69-16372
ISBN 0-87011-364-X
ISBN 4-7700-0695-0 (in Japan)
First edition, 1969
First paperback edition, 1979
96 97 98 99 22 21 20 19

TRANSLATOR'S PREFACE 🌿

When I was first asked to translate Masuji Ibuse's *Kuroi Ame* I had considerable doubts. I knew that the work had been acclaimed in Japan, but suspected the critics of prejudice in its favor on account of its subject. Could the author possibly have avoided stridency, sentimentality, melodrama, monotony, and all the other pitfalls? Could such a theme yield, in the widest sense, beauty? Could it, in short, be fashioned into a work of art?

In my ignorance, I underestimated Ibuse. My work has left me with a sense of deep respect for the author, a new understanding of some aspects of the Japanese novel, and fresh insights into a country in which I have lived for fifteen years. However difficult it may have been to render the subtlety of Ibuse's language into English, I believe that the work itself is important both for Japan and for the world.

The work is woven from many different strands. Given such a theme, a lesser author might—to borrow a metaphor from music —have produced no more than a steady, discordant fortissimo. In *Black Rain,* we have a subtle polyphony. That is not simply to say that Ibuse weaves together, around a central theme, the stories of several different people. More important, he creates an interplay between varying moods and between his main and secondary themes. It is from this interplay, rather than from the significance of its theme, that the work derives its value as literature.

The basic material, of course, is drawn from actual records and interviews—to the extent that *Black Rain* might even be called a "documentary novel." It is interesting to know, for example, that Shigematsu Shizuma and his journal really exist, and that Dr. Iwatake is, indeed, alive and practicing today in Tokyo. The horrors, too, are described as they were, without exaggeration (the author, in fact, has been accused of playing them down; but to set down more than he has here was unnecessary and irrelevant to his purpose).

Against its basic theme, the work creates many contrasts. These serve to give the work variety; they are also, I feel, the essence of its success as art. It is the distillation of these conflicting elements that gives it its depth—its beauty, even. A typical example is the way the author invariably balances the horrors he describes with the wry humor for which he has long been famous. At times, the effect this creates is quite indescribable; indeed, until one has become attuned to the characteristic flavor of the work it is sometimes difficult, almost, to accept the humor as really intended. In the same way Ibuse, with infinite nostalgia, sets against the violent destruction of the city the beauty of the Japanese countryside and the ancient customs of its people. Against the mighty, brutal purposes of state, he lays the small, human preoccupations and foibles. Against the threat of universal destruction, he sets a love for, and sense of wonder at life in all its forms. Significantly, it is often at the points in the narrative where one feels these contrasts most strongly—where humor and horror, gentleness and violence come into sharpest conflict—that there occur those moving human vignettes that linger so strongly in the memory after one has finished reading.

It is a truism that the Japanese are not much given to the explicit statement of personal feelings or to extravagant emotional gestures. Ibuse, one of the most Japanese of authors, is no exception. The scene of Shigematsu's reunion with his wife after the bombing may seem at first almost brutally casual to the Western reader. Yet to the sensitive Japanese reader, the spare exchange of questions and answers will be immensely moving, and the rice-cooking pot and small pan that stand by Shigeko's side will symbolize a whole world of traditional values and feeling.

Not only is this approach intensely Japanese—and here, probably, artistically necessary—it is also most effective if one considers the work as a protest against the bomb. More than twenty years later, the author has succeeded in ordering the violent emotions that, as he himself has admitted, the subject once aroused in him. On the one hand, he avoids all emotional political considerations, all tendency to blame or to moralize. On the other, he refrains from bludgeoning the senses into apathy with an unvaried repetition of horrors. In a way that no other book has done, *Black Rain* succeeds in relating the bomb to our own, everyday experience, wherever we may live.

The skill with which the varied elements making up the work are organized becomes more and more apparent as one's reading progresses. The narrative moves backwards and forwards in time, the moment of the bomb's dropping, the crucial point around which the whole work revolves, occuring to great effect in many different guises throughout the book. The Imperial broadcast ending the war, mentioned in the very first chapter, is reintroduced in the last chapter in a moving scene that creates the effect of a wheel that has turned full circle. In the same way, themes at first apparently irrelevant—such as the carp-rearing scenes—gradually reveal their symbolic significance for the author as the work progresses. The work is in the tradition of the discursive "I-novel"—a chunk of life is presented for our inspection without overt comment or a very obvious "plot"—but its "discursions" are peculiarly well organized. And the suggestion of life going on after the novel is finished has, in this context, a fresh significance, together with an added poignancy in the awareness that, for the first time, that continuity is actually threatened.

Black Rain is a portrait of a group of human beings; of the death of a great city; of a nation crumbling into defeat. It is a picture of the Japanese mind that tells more than many sociological studies. Yet more than this, it is a statement of a philosophy. Although that philosophy, in its essence, is neither pessimistic nor optimistic, it seems to me to be life-affirming. Dealing with the grimmest of subjects, the work is not, in the end, depressing, for the author is ultimately concerned with life rather than with death, and with an overall beauty that transcends ugliness of detail. In that sense, I would suggest, *Black Rain* is not a "book about the bomb" at all.

JOHN BESTER

CHAPTER 1 🍂

For several years past, Shigematsu Shizuma, of the village of Kobatake, had been aware of his niece Yasuko as a weight on his mind. What was worse, he had a presentiment that the weight was going to remain with him, unspeakably oppressive, for still more years to come. In Yasuko, he seemed to have taken on a double, or even a triple, liability. That no suitable marriage was in sight for her was a circumstance simple enough in itself. The real trouble was the rumor. Towards the end of the war, it ran, Yasuko had been working in the kitchens of the Second Middle School Service Corps in Hiroshima City. Because of that rumor, the villagers of Kobatake, over one hundred miles to the east of Hiroshima, were saying that she was a victim of radiation sickness. Shigematsu and his wife, they claimed, were deliberately covering up the fact. It was this that made her marriage seem so remote. People who came to make inquiries of the neighbors with an eye to a possible match would hear the rumor, would promptly become evasive, and would end up by breaking off the talks altogether.

On that morning—the morning of August 6—the Service Corps of the Second Middle School in Hiroshima had been listening to an exhortatory address on Temma Bridge, or some other bridge in the west of the city, when the atomic bomb fell. In that instant the boys were burned from head to foot, but the teacher in charge had got the whole party to sing, pianissimo, a patriotic song: "Lay Me Beneath the Waves." When they had finished, he gave the command "Dismiss!" and himself led the way in jumping into the river, which happened to be running high with the tide at the time. The whole party followed suit. Only one pupil had struggled home to tell the tale, and he too, it was said, had died before long.

It seemed likely that this account had come from a member of the Patriotic Service Corps from Kobatake who had got back alive from Hiroshima. Even so, the story that Yasuko had been working in the kitchens of the Service Corps of the Second Middle School in Hiroshima was pure fabrication. Even had she been in the kitchens, it was hardly likely that a girl would have been on the spot when they sang "Lay Me Beneath the Waves." The truth was that she had been working in the Japan Textile Company works at the town of Furuichi outside Hiroshima, where she served as messenger and receptionist to the manager, Mr. Fujita. Between the Japan Textile Company and the Second Middle School there was no connection whatsoever.

Since starting work at Furuichi, Yasuko had been sharing the Shizumas' temporary home at 862, 2-chōme, Senda-machi, Hiroshima, and had traveled to and from the factory on the same Kabe-bound train as Shigematsu. There was no connection whatsoever either with the Second Middle School or with the Service Corps. The only link, if any, was that a former pupil of the school —an army man with the forces in northern China—had written Yasuko a rather fulsome letter of thanks for a gift parcel, and had followed it up with five or six poems, all written by himself. Shigematsu still remembered how, when Yasuko had showed them to his wife, Shigeko had blushed inappropriately for someone of her age, and had said, "Yasuko, these must be what they call '*love poems.*' "

During the war, of course, "irresponsible rumors" had been forbidden by an army edict controlling freedom of speech, and topics of conversation were regulated by means such as the bulletin-boards that were circulated among the inhabitants of each district. Yet once the war was over, rumors and stories of every kind—of holdups, robbery, and gambling, of army stockpiles and men who became rich overnight, of the occupation forces—ran wild, only to be forgotten again, rumors and stories alike, with the passage of time. All would have been well had the rumors about Yasuko likewise passed away once they had had their day. But they refused to do so, and whenever somebody came with inquiries relating to a prospect of marriage, the same well-worn story that she had been in the kitchens of the Hiroshima Second Middle School Service Corps would be served up yet again.

For a while, Shigematsu had entertained an idea of hunting out the arch-villain who had first touched off the irresponsible talk. But apart from Shigematsu and his wife and Yasuko, the only people from Kobatake who had been in Hiroshima when the bomb fell were young men belonging to the Patriotic Volunteer Corps and members of the Service Corps. The Patriotic Volunteer Corps was organized from young men drafted from country districts of the same prefecture to work as laborers on the compulsory dismantling of houses, which was carried out to create fire-breaks in the built-up areas of Hiroshima. The young men from Kobatake were incorporated in a unit known, rather pompously, as the Kōjin unit, because it drew its members from the two districts of Kōnu and Jinseki. Their job was to pull down people's houses. They would saw about four-fifths of the way through every pillar of any size in the house, then attach a stout rope to the ridge-pole and tug, twenty or thirty of them, till the house came tumbling down. Single-storied houses were hard work, and came down piecemeal, with much fuss. Two-storied houses were more obliging, and collapsed in one mighty crash, though the cloud of dust they sent up made approach impossible for a good five or six minutes at least.

Unfortunately, the members of the Kōjin unit and the Service Corps had barely got down to work, having arrived in Hiroshima only the day before, when the bomb fell. Those who were not killed outright were taken, their bodies burned raw all over, to reception centers at Miyoshi, Shōbara, Tōjō, and other places round about Hiroshima. The first party sent from Kobatake to the ruins of Hiroshima consisted of the village firemen, who went there in a charcoal-burning bus. They were followed, early on the morning of the day the war ended, by a party of volunteer workers from the Young Men's Association, who went to the temporary reception centers at Miyoshi, Tōjō and elsewhere to search for injured from the village.

The members of the Young Men's Association who were offering their services were given an official send-off by the village headman, in the presence of the acting president of the Association.

"Gentlemen," he said, "you have our deepest gratitude for giving thus of your services in these busy wartime days. I scarcely need to remind you that the injured whom you will be bringing back with you are blistered with burns over their entire bodies, and to request you, therefore, to take every care not to cause them yet further suffering. It is said that the enemy used what is referred to as a 'new weapon' in his attack on Hiroshima, which instantly plunged hundreds of thousands of blameless residents of the city into a hell of unspeakable torments. A member of the Patriotic Service Corps who escaped with his life from Hiroshima has told me that at that moment when the new weapon wiped out the city he heard countless cries for succor—the voice of those hundreds of thousands of souls—seemingly welling up from beneath the earth. Even the Fukuyama district, which he passed through on his way back, was a burnt-out waste; the keep and the Summer Gallery of Fukuyama Castle had been destroyed in the flames. His heart was wrung, he told me, by the realization of the awfulness of war. . . . Be that as it may, however, it is an unquestionable fact that a war is in progress, and you, as members of a voluntary

labor unit, are proceeding henceforth to bring home your com-
rades-in-arms. I must request you above all, therefore, to take care
not to drop those symbols of your invincible determination to fight
on to the bitter end—your bamboo spears. It is most unfortunate
that I should have to see you off in this hole-in-the-corner manner, addressing my parting words to you in the predawn darkness
without so much as a light, but in view of the prevailing situation I
feel sure that you will understand."

His speech over, he turned to the eighty-odd people who had
come to see the party off. "I hope you will join me," he declared,
raising his arms ready to beat time, "in three rousing cheers to
speed the members of the voluntary labor unit on their way!"

The party split into three groups as it set off, one to go to
Miyoshi, one to Shōbara, and one to Tōjō. They walked in silence
in the wake of the horse-drawn carts carrying their baggage. The
members of the unit bound for Tōjō stopped to eat their lunches
at Yuki, about halfway between Kobatake and Tōjō, seating
themselves for the purpose on the veranda of a farmhouse that
stood by the roadside. As they were eating, an unprecedented
broadcast by His Majesty the Emperor came over the radio inside
the house. When it was finished, they sat for a while in silence.
Then the man who was leading the horse by the reins said:

"The headman's parting speech this morning was rather long,
wasn't it?"

This led, in the natural course of events, to a discussion on what
to do with their bamboo spears, and it was finally decided, by
unanimous agreement, to leave them as a parting gift to the farmer
whose veranda they had made free with.

The reception center at Tōjō was an old building that had
happened to be available. It had two superintendents, but no one
had the least idea of how to set about things. The victims were
sprawled about on the tatami; visual identification was impossible
since their faces, without exception, were burned raw. One of them
was as bald as an egg where he should have had hair, with a single
band of normal skin left; he had apparently had a cotton towel
round his forehead. His cheeks were dangling like an old woman's

breasts. Fortunately, the injured could all hear, and people went round asking each of them his name, which was written in Chinese ink on his bare skin if he was naked, or on any tatters of cloth he might have retained about him. This method, though crude, was necessary if identification was to be possible, since the injured were constantly shifting about in their suffering, groaning all the while.

"What does the doctor think he's up to?" one of the volunteers demanded of a superintendent. "Isn't he going to do anything for them?"

But the doctor himself was reluctant to risk touching patients whose sickness he did not know how to treat. Having no idea of the source of their suffering other than the pain of the burns, he injected six of the injured with a medicine called "Pantopon," which relieved their suffering temporarily. After that, he said, he had no more of the medicine left.

This account had been given to Shigematsu later, after he had come back from Hiroshima, by a member of the volunteer work party. By that time, Shigematsu himself was showing symptoms of radiation sickness. Whenever he applied himself too enthusiastically to working in the fields, he would be overcome by sudden lethargy, and small pimples would appear on his scalp. If he tugged at his hair, it came out, quite painlessly. At such times, he would take to bed for a while and eat plenty of nourishing foods.

The symptoms of radiation sickness usually began with an unexplained lethargy and heaviness of the limbs. After a few days, the hair would come out without any pain, and the teeth would come loose and eventually fall out. Finally, collapse set in and the patient died. The essential thing if one felt lethargy in the early stages of the sickness was to rest and eat well. Those who forced themselves to work gradually wilted, like a pine tree transplanted by a bungling gardener, until finally they expired. In the village next to Kobatake, and in the village beyond that, there had been people who had come home from Hiroshima in the best of health, congratulating themselves on their escape, and had worked their hardest for a month or two, only to take to their beds and die within a week or ten days. The sickness would set in in one particular part of the body, producing the excruciating pain so characteristic of it. The pain in the shoulders and back, too, was incomparably worse than with any other disease.

The visiting doctor diagnosed Shigematsu's case quite explicitly as radiation sickness. Dr. Fujita in Fukuyama pronounced the same diagnosis. Yasuko, however, was a different matter: Yasuko was in no sense sick. She had been examined by a reputable doctor, and she had submitted to one of the periodic check-ups for survivors of the bomb that were given at the local health center. Everything was completely normal—corpuscle count, parasites, urine, sedimentation, stethoscopy, hearing, and so on. This was four years and nine months after the end of the war, when Yasuko had the chance of a match which seemed, if the truth be told, almost too good for her. The prospective husband was the young master of an old family in Yamano village. He must have seen Yasuko somewhere, for a tentative proposal was duly made via a go-between. Yasuko herself had no objection to the match. Shigematsu, who was anxious to ensure that for once things should not be spoiled by rumors of radiation sickness, had a reputable doctor draw up a certificate of health for Yasuko, which he mailed to the go-between.

"This time it'll be all right!" he said somewhat self-importantly. "There's nothing like making doubly sure! People nowadays like to exchange health certificates before they get married. I'm sure they won't think it at all odd. The go-between's the wife of a former army officer, it seems, so she's sure to be used to the modern way of doing things. It'll be all right this time, you'll see!"

In the event, though, he proved to have shown more care than wisdom. The go-between must have come to someone in the village to inquire about Yasuko's health, for a letter came asking about Yasuko's movements in Hiroshima from the day the bomb fell until her return to Kobatake. This was only for the go-between's own information—the letter hastened to add—and was not the result of any contact concerning the subject with the prospective husband.

It dawned on Shigematsu that he had incurred yet another

liability. His wife read the letter and handed it to Yasuko without speaking; she herself sat still for a while, gazing down at the *tatami,* then got up and retired to the box room. Yasuko followed her there. After a while, Shigematsu went and peered in. His wife's face was buried in Yasuko's shoulder, and they were both sobbing quietly to themselves.

"All right, then—I was wrong for once," he said. "But it's disgraceful, to treat someone like a chronic invalid just because people gossip. Let them gossip, then! We'll rise above it. We'll find some way out, mark my words!"

But he knew, even so, that he only said it to make himself feel better.

Slowly and wearily, Yasuko got to her feet and, taking a large diary from the chest of drawers, handed it silently to Shigematsu. It was her private journal for 1945, and the cover had a design of two crossed flags—the national flag, and the Rising Sun flag used by the navy. During their stay in Senda-machi in Hiroshima, she had written up the day's events in it every evening after supper, using the round meal-table as a writing desk. She had written it up unfailingly every day, however tired she might be.

Her way of keeping a diary was to deal with the day's events in a brief five or six lines for four or five days, then, on the fifth or sixth day, to devote one entry to describing the past few days in greater detail. In this she was carrying on Shigematsu's own method, which he had followed for many years past and which he had taught his niece. He had first devised this scheme, which he liked to call his "stopstart" method, so that on evenings when he was late home from work and too sleepy to do anything more, he could allow himself to dismiss the day in a few lines.

It occurred to Shigematsu that he must copy out the relevant parts of this diary of Yasuko's and send it to the go-between. Setting to work, he transcribed several days' entries just as they stood, beginning with August 5.

August 5
Gave notice to Mr. Fujita, the factory manager, that I should be

absent tomorrow, and went home to get our belongings ready for sending to the country. List: Aunt Shigeko's summer and winter formal kimonos (one of them—very precious—a yellow-striped silk which great-grandmother is supposed to have worn when she first came as a bride), and four summer kimonos; Uncle Shigematsu's winter morning coat, winter and summer formal kimonos and a formal *haori*, two winter suits, one shirt, one tie, and his graduation diploma; my own summer and winter formal kimonos, two sashes, my graduation diploma. Did them all up in a straw mat. In a bag to carry over my shoulder, I put three measures of rice, my diary, a fountain pen, my seal, mercurochrome, and an all-purpose triangular bandage. (Note added by Shigematsu: Our belongings were sent back to us from the country, still done up, more than a year after the end of the war.)

An air raid warning in the middle of the night, and a B-29 squadron flew over without doing anything. All-clear around three. When Uncle Shigematsu came back from night watch he said he'd been told that the other day the B-29's dropped propaganda leaflets saying "Don't think we've forgotten to raid Fuchū-machi, will you? We'll be there before long." The phrasing manages to sound affable yet threatening at the same time. Will they really bomb Fuchū, I wonder? According to someone who came from Yamanashi Prefecture the other day, the B-29's dropped a kind of propaganda pamphlet printed on real art paper before raiding Kōfu. One passage apparently claimed that on Saipan or some other island occupied by the Americans the Japanese were living quite contentedly, with plenty to eat. One never even *sees* art paper in Hiroshima these days. To bed at 3:30.

August 6

Mr. Nojima came in his truck at 4:30 to take our belongings to the country. At Furue there was a great flash and boom. Black smoke rose up over the city of Hiroshima like a volcanic eruption. On our way back, we went via Miyazu and thence by boat up as far as Miyuki Bridge. Aunt Shigeko was unhurt, Uncle Shigematsu injured on his face. An unprecedented disaster, but it is impossible to get any overall picture. The house is tilting at an angle of about 15 degrees, so am writing this diary at the entrance to the air raid shelter.

August 7

We decided yesterday to move to the workers' dormitory at the Ujina works, but it proved impossible, and at Uncle Shigematsu's suggestion we took refuge at Furuichi. Aunt Shigeko accompanied us. Uncle Shigematsu shed a few tears in the works office. Hiroshima is a burnt-out city, a city of ashes, a city of death, a city of destruction, the heaps of corpses a mute protest against the inhumanity of war.

Today, inspection of damage done to the works.

August 8

Frantically busy cooking rice for everybody's breakfast.

The main points which were decided on at a conference on the running of the works have been published.

August 9

More survivors arrived seeking refuge today. Among them, some people who are quite unconnected with any of the workers here. Almost all of them are injured. Not one of them has any proper clothes. One of them came clasping a parcel containing a box with somebody's ashes, which he hung on a cord under the eaves over the window, muttering a prayer to himself as he did so. There was a middle-aged man too, with his throat bandaged in a grubby cloth, and a heavy, coarse face. He had a kind of desperate humor, and distributed three unused postcards each to everybody, saying "Don't hesitate, now. Drop a line to the people who'll be worrying about you. You can have as many of these cards as you like—I make them at my place. But keep it to yourselves, will you?" I imagine he had found the cards lying around at a bombed-out post office or somewhere.

It is 1 p.m., and most people are resting, fast asleep. Today, I feel I have recovered the power to think somewhat, so will go over again in my memory what has happened since the sixth. At 4:30 on the morning of the sixth the truck came with Mr. Nojima driving and loaded our belongings to take to the country. Our party were all from the same district association, or from the next district—Mrs. Nojima, Mrs. Miyaji, Mrs. Yoshimura, and Mrs. Doi. Everyone got in next to her own belongings. Off at 5:30.

On the main road on the way from Koi to Furue, we saw a dark brown, life-size figure of a man set up as a scarecrow in a tiny vacant lot being used to grow millet. Mr. Nojima slowed down the truck and tapped on the bar of the partition, as if to say "Look at that! There's something queer for you!" It was only a figure, but the face, hands, and feet were done in detail, as though modeled in clay, and it had a straw mat wrapped round its hips. It may well have been papier-mâché, but Mrs. Nojima said: "Do you think it's a scarecrow made by natives that somebody's brought back from the South Pacific?" And Mrs. Miyaji said, "I expect it's a wax dummy from a department store that got blackened with smoke from an oil bomb or something." But Mrs. Doi said, "It gave *me* a proper turn. I thought it was a *real* human being all burnt black!"

It was 6:30 a.m. when we reached Furue. The farmhouses still had their shutters closed, but at Mrs. Nojima's parents' home the old lady and gentleman had got the doors of the earthen-walled storehouse open ready for us. We unloaded our belongings and put them in the storehouse. Mrs. Nojima wrote out a receipt for us—just to make sure, she said—then took us into a room in the main house and gave us each a small cucumber with some bean-paste, since there weren't any proper cakes for serving with green tea, she explained. They were all very nice to us. Mrs. Nojima's father seemed to prefer to leave things to his son-in-law, Mr. Nojima. "Our peaches are still rather green," he said with old-fashioned politeness, "but I hope you'll try them. They're still cold from the night dew, you know." He disappeared outside and was back in no time with about ten peaches in a basket. A variety called "Ōkubo," he said. They were still rather green, but Mrs. Nojima peeled them for us.

Both Mr. and Mrs. Nojima are always doing things for the other people who live in the same district. People say that Mr. Nojima has been friendly for years with a left-wing scholar called Mr. Matsumoto, and that since the war got more serious he's been making himself especially nice to everybody in the district so that the authorities won't get suspicious. Mr. Matsumoto, who went to an American university and used to correspond with Americans before the war, has been called before the military police any number of times. So he, too, is always on his best behavior with people at the city hall, the officials of the prefectural office, and the members of the civilian guard, and whenever there's an air raid warning he's always the first to dash outside and rush around calling out "air raid! air raid!" He's never been known to take off his puttees, even at home. They say he even offered to take part in bamboo spear practice with the women. It's really pathetic to see a reputable scholar like him trying so hard to please. Once, when we were talking about his behavior, Uncle Shigematsu said: "It shows there's something wrong with the world when a man like Mr. Matsumoto can let himself be put on so by officials. It reminds me of the saying that 'the finest barge sometimes conceals a load of turnips'— but I don't feel that quite fits his behavior. Or you could compare him to that story of the great hero, the man of action, whom circumstances obliged to turn to growing flowers for a while— but that's not quite it, either. Nor is he one of those 'political turncoats.' No, it's spy phobia—that's what's the matter with people like him! But what I say is this: there's a time for every man to show his true colors, and when that time comes he should do it like a man!"

Although Mr. Matsumoto could be evacuated any time he liked, he's too afraid that he might be suspected as a spy, and dashes around all day frantically doing things for other people in the district. Even supposing that Mr. Nojima is acting on the same principle, I wonder whether we really ought to take advantage of it and get him to drive trucks and look after clothing for us? I expect my kimonos, graduation diploma and the like would have seemed so much worthless trash to him before the war.

Mrs. Nojima's parents' house had an air of gracious living. How many acres of farm land—or rather, how many dozens of acres—would go with a residence on this scale? I was wondering about it and looking out at the rockery in the garden when the all-clear siren sounded. My watch said eight o'clock. Every day at this time an American metereological observation plane had been coming and flying over the built-up area of Hiroshima without doing anything, so I assumed it was the same thing again, and thought no more of it. Four or five of the neighborhood children who had strayed into the garden were playing around the truck, which had been driven inside the gate, and were sitting on the frame or dangling from it. Mrs. Nojima's father brought all kinds of utensils for the tea ceremony, saying he was going to offer us a cup of powdered tea. Not knowing the etiquette for the ceremony, and being the youngest, I sat in the humblest seat.

It was pleasantly cool in the room. The old gentleman took the lid off the iron kettle, which had begun to boil, and as he did so there was a terrible flash of bluish-white light outside. It seemed to rush past from east to west—from the built-up part of Hiroshima, that is, toward the hills beyond Furue. It was like a shooting star the size of hundreds of suns. Almost simultaneously, there came a great roar of sound. "Why, something bright flashed past!" I heard the old gentleman exclaim. We all leapt to our feet and dashed outside, where we crouched down in the shelter of the rocks in the rockery or behind the trunks of trees. The children had leapt down from the truck and were falling over each other to get out of the gate, as though someone were after them. One of them, who had fallen over on the ground, scrambled to his feet and ran away limping—he must have been sitting on the frame of the truck, and been blown off.

"The shelter's round the back," said Mr. Nojima, but nobody got up to go there, nor did he himself make any move.

In the direction of the city, smoke was rising high up into the sky. We could see it above the white clay wall of the garden. It was like the smoke from a volcano, or a column of cloud with sharply etched outlines; one certain thing was that it was no ordinary smoke. My knees as I squatted there shook so uncontrollably that I pressed them against a rock, heedless of a small white flower clinging to it.

"They must have dropped some new weapon," said Mr. Nojima from behind a rock. "Do you think it's safe now?" said Mrs. Nojima. Little by little, like freshwater crabs creeping out from between the stones, we poked our heads out from behind the rocks. Finally, we left the rockery and, running to the gate, gazed in the direction of the city. The smoke had climbed high into the sky, spreading out wider the higher it went. I remembered a photograph of oil tanks burning in Singapore that I had once seen. It had been taken just after the Japanese army had brought about the fall of the city, and the scene was so horrifying that I wondered at the time whether such things were really justified. The smoke climbed higher, ever higher, into the sky, and put out a horizontal bank of cloud around it, forming a great, umbrella-shaped mass that loomed over everything like some top-heavy monster. It made me wonder if the B-29's had dropped some kind of oil bomb. All the married women agreed with Mr. Nojima's theory about a new weapon. A thatched cottage visible at the foot of the slope outside the gate had collapsed. The houses with tiled roofs had had their tiles stripped off.

Mr. Nojima stood talking for a while with his father-in-law, then they walked down by the ornamental spring and stood talking a while longer. Finally, Mr. Nojima came over to where we were standing, a resolute expression on his face.

"I'm sure you're all worried about your families," he said. "If you like, I can take you to the city now. My wife is worried about the children, and wants to go back to Hiroshima at once."

I looked at that monstrous cloud and wondered whether I could bring myself to go home beneath its shadow. To do so seemed like inviting disaster. But there was a chorus of "Oh, please," "Thank heavens!" "We're in your hands, Mr. Nojima," with the result that it was decided to set off for home at once. We had already said good-by to the old lady and gentleman when I suddenly noticed the lid of the tea ceremony kettle, lying where it had rolled down onto the stone below the veranda.

The old lady gave each of us some rice balls wrapped in a piece of bamboo sheath. "I'm afraid it's only ordinary boiled rice," she said. "I feel it ought to be millet dumplings, like those that Momotarō took with him when he went to conquer the Island of Devils in the fairy tale." She had an elderly manservant put three or four dampened straw mats in the back of the truck, for use in case of fire.

We set out about nine. As we came out onto the main road, black clouds gathered in the sky over Hiroshima, and there was a rumble of thunder. Mr. Nojima saw a man on a bicycle pedaling furiously along the road from the opposite direction. He stopped the truck, and he and the man had a whispered conversation. I think he must have been asking about traffic conditions on the main road, but didn't want to alarm us. At a place where three roads met he turned the truck back in the direction we had come from. When we got to the sea at Miyazu, he hired a black market boat at the house of a fisherman, apparently someone he knew, and left the truck there as a pledge. The boat, which he said was about two-and-a-half tons, was a sail boat only a little larger than a fishing boat, but the fisherman's sturdy build and the look on his face were somehow reassuring. I felt that Mr. Nojima was a man to depend on too, to be able to produce someone like the fisherman out of a hat.

The married women kept their faces averted from the direction of the city, avoiding looking at Hiroshima as though they had made a pact not to do so. I myself kept my eyes turned towards the islands of Ninoshima and Etajima. Mr. Nojima was holding a hand net, and from time to time would lean out over the gunwale to scoop up refuse from the surface of the water, obviously to see what was being washed along by the sea. "Hey, Tanomura!" he called suddenly to the master of the black market boat. "The tide's going out by now, isn't it?"

He was staring at a piece of board he had just netted. It was no more than a fragment of wood, about three inches wide and six inches long, that had been wrenched off somewhere, but his face was grim. I edged along toward him to see what was the matter, then, almost instinctively, I averted my eyes. It was unmistakably recognizable as a piece of floor-board from the corridor of a house. It was scorched black all over except for a design of Mt. Fuji with a sailing boat and pine trees, standing out white in unburned wood on the surface. The floor-boards must have been scorched by the heat when that monstrous ball of fire had flashed high over Hiroshima, leaving only the pattern from the frosted glass standing out on the wood; then the blast had lifted the fragment up and away and deposited it in the river or the sea.

Mr. Nojima flung it back into the sea.

The boat arrived at the foot of Miyuki Bridge, on the right bank of the Kyōbashi River. Above the bridge, the river was shrouded in black smoke. It was impossible to tell what was happening in the direction of the city hall, though there were flames wherever one looked. The air was murky, as though night was already drawing in. Senda-machi still stood undamaged, so we went ashore, only to encounter a barricade of military police who were refusing to let people through. Mrs. Doi thrust her face into that of a policeman. "We live here in Senda-machi," she said. "We have children at home. Why don't you let us through? I *am* going through!"

"This is an emergency barrier," he said harshly. "When I say get back, you get back!"

Mr. Nojima retreated dejectedly from the barricade. But then, acting as though he were going away, he muttered to us in a low voice: "Follow after me, everybody. We'll borrow the wisdom— or should I say the cunning?—of the ancients. This is a trick that a famous hero thought up during the Teiyū civil war. Come on, after me!"

He stepped into the passageway of one of those houses that have an unfloored passageway running from front to back. He walked straight through the house, and out at the back. Next, he went in at the rear entrance of a house backing onto the first, walked straight through the passageway, and out into the broad street beyond. All the houses were leaning at an angle, and plaster had fallen away from the walls. They were unoccupied.

"Well I never!" said Mrs. Miyaji.

I admit I was rather startled myself. For all Mr. Nojima's resourcefulness, what would have happened if there had been somebody in the houses we had passed through? Fortunately, everybody must have fled for fear the flames might spread in this direction. My heart was thumping faster when I came out of the passageway than when I had gone in.

CHAPTER 2 🌿

At this point, Shigematsu decided to get his wife Shigeko to help in transcribing the remainder of his niece's diary. She wrote in a better hand than he, for one thing. Besides, three days previously he and Shōkichi and another man called Asajirō had begun trying to rear carp, and somehow he felt uneasy unless he went to make a quite unnecessary inspection of the pond in which they were keeping the fry. He had been twice the day before yesterday, and three times, braving the rain, yesterday.

At suppertime the previous day, Yasuko had said to him sympathetically, "Going to inspect the ponds is a kind of act of homage for you, isn't it Uncle? I don't expect it's such fun as it looks to the outsider."

But she was wrong: it was a pleasure that no outsider could possibly know, a pleasure only comparable to that of fishing.

"Shigeko!" he called to his wife as he was going out. "I'm going to 'pay homage.' Will you go on copying out this diary for me? But you'd better not write in that calligraphy-teacher hand of yours—do it in ordinary writing as far as possible. Those fancy styles aren't very practical, you know. The go-between might find it hard to read."

He went off to visit the pond at Shōkichi's place beyond the hill, the private nursery in which he, in cooperation with Shōkichi and Asajirō, were to raise the baby carp, feeding them on rice bran and silkworm pupae throughout the summer in order to release them in the lake at Agiyama.

There had been a dozen or more people suffering from radiation sickness in the village, but now only three survived—mild cases, of whom Shigematsu was one. All three had checked the progress of the disease by taking care always to get plenty of food and rest. Where the rest was concerned, however, it was not enough—nor was it tolerable for the patient himself—simply to lie in bed all day. The doctor had suggested doing light jobs about the place, supplemented by "walks." Unfortunately, it was out of the question for the head of a family, to all appearances in the best of health, to stroll idly through the village. For someone to "go for a walk," in fact, was quite unheard of. A "walk" was unthinkable in terms of traditional custom, and thus unthinkable in principle.

Why, then, should they not go fishing instead? Both the doctor at the clinic and the heart specialist in Fuchū had said fishing was very beneficial in mild cases of radiation sickness, both psychologically and because it provided an added source of fat in the diet. Fishing from a boat—for sweetfish, for example—was too chilly, but fishing from the embankment of a lake was the ideal way (therapeutically speaking) of killing two birds with one stone. While one was fishing, one's powers of thought were temporarily paralyzed, so that it had the same effect in resting the cells of the brain as a deep sleep.

Even so, for someone to go fishing at an age when he should have better things to do was liable to cause bad feeling among others who were busy at work. Shigematsu and Shōkichi had themselves been subjected, to their very faces, to a piece of unpardonable sarcasm on that same score.

It was during the busiest season on the farms, at a time when everybody was hard at work cutting the wheat and planting the ricefields. It was the best time of year for fishing, both in the river and the lakes, and the weather had just cleared up after a spell of rain. Shigematsu and Shōkichi were fishing on the bank of the lake at Agiyama when the woman from Ikemoto's hailed them:

"Lovely weather we're having!"

So far, so good; but she halted in her tracks and went on disagreeably:

"Both fishing, eh? Some people *are* lucky, I must say, seeing how everybody else is so busy."

She wore a cotton towel over her hair and carried an empty bamboo basket on her back.

"What are you getting at?" said Shōkichi, keeping his eyes on his float in the water. "It's the woman from Ikemoto's isn't it? Just what would you mean by that, woman?"

Instead of getting on as she ought to have done, she deliberately came closer to the foot of the bank.

"Well, what do you mean, some people are 'lucky'?" went on the normally mild and gentlemanly Shōkichi. "If you mean *us,* you're barking up the wrong tree. Quite the wrong tree, I can tell you! Come now, woman, let's see if you can't put things more civilly."

The tip of his fishing rod was quivering with indignation.

"Look here," he continued. "We've got radiation sickness, and we're fishing for roach at the doctor's orders. . . . You think we're 'lucky' to be sick, do you? *I'd* be only too glad to do some work, I can tell you—any amount! But people like us have only to do a bit of hard work and their limbs start to rot on them. This damned disease comes out."

"Well, fancy that now . . . ! Of course, you wouldn't be taking *advantage* of being caught in the raid, would you?"

"That's enough! Shut your mouth! A joke's a joke. . . . I suppose you've forgotten how you came to see me when I got back

from Hiroshima, have you? Or were they crocodile tears? I remember you blubbering and calling me a 'precious victim' at the
time."

"*Did* I now? But that was before the end of the war. Why—
everybody said that kind of thing during the war. If you ask *me,* I
think you're trying to pick a quarrel or something, to start bringing
up things like that now."

Still she refused to get on, a typical widow in her determination
not to be got the better of.

"And you're a fine one aren't you, Shōkichi—" she went on,
"reminding me about going to see you when you were sick. Whose
place do you think it is to talk like that? You'd do well not to
throw people's kindnesses in their faces."

"People's kindnesses? What do you mean? I suppose you
think you own this lake, do you, just because you're in charge of
the lock? You're wrong there—quite wrong, woman! Anybody
on the irrigation committee for this lake can fish here as he pleases.
Didn't you know that?"

"Isn't that just what I'm saying—that it's very *nice* for you?
That's why I said you were lucky—"

"Why, you damned widow bitch!"

He made as if to jump up, but his lame leg thwarted him. His legs
were dangling over the inner slope of the embankment, and he
could not get up in a hurry. He began easing his buttocks round
towards the water so that he would not slip down the embankment, but the woman in the meantime had got down to the path
that sloped away from its foot. Not content with that, she had
rakishly flung the rope of her empty basket, which had originally
been over both shoulders, over one shoulder only, so as to cut a
dash with her back view as she went.

"Did you ever hear the like! My God!" stormed Shōkichi,
glaring at her retreating form. "It makes my blood boil." He was
so carried away that he was actually stirring the waters of the lake
with his rod.

"The people at Ikemoto's have forgotten that Hiroshima and
Nagasaki were atom-bombed. Everybody's forgotten! Forgotten

the hellfires we went through that day—forgotten them and everything else, with their damned anti-bomb rallies. It makes me sick, all the prancing and shouting they do about it."

"Come, now, Shōkichi—you mustn't say such things. . . . Why, look—you've got a bite! Your float's bobbing!"

Wondrous to behold, the float of the rod with which he had been stirring the water was being tugged down vigorously below the surface.

Shōkichi raised his rod and drew it to him, revealing a large roach with the hook embedded deep in its throat. Needless to say, this deus ex machina successfully assuaged his wrath, and he fished steadily throughout the rest of the day, catching nearly eight pounds of fish in all. Even so, both he and Shigematsu decided that they would not go to fish in the lake for a while.

The third friend, Asajirō, had been in Hiroshima as a member of the service corps when the bomb fell, having himself volunteered for work there. His symptoms were the same. If he pulled a heavy cart or worked in the fields, he got an ominous rash of small pimples among the hair on his scalp, but they dried up if he ate nourishing foods, went fishing, and took other mild exercise. His particular method of taking nourishment did not follow the intructions of the visiting doctor, but was something he had got from a practitioner of moxibustion. He ate three meals a day, invariably including two bowls of bean paste soup with fried bean curd and dried, shredded giant radish, plus a raw egg and, once a day at least, some garlic. Medical treatment for him consisted of a weekly moxibustion session. The lower, unfloored part of his barn was hung with row upon row of giant radishes, both whole and shredded, waiting to be eaten.

Asajirō had been fond of fishing since childhood, and was adept at catching eels using a special contrivance made from a bamboo tube. On the night before the bomb had been dropped on Hiroshima, he had left his lodgings after dark (being a member of a voluntary labor unit, he was free to move about as he pleased) and had gone down to the river from the west end of Sumiyoshi Bridge, where he set his bamboo-tube trap on the river bed. The next morning, his unit had gone to work as usual with the foreman at its head, but, hearing distant explosions, Asajirō and his friend Shōkichi had taken refuge under the bridge, hiding in a covered boat tied up there. It was high tide, and there was six or seven feet of water in the river. The all-clear sounded almost immediately, so Asajirō came out of the boat, hauled up the bamboo trap, and went back under the cover so as to take out the eel without being seen. Shōkichi got in with him.

The cover of the boat, a piece of old sail-cloth covered with patches, was dyed a virulent yellow. The broad flap that hung all round it was similarly dyed yellow. Asajirō's bamboo trap, which worked on a special principle of his own, was a good six feet long. The tube was wet and slippery, and Shōkichi was wiping and rubbing at it with a cotton towel when there was a flash, bluish-white like a will-o'-the-wisp, and a terrifying roar. The boat spun round on its bow as though on a pivot, and its gunwale crashed against that of the next boat. They threw themselves clumsily into the bottom of the boat and Shōkichi, rolling head over heels, banged his ankle against the gunwale.

They found later that one side of the part of the bamboo tube that had been projecting beyond the gunwale was blackened— scorched by the flash, or by the heat from the explosion. The other side was still the natural color of green bamboo. When they tipped up the tube, a small quantity of lukewarm water ran out into the bottom of the boat. The gunwale, bow, and stern of the boat were all scorched; the hawser, being chain, was spared. The cover of yellow canvas was not scorched: yellow, it seemed, repelled the flash. Thanks to this, they were both spared having their skin charred or blistered, though they could not escape the after-effects of radiation. Shōkichi's limp was the result of breaking a bone when he banged his ankle against the gunwale.

For a while, Shigematsu and the other two gave up any idea of going to the lake to fish, but at Shōkichi's suggestion they decided to get together to rear carp in the lake. "I'm so eager to give the woman at Ikemoto's a taste of her own medicine," Shōkichi said, "that I thought up the idea just to be nasty." As an idea, there was really nothing out of the ordinary about it. When the rice-planting season came, they were to order carp fry from the hatchery at Tsunekanemaru village. They would feed them throughout the summer in the pond at Shōkichi's place, then release them in the lake at Agiyama before the typhoon season began. They would club together and have about three thousand fry sent to begin with.

"That will mean we've invested capital in it," he said. "Nobody can call it just amusing ourselves to fish for something we've invested good money in. It means we shall be able to fish with a completely easy mind. In fact, it might even be a good thing to spread the story that we've bought twenty or twenty-five thousand fry."

Both Shigematsu and Asajirō approved of Shōkichi's plan, and Asajirō went to the local office to get permission to release fish in the lake. Permission was given on condition that only those who belonged to the irrigation committee for the lake could fish there. Even so, the main thing was that Shigematsu and his friends should be able to fish there without worrying about what other people thought. As Shōkichi said, so long as one had invested even a little money in the fish one caught, it was not just amusing oneself, but a kind of work, or like running a business. The doctor, of course, had insisted on the importance of regular daily walks, but since it was not possible, unfortunately, to invest in walking, the activity tended to be looked down on as merely frivolous. To stand gossiping by the main road, or to take a nap by the side of a path, was something different; these needed no capital either, but they happened to be customs sanctioned by hundreds—if not thousands—of years of tradition.

When they ordered the fry from the hatchery at Tsunekanemaru, the young owner of the hatchery came personally on his motorcycle to inspect the pond at Shōkichi's. He measured the temperature of the pond, the rate of flow, the depth, the area, and so on; checked to see whether any agricultural chemicals were getting in; and even investigated what kinds of foodstuffs occurred naturally in the pond. Then he wrote out a card with details (including some impressive words in English) of the kinds and quantities of artificial feed needed for three thousand fry.

"I imagine the temperature in this pond ranges from 59° in midwinter to 75° in midsummer," he said. "You couldn't do better for keeping carp fry. Just the right temperature. Ideal conditions, in fact."

Having delivered this verdict, he went on to see the lake at Agiyama before going home. A few days later, he came again in a truck bearing a tankful of fry and a cylinder of oxygen. The tanks held tens of thousands of fry, all for release in ponds in the neighborhood. Shōkichi, as he had said all along he would do, brought an abalone shell suspended from a bamboo pole and set it up by the pond—in order, he said, to keep away weasels.

"Well, well—an abalone shell!" said the young hatchery owner, pausing in his task of scooping out the fry. "Takes you back to the old days, doesn't it? An abalone shell. . . . I expect they bring back memories for most of the old folk in these parts, don't they?"

He had put three thousand fry in the pond, taking care not to waste a single one. This had been three days ago, on a day with a warm, damp, almost stifling wind.

All seemed to be well at the pond at Shōkichi's, and no noticeable number of fry had perished. When Shigematsu, having reassured himself on this point, returned home, he found Yasuko rattling a chain in the bathroom chimney to get rid of the soot. Shigeko, who had got the straw mats from the garden in the unfloored downstairs part of the barn, came to the door.

"Mightn't it be better to cut out that one place in Yasuko's diary?" she said. "At the time she wrote it you could still talk to people about the black rain without their getting funny ideas, as nobody knew there was anything poisonous in it. But nowadays everybody knows. If we leave that part in when we send them the copy, mightn't they get the wrong idea?"

"How far have you got with the copying?"

"That's just it, you see—I wanted to ask you, so I waited. Don't you *realize*—it's down there in writing, about her getting rained on."

"Oh yes, the rain. . . . Then, you mean you haven't copied out a single word?"

Quite suddenly, the memories of the day the bomb fell swept over him, and he went off into the house, grumbling to himself as he went. Yasuko's diary and her notebooks were stacked on the table in the box room. Checking the contents, he found that he himself had copied out less than one-fifth of the whole.

"Bother them and their black rain!" he muttered to himself querulously. "*And* people getting the wrong idea! *And* being scared about what people think." He began to read on in Yasuko's diary.

It felt as though night was drawing in, but after I'd been home for a while I realized that it was dark because of the clouds of black smoke filling the sky. My aunt and uncle had just been setting out to look for me. Uncle Shigematsu had been at Yokogawa Station when the bomb fell, and was hurt on his left cheek. The house was leaning at an angle, but Aunt Shigeko was unharmed. I wasn't aware until Uncle Shigematsu told me that my skin looked as though it had been splashed with mud. My white short-sleeved blouse was soiled in the same way, and the fabric was damaged at the soiled spots. When I looked in the mirror, I found that I was spotted all over with the same color except where I had been covered by my air-raid hood. I was looking at my face in the mirror, when I suddenly remembered a shower of black rain that had fallen after Mr. Nojima had got us in the black market boat. It must have been about 10 a.m. Thundery black clouds had borne down on us from the direction of the city, and the rain from them had fallen in streaks the thickness of a fountain pen. It had stopped almost immediately. It was cold, cold enough to make one shiver although it was midsummer. Obviously I had been in a state of shock. I had had the idea, for one thing, that it had started raining while I was in the truck. Actually, the shower had come and gone in a moment, as if to befuddle my wits. A nasty cheat of a shower!

I washed my hands at the ornamental spring, but even rubbing at the marks with soap wouldn't get them off. They were stuck fast on the skin. It was most odd. I showed them to Uncle Shigematsu, who said, "It could be the oil from an oil bomb, after all. I wonder if it was an oil bomb they dropped, then?" Then he looked at my face and said, "Or it might be poison gas —some sort of substance like mud, but more clinging. Perhaps they dropped a poison gas bomb." He looked again, and said, "Or it may not be poison gas, but something that sprayed out of a Japanese ammunition dump that blew up. Perhaps a spy or someone set fire to an ammunition dump. There may have been an arsenal for storing the army's secret weapons. I was at Yoko-gawa Station when it happened, then I walked back along the tracks, but *I* didn't see any black rain. I expect you've been splashed with oil."

If it's really poison gas, I thought, then this is the end. I felt horrified, and then awfully sad. However many times I went to the ornamental spring to wash myself, the stains from the black rain wouldn't come off. As a dye, I thought, it would be an unqualified success.

Yasuko's diary for August 9 ended here. Ideally, he realized, it would be better to cut out the account of the black rain as his wife had suggested. But what would happen if, when they sent a copy of the diary to the go-between, she asked to see the original? Somehow or other, Shigematsu wanted to put off thinking about that question until another day. And yet, he told himself, at something past eight on August 6, when the bomb fell, Yasuko must have been more than ten kilometers from the center of the blast. He himself had been at Yokogawa, only two kilometers from the center, and his cheek had been burned, but even so he was alive, wasn't he? He had heard that some people who had been in the same area but had escaped without burns were now leading perfectly normal married lives.

He began to feel like showing the go-between his own account of the same period, from his own journal, so that they would realize the difference. This time, whatever happened, Yasuko's proposed marriage must not be allowed to founder. Recently, Yasuko's appearance had improved beyond recognition. Her eyes had a new, almost unnatural luster, and she seemed terribly young and fresh. He knew that she was devising every possible way to make herself more attractive without seeming to do so, and he felt desperately that he must not disappoint the enthusiasm she so clearly felt for the match this time.

"Shigeko!" he yelled, his frustration finding an outlet in his voice. "Get out my journal of the bombing, will you? Shigeko! You remember—you put it away in your chest of drawers, didn't you? I'm going to show it to the go-between, so get it out for me."

Shigeko, who was in the next room and could have heard perfectly well without being shouted at, brought the diary at once.

"I should have had to copy it out decently soon at any rate, if I'm going to present it to the Primary School Library for its reference room. I'll show it to the go-between before I give it to them."

"Surely Yasuko's diary will be enough for the go-between, won't it?"

"Yes, but this will be a kind of appendix to it. Either way, if it's going to go in the school reference room, it'll have to be written out properly sometime."

"Won't you just be making yourself more work?"

"I don't care. It's my nature to keep myself occupied. This diary of the bombing is my piece of history, to be preserved in the school library."

Shigeko said no more, so with a smug air he went and got out a fresh notebook, then set about rewriting his own account of the bombing.

Document entitled "A Journal of the Atomic Bombing," written by Shigematsu Shizuma in a room of a rented house in the town of Furuichi, in the district of Asa, Hiroshima Prefecture, during the month of September, 1945.

August 6. Fair.

Every morning until yesterday the familiar voice on the radio would say "A squadron of eight B-29's is proceeding northwards over the sea at a point 120 kilometers to the south of the Kii Channel." This morning, the broadcast said, "One B-29 is proceeding northward," but we paid little heed since it was the same kind of broadcast as we had been hearing every day, day and night, for so long. We had become so used to air raid warnings that they bothered us little more than the midday siren had done in the old days.

On my way to work, I entered Yokogawa Station as usual to board the Kabe train. The train was about to leave. There was a station official whose face I knew at the ticket barrier, but the platform was empty of passengers. As I jumped onto the deck, I heard a voice say "Good morning, Mr. Shizuma." Standing beside me on the deck was the woman who owned the Takahashi spinning-comb works.

"Mr. Shizuma," she said, brushing back a wisp of hair with her fingers, "I shouldn't really ask you in a place like this, but we need your seal on those papers you prepared for us the other day so—"

At a point three meters to the left of the waiting train, I saw a ball of blindingly intense light, and simultaneously I was plunged into total, unseeing darkness. The next instant, the black veil in which I seemed to be enveloped was pierced by cries and screams of pain, shouts of "Get off!" and "Let me by!", curses, and other voices in indescribable confusion. The passengers came pouring out of the car. I was squeezed off the deck and flung onto the tracks on the opposite side from the platform, landing on something soft that seemed to be a woman's body. Another body landed heavily on top of me in turn. More bodies were piled up on either side of me. A cry of pain and rage escaped me, to be echoed in my ear by a similar cry, in a heavy local accent, from a man whose head was jammed against mine. With cries and groans rising all about me, I shook myself free of those lying on me and struggled to my feet. I pushed out with all my strength, thrusting others out of the way, until eventually I found myself being buffeted from behind against something hard. Recognizing it as the edge of the platform, I elbowed people out of the way and clambered up onto it.

Here, the cries of pain outnumbered those of alarm and anger. My eyes shut, my body wedged in a wave of humanity, I took one, then another step forward and found myself up against something hard again. Realizing that it was a pillar, I clung to it, scarcely aware of what I was doing. I wrapped my arms about it tightly, but still I was torn and buffeted mercilessly. Pushed to the right, thrust back immediately to the left, many times I came close to being torn loose. Each time, my arms were squashed, my body and chin ground against the pillar till it seemed that my shoulders must give way with the pain. I knew I had only to let go and join the wave of humanity, yet every time the wave beat against me I clung desperately to the pillar so as not to be swept away. The first opinion I had formed was that the B-29 had dropped a poison bomb that blinded one's eyes, and that the train had been the direct target.

Eventually, quiet descended around me. Slowly and fearfully, I tried opening my eyes. Everything within my field of vision seemed to be obscured with a light brown haze, and a white, chalky powder was falling from the sky. Not a soul was in sight on the platform. Despite the uproar a moment ago, now not even a station official was to be seen in the building. I must have stayed clinging to the pillar with my eyes shut for considerably longer than I had realized.

Dozens of electric wires were dangling loose about the pillar. It occurred to me that they were awfully dangerous. I picked up one of the pieces of board that were lying about everywhere and brought some of the wires together, but there was no sign of a short circuit. Even so, I avoided the places where wires were crossed, pushing them aside with a piece of board as I climbed over a fence of old railroad ties to get out of the station. I was shocked to find that almost every house adjoining the station had been knocked flat, covering the ground about with an undulating sea of tiles. A few houses away from the station a young woman of marriageable age, the upper half of her body emerging from the rubble, was throwing tiles as rapidly as she could lay hands on them and screaming in a shrill voice. She probably thought she was crying "Help," but the sound that emerged was no intelligible human speech.

"Hey, young lady, why don't you get out of there?" called an old man with features like a Westerner, who was passing by. "Nobody can get near you if you throw things like that." He made to approach her as he spoke, but the girl began to fling the tiles at him, and he beat a hasty retreat. She must have been pinned down by a beam or something below the waist, yet it was remarkable that she should be stuck so firmly in the tiles and still move the upper part of her body so freely. The tiles were traveling quite far. She was breaking them, to make them smaller for easier throwing. . . .

CHAPTER 3 🍃

At three o'clock in the afternoon, when Shigematsu went to the kitchen for tea, the spring cicadas were venturing on the year's first song in the pine grove at the bottom of the hill. Shigeko was preparing a snack.

"About your journal of the bombing—" she began. "You're going to present it to the library for posterity, aren't you? That's right, isn't it?"

"That's right. The headmaster asked me to. It's my piece of history."

"Then you ought to take more care over it. Why don't you write it out with writing-brush ink instead of ordinary pen ink? Writing in pen ink gradually fades away with time, doesn't it?"

"Don't be silly. It may fade a little, but not as much as all that."

"But I've seen a letter written in ink around 1870, and it had turned light brown. A letter grandfather got from someone in Tokyo."

"When do you say you saw it?"

"Actually, it must have been over twenty years ago. The day after I came here as a bride, mother showed it to me upstairs in the storehouse. I came here on July 1 by the old calendar, which means she showed it to me on July 2. I remember the date distinctly."

"Then let's go and find out whether ink really turns light brown. Come on, take me to the storehouse and show me."

He brought a flashlight and went with Shigeko into the storehouse, leaving the food uneaten.

Downstairs, the storehouse was divided in two—a section with a hardened earth floor, and a rice store with a stout door of boards. Before the postwar redistribution of agricultural land, the rice store had always been piled high with bales of rice. In years when tithes from the tenants were particularly large, they had been piled in the unfloored space too. The second floor was boarded with red pine, but badly worm-eaten; there was a set of built-in drawers containing a collection of spurious prints and calligraphy, and below it a number of chests. The chests, which were inscribed with large family crests, were said to have been brought by great-grandmother when she came as a bride. They contained, among other things, a memorandum kept by great-grandfather and various other documents which he had considered worth keeping. In the old days, Shigematsu had left the regular airing of the things in the storehouse entirely to his mother; since she had died, he had left it to Shigeko.

"It's in a writing-box in this chest," said Shigeko. "Great-grandfather must have attached a great deal of importance to that particular letter."

She opened the lid of a chest and by the light of the flashlight drew a bundle of papers out of the writing-box. She undid the ribbon and, from amidst letters from the district office and the district officer, a Red Cross membership certificate and sundry other papers, produced the letter in question. The sender was one

Ichiki of Surugadai in Tokyo, and the addressee was Shigematsu's great-grandfather, in the care of Mr. Sonoda, at Uchisange by Okayama Castle in the province of Bizen. The date was "an auspicious day of the eleventh month in the sixth year of the Meiji era."

"According to mother, letters first started coming to the villages in the sixth year of Meiji," said Shigeko. "They were sent care of somebody in Fukuyama or Okayama, then they were given to somebody to bring from there."

Mother would have been right: the sixth year of Meiji, 1873, was the year when the official postal service was first extended to all the nation's major cities.

"Great-grandfather must have set a lot of store by this letter," said Shigematsu. "Look what's in it."

Along with the long, folded sheet of writing paper on which the letter was written, the envelope contained a folded tobacco leaf. By now, of course, it was dark brown and crisp. In 1873, tobacco would not yet have been a government monopoly, and farmers had probably grown it themselves for use as a vermifuge. Another ten or twenty leaves were interspersed among the documents remaining in the box.

"What a waste!" said Shigematsu. "I wish I'd found them while tobacco was scarce during the war. Why didn't you tell me about it at the time?"

"But the nicotine will all have gone out of them, won't it? Besides, they *are* tobacco after all, and to cut them up and smoke them would have violated the Monopoly Law."

"Well put, woman! Why, you're as cut and dried as these tobacco leaves yourself! Aren't you, now?"

Everything on the second floor of the storehouse, which was dimly lit and smelt of dust, was so dry that it seemed to suck at the very moisture in their bodies. The wood was so wormy that they had to tread lightly to avoid putting a foot through the boards.

Shigematsu unfolded the letter and turned the flashlight on it. It was done by brush in an excellent hand, but the writing had faded to a pathetic light brown color:

Sir:

I am in grateful receipt of the two ounces of *kemponashi* seeds which I begged of you last year on the occasion of our tour of inspection to your village of Kobatake. They were delivered to me at my home by S. Murata, Esq., one-time magistrate of the village of Kobatake, on his recent arrival in the capital. I shall in due course have them grown to discover whether or not the tree in question would be appropriate for lining the avenues of the capital, and shall duly report on the matter to those in authority. May I mention that this letter, in accordance with my promise to you at the time, is written in the "ink" commonly in use in the West . . .

The magistrate of Kobatake in the closing days of the feudal era, who after the Restoration had continued to be responsible for keeping the peace in the district until the new district office was established two years later, had finally packed up his bags in 1873 and moved, at least temporarily, to Tokyo. All that now remained on the site of the former magistrate's office was a tumble-down rear gate, half of the living quarters, and the white, clay-walled storehouse; the primary school now stood on what had once been part of the grounds.

"Mr. Ichiki of Surugadai in Tokyo" was doubtless an Inspector for the new Meiji Government, or a member of such an inspector's entourage, who had happened to drop in on the magistrate's office in Kobatake. He must have seen the trees and extracted from Shigematsu's great-grandfather the promise to which the letter remained as witness. It was said that five great *kemponashi* trees had stood in the garden before Shigematsu's house right up to the time of the Sino-Japanese War.

The *kemponashi* is a noble tree. Five such trees in a row must have given Mr. Ichiki a fancy to seeing them lining the streets of Tokyo. He would have summoned Shigematsu's great-grandfather to his lodgings, and commanded him to send him two ounces of the seeds in the care of the former magistrate, when the latter should come to Tokyo. And he would graciously have bidden him name his reward for doing so. Why—great-grandfather would have replied—might he dare suggest (such an honor, indeed!) that his worship send him a letter written in this *ink* of which he had heard so much? How amazed, indeed, great-grandfather must have been at the new-fangled talk of "the avenues of Tokyo" and the like! Small wonder that he had cherished this letter so dearly. . . .

Shigematsu decided to rewrite his "Journal of the Bombing" using a brush and Chinese ink. He would have Shigeko copy out again the part already written with a pen, and would himself go on with the rest on Japanese-style writing paper, using a brush.

He had been so thirsty that day. He would have given anything for a drink of water. He had turned a tap by the roadside, and steaming hot water had come out, too hot to drink directly, too hot to cup in the hands. . . . His head full of such memories, he took up his brush, and set to work.

In the grounds of the Yokogawa Shrine, which lay on the east side of the station, nothing remained of the main sanctuary save a number of naked uprights. The worship hall in front of it had vanished, leaving only its clay foundation, a bare and ugly hump.

The people in the street by the shrine grounds were all covered over their heads and shoulders with something resembling dust or ash. There was not one of them who was not bleeding. They bled from the head, from the face, from the hands; those who were naked bled from the chest, from the back, from the thighs, from any place from which it was possible to bleed. One woman, her cheeks so swollen that they drooped on either side in heavy pouches, walked with her arms stretched out before her, hands drooping forlornly, like a ghost. A man without a stitch of clothing on came jogging along the road with his body bent forward and his hands between his legs, for all the world like someone about to enter the communal tub at a public bathhouse. There was a woman in her slip who ran wearily along the road groaning as she went. Another carrying a baby in her arms, crying, "Water! Water!" and constantly wiping at the baby's eyes between her cries. Its eyes were clogged with some substance like ash. A man shouting at the top of his voice; women and children shrieking as they ran; others crying for relief from their pain. . . . A man plumped down by the side of the road with his arms thrust sky-wards, waving them frantically. An elderly woman sitting earnestly praying with her eyes closed, her hands pressed together in suppli-cation, beside a pile of tiles that had slid off a roof. A half-naked man who came along at a trot, cannoned into her and ran on cursing her foully. A man in white trousers who crept along a little at a time on all fours, weeping noisily to himself as he went. . . .

All these I saw in less than two hundred yards as I walked from Yokogawa Station along the highway towards Mitaki Park.

The street was swarming with people, like the rush hour in front of the station, and I simply let myself walk in the same direction as the throng. Suddenly, I heard a shrill voice calling my name amidst the other varied cries about me: "Mr. Shizuma! Mr. Shizuma!"

"Where? Where are you?" I called, and was pushing my way in the direction the voice had come from when someone seized my arm and flung herself on me.

"Oh, Mr. Shizuma! I'm so glad to see you!"

How she had wormed her way through to me, I don't know. It was the woman who owned the Takahashi spinning-comb works. She put her arms round my waist and her head against my chest, and began to shake all over. I pulled her between two of the collapsed houses by the road, out of the general turmoil.

"Whatever can have happened, Mr. Shizuma? Such a horror!" Her face was ashen, and she continued to shake.

"We've been bombed, that's what."

"Where do you think it fell?"

"Who can tell? We've been bombed, though—that's certain."

"Mr. Shizuma—you've hurt your face, haven't you? The skin's coming off and it's turned a funny color. It must hurt—it *looks* as though it would."

I ran my hands over my face. The left hand came away wet and sticky. I looked, and found the left palm had something bluish-purple like little shreds of damp paper on it. I stroked my cheek again, and again some sticky substance came off on my hand.

It was extremely odd—I had no recollection of hitting my face on anything. It must be ash or dust or something else that rubbed off like tiny rolls of dead skin. I was about to feel it again when Mrs. Takahashi grasped my wrist.

"No you mustn't rub it! Leave it alone until you can put something on it. If you play with it, the germs will get in from your hand."

There was no particular pain, yet a mild horror prickled at the nape of my neck. My left cheek felt as though countless small particles were clinging to it. I made the skin move by opening my mouth wide and shutting it, and the impression of something sticking there grew stronger. Mrs. Takahashi would not let my left wrist go, so I furtively ran my right hand over my left cheek. Again the little shreds stuck to my palm. I rubbed them on the palm of my left hand, and it was like the shreds from a rubber eraser, but more slippery to the touch. A chill struck throughout my body. Suddenly, the uproar about me receded into the distance; it was not exactly faintness, but the mental shock of that moment was quite indescribable.

Something recalled to my mind a phrase from a propaganda leaflet that an enemy plane had dropped early the previous month. Words to the effect of: "We'll be along sometime soon with a little present for the people of Hiroshima." I didn't see it myself, but old Tashiro, the chief technician at the Ujina canning works, told me about it. Yasuko said that one of the people at work told her about it too.

"Something terrible's happened," I said. "Something terrible, so we must keep calm, Mrs. Takahashi. We must think before we act. And keep really calm."

"Whatever can have happened, though—for everything to be like this all at once? Whatever it was—a bomb or whatever— they've gone too far. Yes, it's too much!"

"Say, Mrs. Takahashi," I said. "Your face and hair are all covered with dust. You look like you've got a wig of ashes on."

At this she finally released my wrist and slapped at her hair with both hands. A fine sprinkling of something like ash or dust fell, onto her face and shoulders, so she turned her head, first left, then right, so that she could blow it off. That got it off better than slapping at it with her hands. Then she bent forward and slapped at it again, shaking her head and blowing furiously at the same time.

I tried tapping at my own hair. Powder flew off it, like the cloud of dust that rises if you spill water from the kettle onto hot charcoal in the brazier.

"I don't like the look of this," I said. "Stop that, Mrs. Takahashi, and let's find some water and wash our hair and faces. We'd better wash them properly."

She agreed with me, but all the houses about had collapsed, and the fire tanks used to store water for fire-fighting, which had formerly stood under the eaves, were buried under collapsed walls and piles of eave tiles. We went back to the tap from which boiling water had spouted, only to find it left turned on with nothing, either cold water or hot, coming out of it. We realized now that it was the tap to a tank that had been installed at the entrance to a shop. An oil drum had been set in a concrete stand, apparently for use as a makeshift cistern. The shop itself had been blasted out of existence.

The number of people we passed in the street had grown fewer, and the cries of the injured more scattered. Most people seemed to be going in the direction of Mitaki Park or the Sanjō railway bridge, so we walked in the same direction too. Along the railroad tracks there stretched a long train of refugees like a trail of ants, or like the pilgrims—it occurred to me—who were said to have lined the approaches to the shrines of Kumano in olden days. Seen in the distance, the hill in the park was like nothing so much as a great pale bun with ants swarming all over it.

As we were passing by Yokogawa Primary School, we noticed an emergency water tank in a corner of the grounds. Mrs. Takahashi, who saw it first, ran off towards it. I started to run too, but the shaking of my cheek muscles at once made me painfully aware of my left cheek, so I forced myself to keep calm and walk there. As I went to remove my spectacles to wash my face, I found they had gone. My hat, I realized, had gone too.

"I dropped my glasses and my hat!" I said.

Mrs. Takahashi put her hands to her sides and then to her shoulders.

"And I've dropped my bag," she said in a hushed voice. "That bag had more than three thousand yen[1] in it. My money, and my savings book, and my seal."

"Then let's go and look for it. I expect you dropped it at Yokogawa Station when the fireball burst. Three thousand yen—that's an awful lot of money—!"

Either way, we decided to wash ourselves first, pouring water over each other's hair with a bucket we found nearby.

"Now you mustn't rub your face, Mr. Shizuma!"

I scarcely needed to be warned. I washed my face by thrusting it into a bucket of water and shaking it steadily from side to side without using my hands at all. I filled the bucket full, took a deep breath, and plunged my face into the bucket, breathing out little by little as I shook my head; the bubbles caressed my cheek comfortingly.

I had a raging thirst, so I filled the bucket with fresh water and gargled three times, then drank. I don't think anybody actually taught me to do so, but when I was a child I always made sure to gargle three times before drinking from a well or spring on unfamiliar territory. The other boys said *they* always gargled three times first. Besides preventing upset stomachs caused by drinking strange water, it was supposed to be a mark of respect for the water god who dwelt in the well or the spring.

The number of passers-by in the street had decreased sharply. We retraced our steps, myself in the lead, and entered what remained of Yokogawa Station as though this was the only thing there could possibly be for us to do. Mrs. Takahashi followed behind me tearfully, quailing at the thought of having lost the bag containing her entire worldly wealth.

"It's a patent leather bag with a strap," she said, though she had told me the same thing already. "With gold-colored metal fittings."

1. One yen was then worth about one dollar.

"You'll have dropped it where you were caught in the crush," I said, also repeating myself.

There was not a soul inside the station. Around the ticket barrier and along the platform was strewn a miscellany of objects—shoes, wooden clogs, sandals, canvas slippers, parasols, air raid hoods, jackets, baskets, bundles in wrapping cloths, lunch-boxes—something of everything, like the dressing-room during school theatricals on graduation day. The lunch-boxes were particularly numerous, and I was oddly shocked—no wonder, perhaps, when the food shortage made eating loom so large in one's mind—at the way their contents were all upset. The rice-balls were not good plain rice, but rice mixed with barley, rice mixed with soybeans from which all the oil had already been extracted, rice mixed with vegetables of a kind, rice mixed with the pressed-out leftovers from making bean curd. To go with the rice, pickled giant radish, and nothing else. Everything testified to the mad scramble that had occurred a while ago.

"There it is, my bag! There!"

She jumped down from the platform onto the tracks. It was the place where she and I and the rest had spilled out of the train in that instant when the fireball had flared up in the sky.

"Well then, my spectacles ought to be where I got caught, too."

I was right. I found them at the foot of the pillar I had been clinging to. Luckily enough, the lenses were unbroken, but the celluloid on the left half of the frame had curled up like a spring, leaving the metal core bare and shiny. I twisted off the celluloid, and found myself with a lop-sided pair of spectacles of which the left half, sidepieces and lens frame alike, were of metal and the right half of celluloid.

Mrs. Takahashi picked up the bag and checked over the contents, exclaiming "Oh, thank heavens!" as she did so.

As I went to wipe the lenses of my spectacles on the lapel of my open-necked shirt, I found my hand trembling. It trembled so violently that Mrs. Takahashi must have noticed, for she said, "Shall I wipe them for you, Mr. Shizuma?"

"No, I can manage," I said, wiping the lens with a quivering hand. "I know why my hands are shaking. The enemy's just throwing his weight about by now. That infernal light, whatever it was, burnt my left cheek. I know, because the left side of my spectacles is burnt too. It's unimaginably beastly. It's the act of a vicious bully, if ever there was one."

"Yes, but there won't be any more air raids today, surely?"

"I'd like the enemy to take a look at those lunch-boxes lying there. If only they could see those rice-balls, I doubt if they'd bother to come raiding any more. There's been enough stupid waste like this! Why don't people realize how we feel?"

"Mr. Shizuma, you mustn't say such things!"

I put my spectacles on. I caught sight of a service cap trampled in the dust not far away, and picked it up. It was like mine, but not mine. What difference does it make, I thought, and, putting it on, left the station with Mrs. Takahashi.

"Put a bandage round your face," she said. "It won't heal over properly if the wind gets at it."

I got an all-purpose bandage out of the first-aid kit on my shoulder and wrapped it round my head, tying it under my chin. When I put the hat on again it was too small. Stolen clothes ill fit the thief, I thought, and decided to leave it behind rather than try to keep it on. I hung it over the gargoyle-like end tile decorating the ridge of a house that had collapsed: somebody would be certain to find a use for it.

We walked on, still with no definite goal, in the direction of Mitaki Park. Our encounters with others were far more sporadic now, but the people wending their way in the same direction as ourselves were all much more badly injured. I noticed a woman standing quite still in a disconsolate attitude, with blackish blood spurting through the fingers of her left hand where she clasped her right arm. I turned my head away, unable to look at her, only to see a young boy rush past me shouting "Ichirō! Ichirō!" He was dressed in a short-sleeved shirt, trousers in tatters from the shin down, and canvas shoes.

"It's me, Kyūichi! It's me!" He had halted before a young man in a steel helmet who was coming from the opposite direction. The young man stopped too, but said, "Who are you?" and seemed to shrink away slightly. Mrs. Takahashi and I paused to watch.

The boy's face was swollen up like a football, and was much the same color; his hair and eyebrows had disappeared. He might have been anybody.

"Ichirō, it's me. Me, your brother!"

He looked up into the young man's face, but the young man made a wry expression as though unwilling to recognize him.

"Come on, tell me your name, then," he said roughly. "Tell me the name of your school."

"Kyūzō Sukune, first grade, second class, Hiroshima Prefectural First Middle School."

The young man drew back, suddenly on his guard.

"I see, but Kyūzō—yes, Kyūzō's wearing puttees. And he's got a shirt made from a cotton kimono, with dark blue spots all over."

"But the puttees got blown off. And the spots have all gone into holes. It all happened when the bomb flashed. Ichirō, you *must* know who I am!"

The shirt was indeed covered with holes, but the young man still seemed wary.

"But . . . yes, of course—I could tell Kyūzō by his belt!"

"You mean this one, Ichirō?"

Swiftly, with raw, burned hands, he pulled out his belt and showed it to the young man. It must have been made for him from the leather strap used for fastening a wicker hamper, and it had a crude ring of the same color encircling it by the brown metal buckle.

"It is!" The young man's voice choked. "Oh, Kyūzō. . . ."

He squatted beside the boy to put his belt back on for him, and Mrs. Takahashi and I walked away. Unable to decide where to go, we went back in the direction from which we had come. I myself was in two minds whether to go home or to the works, and Mrs. Takahashi was in two minds whether to go to her spinning-comb factory or to the place with which she did business.

"I'm going home first," I said. "Even if the town's on fire, it should be possible if I go along the railway tracks."

"I'm going to go to my customer's to get my money. If I don't get it in the bank the materials will stop coming."

"What about young Iwashita at your branch?" I said. "Even if there was a fire, he might insist on holding on there, like a captain going down with his ship. He's that kind of fellow, isn't he?"

"I'm sure Iwashita can take care of himself. Either way, if I don't get the money in the bank, the flow of goods will stop dead."

"Don't go, even so. Don't, now! I doubt if there'll be anyone at the bank, at any rate. Or at your customer's, for that matter."

"Whether there is or not, I believe in taking risks. Once a businesswoman, always a businesswoman, I say."

"Well then," I said, "let's say good-by here. If you look in at our works, tell the manager I'll be there tonight or tomorrow morning, will you?"

We parted company and I went back to Yokogawa Station. Fires had started in a dozen places or more, and were spreading from left to right in the direction of Ujina. (Note added later: I heard no more of Mrs. Takahashi: I expect she was caught in the flames). Fires were rising in the direction of Sanjō Bridge, too. There seemed little chance of getting through the streets. The only possible route left was to follow the Sanyō Line tracks over Yokogawa railway bridge, then out along the railway embankment in the direction of Futaba-no-Sato. So deciding, I started walking eastwards along the tracks in the direction of the Yokogawa Bridge. Here too, the refugees from the city were comparatively few, but most of them were badly injured or burned. Among them was a small boy of about seven, plodding along all by himself. Catching him up, I spoke to him.

"Where are you going, sonny?"

He made no reply, his face blank.

"Do you think you can cross the bridge all by yourself?"

Again no reply.

"Then I'll stay with you till you're over the bridge, shall I?"

He nodded, and started walking by my side. Once he was over the bridge, the hills at Futaba would be close at hand, and he would be all right.

Afraid that I might grow fond of him, I refrained from asking him his name or anything else about himself. He was a nice little boy, and it was a relief when he said not a word. He walked with his mouth open vacantly, as though preoccupied with something; occasionally, when we came to a place where the railway ties were burning, he would stop and look at them in a puzzled fashion, then go through the motions of throwing stones at the fire before walking on again.

The burning ties puzzled me, too. As we walked on, we came across more ties smoking and flaring up fitfully, as well as railway poles which were smoking at the top or halfway down. The enemy must have dropped an oil incendiary bomb; to test my theory, I stamped out the fire on one sleeper and got down flat on my face to smell it. It smelt of nothing worse than charred wood. An oil bomb would have had an unpleasant odor. It was most odd.

As I got up from my prone position, the first thing to meet my gaze was a great, an enormous, column of cloud. In its texture, it reminded me of cumulo-nimbus clouds I had seen in photographs taken after the Great Kantō Earthquake. But this one trailed a single, thick leg beneath it, and reached up high into the heavens. Flattening out at its peak, it swelled out fatter and fatter like an opening mushroom.

"Say sonny, look at that cloud!"

The boy's mouth opened wide as he looked up at the sky. Although the cloud seemed at first glance to be motionless, it was by no means so. The head of the mushroom would billow out first to the east, then to the west, then out to the east again; each time, some part or other of its body would emit a fierce light, in ever-changing shades of red, purple, lapis lazuli, or green. And all the time it went on boiling out unceasingly from within. Its stalk, like a twisted veil of fine cloth, went on swelling busily too. The cloud loomed over the city as though waiting to pounce, and my whole body seemed to shrink from it. I wondered if my legs were not going to give out on me.

"That over there, underneath the cloud—it looks like a shower, doesn't it?" said a polite, woman's voice. I looked, and saw standing near me a middle-aged woman with a good natured expression, accompanied by a fresh-faced girl.

"I wonder, now?" I said. "A shower. . . ."

I screwed up my eyes and gazed into the sky, but the impression was less of a shower than of a dense mass of small particles. I wondered if it could be a whirlwind. It was like nothing that I had ever seen before. I wondered, my flesh shrinking at the idea, what would happen if it came in this direction and we were rained on by those particles. The mushroom cloud itself was sprawling out farther each moment toward the southeast. I had been right: my legs were giving way under me.

Seeing the boy with me, the middle-aged woman told me that it was quite impossible to take a child across the Yokogawa railway bridge. About nine-tenths of the way across, a freight train was lying on its side across the tracks, and hundreds and thousands of refugees were squatting on this side of the bridge.

"Why don't they come back this way?" I asked.

"They're all resting," she replied, "so badly hurt they don't have the energy to come back again. Some of them have collapsed where they are and can't go any further. . . . But I'm sure you'll never get across the bridge with a child."

"Did you hear, son?" I said. My voice was slightly unsteady. "They say children can't cross the bridge. Why don't you go with this lady, along the Kabe line tracks toward the hills?"

He turned his gaze on me.

"So you see, sonny, we'll say good-by here, eh?"

He nodded. The middle-aged woman rested a hand on his head and bowed to me.

The child, who seemed to have formed some idea of where he was going, set off ahead of the woman in the direction from which he had come. I watched him go. His spindly legs ended in a pair of black canvas shoes, trodden down at the backs. He wore shorts, and a short-sleeved shirt, and his hands were empty.

The mushroom cloud was really shaped more like a jellyfish than a mushroom. Yet it seemed to have a more animal vitality than any jellyfish, with its leg that quivered and its head that changed color as it sprawled out slowly toward the southeast, writhing and raging as though it might hurl itself on our heads at any moment. It was an envoy of the devil himself, I decided: who else in the whole wide universe would have presumed to summon forth such a monstrosity? Should I ever get away alive? Would my family survive? Was I, indeed, on my way home to rescue them? Or was I seeking refuge for myself alone?

My legs were so unsteady that I could not put one foot before the other, and I shivered uncontrollably.

With a mighty effort, I forced myself to get a grip on myself. Catching sight of a stick of the kind used for hulling ration rice that was lying by the tracks—Heaven knows where it had been blown from—I beat myself indiscriminately on the calves, buttocks, and thighs. Next, I beat my shoulders and upper arms. Then I shut my eyes and did some deep breathing. I did it by the method we were always made to follow in morning exercises at the factory, breathing in and out very slowly, in almost incantatory fashion. It gave me back control of my legs as well as a certain mental detachment, and I set off eastward along the tracks.

Although everything in me told me to hurry, I adjusted my pace so as not to overtake other refugees. Since this was not one of those nightmares where one is held back by invisible forces, I probably could have run if I had wished, but a feeling that it was best to leave everything in the lap of the gods held me in check.

Suddenly, one of a group of refugees who were just then overtaking me cried out, "Parachute! Parachute!" and broke into a run. Then, just as suddenly, he reverted to the same plodding, lifeless gait as before. It was a parachute, no doubt. Ahead of us and to the left, a clump of white clouds floated over the farthest hills, and way up in the sky above the clouds was a single white parachute, drifting gently toward the north.

I was walking on, still worrying about it vaguely, when there was a sudden, loud boom. The ground shook, and a column of black smoke rose up about seven or eight hundred yards to the northwest. As one man, the refugees on the tracks began to run, but almost at once reverted to their former leaden tread, the tread of men utterly exhausted both physically and mentally.

There was another explosion, and another. With earth-shaking roars, columns of black smoke shot up a full three hundred feet. At each explosion, the refugees began to run. Finally, someone called out, "It's oil drums going up. Oil drums!" and their pace became even more lethargic than before. No one made any verbal response to the voice.

When I got to the near side of the Yokogawa railway bridge, I found over two thousand refugees squatting on the grass embankment below. Almost no one except the young made any move to cross. The bridge must have been more than a hundred feet up, and a glimpse of the river below was enough to make one's limbs go weak. Even so, it was the only way to get to the other side. The people squatting there, almost all of whom were injured, seemed to be in a state of apathy, without even the will to get across. Some of them simply sat in silence, gazing at one fixed spot in the sky.

Most of them, however, kept their eyes averted from the mushroom cloud. Quite a few of the injured lay sprawled on their backs on the bank. The one exception was a woman who had her arms stretched out toward the cloud and kept screaming in a shrill voice: "Hey, you monster of a cloud! Go away! We're non-belligerents! D'you hear—go away!" Oddly for one who seemed so lively, she made no attempt to cross the bridge.

Suddenly, I could no longer bear waiting about indecisively. I made up my mind: I would cross the bridge. I set off in the wake of a young man who was bleeding from the shoulder, avoiding as far as possible looking at the waters below. About nine-tenths of the way across, passage was blocked by the freight train lying on its side, but after much difficulty I succeeded in getting past by crawling flat on my face. About halfway along the train, where the river below was shallow, I spied a mass of onions that had tipped out and lay in heaps below.

The refugees who had got over the bridge were going up the hill from Futaba-no-Sato in a long procession as though being steadily sucked up toward the higher parts. In two or three places higher up the hillside, forest fires were visible. It seems that only those who live in the hills themselves realize the very special horror of hill fires. To walk in droves in the direction of a hill fire reminded me terribly of moths dashing themselves against a lamp at night. I myself knew the fearful danger of hill fires, from having seen them when I was a child; I remembered, too, how many victims they had claimed. I said to a group of four or five refugees as they went past: "Hill fires are dangerous. They may look small, especially in the daytime, but they're really quite large, and cover a large area. The flames roar downwards, and red-hot stones and rocks come rolling down." But they went on up the hill without seeming to heed.

Eventually, I came out at the corner of the West Parade Ground. Here, there seemed to be refugees as far as the eye could see, and the whole great expanse was swamped beneath a sea of humanity. Yet here too, the fleeing crowds were pressing on with the one idea of getting to the hills. I remembered what I had heard of tidal waves—how they ooze on in muddy swirls, on up to the higher ground beyond. . . .

In accordance with my plan of getting first to Hiroshima Station, I walked along the edge of the parade ground, cutting diagonally across the flow of people going to the hills. Need I say how varied in appearance and condition were the hundreds, the thousands of people I saw on the way? I feel compelled—unnecessary though it may be—to set down here some of my memories of them, just as they come back to my mind today:

The countless people who had blackish dried blood clinging to them where it had flowed from their faces onto their shoulders and down their backs, or over their chests and down their bellies. Some were still bleeding, but they seemed to have no energy to do anything about it.

The people staggering along in whatever direction the crowd carried them, their arms dangling purposelessly by their sides.

The people who walked with their eyes shut, swaying to and fro as they were pushed by the crowd.

The woman leading a child by the hand who realized that the child was not hers, shook her hand free with a cry, and ran off. And the child—a boy of six or seven—running, crying plaintively, after her.

The father leading his child by the hand who lost hold of him in the crush. He pushed through the crowd calling the child's name over and again, till finally he was struck brutally and repeatedly by someone he had thrust out of the way.

A middle-aged man carrying an old man on his back.

A man carrying a young girl—an invalid, I should say, and his daughter—on his back.

A woman with her belongings and a child loaded on a baby carriage, who was engulfed in a sudden wave of humanity that crushed the baby carriage and felled her on top of it, so that twenty or thirty others coming behind her toppled like dominoes in their turn. The cries at that moment had to be heard to be believed.

A man who carried, held like an offering before him, a clock that emitted a dull, broken noise as he walked.

A man who carried over his shoulder a fish-basket attached to the cloth case of a fishing rod.

A bare-footed woman shading her eyes with both hands, who sobbed helplessly as she walked.

An elderly man half supporting about the waist, half dragging, a woman whose face, arms, and chest were covered with blood. At each step the man took, the woman's head lolled heavily backwards and forwards or from side to side. Both looked as though they might expire at any moment, but they were jostled mercilessly by the throng.

A young woman who came along almost naked, with a naked baby, its face almost entirely covered with blood, strapped to her back facing to the rear instead of the normal way.

A man whose legs were moving busily as though he were running, but who was so wedged in the wave of humanity that he achieved little more than a rapid mark-time. . . .

CHAPTER 4 ✍

Shigematsu had reached this point in his copying when Shigeko called from the kitchen: "Shigematsu! Whatever time do you think it is? I'd be grateful if you'd call it a day and come and have your dinner."

"Right! Just coming." Getting up, he went to the kitchen. He had been putting off dinner until now, staving off hunger while he copied out his journal of the bombing by munching home-made salted beans. Shigeko and his niece Yasuko had had their dinner long ago, and Yasuko, who was catching the first bus to Shinichi-machi in the morning to go to the beauty parlor, had already gone to bed in the box room.

Shigeko was dishing out loach soup from a saucepan into his bowl.

"Well," he said, "I got through a lot today. I've copied it all out up to the place where the West Parade Ground is jammed with people taking refuge from the mushroom cloud. Even so, I haven't got down on paper one-thousandth part of all the things I actually saw. It's no easy matter to put something down in writing."

"I expect it's because when you write you're too eager to work in your own theories."

"It's nothing to do with theories. From a literary point of view, the way I describe things is the crudest kind of realism.   By the way, have these loach been kept in clean water long enough to get rid of the muddy taste?"

"Kōtarō brought them for us a while ago. He said they'd been in clean water for about half a month. He caught them in the ditch below the temple, and kept them in running water in his hundred-gallon jar."

During the war old Kōtarō's family had given up the great gingko tree that grew by their house, for the sake of the war effort. As they were digging up the stump, they had uncovered the jar, an enormous affair in Bizen ware of the type once used for storing rice. It was broken in five or six pieces, but had been patched up with a liberal application of cement.

Shigematsu seated himself in front of the small individual table set for him, and picked up a clumsy earthenware cup containing a brownish liquid. This was his regular preprandial drink, an infusion of dried geranium, chickweed, plantain, and other plants. The food on the small table before him consisted of fermented bean paste mixed with chopped trefoil root, an egg dish, and pickled radish, with the bean paste soup with loach floating in it.

"This is what I call eating in style!" he said as he lifted the lid from the bowl of soup. "There's always something in the jar at old Kōtarō's place, isn't there? Do you know, when I took a look in it one day it was quite dry, but he'd got sand from the river bed in the bottom and was trying to hatch some turtle eggs! Not that they ever did hatch out in the end, it seems. . . ."

"When I was over there at the end of last year, he had seven or eight live eels in it," said Shigeko.

"You never know what's going to come out of that jar. It's a kind of cornucopia. Perhaps we ought to follow his example?"

Shigematsu was only talking for its own sake; their house stood on the higher part of the hill, and it would have been impossible to bring water there by means of hollow bamboo pipes, as Kōtarō did. Kōtarō had built a dam on a stream flowing from one of the higher hills at the back, and got water for the jar from it, via a bamboo pipe. By a fortunate coincidence, just the right amount of water leaked from the jar through the cracks where it had been pieced together. Conditions, thus, were ideal, and it was quite possible to keep fish alive in it—eels, sweetfish, trout, or anything else one fancied.

Kōtarō was a full decade older than Shigematsu. During the war, he had made it his business to hunt out extra food for the neighborhood. Twice his expeditions had taken him to Hiroshima, and on both occasions he had called at Shigematsu's house with a present of salted cherry blossoms from the country. The first time, he had come to buy emulsion for use as soap substitute, and edible fat. The emulsion, a black market commodity that was not controlled by the ordinance controlling washing materials, was produced by some firms in defiance of the law. It was the sticky liquid produced on the way to making solid soap, and it came in a can. The fat was the fat cut off meat before they canned it at the Provisions Depot. It was already seasoned and was available at about ten *sen* for a box about three inches square and four inches deep.

Kōtarō would wrap up these black market goods in an extra large wrapping cloth at Shigematsu's house and carry them on his back all the way to the station. "Commercial traveling's been in our family ever since my grandfather's days," he would declare. The second time he came, the only thing for him to buy was some edible fat in an old can, but he had been so pleased with it that, as a parting gesture to Shigematsu, he had set a trap for catching birds on a nearby stretch of open land where houses had been pulled down to create a firebreak.

For some time afterwards, going to look at the trap had been almost a daily routine for Shigematsu, but never once had he found a bird caught in it. It was on the same vacant site, he recalled, that his wife had so often picked pigweed shoots. They had eaten them, boiled in soy.

"Remember that trap old Kōtarō set for us in Hiroshima?" he said. "I wonder what became of it? On the vacant land that used to be grown all over with pigweed in the summer."

"Actually," said Shigeko, "Kōtarō's traps never caught a single bird, did they? Perhaps he didn't set them properly."

Shigematsu could still remember Kōtarō grumbling to himself as he whittled down a piece of split bamboo for the trap. "This food shortage is something awful," he'd said. "Even at the Provisions Depot, the people in the kitchens were in a state because they didn't have enough bean paste to go round for the soup. They told me they'd no idea until the actual day whether they'd be making bean paste soup or 'salt water soup.' It seems they can't plan the meals properly even if they want to." In those days, everybody had been as short of food as the next man.

"Say, Shigeko—" Shigematsu called. "I've an idea! You must jot down some notes about our family's meals during the war. A list of all menus for a week would be better still, but I don't expect you can remember all of them. Just jot them down, will you?—tomorrow, if possible."

" 'Menus,' indeed! 'Boiled chickweed with soy, wild leek with bean paste and vinegar'—that's about all there is to write, isn't it?"

"But that's just what I mean—that you should write about the abominable kind of stuff we ate. 'The unbelievably meager diet of the Shizuma family in wartime,' you can call it. Then I can include it in my 'Journal of the Bombing.' Why didn't I think of it before now?"

"If that's how you feel, I've a suggestion," she said. "Every year on the anniversary of the day the bomb fell, why don't we have the same things for breakfast as we had that August 6? I can remember what we had *that* day all right. Very clearly, I can."

"What was it, now? That morning. . . ."

"Watery stock with clams, and soybeans with the oil extracted, in place of rice. That was all. Only six small clams for three people, mark you. Yasuko and I had dug them out of the sand under Miyuki Bridge the day before. . . ."

Yes, he remembered them: skinny little clams, with a transparent look to the flesh. He had grumbled to Shigeko, in all seriousness, that even the clams were suffering from malnutrition nowadays.

"You know, Shigeko—what the family eats is really your affair, as mistress of the house. So get it down on paper, will you? Tomorrow, if you can. It doesn't matter whether you write it as a kind of memo or in letter form. . . ." He paused. "Anyway, I've had enough for today. I'm off to bed."

The next day was a festival in the agricultural calendar, and Shigematsu set about putting the agricultural implements in order, as tradition required of the head of a farming household. He washed the spades, hoes, and crowbars, and hammered new wedges into the handles. The axes and sickles he sharpened. The saws he reset. He even sharpened the rice-reaping sickles, and coated them with rapeseed oil. He weeded around the family shrine that stood in one corner of the garden, and went to "pay homage" at the pond at Shōkichi's for good measure. All this accounted for a full half day.

Yasuko, who had gone to the beauty salon in town for a permanent wave, came home around five exuding an unfamiliar air of glamor. By this time, Shigeko had finished writing her account of what she had called "Diet in Wartime Hiroshima." It was done in brush and ink on handmade writing paper, and it ran as follows:

Diet in Wartime Hiroshima
What I'm really writing about here is the food situation in Hiroshima before the bomb, but first of all I must just say something about our everyday lives and the way people behaved.

Under the control ordinances in force at the time, rice, rice substitutes, fish, and vegetables were all rationed. Information about rationing, as well as other notices, was either put up on the district notice board or passed around from family to family on the local bulletin-board. This bulletin board was particularly important, and served as a way of circulating official directives to every corner of society. The authorities must have attached a great deal of importance to it, and to get the system working really smoothly they used the movies and phonograph records to popularize a song about the spirit of the neighborhood association. I remember the first verse, it went—

> Tap, tap, smartly at the door—
> Now, whoever can it be?
> Just a neighbor's well-known face
> When we open up and see.
> Pass the board on with a will—
> News for you and news for me.

On ration days there was always a line of people in front of the rationing center well before time. No wonder, either, as the food shortage was really quite unspeakable. Sometimes a line of customers would even form in front of one of the ordinary shops, which because of the shortage of goods were "open, but not for business," as they said. Sometimes, you'd hear someone at the back say to someone at the front, "By the way, what are they selling at this shop?" And the answer would be, "You know, I'm not certain. But I'm sure they're selling *something*." Everything was so scarce, you were glad to get hold of anything, whatever it might be. You couldn't afford to waste even an ordinary piece of paper.

The value of money had gone down. Sometimes when I went to buy vegetables at farms just outside the town, they'd be unwilling to sell for money, and would ask for clothing instead. Naturally, middlemen and retailers began to dabble in undercover business to avoid the controls, and people used to refer to them contemptuously as "black marketeers." If ever there was a typical product of war, that word "black marketeer" was it—a hateful word that I can never hear now without thinking of wartime austerity.

With the basic foods, rice and barley, the ration at first, as I remember it, was about 3.1 *gō*.[1] Before long, though, quite a large part of the rice and barley came to be replaced by soybeans, then they began to dole out foreign rice and, worse still, those dreadful pressed-out soybeans. The quantity gradually went down, and in the end the ration was about 2.7 to 2.8 *gō* of those beans a day.

At first the ration rice was brown, unhulled rice, which was unpleasant to eat, so we used to put it in a bottle and pound it with a stick to make it into white rice. We would do the hulling at night. It would make extra work for us in the evening, and we used to complain about it all the time. The rice got less when it was hulled, and even when the ration was about 3.1 *gō* per person it ended up only a little over 2.5 *gō*.

I believe it was around that time that Mrs. Miyaji was summoned by the authorities for an official talking-to. She was going out to a farm to buy food one day when she said to someone in the next seat to her on the Kabe train, "Now the rice ration has gone down to three *gō*, they've altered some of the words in a textbook our boy uses at school." It seems a line of verse in her child's poetry book which had said "To each his four *gō*/Of unhulled rice a day" had been changed to "To each his three *gō*/Of unhulled rice a day," so as to make it fit in with the actual amount of the ration. According to what she told me later, the poem is one of the most famous pieces by a poet called Kenji Miyazawa, a fine piece with a kind of austere beauty that gets over wonderfully the hardships of the farmer's life.

"To change 'four *gō* of rice a day' to 'three *gō*' is an insult to learning," Mrs. Miyaji said. "Whatever would happen if the child got to hear about it? Why, I wouldn't be surprised if he even started getting ideas about the Japanese history they learn at school. It would be different, now, if Kenji Miyazawa came to life again and rewrote it *himself*. . . ."

The fact remained, though, that the textbook was a government one compiled in accordance with major policies of state, and it seems the authorities told her to "keep a curb on her

1. One *gō* equals 0.381 U.S. pints.

irresponsible talk." "We know quite well you've been going to buy black market goods," they said. "Such people have no business making impertinent remarks about textbooks. Irresponsible talk in wartime is a matter that's too serious for the ordinary civil or criminal code." The way they spoke, it was almost as though they were suggesting it was a breach of the National General Mobilization Law, which was a capital offense, of course. By that time, everybody was taking care what they said in front of others.

In our family, my husband and Yasuko had their lunch at work. They bought their meals there, without taking any of their own food, which meant that we saved on two meals a day. Besides that, I made do with potatoes for my own lunch, so that altogether we gained three meals a day, which made things a bit easier. Then we had a way of getting rationed buckwheat noodles that sometimes got onto the black market, so that altogether, I suppose, we had the equivalent of three or four *gō* of rice or barley.

Besides this there was sometimes a ration of very poor quality dried bread, about thirty or forty grams to each household. There was a ration of about one bundle of noodles per person three or four times every month, but the rice or barley ration was always cut down correspondingly.

Sometimes the ration rice had soybeans mixed in with it. The trouble was that if you cooked it in the usual way with the beans in it, they gave it an unpleasant taste, so we used to pick out the beans—more than one *gō* of them—and soak them overnight in water. Then the next morning we'd mash them, strain the liquid through a piece of cotton, and use it for things like bean paste soup or soy sauce soup. Sometimes, too, we would use it by itself as a drink, with a certain amount of sweetening added. Occasionally we would cook the remains of the soybeans in soy sauce and eat them with our rice or rice substitute.

The bread that took the place of rice was a valuable means of stretching the ration. We toasted it and ate it with bean paste on it, or spread it with bean paste before toasting. Whenever we had bread, we missed the taste of butter and corned beef dreadfully. All the same, it gradually made us realize that where the traditional Oriental flavorings were concerned, bean-paste was at least far more substantial than salt or soy sauce. Here is a list of one day's rations of foodstuffs, apart from the basic rice or rice substitute. Actually, this was the ration for the eleven families in our neighborhood association, thirty-two people altogether, so many of the items were difficult to split up, and we used to divide them up among two or three families at a time:

> One cake of bean curd
> One sardine or small horse-mackerel
> Two Chinese cabbages
> Five or six carrots, giant radishes, leeks,
>   burdock roots, bundles of spinach, or marrows
> Four or five eggplants
> Half a pumpkin

Once the air raid warnings started, the food situation began to get worse and worse. Almost every day, I used to go to the place where houses had been cleared away to pick pigweed, trefoil and other leafy plants. At other times I would go to collect clams under Miyuki Bridge or, when the tide was out, would take an old writing-brush and trowel and go to catching squillas. At first, I would get about five *gō* of clams and from ten to twenty squillas. But they both got scarcer and scarcer, and by the end of the war I was only getting about ten clams and no squillas at all.

We grew a few green vegetables on the vacant lots, and pumpkins in the garden, in line with the authorities' slogan: "There's always a place for a pumpkin." When the stalks grew long, we would cut them off, peel them, and boil them for eating. In summer, the pumpkin plants would spread all over the garden so that you could hardly set foot in it, but we were disappointed at the number of actual pumpkins, a bare dozen or so each year. Sometimes, with our rice or rice substitute, we had dried shredded giant radish, dried fern, or bracken sprouts that were sent to us from my family who were living in the country.

On the day war was declared, December 8, 1941, I'd bought up a whole stock of matches and salt, so our family never went short of either, right up until the end of the war. I did this because my grandmother had told me as a child what happened at the time of the Russo-Japanese War. The salt came in very handy. I would make a substitute for soy sauce by adding table salt to a meat extract made by refining the broth from the Army Provisions Depot and canning factories. I can still remember how good cooked food or soup tasted with a spoonful of this substitute soy sauce in it. The only trouble with it was that unless you gave it a rest, after two weeks or so of continual use your stomach somehow just refused to take it.

We would cook the whole day's rice or rice substitute in the morning, and make any leftovers from breakfast, along with that for the evening meal, into balls which we did up in a coarsely-woven wrapping cloth and hung up somewhere airy. This was so that we could take it with us when we went to the air raid shelter if the warning sounded. Along with the rice balls in the bundle, we always put some parched rice that my family in the country had sent us for use in an emergency, and also a document listing the names of our ancestors.

The only fish we felt free to broil as we pleased was what we got on the ration. We didn't like to broil fish we had bought on the black market in case the smell got to the neighbors, so we boiled it or made soup with it instead.

We were not too badly off for sweet things as Yasuko bought some on the black market through somebody she worked with. The stuff was a kind of candy made by a farmer living in the hills behind Furuichi, who used starch got by soaking the roots of a plant related to liquorice. Yasuko's friend used to buy it from this farmer, and would let her have some of it. We only used it for sweetening things a few times, though. Most of it we sucked as it was, to stave off hunger, though we felt it was an awful waste. As for saké, the same thing happened in our neighborhood association as everywhere else—once it went on the ration, people who had never touched it before the war started drinking. A peculiar thing to happen.

Besides the cigarette ration, someone at the works would let us have a share of leaf tobacco he bought on the black market. We would hang it under the floorboards for a while to moisten it, shred it with cloth shears, and wrap it in the thin, fine paper from an English dictionary—"Indian paper," I was told it's called. In the years before and after the end of the war we smoked a whole pocket dictionary in our house.

In the last years of the war every household in our neighborhood association was supplementing its food with wild plants. In families with small children they would wait till the shoots of various kinds of brambles had grown a bit, then collect them, peel off the skin, and give them to the children for their afternoon between-meals. In some families they gave them knotweed shoots. You could find these plants on the banks of the Ōta River, on the outskirts of the city, and some families who went out to work would ask people commuting from outside the city to gather the plants for them. In every home, parched beans made up ninety percent of such snacks for the children, and the wild plants made a kind of change.

You could get sorrel if you asked someone commuting from outside the city. We used to leave it in brine overnight and use it instead of pickles, or as a main dish with our rice substitute.

Reed root, chickweed, pigweed, tugwort, and barweed (these may not be the scientific names) we used to parboil and serve with soy sauce, or fry for use as a side dish. Vegetables such as carrots and burdock stem were considered a real luxury. Children who were undernourished or prone to bed-wetting were given the grubs found in figs or the fruit of a certain shrub, broiled in soy. Actually, these grubs are the young of the long-horned beetle. In the summer when I was a child in the country, there was a woodcutter who used to come selling them, and sometimes I was given them to prevent worms. I remember them as savory and rather nice.

The wife of one of the neighbors who suffered from headaches because of the change of life used to take a couple of ant-lions in a cupful of cold saké. She said they were remarkably effective.

Actually, I had intended to write out our family's actual wartime menus for a week at least, but since I was doing the same kind of thing in the kitchen every day, everything's mixed up in my mind, and I can't recall things accurately. I wonder if even the cooks in the leading hotels up in Tokyo—in the Imperial Hotel, say—can remember exactly their menus on the day the war ended! They say that around that time the envoys of the countries of the Greater East Asia Co-Prosperity Sphere and members of the various organizations connected with the Foreign Ministry were staying at the Imperial Hotel. I wonder what they had to eat? Either way, sixty or seventy per cent of *our* diet in Hiroshima during the last years of the war was rice with soybeans, and pressed-out soybeans boiled down in soy sauce, without sugar.

Animal protein other than fish was almost unobtainable. Instead of tea, we used cherry blossom buds pickled in salt.

Charcoal and charcoal balls were hard to come by too, so in our house we kept warm in winter by roasting flat stones or tiles in the stove when we were cooking, then wrapping them in old newspapers, doing them up in cloth, and putting them down our backs. When we were sitting Japanese style we would keep them between our legs, and when we were sitting on the sofa we would put them under our feet to keep them warm. As the stone gradually cooled off, we would take off the newspaper one layer at a time to get at the remaining warmth, then when every bit of warmth had gone we would put it back in the oven and use it again in the same way.

For soap, we would use the stuff we were given, made with rice bran and caustic soda, or buy emulsion on the black market.

Sometimes, even, we used to put out the fire under the stove after we had finished cooking and collect the half-burnt embers. When we had enough, we would powder them, mix the powder with a trace of clay and paste to bind it, and shape it into balls which we used for fuel once they were dry.

When tooth powder became unavailable, we used salt.

Oh, yes—and when there was a ration of onions we used not to eat them but planted them in the ground instead, and picked the leaves as they grew to use in soup.

That ends my sketch of the food situation in Hiroshima during wartime. I imagine you could call our family's diet "lower middle grade" as far as ordinary white-collar workers' families went. Before the war, Hiroshima was known as a place with plenty of produce both from the sea and the country, and although it was so big, there were no slums. But living in Hiroshima I realized, as they say, that in a long drawn out war it's a case of the larger the town, the shorter its inhabitants go of food. And I realized, too, that war's a sadistic killer of human beings, young and old, men and women alike.

By Shigeko Shizuma

Shigematsu fastened this account away as an appendix to his "Journal of the Bombing." Then, at Shigeko's request, he set off for Kōtarō's place with rice dumplings for the Mass for Dead Insects. The lacquer box containing the dumplings was inside the metal wash-bowl in which Kōtarō had brought the loach, and the whole was encased in a wrapping-cloth.

The Mass for Dead Insects was a rite performed on the day after the festival, when farmers would make rice dumplings as an offering to the souls of the deceased insects they had inadvertently trodden on as they worked in the fields. On the same day, custom also demanded that they should return any articles that they had on loan from their neighbors.

CHAPTER 5 ✍

Kōtarō's home stood by the side of the slope leading up the hill. As Shigematsu approached, he caught sight of a gleaming new, medium-sized automobile parked at the foot of the slope. This was something he had not bargained for. The car was empty, and a middle-aged man who seemed to be the driver, with a peaked cap pushed back on his head, was peering into the great jar into which water flowed from the bamboo pipe. It was clear that Kōtarō had some rather special visitor.

Shigematsu's heart had begun to pound at his first sight of the intruder. "Lovely weather we're having," he said, affecting an air of vagueness, as he approached the jar. "That's the car belonging to the Fujita Clinic in Fukuyama, isn't it?" he went on disingenuously. "Has your passenger come from Fukuyama?"

"No, this is a hired car," the man in the peaked cap replied.

"I'm just the driver. I've brought a lady over from Yamano."

"You mean a lady doctor? Of course, if it's something sudden, one has to send a car for the doctor, I suppose. What's up with old Kōtarō, then?"

"No, that's not it—the lady's here to make inquiries about some marriage prospect or other. At least, that's the impression I got from what she said. I've been waiting here for more than an hour."

If she had come from the village of Yamano to inquire about a marriage, it could only be about Yasuko. The village was too small for it to mean anything else.

Again Shigematsu's heart started to beat faster. But he peered into the jar with feigned unconcern.

"All these loach are black, aren't they?" he said. "When I was a kid, there used to be a brown kind with black spots called *sunahami*."

"I expect that's the kind we call *sunamuguri*. You used to find it in mountain streams. By now, though, they've all been killed off by agricultural chemicals."

"In our village here it's not only the *sunahami*. All the *gigichō* have been killed off too."

"That would be what we call *gigi*, I suppose. A pale reddish fish, with fins on its back and belly that stick into you? Yes, they've all disappeared from the stream in our village too."

Peering through the foliage, Shigematsu could see that the papered sliding screens facing the veranda of Kōtarō's house were shut, and those inside the entrance too. He wondered what kind of things Kōtarō and the woman were saying about Yasuko. It occurred to him, though, that by now she might well be winding up her business. She might even be getting up to go at this very moment.

"Well, I mustn't keep you talking," he said, suddenly fearful of getting caught. "I just hoped it might be the doctor's car, as there's someone sick near us. Good-day to you."

He walked up a path that led into a grove of oak trees and seated himself on a flat rock that lay there. Very well—he told himself—he would be patient and wait here until the woman went home. He could hardly leave without giving Kōtarō the dumplings. If he took them back home, the womenfolk would want explanations, and he didn't want Yasuko to find out that a woman had come from Yamano especially to make inquiries about her.

The rock on which he sat was about the size of two tatami mats. In the old days, the trunk of a great red pine all of 180 feet high had towered by its side, but the pine had gone for the national effort during the war, and so had the gingko tree at Kōtarō's, which people said had been the same height. On sunny mornings in late autumn and on into the winter, the shadows of the pine and the gingko tree would reach out all the way to the foot of the hill on which Shigematsu's house stood.

As a boy, Shigematsu had seldom come to the flat rock to play, but he had often been to play under the gingko tree at Kōtarō's place. When the frosts came and the gingko tree began to shed its leaves, the roof of Kōtarō's house would be transformed into a yellow roof, smothered with dead leaves. Whenever a breeze sprang up, they would pour down from the eaves in a yellow waterfall, and when it eddied they would swirl up into the air—up and up to twice, three times the height of the roof—then descend in yellow whirlpools onto the road up the slope and onto the oak grove.

This always delighted the children. As the wind dropped and the leaves came dancing down, the boys would stretch up their hands to clutch at them, and the girls would catch them in their outspread aprons. Then they would total the number of leaves they had caught. "One-for-me, two-for-me, gingko yellow," they would chant, throwing away a leaf at a time—that made four leaves. "Flittery, slippery, gingko fellow"—that made another four. Over and over again they would sing the same refrain, until only one child had any leaves left, and he became the winner.

At such times, old Ruigorō from Kōtarō's place would often appear from the house with a broom to sweep the road up the hill, since it worried him to think the children might slip on the piled-up gingko leaves on the slope.

The old man had still been working as a mail carrier for the

Kobatake post office in those days. Every day for more than twenty years, come rain, come shine, he had gone to and fro with the mail on his back between the Kobatake and Takafuta post offices. He had even been given an award by the Minister of Communications for his services. He wore a round wicker hat and a loose, dark blue cotton jacket with the words "Kobatake Post Office" picked out in white around the collar, with puttees on his legs and straw sandals on his feet, and the pouch containing the mail slung on the end of a pole over his shoulder. When the road was blocked by children at play, or if there was a cart or a horse-wagon in the way, he would clear a path for himself by crying: "Way for the mail! Here comes the mail! Official business! Make way there!" The children would gather by the side of the road and chorus after him as he went: "Way for the mail! Here comes the mail! Official business! Huff, puff, huff, puff, huff. . . ."

A car door slammed, and there came the sound of an engine starting up. The sun was beginning to set. Shigematsu came out of the grove and went over to Kōtarō's house. The sliding doors on the veranda were still shut, but those inside the entrance were open now. He went in, and found Kōtarō sitting on the step up from the hall with his arms folded, staring down at the floor. He must have been sitting there, quite still, ever since seeing his visitor out.

"Good evening," Shigematsu said.

Kōtarō looked up as though startled. "Oh, good evening." Seeing Shigematsu, he returned the greeting, but immediately dropped his eyes again. He seemed ashamed of himself: this much at least Shigematsu could tell, despite the gloom inside the entrance hall. Obviously Kōtarō had been pressed to answer all kinds of questions about Yasuko, had been made to say things against his will, and was feeling worn out as a result. Sensing how things were, Shigematsu thanked him for the loach he brought for them, got him to transfer the dumplings into a bowl, and went home without further ado.

The incident had left him with an unpleasant taste in his mouth. He felt an intolerable pity for Yasuko at being exposed, as it were, to the public gaze like this. There was only one thing for him to do: he must finish copying out his journal of the bombing as soon as possible. He must show it to those concerned, and let them compare it with Yasuko's diary. It was a matter of normal self-respect. By now, he realized, he had been driven into feeling it as his own personal problem.

For dinner, he had a simple bowl of rice mixed with green tea and pickles, then got down to his transcription again.

Skirting the edge of the throng, I managed somehow to get through to the East Parade Ground. The road from the street to the ground was filled with a continuous stream of refugees. Most of them had only the clothes they stood up in, but one family had its household belongings piled on a wheelbarrow, with a child on top of them. They were arguing noisily among themselves, unable to make any progress through the dense stream of humanity but equally unable, it seemed, to bring themselves to abandon their belongings. There were a husband and wife carrying several large bundles in wrapping cloths, together with a suitcase and Gladstone bag which were threaded on a pole slung over their shoulders. There was a group of about twenty schoolboys walking in single file, all holding onto a rope in case they got separated.

I looked back. The road from the street to the parade ground entrance was a broad, continuous belt of humanity.

When I reached Hiroshima Station, the trains in the marshaling yards backing onto the East Parade Ground were all, freight and passenger trains alike, jammed with refugees. On one passenger train near the station itself, people were hanging onto the roof in clusters shouting "Get going! Get going!" No station official was in sight, and there seemed little chance of the train starting, but still the refugees pressed on toward the station. The windows, window frames, and doors of the station building had disappeared, and here and there the outer walls gaped in holes. As I passed by the building, I saw that a large chunk of wall on a level with the second-floor windows had been blasted out and was hanging in the air, suspended from a thick strand of the metal reinforcement. I ran as I passed beneath it.

When I reached the place where the switches were, I saw a young station official not much over twenty busily clanking levers up and down. "Not one of them that works!" he suddenly declared to himself, and set off running in the opposite direction from the station.

The streets in front of the station were on fire and unapproachable, so I set off round the back of Hiji hill. Gobenden Shrine no longer stood in its accustomed place on the hill, but I did not doubt the road I had taken: Hiji hill was Hiji hill, even without a shrine on it.

Matoba Bridge was on fire and impassable. I crossed Taishō Bridge, passed the southern side of Hiji hill, and came out by the side of the Women's Commercial College. This was a residential district, but all the houses I passed seemed to be empty, and few people were in the streets. The place felt empty and deserted, and a dog was howling in the distance. A small group of housewives stood by the roadside, talking. There was no water in the taps, I heard them saying; you couldn't even wash your hands.

At the word "water," I suddenly felt thirsty again, and my throat began to hurt. I looked up at the sky, and saw that part of the head of the jellyfish cloud, whose color was fading by now, was reaching out over the western extremity of Hiji hill. It looked as though it might come after me, over to the north of the hill. Whenever the wind blew from the east, the jellyfish was obscured by smoke from the fires, but as soon as the wind changed it reappeared again.

I had one hundred and twenty yen and some small change in my purse. If somebody had been selling water, I would have given him the lot. I'd heard that at such times it helped to chew tea leaves; I would gladly have chewed leaves off the bush in the state I was then. As it was, I walked on, hugging my thirst to myself, till I found a bucket left standing by a communal tap. It was about seven-tenths full of water. I leaned over the bucket, putting my hands on the wash-place, and, thrusting my face in as a dog does, drank ecstatically till I had had my fill. By now I had forgotten that one should take three separate mouthfuls first: I just drank. It was very good. I felt cooler immediately. Quite suddenly, though, all the strength drained out of my body, and my two outstretched arms threatened to give way, so I pressed down on the rim of the bucket and, putting all my strength into my legs, stood up. A wet cloth was hanging down over my chest. It was the triangular bandage; somehow, without my noticing, it had slipped off my head and become a neckerchief.

When I started walking, the sweat began to pour off me, and my whole body was soon drenched from head to foot. My spectacles steamed over. Time and again, I stopped and wiped them, or wiped them as I walked. When I got near the front gate of the Army Clothing Branch Depot, the jellyfish cloud had swollen up to five or six times the size it had been when I saw it at Yokogawa. All the color had faded out of it by now, though, and it was only a misty mass blurred at the edges. Once so terrifying, it was now no more than a shadow of its former self, and seemed to have little power left to do anything. As I watched it, human voices came drifting out of the Branch Depot—"Hey—how much longer? Have you contacted the chief of the Defense Section?" "Yes sir, I've been to contact him"—and there were signs of two or three people moving busily to and fro. I felt a great deal reassured.

One thing I worried about was fire. I did not know where was burning, or how, or to which areas the fires were spreading. I had no idea what had happened to my own house. If Senda-machi was on fire, my wife Shigeko should have taken refuge in the university sports ground; we had long ago agreed on this in case of emergency. There was no need to worry about Yasuko, since she had gone to Furue with the women from the neighborhood association.

I was walking on, looking for somewhere to take a short rest, when my ears caught the sound of a cat miaowing. I turned, and saw a tortoiseshell cat walking along at the feet of a man in boots. "Hey, tortoiseshell!" I ventured. The cat would have walked on past me, completely indifferent, but the man in boots stopped, whereupon the cat, too, stopped and went up to the boots.

The man in the boots spoke. "If it isn't Mr. Shizuma!" he said· "Well, Mr. Shizuma!"

"Why, if it isn't Mr. Miyaji!" The coincidence was almost un-
believable, but there was no mistaking Miyaji, of our neighborhood
association. During the past two months or so, he had taken to
going around in boots of the kind worn by army personnel, and to
wearing, despite the heat, a khaki polo shirt. This was his dress
for doing the rounds of firms and government offices, taking
orders in connection with his business. Today, he was wearing his
army breeches as usual, but above the waist he was naked, and he
had no hat.

"How are you? You're not hurt?" I asked.

"Awful! I caught it, all right." He turned around to show me. The
skin of his back had come clean away from his shoulders, and was
hanging limply, like a piece of wet newspaper. The skin on the back
of his hands had peeled off and was hanging in the same way. His
face was ashen but unscathed.

I assumed he had been caught in a fire and got his back burned
by the flames, but I was wrong. Early that morning, he had gone
to call on an acquaintance who lived somewhere within sight of the
keep of Hiroshima Castle, and had been taking off his polo shirt
before going inside. (I suspect he had gone to see a special woman
friend; rumor always said that he had a woman somewhere.) He
had been hurrying, he told me, and was soaked in sweat. But just
as he got the shirt over his head there was a terrifying roar and
flash. His head and face were muffled in the shirt, but he could
tell the brightness of the flash right through the material and his
closed eyelids.

He did not know what had happened after that. The first thing
he knew, he was running in the direction of the inner moat of the
castle on the other side.

"I didn't know or care what I was up to," he said, staggering
along by my side. "I only knew that I ought to go in the direction
of the hills. So I went to Yokogawa Bridge, then past the front of
the Second General Army Headquarters. That was when this cat
started following me. Do you think it means good luck or bad
luck? I keep wondering."

The Second General Army Headquarters was on the north side

of the East Parade Ground. That meant that from the Yokogawa area to here Miyaji had fled along the same route as myself.

We walked from the Clothing Branch Depot toward the Regional Monopoly Office. It was a district of wealthy homes, completely laid waste. Broken telephone wires hung in great fringes and the road was covered all over with tiles, sliding doors, and other debris.

Sometimes the cat was ahead of Miyaji, sometimes behind. Miyaji was in a pitiful state. He seemed on the verge of collapse, and was hardly aware of what he was doing. I felt a desperate urge to make haste. I picked up a piece of bamboo for him to use as a stick, then threw it away again: with the skin off the back of his hands, it would have been unkind. There was nothing to do but pick our way ahead slowly, treading on tiles, pushing doors and screens out of the way, stooping to pass beneath dangling cables.

The tiles crunched under our feet. Our shoes would slip on them, and we would fall forward. We would put our hands out to save ourselves, but to stand up again was a sore effort. Nobody was about but the pair of us, and the cracking of tiles beneath our feet rang unnaturally loud in the silence. I noticed a large chest of drawers lying tumbled on the undulating mounds of tiles. A young woman in nothing but a loincloth sat propped against it, with her legs flung out before her and one of her breasts torn off. She may well have been dead.

The tortoiseshell cat, it occurred to me, was probably taken with the smell of the boots. It continued to shadow Miyaji, and was still with him when we came out on the broad road along which the streetcars went to Ujina.

The streetcars were all stopped. Here, though, the streets took on a completely different appearance. Trucks loaded with the injured passed by unceasingly. There was a car carrying army officers. A hand-drawn cart went by, the injured hauling the injured. The many maimed who went on foot were in much the same condition as the refugees I had seen on the railway embankment and the East Parade Ground, but here many of them were using pieces of wood or bamboo as sticks. Here, there were few calls for help or cries of pain, and almost none of the injured were running. Why run, indeed, when to run was only to hasten to the world of shadows? Among the refugees I saw a cripple in a chair. He pedaled his chair with his hands, zooming past the injured with an almost contemptuous indifference.

Miyaji felt his way with his hands along the wall of the Monopoly Office as though he might collapse at any moment. When the wall gave out on him, he groaned "Water! Water!" and the next moment had staggered out into the road and halted by a stranded streetcar. I felt myself on the verge of fainting, but followed him up to the streetcar and half crawled onto the deck. Miyaji sat on the step. Inside the car, in a corner of a seat, were a charming small boy barely old enough to walk, a girl of seven or eight, and a boy who looked like a primary school pupil and held a ping-pong paddle. I dropped a triangular bandage from my first-aid kit over the raw flesh on Miyaji's shoulders, and tied the two corners round his throat. It looked like a white shawl.

"Mr. Miyaji, I have some mentholatum at least," I said. "What shall I do—shall I put some on?"

He shook his head. "But I *should* like a drink of water," he said. He pointed at the sky. "Why—look at that fire!"

A tremendous funnel of flame was shooting up into the sky from somewhere around the center of the city. A truly huge column of fire, it sucked together the smoke and flames gushing from different parts of the district, and fashioned them into a single great whirlpool, at the same time spreading out the smoke into a cloudlike shelf above. Around the twisting column of flame that pierced this cloud I could see, scattering and falling, small gobbets of fire and shapes that emitted flames. It dawned on me that they were the pillars and beams and other timbers of houses. They had been drawn up into the whirlwind, and were burning as they fell.

Although the wind did not seem to change direction, the flames from time to time would creep out over the roofs of buildings. At one moment, the fire would stretch out as though a huge rope were being twisted out of the flame, then the next moment it would surge forward in a great wave. With the pointed tongues of its flames, it licked at the windows of the larger Western-style buildings.

"Look—" said Miyaji in a shaking voice, "the tips of the flames are like snakes—they flicker their tongues in at the windows first, then they crawl right inside. Do you see that building that's just started burning—that's the Fukuya Department Store isn't it?"

Every time one of the great waves of fire broke against the Fukuya Department Store, the Chūgoku Power Supply Corporation, the Chūgoku Newspaper Office, the City Hall, or any other large building, its flames would burst out in a southwesterly direction from countless windows at once. One such surge of flame would almost certainly have consumed a dozen or two dozen ordinary wooden houses. Suddenly, though, the wind must have changed, for a part of the fire suddenly bulged out from the center and, first spindle-shaped, then spherical, drifted up into the sky on its own. Then, even as we watched, the center of the sphere on its upward journey split, and gaped wide open.

A remarkable phenomenon. I pressed my hand against my chest. Possibly I was past fear, for my heartbeat was normal. My state of mind was definitely not. I felt, at one and the same time, as though I were being pressed inexorably backward, as though I were being swallowed up into the earth, as though my brain were going numb to all feeling.

Miyaji stood up. "Mr. Shizuma—let's go home," he said. Getting off the streetcar, I glanced back inside; the three children had disappeared.

As we reached the front gate of the Monopoly Bureau, the roof of our home came into sight amidst the houses still standing unburned on the other side of the river. The only smoke to be seen was still far in the distance. The house had survived; quite suddenly, all the strength went out of my limbs, and I sank down onto the ground. Miyaji's house, which was one-storied, was not visible.

"Mr. Shizuma—I'm worried," Miyaji said. "I think I'll hurry on. The way that fire's burning, everything's certain to go up in flames sooner or later."

He went off across Miyuki Bridge on unsteady legs, and disappeared from sight. (They say he died the next day.) I had got halfway across the bridge myself before I noticed that there was no parapet left. On the north side, it lay collapsed along the bridge, but on the south it must have been blown into the river. The posts were of granite—a foot square and about four feet high, I should say. They had stood at intervals of some six feet, each capped with a block of stone about twice the area of the post itself. There had been dozens and dozens of these massive posts, and they were all blown down or blown away.

A man lay at the northern end of the bridge. It was not Miyaji. Several more bodies were floating in the water beneath the bridge. I hastened on towards the university sports ground. Our pre-arranged assembly point was by the side of the swimming pool. It was four or five hundred meters from Miyuki Bridge to the pool, and all the way I felt my chest constricted, almost as though I were approaching some fierce animal that had escaped from its cage. Nor can I believe that it was just because I walked too fast.

The sports ground was a turmoil of refugees. Threading my way through them, I reached the edge of the pool, and there on the other bank, seated on her heels on the ground with a knapsack on her back and a blanket over her knees, I saw my wife. Scooping up water from the pool with my hands, I drank, then made my way around to the other side. I had always instilled into her that she must use a knapsack when taking refuge in a raid, since a suitcase would catch on other people in a crush. And she must go to the side of the pool, I had said, where one could jump in if the fires got too close. She had obeyed my instructions faithfully. Beside her where she sat stood a rice-cooking pot and a small pan.

"You're not hurt?" I asked.

"No." Seeing my face, she looked down and said no more.

"What about the house?"

"It tilted, but it's still standing."

"No fire?"

"The top of the pine tree in the garden started to burn, but it was too high to do anything about it."

"I expect Yasuko's all right. She's at Furue, isn't she?"

"I expect she's all right."

"Not hungry?"

"No, I'm not hungry."

"How about the neighbors?"

"I came here right away, so I didn't see very much."

She seemed to be in a rather dazed state, so I decided to make sure by going to look at the house myself. With a strict injunction to her not to leave the spot until I returned, I set off home.

The fire on the pine tree had gone out, but the props of the telephone pole were burning at the base. I extinguished them by beating them with a bamboo broom.

The house was leaning in a south-southeasterly direction at an angle of about fifteen degrees. The sliding screens and outer shutters on the second floor had all been blown out. I stepped up into the drawing room, and found it strewn all over with pieces of glass, and the sliding doors pushed into a slightly rhomboid shape. I went round all the rooms in turn—the big room, the two smaller rooms, and the one smallest room, as well as the two rooms upstairs—and everywhere the sliding doors were lop-sided and stuck fast in their grooves.

I went through the kitchen into the bathroom, and found that the kitchen from the Hayamis' place, our neighbors at the back, had been blown, wall and all, into our bathroom. The bath-tub was buried in a litter of cups, ladles, chopsticks, gridirons, china bowls, and the like, and the wall of the dressing room was plastered with some blackish food boiled in soy, pickled vegetables, and used tea leaves. There was even a piece of dried cuttlefish lying on the boarded floor, also presumably blown over from the Hayamis. I was tempted to try it, but cuttlefish was such a luxury that I put it in my first-aid pouch instead.

I went back to the smaller room and helped myself to the cold tea in the teapot, drinking from the spout. I rummaged in the medicine chest for something to put on my burned cheek, but there was nothing that could be used as an ointment. The full-length mirror lay broken on the floor. I glanced at the calendar with its message for the day. "Never say die," it said.

CHAPTER 6 🌿

Early the next morning, Shōkichi and Asajirō, dressed as for a journey and carrying Gladstone bags, came to ask Shigematsu whether he would care to join with them in making a pond for hatching carp in. They had already bought fry from the Tokikane-maru hatchery, of course, but this time they wanted to rear much larger numbers of them from the very earliest stage, for release in the large pond at Agiyama.

"As I hear," said Shōkichi, "they begin spawning on the Eighty-eighth. They start when the water gets a bit warm, and go on into July, or August even, so long as the temperature of the water's right. We're going to go to the hatchery at Tokikanemaru to learn how to hatch them."

"So Shōkichi and me, we're just off to Tokikanemaru to learn how," put in Asajirō. "We're going for a period of study, you might say. Then, when we've done our stint, the idea is to make a pond for hatching them in. We two are already set on the idea. So do you agree, or don't you?"

Shigematsu agreed readily. The "period of study" would probably only last three or four days altogether; he could use the time to get on with the transcription of his journal.

Shōkichi and Asajirō went off without further ado to catch the first bus of the day, taking their heavy-looking Gladstone bags with them. They were so active today that it seemed hardly possible they were victims of atomic disease. Shigematsu decided to follow their example, and to press ahead with the copying of his journal.

I went over to the pond by the rockery in the back garden. A parasol and mosquito net were floating on the water. Of late, it had become a kind of ritual after dinner in our family to put a board across one corner of the pond and to stand on it the crockery, the pots, and the other utensils we used every day, so that in the event of an air raid we had only to raise one side of the board with one hand, and the whole lot would disappear under the water. Shigeko must have taken a hint from this and, on the spur of the moment, done the same to the parasol and net.

Taking some bricks from where the wall had collapsed, I loaded them on the mosquito net and parasol to sink them. The net was a valuable piece of property that could be traded for 50 *gō* of rice, and I weighted it with plenty of bricks to make sure it would not come to the surface. As I was doing so, I spotted, in a corner of the pond beneath an overhanging aloe branch, a carp about a foot long and a roach of about six or seven inches, both floating dead in the water with their bellies all swollen up. I fished them out and threw them away at the foot of the brick wall, in case they decomposed and made the net and other things smell. Both their bellies, I found, were distended quite hard.

Years before, when I had been living in a rented room, an earthquake had brought a bank in the garden crashing down, and several carp in the pond had died. I had dissected one of them, a black carp about a foot long that they gave me, and was surprised to find its air bladder blown up tight, like a balloon. I recalled the incident now. It seems that when fish are subjected to some sudden, sharp shock, it paralyzes the machinery regulating their air bladders and their nervous systems, so that the air bladders fill with a mixture of gases which exerts a sudden pressure on the internal organs and stops the functions of the whole body. I remembered, too, how as a child in the country I had caught fish in a mountain stream by hitting a rock with a large, flat-headed hammer. The method was only possible in the winter, when the flow was small. I would raise the hammer high, and bring it down with all my strength on the side of the rock. There would be a great clang of metal on stone, and a gunpowdery smell, and at the same instant the fish would emerge from under the rock and stop quite still, stupefied, in the water. You could get hold of them and they wouldn't try to get away; their nerves had stopped functioning for the time being, paralyzed by the shock.

I, though, who had been on the deck of a train in Yokogawa Station, had registered nothing with my senses apart from the ball of light and the blast. That fish should die, great granite posts be blown down, and walls be broken through, yet human beings on the ground come through almost unscathed, was beyond my understanding. Even though I knew that fish had skins more sensitive to sound than human beings, a nameless dread still filled me whenever I wondered what type of bomb the ball of fire had been, or what its scientific effects might be.

I went around the neighbors' houses, peering about me as I went. I visited each house in turn—the Nozus and the Nakanishis in front of us, the Nittas on the west side, the Miyajis, the Ōkōchis, and the Sugais on the east—but there was no sound from anywhere. Next, I went to the houses on the street at the back. Of the people in our neighborhood association, Nojima, Mrs. Yoshimura, and Mrs. Miyaji had gone to Furue with Yasuko, and should be safe. But here all the houses stood vacant, leaning at an angle of fifteen degrees or more. I called again and again to Miyaji, with whom I had been walking only a while before, but even here there was no reply. The Nakamuras' house had collapsed.

"Mr. Nakamura! Mr. Nakamura!" I called, but there was no reply. "Mr. Nakamura!" I called again. "Master Nakamura! Mrs. Nakamura!" I pricked up my ears for a possible groan, even, but there was no reply of any kind. A silent collapsed house is still more unnerving than a silent empty one.

The members of the neighborhood association must have taken refuge somewhere. The doors and shutters were all left unfastened, with the same complete indifference to the dangers of theft as in the houses I had seen on the way. All those hours of firefighting drill with the members of the association had come to nothing now. Not a single lookout posted, much less anyone to bother about bucket relays, stretchers, or the like. . . . Suddenly, all the things we had done up to now seemed to me so much children's play, and my own life, too, a toy life.

"All right," I told myself, "so everything's kid's play. All the more reason, then, to throw yourself into it wholeheartedly. Do you get it, now? No throwing in the sponge!"

I went back to our own house and walked round it to see where the tiles had come off. The roof on the north side had been stripped completely, while the south side had a score or so left. The ridge tiles had all gone, except for one that I had once secured with copper wire when I did some repairs. On top of the collapsed wall by the pond, a piece of timber more than six feet long and four inches square was resting, and three logs about nine feet long were lying on the inside of the wall. Some of the local timber merchant's wares must have come flying over the Hiroshima University vegetable gardens and landed there, which meant they had been blasted a distance of four or five hundred feet at the very least. I was appalled. With a flash of inspiration, I used the timber and the logs as buttresses to shore up the tilting house. A buttress is designed to afford a constant and powerful check to the impulse of a building to fall down; my own buttresses, I thought, had a plucky air about them.

I was looking out through the wall where it had collapsed, to see if I could find another log somewhere, when I saw a young man sitting on a piece of timber, rewinding his puttees. It was the student from the Hiroshima Industrial College who lodged with the neighbors.

"Hashizume!" I called. "What are you doing there?" He looked round as though startled, and said "Yes."

"What's happened to Mrs. Nitta and everyone?" He only stared at me and said "Yes" again.

"Now, son, pull yourself together," I said, stepping over the collapsed wall and out into the road. "You've come back from school haven't you? What happened to the school? Any damage?"

"The school collapsed," the boy said in an empty voice. "Most of the others were crushed to death. Some of them were caught underneath but got out injured."

Young Hashizume was a relative of the Nittas. He was normally a cheerful, lively youth, but now be seemed almost half-witted. The things he said were rambling and I only half grasped the sense, but I gathered that he had crawled along under desks and chairs, then through the space between ceiling and roof till he found somewhere to get out.

"When I got home there was nobody there," he said.

"Then the thing to do is to look for them before the fires get here," I said. "I imagine most of the people around here have taken refuge in the university sports ground. My wife's there, you know. Now, what shall we do, son? Shall we go and have a look?"

"Yes," he said, and followed me as I led the way.

The sports ground was still a confused mass of injured and refugees. We threaded our way through the crowd and reached the poolside, where we found Mrs. Ōkōchi of the neighborhood association sitting by my wife.

"Why, Mr. Hashizume!" she exclaimed, then seemed to hesitate, at a loss for words. "Oh dear, some people have all the misfortune! It's really too. . . . Mr. Hashizume—your aunt has gone to the Kyōsai Hospital with your uncle."

So it came out. She had seen Mrs. Nitta injured in front of her very eyes. She had stopped in the street to talk with her about seeing off some young men who were going to the front when, all of a sudden, there had been a brilliant flash and a blast, and a tile had come flying through the air and sliced the flesh of Mrs. Nitta's cheek clean away.

Mrs. Ōkōchi had been born in Tokyo; she had been through the Great Earthquake there, and though she had only been at primary school at the time, she knew from her experience then what terrible things tiles could do. In a big earthquake, some force would send them skimming through the air like the pieces of cardboard children sometimes play with. Occasionally, they would travel up to 150 or 200 feet. One could imagine, she said, what an impetus the blast from something like that ball of fire would have given a tile.

As though to prove that he had recovered himself at last, young Hashizume was beginning to weep. "I'll go to the hospital, then," he said. "Thank you for your kindness, and look after yourselves." Reluctantly accepting the five *yen* that Mrs. Ōkōchi insisted on pressing into his hand to help him on his way, he set off alone along the side of the pool.

Working through the possibilities together, Shigeko and I decided that the best thing we could do was to go and contact the Japan Transport branch at Ujina. It seemed to us that even if Yasuko started back to Hiroshima from Furue on the truck, the fires rising menacingly in the east and the increasing number of injured they met as they progressed eastward would convince them that it was impossible to get through to Senda-machi. They would assume that Senda-machi was on fire by now. Since the resourceful Nojima was in charge, they would almost certainly reject the overland route in favor of a boat as far as Ujina. Nojima had always said that if Hiroshima was raided he would get away to Ujina by fishing boat. He told me he had contracts with an angler who lived at Ujina and a fisherman in Miyazu so that he could hire a boat at any time. I had been quite overwhelmed at the extent of his forethought.

"I feel sure Nojima will put ashore at Ujina," I said. "He'll never come back by road once he sees those fires. He couldn't, in fact, even if he wanted to. If they land at Ujina, though, Yasuko's sure to call in at the Japan Transport branch there. There's some urgent business I'm supposed to see the Transport people at Ujina about this evening. I'm obliged to go, in fact, and Yasuko knows it, so she'll show up there for certain."

My wife agreed with my estimate of the situation, and we decided to go and wait at the Ujina offices. Even so, it was a gamble, since there was no definite arrangement that Yasuko should call there. Shigeko turned to face the pool and, pressing her palms together before her, prayed silently for the briefest of moments.

"I only hope your Yasuko really will look in at Ujina," said Mrs. Ōkōchi. "Myself, I'm beginning to feel rather nervous." She was supposed to meet up with her husband, who worked at a bank, by the side of this same pool. They had an only son, a university graduate who was in the army, stationed at somewhere called Palembang in Sumatra.

For want of a better idea, Shigeko put some broken bricks from a wall in the pot and pan and sank them in the pool. I watched them slide effortlessly out of sight beneath the water.

"I mean to come and get that pot and pan one day," I said. "I only hope that day really comes."

"Oh, so do I!" said Mrs. Ōkōchi. "Well then, take care of yourselves. And remember me to Yasuko."

Shigeko and I left the sports ground and made for Miyuki Bridge. The dead body at the northern end of the bridge had flies swarming black at its mouth and nose. There was so much clotted blood about its ears that it was difficult to tell what was ear and what was blood. I was hastening past it when Shigeko said behind me, "Let's just look in at the house. Yasuko may come back while we're away, so we'd better put up a note for her."

She was right. I was disgusted at my own stupidity in not thinking of it. We went back to the house, and were looking for paper to write the note on when Yasuko suddenly arrived home out of the blue. Shigeko crouched down on the tatami amidst the fragments of broken glass and started to weep. Yasuko, who was still outside, seated herself on the raised floor of the corridor between the room and the garden and, with her rucksack still on her back and her air raid hood over her head, shed great tears of joy.

"Yasuko, you shouldn't rub your face," I warned her. "Look—you've got tar or something stuck on your hand. It's lucky you came back now, though. A little later, and we should have gone to the office at Ujina to look for you."

Since Yasuko was in my care—was almost a daughter—it would be inexcusable to my wife's parents if anything should happen to her. Moreover, I had been responsible for bringing her to Hiroshima in the first place. Young women, from country and town alike, were being conscripted for work in military supply factories, where they were set to work ·wielding hammers and turning shellcases. So, taking advantage of my position in the works, I had pulled strings in order to get her appointed messenger to the works manager.

"Oh, uncle!" she exclaimed. "Whatever have you done to your face?"

"Oh, this?—just a little burn," I said.

She told us that Nojima had hired a fishing boat at Miyazu and put them all ashore downstream from Miyuki Bridge, on the right bank of the Kyōbashi River. His wife had wanted to come back with them, but he had left her at her parents' place at Furue and brought back, besides Yasuko, Mrs. Yoshimura, Mrs. Miyaji, and Mrs. Doi. He had insisted that it was his responsibility to see them to their homes, and had negotiated with the fisherman to provide a boat for them. My prediction made by the pool at the sports ground had, in the event, proved to be approximately half correct.

The sky was dusky with the smoke from the fires. There was no water in the taps, so I made Yasuko wash her hands at the pool in the garden, but the marks would not come off. She said they were made by the black rain, and they were firmly stuck on the skin. They were not tar, nor black paint, but something of unknown origin.

Without delay, I went round to the Nojimas, thinking to ask how things were and, incidentally, to thank him for what he had done. I found him hastily preparing to evacuate. He, too, had the marks of the black rain on his hands.

"Do you think it's poison gas?" I inquired.

"No, it's not poison gas," he replied, stuffing food and note-books into a rucksack as he spoke. "They say it's the black smoke generated by the explosion. It mingled with water vapor in the sky and got carried down in the rain. The black rain fell mostly in the western districts of the city. I met someone from the Health Department of the City Hall just a while ago, and he told me about it. They say it's not harmful to human beings."

If someone from the Health Department had said so, I supposed it was all right.

As Nojima saw it, the fires would almost certainly spread to Senda-machi at any moment now. So after arriving home, he had dashed back to the river below Miyuki Bridge and asked the boat-man to wait a while longer so that he could escape to Miyazu by boat. That was why he was so frantically making preparations to get out. If we intended to make our way to Ujina, he said, there was no reason why we shouldn't share the same boat.

"Just the thing!" I said, mentally jumping for joy. "In the first place, I expect this area will be burned down as you say, and besides, I have to contact Japan Transport at Ujina just as soon as possible on some business. Do you think you could get my wife and Yasuko on board too?" Nojima agreed readily. "They're probably safe enough in the university sports ground," he said, "but then, I expect this area will be burnt down at any rate."

According to Nojima, Mrs. Doi and Mrs. Yoshimura had both, on arriving home, taken refuge in the sports ground. Mrs. Miyaji, however, had found a note from her husband waiting for her, and had rushed off to their relatives in Kichijima-chō. Not for the first time, I was astonished at Nojima's ear for the latest news.

The idea that we would get a ride in the boat raised my spirits. I went back home and announced in a loud voice: "We're going by boat to Ujina to take refuge for a while. Nojima's taking us with him." Shigeko and Yasuko were overjoyed.

Together with Nojima, we left Senda-machi behind us and followed the road along the embankment to the place, downstream from Miyuki Bridge, where the boat should have been. But there was no boat.

"What can have happened?" said Nojima, clucking to himself in embarrassment. "The way the tide's running, it can't have gone any farther upstream than this. Perhaps it's a bit farther downstream, then? Will you come along with me?"

"Would that be it?" I asked, pointing to a boat visible downstream.

"No, that's not it. That one's waterlogged. The Miyazu boat is a two-and-a-half ton Japanese-style one. Now, I wonder if I've been taken in?" He trudged off again.

We tagged along after him. As we went farther west, the angle at which the houses in the road below the embankment leaned became progressively smaller. Even so, the damage to roof tiles and the glass of sliding doors was not proportional to the angle at which the house tilted. There were some new, solidly constructed houses, for example, whose roofs were very badly damaged. Others had a single hole yawning in the roof.

Nojima doubtless took the affair as a blow to his personal pride. He had fallen quite silent, though every now and then he would mutter, as though it had just occurred to him, "This is dreadful, you know," or, "I really feel terribly bad about this." Sometimes it was, "I've let myself down badly—at such a time, too."

Many other refugees were walking along the top of the embankment. Nojima went so fast that my throat got dry and my legs hurt. Before long I found myself quite incapable of keeping up with him. Shigeko's knapsack began to look heavier every moment. My own rucksack got heavier. Even Yasuko's rucksack looked heavy.

"I'm sorry, Mr. Nojima," I said, coming to a halt. "I shall just have to drop out."

Nojima stopped too. "*I'm* sorry—really I am," he said with an expression of extraordinary discomfiture. "It's too bad, to lead you on a wild goose chase like this at such a time. But you can see what's happened."

"How could you help it?" said Shigeko. She paused. "Well, then, take care of yourself, Mr. Nojima."

"Well then," he said. "I feel awkward hanging about here, so

I'll get a move on. My apologies again. Look after yourselves."

His hand went briefly to his air raid hood, then, swinging around, he walked off at a brisk pace. It seemed all wrong, somehow, to take leave of the most educated and best-informed man in our neighborhood association in such embarrassing circumstances. To make it worse, he was a proud man, who had always been set up by others as a model of foresight and thoroughness.

My throat was stinging, so I got a bottle of water from the rucksack and drank directly from it. As soon as Nojima had disappeared from sight, I shouldered the rucksack again. "Even so," I said with the idea of sounding out Shigeko's feelings, "It seems we've got to thank Nojima for persuading us to get away to Ujina. The great thing is that we've made a definite decision." Indeed, the fires of Hiroshima were spreading wider and wider, and it was only sensible to get out of their way for a while.

At the Japan Transport branch at Ujina we found almost every pane of glass in the offices broken. Sugimura, the manager, asked me about the Furuichi works of the Japan Textile Company. I told him I knew nothing, since I had turned back halfway on my way to work. Nor could I give him anything but a fragmentary idea of what had happened to Hiroshima. When I told him Miyaji's story of how the keep of Hiroshima Castle had been blown a distance of more than a hundred yards, he gulped and said "Eh? The keep?" I handed him a notification to Japan Transport from the Furuichi works, got a receipt, and transmitted verbally a few confidential matters.

The manager was good enough to provide sufficient food—rice balls made with freshly cooked rice, together with pickled radish and vegetables boiled down in soy and sugar—for three people. It seemed the height of luxury. The meal over, we thanked him, went outside, and set off home together along the road with the streetcar tracks.

The procession of injured had not diminished in the slightest, and the number of severely injured was rather greater than in the morning. Among those I particularly noticed were a man whose shoulder bone seemed almost to be showing; another clutching a bamboo stick and walking on one leg, with the other leg done up in a splint; a man and woman carrying a dead child, covered with blood, on a door panel; and a woman with her hair caked with blood, her face, shoulders and arms covered with blood too, and only her eyes and teeth showing white.

As we passed each of them, Yasuko would stare compulsively. "Oh uncle! Look at that woman," she would say. "Aunt Shigeko— do look at him!" Again and again, I had to tell her: "It's not a show. Anyhow, there's nothing we can do for them, so keep quiet and come on. Keep your eyes on the ground."

When we reached Miyuki Bridge, there was no longer a single house visible in the direction where ours had stood. Smoke was drifting, hugging the ground, toward the east. We had done well to clear out to Ujina for a while. To avoid the residual heat, I led the way through the sports ground, over the small bridge without a name, through the vegetable gardens, and out behind our home. Shigeko and Yasuko followed in silence.

Our house was no more. Beyond the heavy drift of smoke, a grove of camphor trees showed in the distance, green and luxuriant as ever. The only thing in the foreground between us and them was a willow tree, drooping what looked like black needles over the embankment of the river. Again and again, as we walked away, I turned to look at where our home had stood. I must have turned round, literally, seven or eight times.

The crops in the vegetable gardens were scorched by the heat and hung withered and lifeless. A telephone pole in one corner of the field, half burnt down, was spouting smoke, with a flame about a foot high as though someone had set up a huge candle there. Now and then, when a hot gust of wind sprang up, the flame would emit a faint humming sound, and the blackened timbers on the burned-out ruins of our house would suddenly glow red. Smoke would billow up, only to be dispersed at once by the wind.

"Aunt Shigeko, where are we going to sleep tonight?" asked Yasuko.

Shigeko did not answer.

"The only thing possible is to go to the works," I said. "If we can't get there, we'll have to spend the night on the river bank or somewhere. There's no other alternative."

We crossed the field to the river bank. We followed it upstream, and were approaching the grounds of the Senda Primary School when we caught sight of a horse lying on the bank with its four legs stretched out in front of it. From time to time, its blackened, unnaturally large belly gave a heave, then subsided again. It was breathing—short, sharp breaths, as if to prove that it was still, if only just, alive. In the school grounds, we found a fire-fighting bucket with water in it, so we decided to moisten our towels and cover our noses and mouths with them when the smoke came billowing against us.

Giving careful thought to the shortest route to the firm at Furuichi, I led the way to the main street leading from Hijiyama Bridge through to Sagino Bridge. Whenever the wind cleared the smoke away, the ruins of the large Western-style buildings would loom into sight and spew smoke out of their windows on one side. Then, when the wind changed, smoke would float lifelessly out of the windows on the other side too. There were other concrete buildings with their window frames dangling, and yet others still on fire and spouting smoke. Whenever there was a strong gust of wind, the smoke would thin out and the street would appear, with dim human forms moving here and there on it. At one moment, we would be able to see far into the distance; at the next, we would be enveloped in smoke and forced to put the towels over our mouths and noses. By the time we had walked a quarter of a mile or so, all the moisture in the towels had gone.

Whenever the smoke completely enveloped us, it was too dangerous to go ahead. To blunder into red-hot cinders lying on the ground would mean getting badly burned. "Don't move! You'll get hurt," I would shout, stopping and signaling to the others to halt too. We would wait until the smoke cleared, then walk rapidly on again as soon as we could see what lay ahead. Quite possibly we spent more time standing still than walking.

Once, Yasuko stumbled on something and fell forward with a cry of "Uncle!" When the smoke cleared again, we found that the obstacle was a corpse clasping a dead baby in its arms. I took the lead henceforth, and watched out carefully for anything black that lay in the way. Several times, even so, we stumbled on dead bodies, or fell forward, jamming our hands into the hot asphalt. Once, when my shoe caught on a body half consumed by fire and the bones of the legs and thighs scattered in all directions, I shrieked despite myself and halted, petrified with horror.

Sometimes the asphalt, softened by the heat, stuck to the soles of our shoes and made walking difficult. There were dozens of places like this. However much I tightened my shoelaces, my shoes came off, and—maddeningly at such a moment—precious time would have to be spent getting them on again.

The wind gradually dropped, and the smoke ceased moving, which made breathing more and more difficult. I was foolhardy, perhaps, to have brought my wife and niece into such heat. I could not be absolutely certain, even, that we should come through alive, though occasionally people would come walking from the opposite direction, which gave me a certain reassurance. Yasuko, at least, I wanted to see through it all safely. To bring her to Hiroshima in order to escape mobilization had been my own ill-considered idea. I could not consider her in the same way as my wife. Once when we were brought to a halt, blinded by the smoke, the smoke and heat pressed in on us, and breathing would have become unbearably difficult if the wind had not changed just at that moment. Yasuko gave a shrill, suffocated cry, and I had to shout at her: "Don't move! If you move, you'll fall into the fire. That's hell, right there ahead. You'll be burnt to death!"

Reaching Sagino Bridge, we found that the smoke there was already thinning, since the northeastern districts of the city had been burned earlier than the rest. Over to the right, we could dimly discern Mt. Futaba. The mushroom cloud had disappeared.

"We're safe!" I called back to them, hoping to give them heart. "We shall live! Live!" But they were too exhausted to reply. Both of them had bloodshot eyes, eyes like crimson pools of blood. This was no time to think of resting, though, so I led the way on again.

All around was a sea of charcoal. Innumerable pieces of half-burned timber were still smoldering, and small columns of smoke were climbing lazily into the air. A great fire was still raging to the northeast, around Yokogawa, and huge columns of flame were swirling up into the sky.

Nothing was left of the Hakushima Shrine but its stone wall. The camphor trees at the Kokutaiji Temple, which must have been easily six feet in diameter, had all three been uprooted and had fallen to the ground, where they lay, burned through and carbonized but still preserving the shape of trees, with their great roots thrust upwards into the air. The memorial tablets to the loyal samurai of Akō, which had stood nearby, had all fallen over backwards to the south, but the tombstones of the Asano family opposite them had been sent tumbling in all directions, and lay mingled in confusion on the ground. The camphor trees were said to have been more than a thousand years old, but today they had finally met their fate.

Even here, the asphalt sticking to the soles of our shoes made it difficult to walk. The lead of the power cables had melted and dripped down onto the ground, where it lay along the roadside in a procession of silver droplets. On the main road, the iron poles supporting the overhead wires for the streetcars had been bent over, snapping the wires and leaving them hanging down loose. I would not go near them, having the feeling that one or the other of them must still be live.

In this area, the bodies in the roadway were rather fewer. They lay in a hundred and one different poses, but most of them—more than eighty percent of them—were alike in lying face down. One exception was a man and woman who lay face up by the safety zone at the Hakushima streetcar stop, with their knees drawn up and their arms stretched out diagonally to their bodies. The bodies were completely naked and scorched black, and the buttocks of each rested in a great pool of feces. Nowhere else had I witnessed such a scene. The hair on their heads and elsewhere was burned away, and it was only by the contours—of the breasts, for example —that I could distinguish man and woman. How had they come to meet such a grotesque death? The question continued to trouble my mind. Shigeko and Yasuko passed by the two corpses without so much as glancing at them.

Still we came upon corpses, and yet more corpses. Driven by the heat and trapped by the smoke, they had flung themselves face down in their suffering, only to be unable to rise again and to suffocate where they lay. So much was certain from the experiences of our own flight. Had not we ourselves hovered on the brink of a similar fate?

CHAPTER 7 🌿

Still Shigematsu continued the transcription of his "Journal of the Bombing." This month, he reflected, was a succession of festivals. The Mass for Dead Insects had gone by already; the Rice-Planting Festival came on the eleventh, and the Iris Festival, by the old lunar calendar, on the fourteenth. On the fifteenth there was the River Imp Festival, and on the twentieth the Bamboo-Cutting Festival. In all these countless little festivals he seemed to sense the affection that the peasants of the past, poor though they were, had lavished on each detail of their daily lives. And as he wrote on, and the horrors of that day came back to him ever more vividly, it seemed to him that in their very insignificance these farmers' festivals were something to be loved and cherished. . . .

We reached the streetcar stop at Kamiya-chō. The streetcar tracks crossed each other here, and broken overhead wires and cables hung down in tangled profusion over the road. I had a terrifying feeling that one or the other of them must be live, since these were the same wires that one usually saw emitting fierce, bluish-white sparks. The occasional refugees who passed to and fro had the sense to crouch down as they passed beneath them.

I wanted to take the left-hand edge of the road across Aioi Bridge to Sakan-chō, but the heat from the still-smoldering fires seemed likely to bar the way. I tried turning to the right, but a blast of hot air swept over me with an authority that would have made the bravest man waver, so I turned back again. Even so, as I approached a Western-style brick building, a great lump of glowing charcoal came hurtling down from what had been the window frames.

The only alternative was to go along the middle of the road. Since the overhead wires were cut at various points, there was no likelihood of their being live, but the very fact that they were crossing and touching each other made one fear some display of the mysterious properties of electricity. Beneath one of the dangling wires lay the blackened bodies of a man and two women. We, too, numbered two women and one man.

"Come on, under the wires after me!" I called. "Whatever you do, don't touch the wires. I'll hold them out of the way. If I get a shock don't touch anything except my clothes. Do you understand?—you get hold of the end of my trouser leg and drag me away." I followed the example of the other refugees, and pushed the wires away to either side with a piece of stick, crawling on all fours when necessary, crouching down when necessary.

"Look," I yelled back again. "Wrap a towel round your left elbow like those people have done. Your left elbow goes on the ground."

Time and again it was necessary to crouch down beneath the wires, but at last we were safely past. We stopped and took stock of each other. Shigeko was completely unscathed, but Yasuko, who had wound the towel round her arm in the wrong way, had a painful-looking graze on her elbow.

Shigeko sat down beside her on a stone by the roadside and attended to her elbow with mentholatum and a triangular bandage. Suddenly, it occurred to me that we were directly in front of an entrance that I knew.

"Just a moment—" I said, "Surely that stone's one from Mr. Ōmuro's garden?"

The Ōmuros in question were an old family, said to date back to the Edo period, and the present head was engaged in chemical research on spinning thread. He was a man of property, owning mills in three different places, as well as dabbling in calligraphy, painting, and art-collecting. I had visited the house myself several times during the past year for the benefit of his advice on matters concerning textile products. It had been an imposing mansion, with a splendid old-style garden. Now, however, it was completely razed to the ground. Where the main building and clay-walled storehouse had once stood was an arid waste scattered with broken tiles. The stone on which Shigeko and Yasuko were sitting was almost certainly a rock from the garden inside the grounds. Rock though it was, a thin layer had been burned away all over it.

"That rock's granite, you know," I said. "I expect it was covered with moss only this morning."

"Do you think the whole household was wiped out, then?" said Shigeko.

I did not reply. It was a scene of cruel desolation. Where the ornamental pond had been was an uneven stretch of blackish mud, and at the foot of a rounded hillock of earth lay the blackened skeletons of three large pine trees. Beside the trunk of the thickest of the three stood a narrow, square pillar of stone. Why it alone should have remained standing was a mystery. Mr. Ōmuro had once told me that an ancestor of his, several generations back, had had it erected there. It was somewhat over ten feet tall, and instead of the usual long inscription it had the single character "Dream" carved on it, about two and a half feet from the top. Some high-ranking priest was said to have written the original, and the effect was doubtless considered stylish and rather sophisticated in its day, but at present, style and sophistication alike failed utterly.

Both Shigeko and Yasuko were deathly pale. My throat was so dry it felt as though it might close up entirely, and a slight tic affected my eye as I walked.

We reached the entrance to the West Parade Ground. The grass on the west side of the embankment had been burned away, leaving the earth smooth and bare. The trees seemed to have been carbonized where they stood, and retained their branches, but not a single leaf. The divisional commander's residence, the temporary army hospital, the Gokoku Shrine and, of course, the keep of Hiroshima Castle, were all gone.

My eyes began to hurt, so I massaged them as I walked by rubbing the eyelids with my fingers. They smarted, and at the same time felt as though there was grit in them. Shigeko and Yasuko had cheered up a little, and were talking about the now vanished mushroom cloud—its size, its shape, its color, the shape of its stalk, and the way it had moved. Concluding that my eyes hurt because I had too much blood in the head, I had Yasuko give me the treatment they used to give children who had nosebleed. It consisted of no more than pulling out three hairs from the back of the head, but it helped the pain a little.

The West Parade Ground was an unbroken expanse of sand. It reminded me of a vast desert I had seen in a movie called "Morocco." Even in the film, the desert had seemed to exhale a smell of sand, and it had been quite empty, with not a single footprint visible. The sandy waste of the parade ground, however, was rather different: the hot breath it gave off stank of smoke, and there were a number of human trails leading away in the direction of the hills. It must have been raining. The sand was fine enough for holes the size of broad beans to be visible all over its surface, and the newspapers scattered here and there were covered with countless bean-sized black spots. The black rain had evidently fallen here. I had realized that the stalk of the mushroom cloud was a shower, but I had not imagined that the drops were as big as this.

At the western edge of the ground, we found a number of what looked like round black balls lying in the sand. At first I could not identify them, but as I got closer I realized they were lumps of what had been tin sheeting. They must have been torn away by the blast and have risen up into the sky, where they had been softened by the intense heat, then kneaded into balls by the wind before falling. To have gone quite round, like dumplings, they must have been sucked up into the great whirlwind of flame and have spun round and round furiously before finally descending to earth.

I glanced back across the sandy waste. A solitary figure—a boy wearing his underpants and an undershirt that flapped in the breeze at the front, exposing his naked belly—was walking rapidly in the direction of the hills. "Hi!" he called, turning in our direction and waving his hand at us. It seemed a peculiarly pointless gesture.

We walked on northwards. By the bank skirting the Gokoku Shrine a sentry stood with his rifle at order. Closer to, we found he was dead at his post, his back propped against the embankment, his eyes wide and staring. The badge on his collar showed him to be a private first-class in the army. He was about thirty-seven or eight, and old for a ranker, yet his features had an indefinable air of breeding.

"Why—just like the soldier with his bugle," said Shigeko.

"Come woman, mind your tongue," I said sternly, though if the truth be told I, too, had been reminded of the same story—of the bugler found dead at his post during the Sino-Japanese War, with his bugle still held to his lips.

The area was near the point where the bomb had been dropped. We saw another of them at the west corner of the grounds of Hiroshima Castle: a young man, still on his bicycle and carrying a wooden box as though on his way to deliver an order from a restaurant, propped dead against the stone ramparts. This one was a mere youth, and as skinny as a grasshopper.

We had often been taught during air raid drill that one must always breathe out steadily while a bomb was falling. Perhaps the sentry and the delivery boy had been breathing in at the moment the bomb burst? I did not understand the physiology of it, but it occurred to me that a blast just as one had filled one's lungs to capacity might well press on them and cause instant death.

We were taking a rest just this side of the embankment when we were hailed by an acquaintance, Police Sergeant Susumu Satō.

"Hello—I'm glad to see you safe," I said.

"Why, your face has caught it, hasn't it?" he said.

I spoke to him for a while before joining the others, and he told me that Superintendent-General Ōtsuka of the Chūgoku District Commissary had been trapped under his home and burned to death.

I had not known that Satō had been transferred from the police station to the Chūgoku District Commissary. I had not even known, in fact, that there existed a government office of that name. It was most remiss of me. I learned for the first time from Satō that the enemy's attacks had grown so fierce recently that it had been decided that Japan must prepare to do battle on home territory. Local governing agencies known as "district commissaries" had been set up, so that the struggle could be continued in each region independently should the country be split up by enemy forces. With the same objective, war materials had been stored at factories and primary schools throughout the area in which Hiroshima stood.

"So that's what it meant—" I said, "the slogan about the war only just beginning."

"Yes," said Satō, "the idea is to go ahead with the grand policy of a wealthy and militarily powerful nation launched over half a century ago. It's not for you or me to assume that this is a kind of tragic finale. *This* is precisely what we've been brought up for. It's fate."

The Chūgoku Commissary, located in the Hiroshima University of Liberal Arts and Science, had had responsibility for the five prefectures of the Chūgoku district. The Superintendent-General himself—Isei Ōtsuka, a man with the bearing of an old-time samurai—had been in the Superintendent-General's official residence at Kami-Nagaregawa-machi when the bomb fell, and had been caught beneath the house. His wife had managed with great difficulty to crawl out of the wreckage, but the Superintendent-General had been hopelessly trapped. The good lady had been beside herself, but the Superintendent-General had insisted on her leaving him. "I'm ready for whatever comes," he had said. "Get yourself away, woman, as fast as you can." The flames were already close at hand, so she had had no choice but to flee.

"The Superintendent-General was cremated where he lay. A ghastly business," Satō said. "I myself didn't know which way to run from the flames." His eyes filled with tears. Normally, his manner of speech was cheerful and his face gave an immediate impression of openness and sunniness, but today his eyes were bloodshot and his face grim.

Arriving on the embankment, we found the middle section of Misasa Bridge missing. Changing my plan, I set off along the embankment downstream with the idea of crossing Aioi Bridge. Countless dead bodies were lying in the undergrowth at the foot of the embankment on our right. Other bodies came floating in steady succession along the river. Every so often, one of them would catch on the roots of a riverside willow, swing round with the current, and suddenly rear its face out of the water. Or one would come along rocking in the water, so that first its upper half then its lower half bobbed to the surface. Or another would swing round beneath a willow tree and raise its arms as though to grasp at a branch, so that it almost seemed, for a moment, to be alive.

We had sighted from some way off the body of a woman who lay stretched out dead across the path on top of the embankment. Suddenly Yasuko, who was walking ahead of us, came running back with a cry of "Uncle! Uncle" and burst into tears. As I drew closer, I saw a baby girl of about three who had opened the corpse's dress at the top and was playing with the breasts. When we came up to her, she clutched tight at both breasts and gazed up at us with apprehensive eyes.

What could we possibly do for her? To ask ourselves this was our only recourse. I stepped gently over the corpse's legs so as not to frighten the little girl, and walked briskly on another ten yards or so downstream. Here I spotted another group of four or five women dead together in the undergrowth, and a boy of five or six crouched on the ground as though caught between the bodies.

"Come along," I called waving with both arms to the others, who were still hesitating. "Just step over it as quietly as possible and come on." Shigeko and Yasuko stepped over the body and joined me.

At the end of Aioi Bridge we found a carter and the ox harnessed to his cart both seated, dead, on the electric car tracks. The ropes around the load had come undone, and the goods had been rifled.

Here, too, the corpses came floating one after the other down the river, and it was a sickening sight to see them butt their heads against the piers of the bridge and swivel round in the water. Near its center, the bridge reared in a hump about a yard high, and on what one might have called the crest of the wave a young foreigner with fair hair lay dead with his arms clasped about his head. The surface of the bridge was distorted and undulating.

Around Sakan-chō and Sorazaya-chō, it was clear that the flames had swept evenly across the whole area. The corpses lay scattered in every conceivable condition—one with only the upper half of the body burned to the bone, one completely skeletonized save for one arm and one leg, another lying face down, consumed from the knees down, yet another with the two legs alone cremated—and an unspeakable stench hanging over all. Nauseating though the odor was, there was no way to escape it.

In Tera-machi, the "temple quarter," not a single temple was standing. All that remained was clay walls crumbled and collapsed till they were barely recognizable, and venerable trees with their limbs torn open to expose the naked wood within. Even the branch of the Honganji temple, famed as the greatest temple building in the whole quarter, had vanished without trace. The smoke still rising from the embers drifted menacingly over the crumbling walls, then crept low over the surface of the river till it vanished at the other bank.

On the other side of Yokogawa Bridge the flames were still rising. Fanned by the wind, fires were swirling white-hot up to the skies from the whole area on the opposite bank. To approach was out of the question.

We found the road ahead completely blocked on this side of the bridge. The iron girders forming the bow-shaped framework of the bridge were discolored up to a height of some twelve to fifteen feet, and close to one of the piers of the bridge that rested on a stretch of grass stood a horse badly burned on its back and the back of its head. It was trembling violently and looked as though it might collapse at any moment. Close by its side a corpse, the upper half burned away, lay face downwards. The lower half, which was untouched, wore army breeches and boots with spurs. The spurs actually gleamed gold. If the owner had been an army man, then he had been an officer, for only an officer could wear boots with gold spurs like that. I pictured the scene to myself: the officer running to the stables, mounting his horse barebacked, rushing outside. . . . The horse must have been a favorite of the soldier's. Though it was on the verge of collapse, it still seemed—or was it my imagination?—to be yearning for some sign from the man in the spurred boots. How immeasurable the pain it must have felt, with the west-dipping sun beating down unmercifully on its burned flesh; how immeasurable its love for the man in the boots! But pity eluded me: I felt only a shudder of horror.

Our only choice was to walk on through the river. Close to the bank there were grassy shoals, but in places they were too far apart for us to tread dry ground all the time. We stepped into the flowing water and set off walking upstream. Even at its deepest, the water only came up to our knees. The district we were passing through would have been Hirose Kitamachi or thereabouts. On the sandy parts, where the river had dried up, our shoes spouted water with a squelching sound. No sooner did the water empty out of them a little, and walking become a little pleasanter, than the sand would start getting in our shoes and almost lame us with the pain.

We decided it was actually better to walk in the water, and splashed on regardless. On a pebbly shoal a man lay with both hands thrust in the water, drinking. We approached, thinking to join him, and found he was not drinking water but dead, with his face thrust down into the water.

"I wonder if the water in this river is poisonous, then?" said Yasuko, voicing my own unspoken question.

"There's no telling," I replied, setting off through the water again. "But perhaps we'd better not drink it."

The smoke blowing across from the town gradually diminished, and paddy fields appeared on our right, so we clambered up a crumbling stone wall and onto the bank.

We reached the rice fields. Walking along the raised paths between them in the direction of the electric car tracks, we came across a number of schoolgirls and schoolboys lying here and there in the fields, dead. They must have fled in disorder from the factory where they had been doing war work. There were adults lying about too. One of them, an elderly man, had fallen across the path, and the front of his jacket was soaked with water. He had evidently drunk to bursting point from the paddy field water, then —either unable to care any more or in a fit of vertigo—subsided onto the ground and expired where he lay.

We stepped over the body and wound our way, first left then right, along the paths between the fields, till finally they led us into a bamboo grove. The grove must have been kept for the purpose of gathering bamboo shoots, for the undergrowth was well cut back. Finding ourselves in cool, leafy shade at last, we sank to the ground without exchanging a word.

I unfastened my first-aid kit, took off my air raid hood and my shoes, and sprawled out on my back. At once my body seemed to be dissolving into thin air, and before I knew it I had slipped into a deep slumber.

I awoke, I knew not how long after, to a raging thirst and a pain in my throat. My wife and Yasuko were both lying with their heads pillowed on their arms. I rolled onto my belly, and, filching the quart bottle of water out of my wife's rucksack, drank. It was a heaven-sent nectar. I had had no idea that water was so good. The ecstasy was touched, almost, with a kind of pride. I must have drunk all of a third of a pint.

My wife and Yasuko awoke too. By now, the sun was sinking toward the west. Without a word Shigeko took the bottle I handed her and, lifting it with both hands, drank greedily. She probably drank another third of a pint. Then she passed the bottle to Yasuko, also without a word. Yasuko in her turn raised it with both hands. She paused between each mouthful, but every time she upended the bottle a stream of bubbles ran up through it and the remaining water decreased visibly. I was almost despairing of her leaving any at all, when she finally put the bottle down with about one-third of a pint still in it.

From her rucksack, my wife took out the cucumbers she had brought for want of anything better, and opened a packet of salt. The cucumbers were blackened and discolored on one side. "Where did you buy these?" I asked. "Mrs. Murakami from Midori-chō brought them for us this morning," she said.

Early that morning, apparently, Mrs. Murakami had brought us three cucumbers and a dozen or so tiny dried fish, of the kind used in flavoring soup, in return for a share of some tomatoes that Shigeko's people in the country had sent us. Shigeko had left the cucumbers in a bucket of water by the pool in the garden, and the flash from the bomb had discolored them.

"It's funny," I said. "When I went back to the house from the university sports ground, the basket worms were eating the leaves of the azalea. The cucumber was burned, but the insects were still alive."

I dipped the cucumber in the salt and turned the question over in my mind as I ate. Some physical reaction had obviously taken place on the surface of the water in the bucket. Could it be that reflection inside the bucket had stepped up the amount of heat and light? Glancing at the pond as I went to sink the mosquito net in the water, I had noticed basket worms on the azalea that grew out over the water, busily eating the new summer buds. I shook the branch, and they drew back into their baskets, but when I got back from collecting pieces of brick to sink the net with, they were busily eating once more. The buds themselves were not discolored, nor were the worms' baskets burned, which suggested that light and heat had caused some chemical change when it came up against metal. Or had the basket worms and azalea been sheltered by the house, or by some other obstacle, when the bomb had burst? The rice plants in the open paddy fields seemed to have been affected by the flash. It seemed likely that they, too, would have turned black by the following morning.

I washed my small towel in a ditch at the edge of the bamboo grove, wiped my right cheek and the sinews of my neck, then rinsed the towel time and time again. I wrung it out and rinsed it, wrung it out and rinsed it, repeating the same seemingly pointless procedure over and over again. To wring out my towel was the one thing, it seemed to me, that I was free to do as I pleased at that moment. My left cheek smarted painfully. A shoal of minnows was swimming in the ditch, and in a patch of still water the flags were growing in profusion. Here is shadow, they seemed to say, here is safety. . . .

Smoke came drifting from deep within the bamboo grove. Going to investigate, I peered through the bamboos and saw a group of refugees who had built a shelter of green bamboo and branches and were preparing a meal. They seemed to have been burned out of their homes and to be making ready to spend the night out.

I strained my ears to catch their conversation. It seemed from what they said that the houses along the main highway had all closed their shutters in order to keep out refugees. At one sundry goods store this side of Mitaki Station on the Kabe line, they had found a woman who had got in unnoticed and died in one of their closets. When the owner of the store dragged the body out, he found that the garment it was wearing was his own daughter's best summer kimono. Scandalized, he had torn the best kimono off the body, only to find that it had no underwear on underneath. She must have been burned out of her home and fled all the way there naked, yet still—being a young woman—sought something to hide her nakedness even before she sought water or food. The refugees were wondering whether bombs like today's would be dropped on other cities besides Hiroshima. What were Japan's battleships and land forces up to, they were asking each other. It would be a wonder if there weren't a civil war. . . .

I made my way back quietly through the bamboo, and with a "Come on" to the others started to get ready. I had a stabbing pain in my toes. "Come on," I urged them again, but neither Shigeko nor Yasuko made any reply. They seemed utterly exhausted. "Well, then, I'm off!" I said sharply, and this time they reluctantly got to their feet and started to get ready.

Walking made my toes hurt so that I nearly danced with the pain. The others were complaining of the pain too. I myself must have walked some ten or eleven miles already. My wife had walked five or six, and Yasuko about five. We ate parched rice as we walked. We would thrust a hand into the cloth bag my wife was carrying, take out a handful and, putting it in our mouths, chew on it as we walked. It gradually turned to sugar, and tasted sweet in the mouth; it was better than either the water or the cucumber. The most effective way seemed to be to chew as one walked, and I could understand why travelers in olden times took parched rice with them as rations for the journey. Finally, one gulped it down, then took another handful out of the cloth bag and put it in one's mouth. Parched rice may be very unappetizing-looking, but I gave thanks in my heart to my wife's folk for sending it.

The main highway was dotted with refugees. Just as I had overheard the people in the bamboo grove saying, the houses by the roadside all had their doors and shutters fastened. Where there was a roofed gateway, its doors were shut fast. Outside one of the gates with shut doors lay a bundle of straw scorched by fire. I wondered if passing refugees had set fire to it.

However far we went, still the houses along the road had their doors shut. Here the breeze was cool, unlike the hot breath of the town, and ripples were running over the rice plants in the paddy fields. The fathers from the Catholic church on the north side of Yamamoto Station went running past us at top speed, carrying a stretcher. With them was one father, a man past middle age, whom I had often seen on the Kabe-bound train on my way to work. He came panting along far behind the others carrying the stretcher, and as he passed me he glanced into my face and nodded briefly in recognition. "Good luck to you," I called after him.

At last, we reached Yamamoto Station. From here on, the trains were running. A train was standing in the station, every coach full, but we managed to squeeze our way into the vestibule of one of them. Wedged tight, I tried to make more room by nudging at a bundle directly in front of me. Wrapped in a cloth, it rested on the shoulders of a woman of about thirty. Somehow, it felt different from a bundle of belongings, so I tried touching it furtively with my hand. I contacted what felt like a human ear: a child seemed to be a in the bundle. To carry a child in such a fashion was outrageous. It was almost certain to suffocate in such a crush.

"Excuse me Ma'am," I said softly. "Is it your child in here?"

"Yes," she said in a scarcely audible voice. "He's dead."

"I'm sorry," I said, taken aback. "I didn't know. . . . I really must apologize, to be pushing and. . . ."

"Not at all," she said gently. "None of us can help it in such a crowd." She hitched the bundle up, bent her head, and was seized with a fit of weeping.

"It was when the bomb burst," she said through her sobs. "The sling of his hammock broke, and he was dashed against the wall and killed. Then the house started to burn, so I wrapped him in a quilt cover and brought him away on my back. I'm taking him to my old home in Iimori, so I can bury him in the cemetery there."

She stopped weeping, and ceased talking at the same time. I could not bring myself to address her any further.

A kite was wheeling in the air above the wires. The cicadas were chirping, and a dabchick was bustling about the pond with water-lilies by the side of the highway. A perfectly commonplace scene that somehow seemed quite extraordinary. . . .

The conductor announced the train's imminent departure, and a fiercer clamor arose from those who had not succeeded in getting on. The train lurched forward and stopped, lurched and stopped again.

"What the hell're you up to? Are you starting or aren't you?" bellowed a voice, to be followed by another voice that launched into a speech somewhere inside the coach: "Ladies and gentlemen, you can see for yourselves how sadly decadent the National Railways have become. Concerned only with carrying black market goods, they have nothing but contempt for the ordinary passenger. . . ." But this time the train glided smoothly into motion, and the rest of the speech was lost forever in the clatter of its wheels.

CHAPTER 8 🍂

The train tracks and the main road to Kabe ran parallel to each other, and on the main road we could see the refugees trudging along on foot or being carried on hand-carts. All were heading in the direction of Kabe. The train carrying us must have outstripped several hundred of them when, without warning, the engine or something gave out and we jarred to a halt.

"What the hell!" said a voice. "This isn't a station! No wonder people say the National Railways are going to the dogs!" Another passenger jumped down from the platform of the coach. A healthy-looking man in his middle years, he got onto the main highway, adjusted the net haversack on his back, and without so much as a glance back set off walking in the direction of Kabe.

The train showed no inclination to start again. We were jammed together like sardines, and the heat was insufferable.

"Come on, National Railways!" came another voice from some-where inside the coach. "Are you starting, now, or aren't you? If not, I'm going to walk too." And someone, apparently the owner of the voice, climbed out of the window. I could not see them from where I was standing, but three or four other people seemed to be climbing out of the windows after him. Before long, at least a dozen more had gone. Thanks to this, we had a little more room inside, and I gradually got myself away from the vestibule and half inside the coach. My wife and niece were already completely in. The woman carrying the dead child in the white cloth was still standing in the vestibule.

From outside the window came the voice of the conductor call-ing as he went past: "Owing to a breakdown, the train is unavoid-ably delayed." At this, another three or four people left via the windows. A group of people who seemed to be a family helped each other out of a window, then, with a "the child, if you wouldn't mind," had a child passed out into their waiting arms by the people still inside.

Still more came pushing their way out through the crush to the exit. The result was considerably more space, and passengers who had remained silent so far began sporadic attempts at conversa-tion. Without exception, they talked of the bombing. Each told what he had seen or heard as an individual, without relation to the others, so that even synthesizing their stories it was impossible to get an overall picture of the disaster. Even so, I have set some of them down here just as I remember them.

The man in his forties who stood on my right, with his air raid hood dangling down his back on a string, had had the left half of his face burned, and the skin had peeled clean off; he was far more badly hurt than I. Even his eyebrows were burnt away. His eyes were extraordinarily deep-set—so deep-set that that may well have been what had saved them. He had been glancing at my face from time to time, and now he suddenly said:

"Where did you get caught, may I ask?"

"Yokogawa Station," I told him.

"I come from Fukushima-chō," he said. "I was just coming out of the air raid shelter when I caught it."

He had gone back to fetch his cigarettes and matches, which he had left in the shelter, and had just come out again when he was aware of a sudden flash and found he could see nothing about him. However, he soon discovered that he could still move his arms and legs, so he more or less groped his way to the front entrance of the house; whether he walked or crawled, he wasn't sure. The first thing he knew, he had recovered his sight and could see the house, which had been knocked flat. He assumed it had received a direct hit from a bomb. His small daughter in primary school and his wife had been evacuated to Kobe, but his elder daughter, who attended the Municipal Girls' High School, had gone to work at Nakajima Hommachi to help pull down houses to make firebreaks. Worried about her, he started running, but had only got as far as the near end of Fukushima Bridge when he met an acquaintance called Yoda running from the opposite direction.

"How's your place?"

"Knocked flat. I'm worried about my daughter—I'm going to where they're working at Nakajima Hommachi."

"You mustn't, you mustn't! All the girls at the Municipal High School were wiped out, I tell you. D'you mean to give up your own chance of getting away and run into a sea of fire?"

"I'm sorry, I must get on. . . ." And he had made to run on past Yoda. But it was useless. Wherever he looked ahead of him the fires were rising.

"You mustn't, you mustn't! Come away!" said Yoda, tugging at his hand, so he threw everything to the winds and fled with him as far as Koi-machi.

Yoda had been in his home at Temma-chō when the bomb fell, and had no visible injuries, but was bleeding at the mouth. The man with deep-set eyes looked inside his mouth, and found two teeth were missing. His hands and legs felt chilly too, he complained. What had he hit his teeth on? He hadn't hit them, he said —they'd been blown out. It was funny how they wouldn't stop bleeding. . . .

Yoda had relatives in Koi-machi. They called in at their house, and the relatives were applying a bandage soaked in rapeseed oil to his burned cheek, when Yoda's cousin had turned up with his back badly burned. He had been at Temma-chō when the bomb fell. His back was red and lumpy like a turkey's comb, and the skin had come off like a sheet of oiled paper.

"It must hurt dreadfully," Yoda had said to him. No, it wasn't painful, he said, but if it got too dry the flesh pulled and he had a stinging sensation. The only treatment for him, too, was to apply rapeseed oil.

"I wonder what it means?" concluded the man with hollow eyes. "*I* don't feel any pain, either."

"Nor do I—not the slightest," I said.

If our burns had been due to hot water or fire, the pain would have been unbearable for two or three days at least. In fact, all we felt was a kind of stinging in response to any particularly strong stimulus. It was rash to generalize from this, but I suspected that the intense heat had numbed the nerves under the burnt skin so that no pain was felt. Those passengers on the train who were suffering pain from burns were all people who had been burned in fires other than the direct heat of the bomb. (I found later that there were in fact others who felt intense pain from burns inflicted directly by the bomb.)

A passenger standing next to me suddenly said, "Excuse me," and vomited from the window. Then—resigned, it seemed, to the fact that he was going to vomit again—he went out onto the platform of the coach. By then, most of the passengers with diarrhea were already assembled out there. No doubt the people who had climbed out of the windows earlier had been having frequent attacks of the same symptoms. I was suffering slightly in the same way myself, but counting from the morning my attacks seemed to come only once in about three hours. The man with deep-set eyes said he was having diarrhea at about the same rate. My wife and niece said they had no such symptoms at all.

I myself put it down to a sudden epidemic of dysentery, but the man said he imagined it was an after-effect of the bomb. According to him, whenever human beings or animals had drunk or eaten too much, or ingested something bad for the system, the body expelled the offending substance by means of physiological phenomena such as vomiting and diarrhea. It also expelled things in the same way when the body was too tired for the digestion to work properly. Many of those exposed to the bomb were suffering from diarrhea, even though their cases did not seem to fit either of these circumstances. In his opinion, therefore, some substance harmful to the body had penetrated through the skin and upset the working of the various organs, inducing indigestion. The juices inside the stomach and intestines would probably expel it from the body along with the food.

"You see," the man with deep-set eyes said, "the organs of the body are obviously organized like a clever piece of mechanism. So if you have an attack of diarrhea, you should yield to it. If you try to hold out for the sake of holding out, the mechanism will probably get upset."

A boy who had been sitting down gave up his seat to an old woman standing next to the man with the deep-set eyes. He would have been in his third or fourth year at middle school. The old woman, presumably out of gratitude or in a fit of curiosity, insisted on talking to the boy—who showed no inclination for conversation—trying to get him to tell what had happened to him when the bomb fell. She pressed rather too hard, I felt.

Quite suddenly the boy, with an expression of great revulsion, came out with his story. He had been at home when the ball of fire had burst. There had been a sudden flash and a mighty roar, and he had started to run outside. On the instant, the house had collapsed and he had lost consciousness. When he came to, he found himself trapped between beams or other timbers, and his father trying to get them off him. He was using a log as a lever to raise the timbers trapping the boy's leg, urging him all the while to be brave. The flames were drawing in on them and the wreckage of their own house had already caught fire.

"Come on, pull your leg out, boy," his father said. But his ankle was held fast by the wood. By now the fire was closing in on three sides. His father took one look about him and said, "It's no use. Don't think ill of me—I'm getting out. You won't think ill of me, son?" And flinging the log away, he fled. The boy shouted, "Dad, help me!" but his father only looked back once before vanishing from sight. In despair, the boy sank down among the timbers—whereupon, quite suddenly, he no longer felt the restraint on his ankle, and found himself free to crawl out from between the timbers. His leg had slid out from the timbers, just like one of those Chinese puzzles that seem impossible to undo until one chances on the solution. So he ran along a road that led toward a gap in the fires, then all the way to an aunt's house in Mitaki-machi, where he found his father. The reunion of father and son produced such mixed feelings that all of them, the aunt included, had been at a loss for words. The father had looked acutely uncomfortable. The boy had fled the scene and had got on the Kabe-bound train with the idea of going to his dead mother's home in the country.

His story told, the boy wrinkled his forehead in a frown and clamped his lips tightly together. The old woman sat primly with her head bowed, and said no more, almost as though she had been reprimanded. She was a genteel-looking old person of sixty or thereabouts, with a cotton towel tied round her forehead.

In a seat next to the window on the side from which the highway was visible sat a woman of around thirty and a man of about fifty. The woman wore a white shirt with a pattern of small dark blue crosses, and baggy wartime breeches of a stiff yellow material. She had a plump face, with rather nice eyes. The man was wearing a linen shirt with a family crest on it, apparently made over from a kimono that had belonged to his great-grandfather or somebody. He wore baggy breeches also in the same material, and rubber boots. Both seemed to come from families that carefully preserved old clothes even when they were no longer fashionable.

"Why—surely that's young Yukio?" the man in the crested shirt said to the woman. She looked, and started calling after a child, a boy of eight or nine, who was walking along the highway.

"Yukio! Say, Yukio! Where're you going? Aren't you going by train? Why don't you get on the train?"

The boy halted and looked in her direction, then, without so much as a nod or shake of the head, went trudging on again. On the fire bucket he was carrying I could make out the words "Squad 3, Nakahiro-machi." In all likelihood he had grabbed the bucket without realizing what he was doing when the bomb fell, and had clung to it ever since.

"Yukio! Hey! This train's going to Kabe, don't you know? *Yukio!* What's the matter with you!" The woman hung out of the window calling to him, but there was no response.

"Well—he's gone," said the man in the linen shirt. "Fancy, carrying a bucket like that, too!"

Conversation had sprung up in various parts of the coach, but I could hear what the man in the linen shirt said particularly clearly. He was complaining that the Defense Section of the Municipal Office had been slack in its duties at the time of the bombing. The officials of the section, he was saying, had neglected even to report to divisional headquarters after the attack. (*The Truth About the Atomic Bomb,* a work by Shigeteru Shibata published later, on the tenth anniversary of the bomb, has something rather different to say: "In the afternoon of the day the bomb fell, it occurred to Mr. Noda, chief of the Defense Section, that in accordance with pre-arranged plans for wartime emergencies, he ought to report to Fifth Divisional Headquarters on the extent of destruction at and around the City Hall, and he dispatched an official message. As yet, of course, he had no idea that the whole city was destroyed. In time, the message came back again. 'There is no divisional headquarters,' the messenger reported. 'What do you mean—no headquarters?' 'Just that—there's nothing there.' 'What's happened to it?' 'I don't know.' The messenger also added that the moat around the divisional headquarters—it was near the castle keep, inside what had, in feudal days, been the inner moat—was full of the charred corpses of soldiers. At this, it dawned on the Defense Section chief for the first time that this had been no ordinary calamity." The man in the white shirt, in other words, would seem to have been misled by inadequate information. The author of the book, incidentally, subsequently died of radiation sickness himself.)

The linen-shirted man's dislike seemed to extend not only to the bureaucracy, but to the military also. "Only a few days ago," he was saying, "I saw a little scene that just about summed up relations between the military and civilians."

On a train on which he had come back to Hiroshima from Yamaguchi two or three days earlier, an army lieutenant had taken his boots off and was sprawled out over a whole seat, even though the train was jammed with passengers. The outrageousness of his conduct was plain, yet nobody took it upon himself to remonstrate with him. Even the conductor who came to inspect the tickets pretended to have seen nothing. Some time passed, and the train was drawing into Tokuyama, when one of the passengers tipped half a cooked rice-ball into each of the officer's boots, then proceeded to get off with the most innocent air in the world. At this, another passenger carefully shook each boot in turn, to make sure the rice had gone right down to the toes, before alighting from the train in his turn. He had shaken the boots, of course, to make sure that a sacrifice so noble—considering the scarcity of food—should have the very maximum effect. The army man remained fast asleep. The passengers standing nearby who had witnessed the scene looked at his sleeping form with grins on their faces, though several of them moved along to other coaches for fear of getting embroiled. The soldier awoke around Ōtake, and shortly after, as the train approached Hiroshima, stood up, put on his boots, donned his peaked cap, and threw out his chest. An odd expression crossed his face, as though something inexplicable had occurred. Hastily he took his boots off, gave one look at the grains of rice sticking to his socks, and let out a bellow. . . .

Feeling the woman's elbow nudging him, the man in the linen shirt stopped. But he seemed to feel the need to round things off with dignity, and turned to a woman, a shopkeeper type, who was sitting near him.

"Excuse me, madam," he said. "How far are you going?"

The woman nodded with a look of resignation and explained that she had nowhere to go. Her husband, a workman, had been killed in the war, and so had his younger brother. Her own younger brother was at the front, and she had no one to turn to. Her only child, a boy of eight, had been blown off a stepladder and killed by the bomb that morning.

She had been living in one of a row of poor houses standing next to the clay wall of a restaurant. The branches of a pomegranate tree in the grounds of the restaurant, which spread out over their side of the wall, had borne five or six fruit. The boy happened to have come home from the place in the country where he was evacuated, and before he left he had carried out a stepladder that had belonged to his father and placed it under the branches of the tree. As she watched, wondering what he was up to, he climbed the ladder and, putting his lips to each of the fruit in turn, whispered, "Don't fall, pomegranate, till I come back again!" But then a ball of fire had blazed in the sky and there had been a great roar. The wall had collapsed, the stepladder had overturned, and the child had been killed outright, hit by a flying tile or a lump of clay from the wall.

The year before, she said, the branches leaning over their side had had three or four fruit on them, but they had all dropped while they were still green. The boy had been giving them encouragement to make sure that this year, at least, they would grow up safely. She supposed it was his childish way of dropping them the hint, in case it hadn't occurred to them. The mere thought of it made what had happened seem all the more pathetic. And she started weeping brokenheartedly.

Generally speaking, opinion in the coach was divided between those who believed that the noise that accompanied the flash was a single bang, and those who had heard it as a great roar. Personally, I should not have described it as a bang, but definitely as a roar. The center of the explosion must have been in the area of Chōji Bridge. People who had been within a radius of two kilometers said they had not heard any bang. Even those who had been as much as five kilometers away were agreed that they had heard a roaring noise a few seconds after a flash. Simultaneously with the roar, windows had been blown out and buildings had tottered.

It felt as though the train had been stationary for nearly two hours, but when I asked someone with a watch, I found it had not been much more than thirty minutes. It could not have been so long as I thought, in fact, since I had felt no symptoms of diarrhea. Indeed, I was free of the symptoms all the way from there until we finally reached the works.

At the Furuichi works, the manager and foreman appeared personally in the visitors' room to mark our safe arrival. The tears flowed uncontrollably, inordinately. An office girl drew water from the well for us and brought it in wash bowls and a bucket. A janitor brought me a clean suit. I wrung out a towel and wiped myself all over, but however many times I changed the water in the basin it still turned black, so I called a halt after a while and changed into completely fresh clothes. Shigeko and Yasuko went off into the kitchen.

I went into the office and reported to the manager on the damage to Hiroshima, then, although the sun had already set, went to have a look at the factory. Almost all the windows were broken and the glass scattered about the place, but the building itself and the spinning and weaving machines were intact. The rooms with the cotton scutchers and gins were as usual save for the missing window panes. The kitchen I found not so steamy as usual, since the vapors were escaping from the hole where the ventilator had been blown out. I asked the cook whether there had been any damage. A few nine-inch plates stacked on a shelf had fallen down and broken, she said—that was all.

At the workers' dormitory, I saw a heap of broken glass lying, covered with a newspaper, in a corner of the corridor into which it had been swept. Some of the women workers were getting their belongings out of closets and packing them.

The dormitory supervisor informed me that the management was giving leave to workers commuting from within the city, so that at least those whose injuries were not too serious could go back to their homes in the country. The heads of the various sections, who stayed at the works, had all gone to Hiroshima, fearful for the safety of their families, and only the manager and foreman remained, apart from the factory hands and janitors. True enough, operations under such conditions were impossible. What was more certain still, though, was that everybody, myself included, was apprehensive of the next air raid.

CHAPTER 9 🌿

June 30th was the day of the Sumiyoshi Festival in Onomichi harbor. In Kobatake village, the occasion was marked by a festival at which lanterns were set afloat on the river to call the attention of the god of Sumiyoshi and invoke his protection against flood. Four small floats, named after the four seasons, were made of plain, unvarnished wood, lighted candles were placed inside them, and they were set afloat on one of the pools of calm water that occurred along the mountain stream. The longer they drifted about the dark surface of the water, the more favorable the omens were said to be. If the autumn float, for example, was promptly carried away out of the pool, it was believed that there would be a danger of floods in the autumn.

That day, Shigematsu was getting the fire going under the bath when the postman brought an express letter addressed to Yasuko.

Yasuko herself had gone to Shinichi to do some shopping. The sender of the letter was Gentarō Aono of Yamano village, the young man who had proposed marriage to Yasuko. This was the first time that he had made any approach to Yasuko other than via a go-between. The writing on the envelope was exceptionally neat. It was not a bad sign, thought Shigematsu.

"Put this letter on Yasuko's desk, will you?" he said, giving it to Shigeko. "I don't know what it says, but the fact he's written at least shows that the young man himself is interested. I wish everything was done in the same way. . . ."

He abandoned the bath and went off to his room. He must get the copying of his "Journal of the Bombing" completed quickly. He worked at it all the evening, without even going to see the Lantern Festival.

August 7. Fine.
I awoke to find the morning mist blowing in through the broken window and curling about my face. It was a heavy mist, and the fact that I felt its touch equally on both cheeks suggested that sensation had returned to the left, burned side. Both my wife and Yasuko were already up, and their beds lay empty.

A clamor of voices reached me through the mist. "Hey, you with the truck," said a loud voice, "you can still get another one or two on!" "What're you wasting time for?" said another. "It's half-past five already." It seemed that after I had gone to sleep the previous night, a large number of injured had arrived from Hiroshima. In line with the manager's announcement yesterday evening, those employees whose injuries were only slight were to be sent back to their homes, and relief work was to have started before five this morning, two trucks being used for the purpose. The trucks were to deliver the refugees and their belongings to Furuichi Station, and on the way back bring any badly hurt employees of the company who might be at the station or lying by the roadside.

I tried to sit up in bed, but an excruciating pain shot through my shoulders and down my lower back and legs. Even assuming it was due to tiredness, the pain was different in quality from usual. To turn on my side was agony, but I had a bright idea. With my right hand, I tugged at the seat of my pants so as to turn my body on its side. Then I hunched up my body and got my buttocks in the air, then got onto my knees and so succeeded, little by little, in raising the upper part of my body. Sufferers from lumbago get up in the same way. One elbow goes on the bed, while one presses oneself up with the other hand. As one does so, the arm belonging to the elbow on the bed goes into just the same position as when someone doing a classical Japanese dance gets up off the floor. I found myself wondering: perhaps the originator of the Japanese dance had suffered from lumbago?

Having managed somehow to get halfway up, I put one hand on the window frame and, pressing on my back with the other, succeeded in standing upright. When I put my weight on my legs, I had jabbing pains in my toes. When I moved, it felt as though I was treading on needles, but I could hardly stay where I was. Clinging to the window, I went back and forth, back and forth, and only let go when my muscles had got used to the exercise. Finally, I found myself able to walk. It was lucky I had kept my trousers and shirt on in bed; the merits of informal sleeping habits impressed themselves on me most forcibly. But I began having severe belly pains. I went down the stairs on all fours, feet first. The method makes for easy going, since one can take one's weight, as even the tiniest child will tell you, on all four limbs.

A visit to the toilet cured the pain in my belly. The pain in my shoulders and back eased considerably too, but my toes still had me nearly leaping in the air with pain when I walked.

Going to the entrance of the factory, I found that relief work had gone quite smoothly, and only about twenty people were left in the first batch. They were waiting for the truck to come back for them, with their rucksacks and larger belongings stacked on the ground at the foot of the stone steps. As I watched, one of them yelled, "I saw it! I saw it first!" and dashing out into the courtyard picked up what looked like a scrap of paper that came fluttering down from the sky.

"What've you got there?" said someone. "A five yen or ten yen note, I'll bet."

But it was only a scrap of paper after all, a burnt fragment of sheet music. It must have come from somebody's home—or the teachers' room, perhaps, at some primary school—and been carried up into the sky, alight, by the blast from the previous day's raid, then roamed the void for a whole day and night before coming to earth again. Beneath the notes were printed the words: "Cherry blossom, cherry blossom, in the spring sky. . . ." The manager took it from the other man and looked at it. "Terrible," he said. "Really, of all the. . . ." And he put it away in his pocket.

The truck came, and the last band of refugees said good-by to the manager. "Best of luck," they chorused, and as the truck left he waved his hand and called, "Never say die! Keep smiling!" A hollow mockery at such a time perhaps, but what else could one say?

The total number of refugees was around two hundred and fifty. Not only the lightly injured but the other employes as well, provided they had somewhere to go, were sent off to follow their own devices. This was the outcome of an on-the-spot decision by Fujita, the manager. As a result, something over a hundred souls were left—those too badly hurt to move, those who had volunteered to stay and look after them, those who had already been staying in the dormitory, and members of their families.

Employees who had been staying alone in the dormitory, leaving their families in Hiroshima, found themselves not only with no homes to return to, but with no way of searching for their families. They had nothing to do but stand around and wait. I decided to ask the works section to chop some boards into pieces about six feet long and three inches wide, so that we could write their names and addresses on them and set them up on the ruins of their homes. I calculated that fifteen or sixteen, one for each person, would be enough, but one middle-aged employee actually cut himself three extra ones, which he claimed he wanted to put up on the ruins of various aunts' and uncles' homes. According to a man in the works section called Ueda, the employee in question hadn't an aunt or uncle to his name. Ueda, in fact, came specially to the office to tell me. "That's what happens when you chase after ideals like the Greater East Asia Co-Prosperity Sphere," he remarked as he went out of the door. "War widows on the increase, young men on the decrease, while *some* people get unfair shares of certain commodities." I hurried after him, though I knew my toes would hurt. "You ought to keep defeatist talk like that to yourself," I warned him. Not that either of us had really made any attempt to conceal our defeatism from the other. . . .

After lunch, I was drawing up a list of those who had gone back home when one of the factory hands, a man of about fifty called Nonomiya, came running to say that one of the seriously injured had died. "He was throwing himself about the place in his agony," he said, "and spewed up a lot of yellow liquid. Then, all of a sudden, he just went limp."

The dead man, aged fifty and one of our traveling agents, had been leaving for work from his home in Hiroshima City when the bomb fell. His cheeks had swollen up gray and discolored, but his sight and hearing had been unimpaired. I contacted the works section and told them to make the coffin as quickly as possible, and sent an employe called Fujiki to the town hall with a notification of death, and to get instructions on the disposal of the body. Then I dispatched Nonomiya to get a doctor and a priest.

They both came back before long. The town hall was virtually closed down, and refused even to accept notifications of death, much less give advice on things such as the disposal of bodies. The doctor was not at home, having gone to Hiroshima to look for his child. The only other doctor was out too, attending to seriously hurt patients. The priest, who had had three deaths among his parishioners, was too busy to come. Wherever they went, people were far too occupied with their own affairs to notice them.

I was at a loss what to do. I was discussing things with the manager when a janitor who had been out on business came back and reported that smoke was rising from funeral pyres all along the dried-up parts of the river bed. The crematorium was jammed, and there was no time for people to wait their turn.

If ever there was a time of emergency, of course, this was it. There was simply no time to wait for death certificates, cremation notices and the like. Where jurisdiction over the census register and similar matters was concerned, Furuichi and Hiroshima were separate entities, and even in normal times such procedures required a considerable amount of time. The fact remained, nevertheless, that care was needed in the handling of dead bodies, so the manager sent someone from the general affairs section into town to make thorough inquiries. The manager was roughly the same age as myself, but, perhaps because his position was halfway between that of a government official and an ordinary citizen, he was, if anything, more of a stickler for regulations than the average bureaucrat. He was good at English, better at theory than practical business matters, and for his graduation thesis at college was rumored to have written a paper on the inventor of the automatic spinning machine.

On his return, the man from the general affairs section reported that even the police had conceded that burning the bodies on the river bed was an unavoidable necessity. The justifications, ultimately, were hygienic. In short, there was no one to write death certificates, and no one to receive them even if there had been. In this heat, a dead body soon decomposed. The crematorium was so full as to be useless. Haste then, was the order of the day: they must be burnt on the river bed, in the hills— anywhere away from human habitation.

The manager thought for a while. "We can hardly bury them, I suppose. Whether to bury people or to cremate them has always been a matter for the statesmen of the nation to decide, and we ought to go along with national policy. Yes—I suppose we'll have to cremate them on the river bed, like the others." He turned to me. "But look here, Shizuma," he said severely, "We can't just simply cremate them. You can't just say, 'why, he's dead!' and whisk him off and burn him and have done with it. It's a bit hard on the deceased, surely, unless he gets at least something more than that. Personally, now, I don't believe in the immortality of the soul, but I do believe one should dispose of the dead with respect. Look, Shizuma—I want you to take the priest's place and read the service whenever there's a death."

I was at a loss how to reply. Manager's orders or not, reciting the sutras was quite beyond me.

"Quite impossible, I'm afraid," I said. But the manager persisted. It looked, he said, as though the deaths were going to continue steadily, and he told me to go to some temple or other and make notes as to which scriptures the priest read at cremations. I was also told to take down the texts favored by the Shin sect, since many Hiroshima people belonged to it.

"But Mr. Fujita, I'm afraid I can't. However many notes I might make, I'm just not qualified to attend to the welfare of the dead. I'm a complete novice where Buddhism is concerned."

"Then who d'you think *is* qualified? There's no such thing as an expert or a novice in such matters. It isn't as if an amateur saying a service for the dead was the same as an amateur giving a sick man medicine. It doesn't involve breaking the law, either. Even so, if you don't fancy the Shin sect, Zen will do, or Nichiren—anything you like. It's a nuisance for you, but I'm afraid this is an order I'll have to ask you to carry out."

I gave up any further attempt at rebellion, slung my air raid hood over my shoulder so as to be properly dressed for going out, and donned a pair of old *tabi* that I borrowed from the manager to make things easier for my painful feet. I got some name cards and a notebook, slipped on a pair of kitchen sandals, and set off.

I knew a number of temples in Furuichi. I called at one of them where there was a young priest rumored to have distinguished himself as a student at a Buddhist college, but the old woman who came to the entrance told me that he had been drafted and was with the Akatsuki unit. Next, I went to a Shin sect temple where there were an aged priest and a curate. The old priest was infirm and bedridden, and the curate had gone to a funeral. The middle-aged, rather stupid-looking woman who told me this retired into the inner regions with my message, then came back and conducted me to the room where the old priest lay.

In an old-style room twice the size it would have been in an ordinary house, he lay beneath a small, white, child's mosquito net. The thin quilt covering him was almost flat, only the slightest hump betraying the human form beneath. The sliding doors were thrown open, and beyond them I could see pumpkins swarming all over a typical temple garden of craggy rocks and moss and sand.

The old priest listened as I detailed my errand, then turned to the middle-aged woman, who had seated herself on the tatami near his bed.

"My dear," he said, "be good enough to bring the 'Threefold Refuge' and—let me see—the 'Dedication' and the 'Hymn to the Buddha.' And the 'Amida Sutra' and the 'Sermon on Mortality' as well." His voice was thin and reedy. The woman got up and fetched them from the next room.

"Now, then," he went on, "perhaps you would show them to this gentleman here." Faint though the voice was, the woman moved about with alacrity at his bidding.

The five scriptures were printed from wooden blocks. As I set about copying them, the old priest got the middle-aged woman to help him up, and seated himself correctly on his heels, with his hands in his lap, on the tatami near me.

"I'm afraid this is most troublesome for you," he said with infinite courtesy. I noticed how frail were the knees on which his hands rested. "They tell me that Hiroshima is no more. A dreadful thing. Truly a—dear me, how can one put it?—a lamentable thing. . . ."

His voice was somewhat firmer now. I paused in my writing and let my gaze wander out to the garden, but the sight of the cheerful red pumpkins brought the tears springing unbidden to my eyes.

Much of the sense of the scriptures escaped me, but they were written out with signs showing the general intonation to help one in the reading. The "Threefold Refuge" and the "Dedication" were in measured Chinese phrases telling of the Buddha, the Law, the salvation of all beings, and countless aeons of time. The "Sermon on Mortality" was in gentler, homelier Japanese, in a beautiful language that struck home to the heart.

"In our sect at funerals," the old priest said, "we read the

'Threefold Refuge' first, then the 'Dedication,' and then the 'Hymn to the Buddha,' in that order. Next comes the 'Amida Sutra,' and while this sutra is being read those present offer up incense. Then comes the 'Sermon on Mortality,' but this time one reads facing the congregation and not the departed one."

To show me how to read the scriptures, he recited the "Three-fold Refuge" and the "Dedication," his voice unexpectedly strong as he did so. Listening, I made notes on the correct readings here and there alongside what I had copied. Then he read for me from the "Sermon on Mortality." The room was perfectly quiet save for the monotonous chanting of his voice.

I had no qualifications for guiding the souls of the dead in their journey to the next world, yet at the very least, I told myself, my reading of the sutras should be a prayer for their salvation, and I resolved that I would read them with all my heart and soul. The peaceful atmosphere of the room had made it possible for me to feel that way.

On my way back from the temple, I started practicing reciting the sutras, reading them over and over again from my notes in a hasty attempt to get them into my head. At the factory, I found the coffin ready to leave. Some thirty people had gathered in the tatami-floored waiting room of the employees' dormitory. The coffin rested on a low stage normally used for entertainments and speeches, and incense was burning in a toy bucket that someone had found and filled with fine ash for the purpose. There was even a branch of the sacred tree used in Shintō rituals, stuck in a large saké bottle. The manager came in wearing a suit.

Just before I was due to read the service, I put on the jacket of the suit that Fujiki, one of the employes, had lent me. As I seated myself before the coffin, I felt my muscles tense a little, but as I read on, with my eyes on my notebook, I ceased to bother any longer about the congregation. Yet my frame of mind was far from the ideal state of tranquil selflessness, and was much closer to a sense of vacancy and unreality. Two or three times I stumbled in my reading, but at last I got through to the end, turned to those assembled, and bowed.

"Thank you, Mr. Shizuma," said the manager, and a chorus of "thank you's" and "very good of you's" rose from the others. My cheeks flamed and, intolerably embarrassed, I pushed my way through their ranks and retired to the office.

Before long, someone came to report another death. I was telling the works section to make one more coffin, when yet another was reported. As soon as the next body was in its coffin, I went to read the service, and this time, I felt, managed it a little better.

Toward the end of the afternoon, there were four more deaths. The first and second times the message was "Mr. Shizuma, I wonder if you could read the service," but this gradually deteriorated to "Another funeral, Mr. Shizuma—will you come?" Before long, I came to feel that I preferred it that way myself.

When we ran out of wood for coffins, I had to recite the scriptures directly in front of the body. The face was always covered with a white cloth, but the limbs, with the characteristic discoloration of the dead, were in full view. When they were not, they were bound with bandages stained dark red with blood. Properly speaking, one should always read the service after the deceased has been placed in the coffin. So long as this idea persisted in my brain, things tended to go wrong when I was reading before an uncoffined body. Fortunately, I had my notebook to rely on.

The manager facetiously remarked that he would have to give me the "offering" that is a priest's usual reward for conducting a funeral service. What was worse, some of the relatives of the deceased, or those who had tended them, actually brought me money, discreetly folded in white paper as custom demands. "Don't be silly," I would say, thrusting it back at them. "No, please," some of them would say, looking at me earnestly, "if you don't take it, the soul will never attain release."

The office girls apparently took turns to come and hear me read. Three of them actually asked me to let them copy the "Sermon on Mortality." When I asked why, one of them said she liked the language. "I want to memorize it," said another. "I want to learn what comes after 'Sooner or later, to me or to my neighbor, on this day or the morrow. . . .' "

These were the more acceptable of the visits I received between funeral services. I was no match, though, for those who came to discuss the bombing. Little by little, their talk would drag me back unwilling to the reality, till my hair stood on end, my scalp tingled, and the urge to flee became all but irresistible. I cannot well describe the feeling it produced—whether it was distaste or fear— but the result, invariably, was an overwhelming desire to run.

Late that afternoon, as dusk was falling, I went up to a second-floor room looking out in the direction of the city. There were no lights as there had always been before. One lone house, over in the east, showed an uncertain glimmer, but I resented it: it was merely depressing. Utter darkness would have been far less disturbing.

From dawn to dusk, it had been a day given over to funerals.

August 8. Fine and sweltering.
We had changed our lodgings the previous night to a small building, in the grounds of someone's home, that had originally been built for their aged parents. It stood about two hundred yards from the house where Mr. Fujita the manager had rooms. That morning, I was awakened by a voice calling my name from the garden. I got out of bed, and found one of the factory hands, a man called Utagawa, standing outside.

"Two people died last night," he said. "Can you come as quickly as possible?" Before I could reply, he was off back to the factory. I was being treated just like a priest, except that a priest would have been summoned less peremptorily.

I had no real preparations to make. I merely had to wash, eat, go to the factory, and borrow a jacket from one of the hands. Even the funeral required no preparations; once the service was over, the body was taken straight to the river bed and burned. I had sworn that I would put my whole being into reciting the sutras, but my heart was hardly in the task as I set out that morning.

Arriving at the dormitory, I found that the daughter of the factory hand whose funeral service I had conducted yesterday had died. She had been at their home in Temma-chō when the bomb fell, I was told.

The dead girl's mother had raw burns all over her body and seemed to be past caring what was happening. The dead girl's sister, to all appearances unharmed, sat by herself, staring vacantly before her with her mouth open. When I murmured "I'm so sorry," she said "Thank you" mechanically, with no change of expression. There were no tears, no defiance.

The dead girl was laid out face up, dressed in a tattered white shirt. In the hollow between her breasts, someone had laid a few wild flowers doubtless picked in the nearby fields. Small, yellow blooms, they were wilting and drooped as though in grief against one breast. They were the final touch of sorrow. I read the "Three-fold Refuge," and was on the "Sermon on Mortality" when my voice finally choked.

The service over, one of the factory hands said to the younger girl, "Now they're taking your sister to be cremated." "Yes," she said, and gave a slight shake of her head. The mother remained motionless. It was a lonely last journey, attended by neither kith nor kin. The bearers transferred the body onto a straw mat, lifted it onto a handcart, and set off. I followed.

On both sides of the river, the dried-up part of the bed had the aspect of a crematorium. Wherever I looked, upstream or down-stream, the columns of smoke were rising. Here, the blaze would be fierce and the smoke thick; there, mere wisps of smoke would be rising from still smoldering embers.

The handcart I was following came to a halt on top of the embankment, and the men went to look for a suitable spot. "Hey," called one. "The fire's out in this hole. It looks as though they've already taken the ashes home." "We'll use that, then, shall we?" said another, and they took the body and carried it over.

In the center of the hole were two stones, each about one foot in diameter. They laid the body on these, and under and beside it they put coal, which they had brought in two buckets. They propped pieces of timber and old wooden packing cases against it, and on top of it they piled more. The head and face they covered with sawdust, and stood pieces of board on either side. Finally, they swathed the whole in dampened straw and straw mats, and the preparations were completed.

I could still glimpse the girl's hair and forehead through a gap where one of the mats curled upward, and the stony pallor of her face. They were squatting around her on the sand. "Light it, someone," one of them said, and stood up. I read the "Threefold Refuge," and left before the flames began to rise.

From the top of the embankment, countless holes were visible, dug in the sand. I could see bones in most of them, and the skulls especially stood out with strange clarity. The ash that covered the bones after the fire had fallen in must have been cleared away by the breeze blowing across from the river. Some of the skulls gazed fixedly at the sky with empty eye-sockets, others clenched their teeth in angry resentment. In olden times, I suddenly recalled, they used to refer to skulls as "the unsheltered ones."

In some holes, only the head and the legs had been consumed. In others, bright red tongues of flame still flickered fitfully. I remembered the other body awaiting me, and set off back along the embankment, murmuring the "Sermon on Mortality" to myself as I went. This time, I got through it without so much as a glance at my notes.

CHAPTER 10 ✍

The next day, Shigematsu continued transcribing his "Journal of the Bombing." By now, he was halfway through the entry for August 8.

All the way back to the factory I continued to recite the "Sermon on Mortality" to myself, but its precepts had no real meaning for me; in my mind's eye, like a waking dream, I could still see the tongues of fire at work on the bodies of men. Only when I arrived at the entrance to the office did I realize that I was drenched in sweat.

I found the downstairs office deserted. Going to the manager's room, I discovered the kitchen superintendent and a kitchen help, a woman called Mrs. Ariki, seated facing the manager.

"Hello, Shizuma!" said the manager, seeing me. "You've been

hard at work!" He listened to my account of the funeral, then directed me to read a service for another victim who had just died. Her name was Taka Mitsuda, and Mrs. Ariki the kitchen help had been looking after her. She was a black market woman, who used to come to the works kitchen from somewhere in the city to sell clams and various small, poor quality fish. She had been caught in the raid two days before. Injured in the face and on both hands, she had finally arrived at the kitchen early that morning to seek Mrs. Ariki's help. Mrs. Ariki and Mrs. Mitsuda were not related, but Mrs. Mitsuda had always sold things to Mrs. Ariki—so the latter said—a great deal cheaper than the usual black market prices.

I took down details of Mrs. Mitsuda's background in my notebook, just as Mrs. Ariki related them. If we were going to hold a funeral for an outsider, it was necessary to take down her name, address, status, and the names of any relatives, so as to prevent complications later.

Unfortunately, no one knew much about her background, so I had to content myself with the following scrappy notes:

Concerning the Late Mrs. Taka Mitsuda
Address: A side street near the Sumiyoshi Shrine, Kako-chō, Hiroshima City.
Age: 48 or 49.
Height, etc.: About 5′ 2″. Stout; health normally good. Chromium-plated false teeth in upper and lower jaws at the front, four or five in all.
Cause of death: Burns incurred in the raid on Hiroshima. Her face and hands were burned raw and the skin on her left hand was peeling off. She was just taking off her air raid hood at the time, and her hair was not burned.
Time of arrival at the works: About 8 a.m., August 8, 1945. She came staggering into the kitchen and called to Mrs. Ariki to give her water. Mrs. Ariki knew her by her voice, and gave her water in an aluminum cup. Her face was unrecognizable. She drank the water and went into a state of collapse. She made no further response when her name was called, though

Mrs. Ariki felt her chest and found her heart was still beating faintly. She must have passed away around ten o'clock that morning.

Family: According to various remarks made when she came to sell black market goods, her husband had died of disease while on service in China during the Manchurian Affair. Her only son is at a "kind of school" connected with the army, near Yanai in Yamaguchi Prefecture. She always avoided saying just what kind of institution this was, but the fact that her son was there seems to have been one thing of which she was inordinately proud.

Possessions Found on Deceased by Person who Tended Her: A large leather purse containing nine ¥10 notes, twelve ¥5 notes, twenty-two ¥1 notes, and ¥3.49 in coins. One old cotton towel and an imitation leather commuter's pass holder containing photographs of her husband in army sergeant's uniform and her son in a short-sleeved shirt.

All the above details were given to me verbally by Mrs. Ariki and the chief cook.

The money found on the deceased, together with the commuter's pass and the two photographs with it in the case, were placed in the safe in the manager's office in the presence of Mr. Fujita himself, the kitchen superintendent, Mrs. Ariki, and Shigematsu Shizuma, and the manager wrote in the ledger: "One hundred and seventy-five yen, forty-nine sen only, in trust from Taka Mitsuda of Kako-chō, Hiroshima City."

A sum of over ¥170 must have represented the money she was taking with her to buy the clams and fish she would later sell on the black market. Or again, it may have been her total worldly wealth. Either way, the proper thing would be to send it to her son, but since her home at Kako-chō was said to have been burned down, we should have to try to contact him at the school near Yanai in Yamaguchi Prefecture.

"Look here now, Mrs. Ariki," said the manager, "a 'kind of school near Yanai' must mean the place where they train human torpedoes, don't you think? It's a top secret military establishment, I believe. What was the barracks there called, now . . . ?"

"I really can't say, I'm sure, Mr. Fujita," she replied uncertainly. "The clam lady was always saying how it was a military secret. All she would let on was that it was a kind of special college. And sure enough, when you go through in the train they keep all the blinds down on the windows on that side—strict security, you see."

"Fine security it is, too!" put in the cook, a balding, middle-aged man. "With the windows in the toilets all wide open! All this talk of security is so much show, if you ask me. A lot of theory, without the real will to do anything . . ."

"Anyway," the manager said to Mrs. Ariki, ignoring these last observations, "the black market woman's son is on his way to becoming a human torpedo. That means the boy's got courage at least, and a sense of duty to his country. If such a man's mother chooses to pass on at our factory, then we must accord her all the proper rites. And we must have Shizuma here recite the scriptures at her funeral. Mustn't we now, Mrs. Ariki?"

"Why, of course, Mr. Fujita, sir. It's so kind of you, I'm sure, Mr. Fujita. And Mr. Shizuma—you'll read the service for her, won't you?"

Mrs. Ariki had obviously been particularly well disposed toward the woman with the clams. She told me—perhaps to encourage me to take special care in reading the sutras—how, when the clam lady's son had entered the "kind of school" in Yanai, she herself had put one of the stitches in a "thousand-stitch belt" that the women-folk had made for him. She had even joined the rest in signing her name, "Kane Ariki," in her own poor hand, on a Rising Sun flag wishing him good fortune in battle.

They told me that things were ready for the service so, though I was still sticky all over with sweat, I put on the borrowed suit and went to the big room in the dormitory. The dead woman lay on her back on a board, with her face, arms, and legs wrapped in cloths and looking like cloth bundles. I took my place before her, but my throat seemed to choke up, and my voice would not come smoothly. Presumably it was because I had walked home under the blazing sun and had had nothing to drink since. Or again, it might have been because of the fragments of the deceased's life history I had heard. Had this woman who lay dead here—I kept asking myself—made no move to stop her son from volunteering to be trained as a human torpedo?

War, I concluded, paralyzes people's power of judgment. From the first word to the last, the "Threefold Refuge" came out in a hoarse voice, while the "Sermon on Mortality" was no more than a faint whisper. Even so, at the end, as I finally left my place by the body, Mrs. Ariki—chief mourner in the absence of anyone else—came up to me and said "Thank you so much, Mr. Shizuma" in a voice charged with emotion.

I went to the wash-place, drank some water, and rubbed myself all over with a wet towel. I could not wipe the burned left cheek, since it was still covered with a piece of bandage. The cloth felt as though it were stuck fast to the wound. Not having felt the slightest pain since I first received the injury, I had left it as it was, but now I decided to attend to it and to wipe off the sweat at the same time. Fetching my first-aid kit, I stationed myself before the mirror.

I peeled off the sticking plaster holding the bandage in place, and cautiously removed the cloth. The scorched eyelashes had gone into small black lumps, like the blobs left after a piece of wool has been burned. The whole left cheek was a blackish-purple color, and the burned skin had shriveled up on the flesh, without parting company with it, to form ridges across the cheek. The side of the left nostril was infected, and fresh pus seemed to be coming from under the dried-up crust on top. I turned the left side of my face to the mirror. Could this be my own face, I wondered. My heart pounded at the idea, and the face in the mirror grew more and more unfamiliar.

Taking one end of a curled-up piece of skin between my nails, I gave it a gentle tug. It hurt a little, which at least assured me that this was my own face. I pondered this fact, peeling off skin a little at a time as I did so. The action gave me a strange kind of pleasure, like the way one joggles a loose tooth that wants to come out, both hating and enjoying the pain at the same time. I stripped off all the curled-up skin. Finally, I took hold of the lump of hardened pus on the side of my nostril with my nails, and pulled. It came away from the top first, then suddenly came clean off, and the liquid yellow pus dropped onto my wrist.

I could not tell whether the infection was getting worse or better. The only thing I could do was to cleanse the affected spot and apply powdered medicine to the infected place, then cover the whole left cheek with cloth and fasten it with sticking plaster. I had prepared the medicine myself from a formula, consisting mostly of leek leaves, given me by a carpenter back home in the country, who said it was especially effective for cuts and infections.

It was nearing noon. I set off back to our temporary home to get a meal, but as I went up the hill the pain in my leg became so bad that I could only walk gingerly and with great effort. Stopping to rest at a corner of the slope, I glanced up, to see my wife Shigeko looking down at me from the top of the bank.

"Your poor leg seems to be giving you a lot of trouble," she said. "Shall I bring a stick or something?"

She went away and brought back a bamboo spear of the kind people used for training in hand-to-hand fighting. The landlord's wife, she said, had made it for her only a little while before. Leaning on my spear and with one arm around my wife's shoulders, I climbed on up the hill, feeling rather like a defeated remnant from one of the peasant risings of the last century. It was then that I first noticed Shigeko's hair was scorched. I asked her when it happened. It must have been in the air raid on the sixth, she said.

For lunch we had parched rice from our emergency rations, with fermented bean paste fried in rapeseed oil, and tea made from salted cherry blossoms to wash it down. That was all, but for us at the time it ranked as *haute cuisine*.

According to what Shigeko told me now, it was only that morning that she had first noticed her hair was scorched. On the morning of the sixth, the all-clear had sounded, but she could still hear explosions, so she had peered up at the sky out of the kitchen window. At that instant, there had been an intense flash of light, and before she realized it she had thrown herself flat on the wooden floor. (It was then, it seems, that her hair was burned.) After a while, she got up and found everything in the kitchen scattered in disorder. She went out to the back of the house, and found the brick wall collapsed. It looked as though a fire had started somewhere.

Convinced that something awful had happened, she rushed upstairs to get a better view. The window panes were blown out, the sliding doors were all lopsided, and the top branches of the pine tree in the garden, together with the transformer on the telegraph pole next to it, were spurting flames. A tremendous column of smoke was rising from the direction of the city hall. Here and there, other smaller clouds of smoke were rising. The fire seemed to be spreading steadily. Concluding that she should get out, she went first of all to get the silk bag containing the family ancestral tablets, but it was not hanging on its usual pillar. Nor was it on the pillar in the next room.

Giving up the search, she set about seeing to the other things. With the idea of sinking them in the pond for safety's sake, she started carrying bowls and dishes, bedding, mosquito net, shoes, and so on out into the garden—where she found, floating on the surface of the pond, the white bag containing the ancestral tablets. It must have been blown there from inside the house. She fished it out, put it in her rucksack, and threw some of the things she had brought out into the pond, in any order, just as they came to hand. Others she put in the air raid shelter, piling up lumps of brick from the collapsed wall to block the entrance. It was then that she heard cries for help coming from the Nittas' house next door.

She rushed to the house and was horrified to find Mr. and Mrs. Nitta both badly hurt, he in the side, she on the face. She ripped up a "thousand stitches belt" and gave them first aid, then went to fetch the neighborhood association stretcher. She was on her way back when she found that Mrs. Nomura, who lived on the opposite corner, was also badly hurt and seeking help. She dropped the stretcher and bandaged her with a cotton towel. The casualties were far worse than she had realized. The Nakanishis, the Hayamis, the Sugais, the Nakamuras—all the families belonging to the neighborhood association had, she realized, suffered casualties in varying degrees, and she herself was going about alone, the only one left unhurt. There was no hope of being able to use the stretcher.

Before long, Mrs. Nozu's husband, who was a captain in the army, came home with some soldiers and took her off somewhere. Mr. and Mrs. Nitta said they were going to the Mutual Aid Hospital and went off together, a pitiful sight as they helped each other along, both of them covered with blood.

Shigeko went back to the house and put a few more pieces of furniture and other household belongings in the air raid shelter, then took refuge at the university sports ground.

There were some things in Shigeko's story that refused to make sense, either in scientific terms or in terms of common logic. In our district, the blast had passed through from north to south. Yet although the trees in the garden, the house itself, and the doors in the house were all leaning to the south or the southwest, the bag containing the ancestral tablets must have flown from the south towards the north-northwest, traversing some eight yards within the house and about five outside, in order to end up floating on the surface of the pond. It was simply not logical—though it is just possible, I suppose, that it was blown out of the house in a southerly or southwesterly direction, then pulled back to the northwest by the backdraft that followed the blast.

August 9.

At dinner time last night we reached the end of our emergency rations. From today, that meant, we should have to get food from the company canteen. Shigeko went to get our breakfast and Yasuko our lunch, but at lunchtime both of them started complaining; I imagine they had set each other off.

If the food involved were only raw vegetables and rice, they said, it would not be so bad, but to go and fetch cooked food that other people had prepared, and to eat it without so much as lifting a finger themselves made them feel terribly guilty. Yesterday they had had some work to do, helping with the refugees, but from today on they would have nothing at all to occupy them, and they felt too ashamed to go and get the food. The manager had told Yasuko today that she could have a holiday from the office until further notice.

Intensely irritated, I immediately found them something to do.

"Tomorrow you can go to where the house was at Senda-machi," I said. "And you can find out exactly what's happened to the people in the neighborhood association. Then, while you're about it, you might as well get out of the air raid shelter any changes of clothing we're likely to need in the near future, as well as the bottles filled with rice. The rice was for an emergency, so I don't know when we're supposed to eat it, if not at a time like this."

This seemed to put their minds at rest, and they declared that tonight they would go to the canteen together to get the evening meal.

The air raid shelter at the house in Senda-machi contained a radio, blankets, dishes and bowls, kitchen equipment, and various foodstuffs other than rice. In a clear space in the garden, we had buried four half-gallon bottles of rice, a four-and-a-half-gallon can of soybeans, and another can containing underwear and cotton kimonos. I had checked that they were not destroyed by the fire as we were on our way out of the burning city.

Shigeko and Yasuko, who had only the clothes they stood up in, were discussing something in undertones. It seemed they wanted to wash their underwear, but were wondering what to do until it dried. I told them they should go down to the river, take all their things off and wash them, and stay in the water swimming until they dried. So they took their towels and set off.

The tension of my mind must have relaxed, for I suddenly began to feel the heat badly, and sleepiness seemed to steal over me irresistibly where I sat. Yet as soon as I lay down and shut my eyes, the recollection of the countless columns of smoke rising from the river bed and the hills drove sleep away.

Whether I stayed up or lay down, the sweat poured from me steadily, but though I wanted to wipe my face, this was only possible with the right half. The left half, with its bandage, reminded me of the feeling when a hot towel is pressed on one's face at the barber's, only far worse, and there was a suggestion of thick sweat or pus accumulating beneath the cloth. The only thing I could do was to dab at the cloth to help it soak up the sweat or pus. I kept dabbing at it, and the cloth began to feel soggy. I should have changed it, but I had no fresh bandage, so I got a triangular bandage from a first-aid kit, cut it to fit my face, poured boiling water on it, and put it in the sun to dry.

I was leaning against a pillar on the veranda, feeling drowsy, when a man called Tanaka from the general affairs section came to tell me that he had handed over some provisions to a group of soldiers who had come to take them away.

"That's a fine thing you've gone and done!" I said. "When did you give the stuff to them?"

"A while ago—about an hour, I should say."

"What soldiers were they, and where did they take it?"

"They were infantrymen, so I thought they were from the Second West Japan Corps, and gave them what they wanted."

We had been storing the food for the Signal Corps and the Second West Japan Corps. Late at night about two weeks before, Captain Nozu, who lived opposite our house in Senda-machi, had arrived at our place all out of breath, and had asked me to look after some food for him. I asked him why. He said there had been a call from divisional staff saying that things had reached a point where Hiroshima might be bombed any day, and that they were to get army reserve supplies out of the way immediately. Captain Nozu, who was a conscript and knew nothing about army affairs outside his own barracks, entreated me to help him. I called Mr. Fujita at the works before taking charge of the food, then had it taken to the works warehouse that same night.

The following morning, Lieutenant Kokubu of the Second West Japan Corps arrived at our house and asked us to store in the works warehouse some army provisions that they wanted to get out of the way. The matter was urgent, but they couldn't think of anywhere to take the stuff, so in the end they had called Captain

Nozu and asked what the Signal Corps was doing, as a result of which he had come to me.

I checked with the company and agreed to take it again, but there was so much that it would not all go in, and I had to go and ask a local tatami-maker called Tauchi to take care of some of the rice, which was in woven straw bags. It was the rest of this rice, the stuff in the works warehouse, that the soldiers had taken away.

Their story was highly suspicious. They had said that Lieutenant Kokubu had been injured in the bombing, but anybody who came from the Second West Japan Corps to get food stores should have had an introduction from him, or papers of some kind at least. We must resign ourselves, in short, to the fact that we had been hood-winked by scoundrels working under cover of the general chaos. It was too late to doing anything about it.

I gave Tanaka a stern warning. From now on, I said, he must on no account give anything to anybody other than Lieutenant Kokubu or a representative of his armed with the lieutenant's own card. That was one of the conditions under which we had taken charge of the stores in the first place. What complicated matters was that clerical business pertaining to the storage of foodstuffs was out of our hands now, and the Signal Corps was using a small Japanese-style room on the second floor of our office buildings as its quartermaster's office.

I went to the works warehouse and found precisely the number of bags missing that Tanaka had said. It seemed to me that the familiar world had started to come apart at the seams since the bomb had fallen on Hiroshima. In olden times, people used to say that in an area badly ravaged by war it took a century to re-pair the moral damage done to the inhabitants; and it began to seem as though they might have been right.

CHAPTER 11 🌿

I went to the company offices to report on the theft of provisions, taking Tanaka with me as the man in charge on the day in question. We were dealing with the army, so the matter was not one to be taken lightly. Tanaka had undoubtedly been remiss, but the real responsibility was my own, while the ripples of the affair would almost certainly extend to Captain Nozu as well.

The missing goods consisted of seven bales of polished rice and ten cases of canned beef, along with five crates of a white wine known as "Sadoya's Special." It was outrageous for soldiers on active service at such a time of emergency, when the food shortage was at its height, to come along as bold as brass in an army truck and cheat civilians out of army reserve stores that had been left in their charge. The soldiers had come in two trucks, and the lead truck had reportedly had a small, pale blue flag on it.

"When you eat this canned beef you have to cook it with egg-plant," a superior private who looked older than the rest had remarked gratuitously as they loaded the canned beef on to a truck. "It brings some people out in a rash if they eat it straight." The beef was supposed to have been stored ready for use in scorched earth warfare following a possible enemy invasion, but one soldier at least was obviously already familiar with its delights.

"That means that a company officer came with them!" said the manager indignantly when Tanaka gave his account of the episode. "I'd no idea the army had deteriorated so badly." His lips were twitching with suppressed emotion. Tanaka stood stiffly upright and almost motionless before the manager, his face white. A man of forty-eight, he came from Kabe, but was staying in the works dormitory while his wife worked in a foundry in their home town. Both their two sons had died in battle, and they had had a large tombstone erected—so people said—with the two names carved on it side by side.

Although he was standing at attention, Tanaka could only manage a feeble, spineless kind of voice. "Actually, sir," he faltered, "there was one older man, a superior private, and the others had their jackets off. They were all wearing puttees and workshoes."

"But I thought you said they had a pale blue flag on the truck? A pale blue flag should have meant it was carrying a company officer. A red flag would have meant a field officer, and a yellow one a general. You lost two sons in battle yourself, didn't you? So don't tell me you don't know *that* much about the army."

"But you see, the older private was in the infantry, so I simply thought they were soldiers from the Second West Japan Corps. I thought the blue flag meant they'd come at the orders of a company officer. But then, I was stupid. . . . Yes—you must blame me, Mr. Fujita, it was all my fault. . . ." He dropped his head and, without warning, started sobbing, his shoulders heaving with emotion.

"Well at any rate, we shall have to submit a report to the Second West Japan Corps," said the manager, turning to me. "As quickly as possible. And all three of us—Tanaka, and you Shizuma, and myself—will have to sign it."

"Very well," I said. "The usual form for written explanations, I suppose?"

He agreed. Unfortunately, the Second West Japan Corps had vanished, barracks and all, in the raid, and there was nowhere to take the documents. The paymaster's office of the Signal Corps had moved into the second floor of our offices, but I doubted whether it was any good presenting the paymaster's office of the Signal Corps with documents addressed to the paymaster's office of the Second West Japan Corps. We civilians did not know enough about the way things were organized inside the army.

All the same, I drew up the document in the form of a written explanation. The manager and I stamped it with our own personal seals, and I got Tanaka to put his thumbprint on it. Then I took it upstairs to the paymaster's office of the Signal Corps. A chair and table stood on the tatami in the small, Japanese-style room, and a pair of boots that somebody had taken off stood on a piece of newspaper inside the sliding doors. Naturally, I took off my own shoes before going in. Captain Nozu was out on official business, I was told, but there were two army men who looked like non-commissioned officers; I could not tell their rank as they had their jackets off, but one of them who was apparently the senior of the two, with a small toothbrush mustache, took the envelope containing the document that I held out to him.

I said that I was an acquaintance of Captain Nozu, and he said, "Good of you to come, I'm sure." Then he took out the document and started to read it. His expression changed. "Oh dear," he said. "This won't do at all." He thrust the document back at me. "Surely this should be presented to Lieutenant Kokubu of the paymaster's office of the Second West Japan Corps, shouldn't it? This is the paymaster's office of the Signal Corps."

"Yes, but we'd like you to pass it on to Lieutenant Kokubu. You see, we're not sure where the Second West Japan Corps is . . ."

This remark definitely seemed to displease him.

"No nonsense, now," he said. "If this unit passed on that kind of document to Lieutenant Kokubu, it would be as good as putting him in the wrong before the whole corps. And that would affect the record of the whole paymaster's office of the Second West Japan Corps. Anyway, it's quite impossible for us to accept it."

Helpless to do anything further, I retired downstairs and reported to the manager. Tanaka was no longer to be seen. The manager told me that Tanaka had sworn to make amends to the army for the stolen goods, even if it took him all his life to do it.

I went back to the small detached house that we were living in. I was terribly tired. Shigeko and Yasuko had not got back from the river yet, so I decided to have a rest until dusk, and putting up the mosquito net to keep off the flies, lay down.

I slept a while, and awoke with the cry of an owl ringing in my ears. Opening my eyes, I saw the afternoon sun shining on the white clay wall of the storehouse beyond the shrubs in the garden, and the young wife of the house owner walking towards the shrubs. To imagine owls crying was nonsense. In fact, I found, I had woken because my feet were cold. It worried me that I should get cold feet in August, at the height of summer, while the sun was still up. Feeling my toes, I found that the big toe on each foot was rather painful. Somewhat dismayed, I got up, lifted up the mosquito net, and went out onto the veranda. As I did so, something struck cold at my left cheek. I felt at it, and found that the bandage had gone. It was caught on the bottom edge of the mosquito net.

The mirror showed me that the infected place on the side of my nose was gaping open and had dried up crisp and hard. Life was one depressing thing after another. I went and soaked a small towel in water and gently wiped the affected area, replacing the bandage with a new piece which I fastened in place with sticking plaster.

I was folding up the mosquito net when Shigeko and Yasuko came home and fetched dinner for three from the works kitchen. The meal they set out on the borrowed table consisted of sweet potato leaves boiled down in soy, pickles, and boiled barley with bran mixed in it. As we ate, Shigeko and Yasuko talked to me of conditions in the city, as they had heard them from people they met by the river. They had washed their baggy cotton breeches, their shirts and their underwear, then gone and sat in the river while their clothes dried on the pebbly, dried-up part of the bed.

There were three other women doing the same thing, and they had talked of Hiroshima all the while they waited.

In the playground of the First Prefectural Middle School in the city—one of them said—there was a reservoir of water for fire-fighting purposes. Around it, hundreds of middle school students and voluntary war workers lay dead. They were piled up at the edge of the reservoir, half-naked since their shirts had been burned away. Seen from a distance, they looked like beds of tulips planted round the water. Seen closer, they were more like the layers of petals on a chrysanthemum.

In the road with streetcar tracks in front of the Shiratori Shrine, one of the women had seen a streetcar reduced to an iron skeleton, with the half-consumed body of the driver still standing grasping the handle. The half-burned bodies of four or five passengers lay on or near the platform.

On the morning of the sixth, another of the women said, a squad of cadet officers had been drilling on the West Parade Ground under the officer in charge. They had just finished, and were taking off their tunics for physical training, when the great flash came. One of them, at the very rear of the ranks, had been standing with his back against a leafy tree, and claimed to have seen the keep of Hiroshima Castle at the very instant it was blown away—the whole keep, its shape intact, flying off through the air to the southeast.

The next moment, he could no longer see anything. Yet he swore that he had seen the five-story keep of the castle, just as it had always been, up there in the sky forty or fifty yards away from its original position. Even if the story was true, he could hardly have consciously looked at it; the sight, rather, must have imprinted itself on his retina at the instant of the explosion.

People who were there later reported that the keep lay smashed to smithereens on the river embankment, reduced to a heap of clay and broken tiles. It seems that the blast of a bomb has the ability both to push and to lift. The keep of the castle must have weighed some thousands of tons, yet the force moving it was greater than gravity, and it was lifted into the air without being smashed.

Following the dropping of the bomb, the towns and villages around the city had all, sooner or later, sent their own relief parties into the ruins. One of them, from the town of Miyoshi, had set out with the aim of looking for pupils from the Miyoshi Girls' High School and other inhabitants of the town and its environs who had been doing war work in the city. Some of the girls in third grade and above had been mobilized to work as assistant nurses at the army hospital, while others had been assigned to the eleventh Air Force arsenal at Kure to help in the manufacture of planes. The relief party from Miyoshi, with about one hundred members, had entered the city early on the morning of the seventh, but had been trapped in the flames and most of its members had died. One of them, a man called Jitsuo Tabuchi, head of the party's number one squad and a lecturer in the postgraduate course of the girls' high school, had escaped and got as far as Gion, outside the city, before collapsing. The girls who had been in the city when the bomb fell had, of course, all been killed outright.

(I should add here that I myself happened to make Mr. Tabuchi's acquaintance after the war. He told me that on the morning of the sixth, he had been reading the paper before going to work when something like a pale blue spark seemed to cross the sky. He had dismissed it as imagination, but around noon an army announcement over the radio had reported the bombing. By around three in the afternoon, the injured who had escaped from the city were beginning to arrive in Miyoshi by train. The Geibi Line was not running beyond Shimo-Fukagawa, so they had fled as far as Shimo-Fukagawa on foot and boarded the train there.

The local medical association and the Miyoshi fire brigade set up tents in front of Miyoshi Station, where they gave first aid to the injured. Around five in the afternoon the medical association, the staffs of the Miyoshi Middle School and the Miyoshi Girls' High School, the members of the fire brigade, and other citizens from the town and neighboring villages conferred and decided to organize a relief party. Tabuchi was chosen as head of the first squad. Around five on the morning of the seventh, he boarded a train in charge of eighty people—teachers from the girls' high school and volunteers from the town and neighboring villages—and went as far as Shimo-Fukagawa, whence they proceeded into Hiroshima on foot. The time was now about half-past ten in the morning. They were appalled at what they found, but they did not yet know, of course, what kind of bomb had fallen. The horror was so stupefying that they could do nothing but take helpless note of whatever they saw.

They walked from near Hiroshima Station through Inari-chō, Kamiya-chō, Ōte-machi, and Senda-machi, followed all the way by the heat from the smoldering fires, by the stench of corpses, by the cries of the dying. The water in their flasks was soon exhausted and, far from rescuing others, they soon found themselves seeking hither and thither among the burned-out ruins for some place of refuge. After about two hours of such wandering, Tabuchi suddenly realized that all but two of his companions had drifted away from him. They had failed to find a single pupil from the Miyoshi Girls' High School. One of his companions was tottering along half fainting, so they made their way to an acquaintance's at Gion outside the city, which they reached about four-thirty. They rested there for about four hours, and it was not until eight-thirty in the evening that the three of them bestirred themselves and, exhausted though they were, set off home. They were more tired than they could remember ever having been before. They walked from Gion to Shimo-Fukagawa in about three hours, and spent the night in the waiting room there. The next morning around six, they boarded a train jammed with refugees and returned home.

They discovered later that all the pupils from the Miyoshi Girls' High School who had been in Hiroshima doing war work had perished; ninety percent of the other people from Miyoshi and its neighborhood were either killed outright or died before the year was out. Tabuchi himself had wandered around the ruins for something over two hours, and I hear that he is now suffering from a mild case of radiation disease.

In Miyoshi, the hills must have cut off the view of the mushroom cloud over Hiroshima. In Mihara, a city over seventy miles from Hiroshima but with only low hills to the west, it was visible).

The same three women told my wife and niece various other curious things about the stricken city. The wooden bridges in the affected area had almost all been completely consumed by fire, but the way they burned was most remarkable. The planks, first of all, would start smoldering. Then, when they had gone, the fire would spread to the piers underneath. As the tide went out and the water level fell, these piers would gradually smolder away farther and farther down. The strange thing was that though the next high tide ought, in theory, to have put the fire out, the next morning found it smoldering again, so that little by little all the timber was eventually consumed.

At the cemetery at the Kokutaiji Temple, there was a grave where a piece of brick about three inches square had been caught between the square stone base and the stone cylinder that rested on it. The cylinder, which was all of three feet six inches in diameter, must have been lifted up by the blast and, at precisely that instant, a fragment of brick must have come flying through the air and wedged itself in the gap thus formed. The gravestone, which was of smooth-polished granite, was burned raw and rough on the side which had faced the flash, but was as smooth as ever on the side that had been turned away from it. Even granite had been affected like this; ordinary roof tiles exposed to the flash had been transformed from dark gray into a reddish-brown color, and actually had eruptions like small bubbles on their surface. The effect was rather like the texture produced by firing a piece of Koimbe ware in a kiln.

Another story had apparently been told by a first-class private in the engineers when he had stopped for water at a farmhouse in the village of Ōga, on his way to the temporary reception center for victims at Hesaka. The engineers, he said, had lost such enormous numbers of men through the bomb that they were stacking the bodies crisscross on top of each other on the sandy shoals in the river that ran from Hakushima, and setting fire to them. The fires were kept burning even at night, with a guard stationed there to keep watch over them. "Corpse duty," as it was called, was heartily loathed by everybody. Ever since the bomb fell, they said, the army's lines of command had been badly disrupted; discipline had deteriorated, and some officers were beginning to be afraid of their men.

It was Yasuko, for the most part, who related these stories to me. Shigeko, who had griping pains in the stomach as a result of over-immersion in the river, said very little. Both of them had had nothing but towels around their waists as they squatted in the shallow part of the river while their underwear dried.

It was already quite dark when the old father of the owner of the house came to tell us that the electric lights would go on. The power supply had started again that day.

August 10. Fine.
Yasuko and Shigeko fetched our breakfast from the dormitory kitchen, then shaped some of the boiled barley-and-bran mix into "rice cakes" to take with them, and set off for the city. I went with them as far as the station. In the station there were many people who, so far as I could tell, were neither waiting for someone nor buying tickets, but had simply drifted into the waiting room for want of somewhere else to go. When the train arrived a number of them simply stood there without moving, and some of them were sprawled out on the benches again when it left. There were other people asking the station officials how best to set about finding lost children.

I left the station and went back to the company, where I found urgent business awaiting me. I must arrange to secure some coal, and this would necessitate going either to Hiroshima or to Ujina. Mr. Fujita brought a large bundle from an adjoining room. "I hate to bother you," he said, "but I'd like you to get something done about it as soon as possible. The things you'll need in the ruins are in this bundle. Be careful, now—there may be another raid."

I left a message with him for Shigeko. Then I got my air raid hood and a first-aid outfit, shouldered the bundle and set off.

The train took me as far as Yamamoto Station. From here on, services were still interrupted. None of the passengers, fifty or sixty altogether, left the station when we arrived; instead, they set off walking in single file along the tracks towards Hiroshima. The people of Hiroshima are noted for their sociability, but today each of us paced steadily ahead, treading from one railway tie to the next, without exchanging a single word. The only people carrying anything on their backs apart from myself were two women in baggy breeches immediately ahead of me. Less than a quarter of them were carrying anything resembling a packed meal; nothing could have demonstrated so vividly the shortage of goods that affected even the farming villages near the town. How many similar silent parties, I wondered, did the train unload every day into the burned-out ruins of Hiroshima?

As we finally came into the ruined area a dank, malodorous breeze came blowing across the empty waste. One by one, the people walking with us dropped out of file, until eventually only a handful were left going in the same direction as myself. By now, all about was a waste of broken tiles, the road a heavily pitted desert.

I had crossed a bridge when it occurred to me to wonder just where I was. I looked back, and recognized the arched iron framework that had survived the flames: Yokogawa Bridge. Near here, as I had passed along the same road on my way out of the city on the sixth, I had seen three women, almost completely naked, dead in a water tank that stood by the roadside about eight-tenths full. I determined to keep my eyes averted as I passed it, but for all my resolution it was inevitable, perhaps, that I should steal a glance. A length of more than three feet of large intestine had sprouted from the buttocks of one of the women, who floated upside down; it was swollen to about three inches in diameter, and floated in a slightly tangled ring on the water, swaying gently from side to side like a balloon as the wind blew.

On the burned-out site of one of the temples in Tera-machi, I saw a plank propped up with an inscription, written in charcoal, saying "Nekoya-chō Reception Center for Corpses." Inside the clay wall, I could see a pile about six feet high of dead bodies. Some looked as though they had been crushed to death, some were half consumed by fire, some were mere bones. The clay wall had collapsed in places, and so long as one had one's eyes open the corpses came into one's field of vision whether one willed it or not. The mound of corpses was black with swarming flies. As I watched, something —the breeze, perhaps—disturbed them, and they started up with a loud buzzing, only to cluster round the corpses again almost immediately. At the same time, a stifling, penetrating odor that stung at the nose and throat assailed my nostrils. Holding my breath, I made off at a trot. After a while, I slowed down to a normal pace and walked with a cotton towel over my nose, but still the stench that came following after me was enough to make my head reel.

Once I emerged from the ruins of Tera-machi, the smell abated somewhat. It was only a moment's respite, though, and as the number of corpses and skeletons by the roadside increased I was enveloped once more in a vile stench. I was in hell, a hell that tortured with omnipresent, inescapable odor. The one place where it seemed to lessen somewhat was on Aioi Bridge, where a breeze was blowing from the river. Heaving a breath of relief, I propped my load against the stone rampart and took a rest.

Since the city had been almost entirely razed to the ground by the fire, one could take in the distant view at a glance. To the south, I could see the dark grayish-green hills of Ōkawa-chō. To the southwest, the unspoilt woods of Mukai-Ujina and, directly opposite, Shumi-yama at Miyajima; to the west, the low eminence of Eba, and to the east the sacred hill of the Tōshōgū Shrine. Nothing stood on the scorched waste at the center of the city save the skeletons of a few buildings; apart from these, the only thing that met the eye was a litter of carbonized timbers and fragments of tile. The occasional black or white speck moving in the wilderness would be a human being—searching, as likely as not, for the remains of a relative or a friend. It was a scene of unremitting desolation.

At one end of the bridge, a body lay face up with its arms stretched out wide. Its face was black and discolored, yet from time to time it seemed to puff its cheeks out and take a deep breath. Its eyelids seemed to be moving, too. I stared in disbelief. Balancing my bundle on the parapet, I approached the corpse in fear and trembling—to find swarms of maggots tumbling from the mouth and nose and crowding in the eye sockets; it was nothing but their wriggling, that first impression of life and movement.

Suddenly, a phrase from a poem came back to me, a poem I had read in some magazine when I was a boy: "Oh worm, friend worm!" it began. There was more in the same vein: "Rend the heavens, burn the earth, and let men die! A brave and moving sight!"

Fool! Did the poet fancy himself as an insect, with his prating of his "friend" the worm? How idiotic can you get? He should have been here at 8:15 on August 6, when it had all come true: when the heavens had been rent asunder, the earth had burned, and men had died. "Revolting man!" I found myself announcing quite suddenly to no one in particular. "'Brave and moving,' indeed!" For a moment, I felt like flinging my bundle in the river. I hated war. Who cared, after all, which side won? The only important thing was to end it all soon as possible: rather an unjust peace, than a "just" war!

I went back to the parapet, but instead of flinging my bundle into the river made it fast on my back. It was full of things necessary for survival amidst the ruins: a bottle containing stomach pills, a trowel, old magazines, eucalyptus leaves, dried rusks, a round paper fan, and the like.

Nearing Kamiya-chō, I came upon a number of men who looked like soldiers. With gauze masks over their mouths and noses, they were tending to three or four fires which they had built in separate places. As I drew nearer, I saw that they had made the fires in holes about six feet square dug in the ground, and were fetching corpses and throwing them in the flames. For fuel, they were using old railway ties, and the crackling of the ties as they burned gave the pyres an added touch of horror beneath the blazing sun. I looked, and from the trunks of the bodies could see pale blue, slender flames rising, to be caught up at once in the fierce red flames leaping higher all about them.

Body after body the soldiers brought, on door panels and sheets of corrugated iron, to fling them unceremoniously, face up, into the flames before trudging off silently on their next mission. They had bent up the corners of the corrugated iron sheets for ease in carrying. They must have been working under orders from a superior officer; whatever emotions they felt, their expressions gave no clue. The only sign of feeling seemed to be in their military boots, which were slow-moving and leaden. When there were so many bodies in a pit that the flames died down, they would dump the bodies they brought on the ground by the edge. Sometimes, the jolt would bring a mass of maggots and liquid corruption gushing from the corpse's mouth. When a body was dumped too close to the fire, the heat would bring the maggots wriggling out in panic all over it. And occasionally the shock of hitting the ground would do something to the joints of a corpse, so that it reminded me of Pinocchio, in the children's tale, with all the pins removed from his wooden limbs. If even Pinocchio, poor plaything of wood and metal pins, was supposed to have felt pain in his own wooden way when he barked his shin against something, what of these the dead, who had once been human beings?

"These stiffs are getting out of hand," muttered the soldier at the front end of a piece of corrugated iron.

"If only we'd been born in a *country*, not a damn-fool *state*," said his companion wistfully.

That exchange was the only human sound I heard there. The body on the improvised stretcher lay in a tight huddle, a Pinocchio with every single pin removed . . .

All unconsciously, I had started murmuring the "Sermon on Mortality" to myself. Hiroshima was no more. . . . Yet who could have foreseen that its end would be of such horror as this?

CHAPTER 12 🍂

A jabbing pain in the stomach forced me to seat myself on some stone steps, heedless of the thick layer of ash settled on them. It was a dry, powdery ash like buckwheat flour. Dabbing at it with my finger, I found I could draw scrolls and write letters in it. I wrote all kinds of things. I visualized the blackboard at school in my childhood, and started to draw the diagram for Pythagoras's theorem, but gave up halfway.

After a while, the griping pain eased up. I turned around to see where I was, and found it was the front entrance of the city hall, littered now with pieces of charred timbers lying here, there and everywhere. It was a desolate sight: the outer wall, a tasteful shade of cream until only the other day, was burned to a grayish-brown, and all the window frames, not to speak of the windows themselves, were gone. In the corridor leading from the entrance to the back of the building, pieces of steel scrap that might have been broken helmets were lying about the floor. The building, of course, was a desolate, gutted ruin, but at the back I could hear a noise as of empty boxes or something being dragged about the floor. Pricking up my ears to catch the sound, I began to fancy that it was welling up from under the ground.

Feeling suddenly uneasy, I shouldered my rucksack again. Just then, I was surprised to hear someone call my name: "Mr. Shizuma! Where are you going?"

It was Mr. Tashiro, an elderly technologist from the Ujina canning factory.

"Mr. Tashiro! It's good to see you. What do you think that noise is?"

"It's the municipal workers clearing away the charred timbers. You've burned your face, I see. What happened to your family?"

"They're safe, thank you. What's your firm doing for coal? I'm supposed to go to the Coal Control Corporation, but I've not the faintest idea where it is."

"They've had it, the same as everybody else. I don't even know where the employees have gone to. So I tried coming to the city hall."

The Ujina cannery was under the jurisdiction of the Provisions Depot, and like us supplied part of its products to the Clothing Depot, but even so it was having trouble getting coal. According to Mr. Tashiro, more than twenty employees were already doing business at the city hall under the general direction of Deputy Mayor Shibata, but they had refused to accept any petitions concerning the coal ration. Since coal was under the jurisdiction of the Coal Control Corporation, the only outcome if the city hall meddled with it would be a reprimand from the military, and things would become more complicated than ever.

"So the upshot is that I've come to the city hall to complain," Tashiro said.

Whatever happened, I would have to make a report to the manager, so I asked Tashiro to take me to the site of the Coal Control Corporation offices. As chief technologist at the Ujina cannery, the old man was well versed in matters concerning coal, and was on close terms with the head of the Corporation.

"But you know," said Tashiro as we walked, "it puzzles me why an important place like a control corporation still hasn't put up a notice saying where it's moved to. There must be some explanation for it, don't you think?"

At the former site of the control corporation, we found all kinds of messages written up on a piece of concrete wall that had been left standing—but, as Tashiro had said, nothing from the corporation itself.

They were written in every kind of writing, from the careless scrawl to the well-formed hand. "Mr. Fujino," one message said, "please inform address—Mikkaichi Iron Foundry." "Please leave temporary address of your corporation here—Nakabayashi, San-kyō Co." "Mr. Honda: Are you all right? Please leave your present address—Tsutsuki Works, Kaitaichi." "Mr. Murano: Please write your address here—Uchiyama, Koi." All the messages used pieces of charcoal from half-burned timbers, and all gave the date.

"Mr. Tashiro—" I said, "there's not a single reply from anybody in the corporation. Look—some of the dates are three days old already."

"Then it seems as though the worst may have happened, doesn't it?"

"The worst?"

"That the whole corporation was wiped out."

Tashiro had himself been the only one to survive of his family. His young second wife and his infant daughter, trapped beneath their house, had certainly perished in the flames, but at his age, he said, he could not summon the energy to hunt in the ruins for their ashes.

"It can't be helped," he said. "I'll leave them where they are. Wherever a person's remains are, it's the same in the end—so much organic matter in the soil."

What would he do if he wanted to erect a tombstone for them, I asked.

"They still have a photograph of my wife and daughter at my

wife's home in the country. I'm thinking of burying that instead. But then, what if somebody at my wife's home starts saying he's coming to look for the remains? I can hardly tell him to leave them alone as they're organic matter, can I . . . ?"

For a moment, the old scientist's approach seemed too cut-and-dried, and I found it rather repulsive. But then another way of looking at it occurred to me. Tashiro was old, but his wife had still been young and attractive. His daughter too, of pre-school age, had been a charming child. Perhaps he was afraid that, if he were to go looking for ashes and find corpses, it would wipe out forever the image of them he cherished. He too, like myself, must have seen enough of bodies, mangled, half-burned, and decomposing, during the past few days.

"Why don't you have some third person look for the ashes?" I asked.

"About the coal—" he said, ignoring my suggestion. "Why don't we go to the Clothing Depot and negotiate with them about it? There's nothing else left to try, so far as I can see. Besides, there aren't so many bodies in that area, around Sagino Bridge, so I expect the smell will have died down to some extent." And he set off walking, with an unexpectedly firm tread.

The route to Sagino Bridge took us through almost the same scenes of desolation as before. Tashiro made no comment on his surroundings, but related to me what he had heard a while back at the city hall. Of the approximately nine hundred employees in the main offices before the raid, not many more than twenty were there at present. There was not one of them who had not suffered in some way or other.

By now, two men like laborers, half-naked in the heat, had joined the soldiers in shouldering the corrugated iron sheets and disposing of the dead. As we passed by, they were gazing transfixed at a water-tank standing beside a collapsed clay wall. In the tank was a human figure with the head alone reduced to a skull and the rest of the body beneath the water, on the surface of which floated viscous, greasy brown bubbles. As the laborers reluctantly approached the tank with their corrugated iron sheets, the skull, without warning, suddenly tilted forward and sank amidst the bubbles. "Oh, my God!" exclaimed Tashiro, his composure shaken at last.

The mayor, Mr. Kuriya, had died in the raid at his home, Tashiro told me. His deputy, Mr. Shibata, had been hurt on the sole of his right foot and could not walk on it properly. A fragment of glass had also penetrated deep into his left calf, so that he had to go to the city hall on crutches. The mayor's house, being in Kako-chō, had of course been razed by fire. On arriving at work the morning after the day of the raid, Shibata had sent another official to inquire after the mayor at his home. In the ruins of what would seem to have been Mr. Kuriya's living room were found the partly burned bodies of an adult and a small child, lying together. The mayor had always been extremely fond of his grandchild; probably just as the bomb fell he had been lifting the child up in his arms to say good-by before he went to work.

Deputy Mayor Shibata had taken charge of municipal affairs since Kuriya's death, Tashiro said. The twenty-odd employees at their posts in the city office were dealing with business of every kind with the aid of a dozen or so chairs miraculously spared in the fire, one mimeographing machine, and files made by clipping together other documents and using the backs. None of them had anything but the clothes he stood up in, since they had all been burned out of their homes, and along with several dozen of the injured they were living a communal life, doing their own cooking, in the ruins of their office. They had cleared the litter of broken glass, charred wood, scrap metal and the like into a corner of the room, and had rigged up a tent that they had borrowed from the army barracks in place of a window. For offices, they had the defense, health, and relief sections on the southeast of the first floor, which had survived the flames. (I later learned, from the personal account of Mr. Shigeteru Shibata, the deputy mayor, that Lieutenant General Saeki, commander of the Akatsuki Corps' shipping headquarters at Ujina, had called at the city hall at three on the afternoon of August 7 to explain that he had been appointed commander-in-chief for defense in the Hiroshima area, and to notify them that sometime between that night and the following morning a unit from Shimane Prefecture and part of the Akatsuki Corps would be arriving in Hiroshima. This gave Mr. Shibata and the other surviving senior city officers their first hope of taking some concrete emergency measures. On the eighth, an official message came from the West Japan Army headquarters ordering the officials concerned to report there, taking relevant documents on defense with them. Accordingly, a group including auditor Hamai Nakahara, head of the Rationing Section, and Isamu Itō, head of the Sanitation Department, proceeded to the headquarters, which was located in a dugout on the side of Mt. Futaba on the outskirts of the city.)

At the Clothing Depot, I found two or three janitors standing talking at the entrance, but none of the usual coming and going. Together with Tashiro, I obtained an interview with Lieutenant Sasatake of the Control Section and tried to get a ration of coal, but we were told that permission to broach the reserves of coal at Ujina was absolutely out of the question. On all other matters, we met with nothing but equivocation, and our visit proved completely fruitless.

The lieutenant was too overwrought even to listen seriously to our petition. "Concerning coal, as I have said many times already," he said, "we must hold a conference before we can come to any conclusion. Anyway, I have to ask my superiors. The question of transport, for one thing, involves various technical considerations. And we have to weigh your request against the requirements of other firms, too. I'm afraid you'll have to wait until we've held our conference."

Since there was nothing further to be gained here, we asked to see the chief of the Control Section, but he was equally equivocal. In the end, even the normally phlegmatic Tashiro seemed to lose his patience.

"If you'll excuse me," he said to the section chief, "I'll tell you quite plainly what our company would like. *You* go ahead with your conference, but we, for our part, would appreciate some emergency measures in the meantime. If it's absolutely prohibited to touch the coal reserves at Ujina, why can't somebody—seeing that this is a top-priority emergency—be sent direct to the mine at Ube? If they went now, they'd arrive there by the evening, I imagine. It's unlikely, surely, that the control corporation in Hiroshima will be back in business for some time to come?"

"We are in the process of considering such measures ourselves, of course," the chief said. "But we must consult our superiors and get a definite ruling. That's precisely why I say we have to hold a conference."

"If I may say so," I ventured, "I can't help wondering, if you wait until you hold your conference and come to some conclusion before sending someone to the Ube mine, just how long it will be before any coal gets through to this wasteland. We've no knowledge of any temporary office of the Coal Control Corporation, and we're feeling very lost."

"How many days' coal d'you have at your places?" he demanded.

"Four or five days at ours," I said. "Two days at ours, operating at the usual rate," said Tashiro.

"Very well, then—how would this be?" he asked, as though a new idea had just struck him. "Considering that your firms are both producing military supplies, I don't see why you can't do just as you please, without waiting for the military. So why don't you just try to be a bit more cooperative?"

"We're quite willing to try, and to cooperate too," I said, "but on one condition. Could we have a letter of authorization from the authorities? Then we could go to Ube this very minute and negotiate for some coal."

"That would be difficult as far as the army's concerned. But consider, now—your firm's making cloth for army uniforms. You're in a position to do just what you please, aren't you? So I hope you'll see your way to cooperating with us."

I was perfectly well aware that a large number of workers had been put into the mine at Ube in order to raise output there. At the Mine mine too, production had been stepped up to the point where there was not enough transport to handle the coal they turned out, and the anthracite already mined was lying around in heaps. I failed to see why they couldn't agree to hold their precious conference but speed up the transport of the coal in the meantime. If only some coal came, the Coal Control Corporation could get started again in no time. But the section chief had already lapsed into what appeared to be silent meditation, and whatever we said went off him like water off a duck's back. What he had told us, in effect, meant postponing further production of both clothing materials and canned food.

Losing patience with such stupidity, I left the office. Tashiro stayed on; for his firm, which was engaged in processing raw meat and vegetables, a break in production of even a single day could be disastrous.

It struck me that our firm, which undertook official work for the Clothing Depot, had let itself get into the habit of doing far too much for its client. A large part of the reason for this lay in the shortage of commodities. Lawful rations of both foodstuffs and other daily necessities being inadequate, we had to scrounge around for them here, there, and everywhere, trading on our association with the Clothing Depot in order to secure what we needed. This meant, in turn, that we had to provide an indecent degree of service for the Clothing Depot in order to ensure that the firm's affairs kept running smoothly. We were bleeding ourselves white in the effort to please, while the other side sat pretty without lifting a finger.

I had had many unpleasant experiences in this connection. The first time, not long after I joined the firm, was when we got in fifty large tubs of bean paste and were obliged to let the Clothing Depot have just half—twenty-five tubs. Then we bought a wagonload of mortars to present to the mine, and again had to let the Clothing Depot have half. Next, we bought two wagonloads of water jars, and again the Clothing Depot got one wagonload. The same thing happened to a boatload of charcoal cookers, and to thirty barrels of mandarin orange wine. On every occasion the Depot was most pressing.

It occurred to me that rather than stay dependent on the army and get beaten and robbed for our pains, we would do better, at this stage, to devise some independent course of our own. I made up my mind to recommend that we do so to the manager, and cursed my stupidity at having trudged along four miles of road, all for nothing, for fear of a shortage of coal.

Emerging from the main gate of the Clothing Depot, I was struck by the desolation of a lotus pond familiar to me from the old days. The leaves had all collapsed towards the south, and the worst affected looked like broken umbrellas. Not a single one remained whole. Before going to work in my present firm, I had worked for seven years at the Army Provisions Depot, living in rented rooms at the home of a policeman. I had gone to work on foot, taking my lunch with me, and the broad stretch of rice fields and the lotus pond that lay between Asahi-chō and Midori-chō were old friends. Every day on my way to work my eyes were delighted by the sight of crows settled on the dew-damp path between the fields. The glossy black sheen of crows' plumage in the morning blends well with the green of the rice plants, and equally well with the rice fields after they have started to turn yellow. The sight is indescribably pleasant; at daybreak on a really fine morning it is enough to set your heart beating faster.

But today, even the lotus pond had a dead body lying in it. Beside the pond, I noticed a white pigeon crouching in the grass. I went gently up to it and took it in my hands, but it was blinded in its right eye, and the feathers above its right wing were slightly scorched. For a moment, I felt a sudden desire to eat it broiled with soy, but I let it go, tossing it up and away from me into the air. It managed to flap its wings quite well, and flew off just over the tops of the lotus leaves, describing a horizontal parabola that curved steadily towards the left. But then, as I watched, it lost height and plunged into the waters of the pond.

I decided to go straight ahead to the Miyuki highway, and set off along the same road that we had traversed on the sixth. The Mutual Aid Hospital, visible beyond the embankment lined with cherry trees, had lost the glass from its windows, but I could see people bustling to and fro along the corridors. It seemed to be jammed with people, some come to search for survivors, others seeking care for themselves. The houses along the road had tilted or collapsed, but there were some, leaning at an angle, where the owners had cleared away the debris and were putting back sliding doors with all the paper gone from the frames. I could hear people talking inside some of them. Some houses had been buttressed with burned, blackened timbers. I saw someone with a scorched, blackened chair in the unfloored entrance hall to his house, scraping off the carbonized surface with a piece of broken teacup. It reminded me of a clumsy, misshapen chair in a painting by Van Gogh that I had seen in a special issue of a magazine. For some reason, my throat suddenly felt dry.

In the broad thoroughfare along the foot of Hiji hill, I saw two or three injured looking much the same as the refugees I had seen on August 6. They staggered along in the direction of Ujina, supporting themselves with their right hands against the wall of the Hiroshima District Monopoly Bureau. They were all half-naked, emaciated, and pale as ghosts. There was no sign of the tortoise-shell cat that had followed Miyaji on the sixth. The dead bodies at the north end of Miyuki Bridge had been cleared away, but dark, greasy-looking human silhouettes were left where they had lain.

The area around the Miyuki highway was a waste of scorched fields and scorched residential land. The site where our house had stood was quite undistinguished save for the small pond that remained in what had been the garden. Its area was far smaller than I had realized. Shigeko and Yasuko had assembled our belongings from the air raid shelter and the pond, and had already left. A laborer had loaded them on a cart, and was just taking a rest prior to starting off.

The only sign of life among the ruins of the neighborhood associations' homes was a single shack set up on the space where the Nakaos' residence had stood. All the others must have gone to stay with relatives or friends. The laborer told me that the man in the shack had come over to speak to my wife and niece, and had told them that he had lost touch with his son. Mr. Nakao, that meant, must be living there alone with his young daughter.

The Nakaos' shack, roof and walls alike, was constructed of corrugated iron from burned buildings, and occupied four or five square yards of space. The main building of their house—a palatial affair made entirely of cypress, with red glazed tiles—had alone covered more than 180 square yards. Mr. Nakao, who worked in a trading company, owned a lot of shares and bonds. He collected lacquerware as a hobby. The low table in his drawing room had been of black lacquer and was said, I believe, to date from the Muromachi period; it was the kind of table that would not have looked out of place with a Lady Murasaki or Sei Shōnagon leaning gracefully against it.

I went to see how he was, taking with me as presents the eucalyptus leaves, the trowel, the paper fan, and some creosote tablets from my rucksack (I left the canned meat where it was). The firm had entrusted me with them as gifts for the people at the Coal Control Corporation, but since the Coal Control Corporation people were not to be found, I was left with them on my hands. I ought to have taken them home again, but I considered myself old enough to adapt orders to changed circumstances.

Mr. Nakao knew the use of my primitive gifts without waiting to be told. The eucalyptus and the trowel in particular would be invaluable, he said. He was effusive in his thanks.

The eucalyptus leaves served as a substitute mosquito repellent. If one kept them smoldering in the covered-hole kind of air raid shelter, they helped drive away the striped mosquitoes that were rampant even in the daytime. The people living in shacks on the ruins were using the farthest recesses of their air raid shelters as toilets. The onslaught of mosquitoes was terrible, but sometimes it was impossible, they said, to hold out until sundown. The problem must have been an awkward one at the Nakaos', as his daughter was just at the most bashful age.

The paper fan was invaluable in keeping the eucalyptus leaves smoldering. The trowel was an indispensable tool for scratching about in the soil or filling in holes, whether inside the shelter or in the open air.

"Thank you so much," Mr. Nakao repeated over and over

again. He seemed to want to talk. "Before the raid, you know, our shelter used to be full of crickets—no end of them, in fact. Little brown crickets—'rabbit crickets' a man at the Geibi Bank told me they were called. But since the raid we've had a sudden spate of striped mosquitoes. Brutes, they are. Really, though, you couldn't have brought us a more useful present . . ."

"It wasn't I who chose them in the first place," I said, avoiding telling him that I had passed on something intended for other people. "The works manager at our place had heard about the striped mosquitoes, so he gave me these things to bring on the off-chance. I could bring you some more of the leaves next time if you like."

Mr. Nakao was busily sniffing at the eucalyptus. The manager had given me a weeding basket stuffed full of the leaves, and the young oval leaves with their whitish, powdery coating were wilting sadly, while the semicircular older ones were all bent a stiff, awkward shape.

Mr. Nakao told me he intended to stay there for the time being, until he found his son. The city hall was providing them with food, dealing out one large rice-ball a day, with pickled sour plums or pickled radish to go with it. I bade him farewell for the time being and rejoined the laborer. Taking over my shoulder one end of the rope fastened to the cart, I set off, dragging it behind me. At once, I realized that dragging a cart from the front was a stiff task. Every time a wheel rode over a piece of broken tile, the rope gave a vicious heave upwards at my shoulder. I was leaning forward at an angle of forty-five degrees, resting the weight of my body on the rope, but the jerks it gave seemed to be tugging me backwards rather than upright.

"I can't manage it like this, Rokurō," I said to the laborer. "This rope's got no give in it. Scientifically speaking, it's no wonder it's difficult. Four or five miles like this, and the flesh'll be rubbed off my shoulders."

"You should pull with the weight of your body, not your shoulder," he said. "Try it like this." He tied the end of the rope in a loop.

Following his instructions, I slung the loop over my right shoulder and around under my left arm, so that the knot came just in the center of my back. Things were a little better like that, since the shock when the cart went over a bump was absorbed by a larger area of the body.

It looked as though ours was the first cart to pass along the road since the sixth. I looked back, and saw that the wheels had crushed the broken glass scattered everywhere into a powder, leaving two tracks in the debris that glittered white in the sunlight.

The laborer had filled two bottles with water and put them on the cart. We would go a way, then stop to wipe off sweat, start again, then stop to wipe off the sweat again, and every time we stopped we took a pull at the water, which had all disappeared before we even got out of the town. The constant bumping and jerking and the stink that lay over the streets seemed to double the heat from the blazing sun overhead. Once I called back to my companion: "Rokurō! Why don't we have a proper rest somewhere around here?"

But he said, "No—not till we're out of the town."

I pulled the cart along behind me, concentrating my mind on estimating the distance we had already covered. Now we've done two miles, I told myself; now we've done two-and-a-half, or two-and-three-quarters perhaps. . . . After about three miles, we stopped at a house by the roadside and begged some water from their well. We filled our bottles, and enjoyed a leisurely rest. The laborer with me, Rokurō Masuda by name, was a lean man in his early fifties who had undertaken the job at the introduction of a woman in the works kitchen. He was a hardy kind of man, with a good-natured face.

Off again. Around the three-and-a-half-mile mark, the road ceased to be littered with fragments of tile, and to my great relief the jolting ceased. When we at last reached our temporary home, the lights were already on. I was about to seat myself with a sigh of relief on the edge of the veranda when, to my great surprise, I saw two of my brothers-in-law lying sprawled out on the tatami under the electric light, both of them snoring.

I gave Rokurō his wages, then went round to the back, by the well, to look for Shigeko.

"Back from the forced march!" I announced. Yasuko was lighting the fire for the bath in the landlord's house. Shigeko was beside the stream that ran at the back of the house, rinsing the washing in the dark.

"When did our visitors arrive?" I asked.

Shigeko and Yasuko had apparently arrived back from Hiroshima to find the two visitors in the garden, sitting disconsolately on the edge of the veranda. They had come all the way from their village deep in the hills, solely out of concern for our safety. Finding Senda-machi burned to the ground, they had inquired where I worked, and after much wandering had finally arrived.

"I just cried and cried for joy," said Shigeko. "They had all been so concerned about us. And the two of them had a dreadful time getting here. They even had to walk over the railway bridge across the Ashida river." She wept openly and unashamedly, like a child.

CHAPTER 13 🌿

August 11.
Last night I put off attending to our visitors from afar and went
first to report to the manager, over dinner in the works canteen,
on the coal situation in the ruins of Hiroshima. I also recommended that our firm should take steps to secure coal on its own
initiative. And I told him, incidentally, what I had done with the
trowel and the eucalyptus leaves.

"Perhaps I shouldn't say so," he said, "but if you ask me, you've
been fooled around with. Why on earth can't the army people in
the Clothing Depot release the coal reserves at Ube? That's the
question. Don't you think you should have demanded some explanation? It's not as though you were a kid sent on an errand.
If they say they can't release it, you've no business taking it lying
down. Whatever do the military think they're up to at any rate, in

the middle of a colossal emergency like this? It makes me sick."

He was so excited that his hand shook as it held the can-opener to open a can of beef. The meal was good, despite everything. There was no rice, admittedly, only a mixture of seven parts of barley to three parts of bran, but to go with it we had the beef that should have gone as a present to the Coal Control Corporation. It was many a month since I had eaten anything so good. The rich-looking marbled brown of the meat, the thick, luscious amber of the gravy, the mouth-watering aroma . . .

It would have been a waste to eat anything so good amidst the ruins of the city. A great swarm of flies would have been sure to gather the moment one opened the can. Tashiro from the Ujina cannery told me yesterday that when he ate his lunch among the ruins he had hardly got a can open before the flies flocked round and turned the meat yellow. They laid yellow eggs all over the surface. The tremendous number of flies was enough to put you off your food completely, even without the dreadful smell every-where. Seen from behind, the washed-out linen rucksack on Ta-shiro's back had looked as though it was embroidered all over with black wool, on account of the flies clustering thick all over it. I expect mine was the same.

The manager and I divided the meat equally between us. We each had a second bowl of the substitute rice. We were still eating when a worker called Nishina from the Works Department came to ask me to read another funeral service. The death had only just occurred.

"Then I'll come after I've finished," I said. "I'll be there in half an hour or an hour's time."

Nishina directed an accusing glance at the empty can standing on the table. At this point, the manager could well have explained that it was a can of beef that he had been keeping as a present for our customers, but instead he just said affably, "When the meal's over, you see, Mr. Shizuma will have to go and gargle to purify himself before he comes, having eaten meat. I expect he'll give you the 'Sermon on Mortality' today." Nishina gulped, but said nothing.

The deceased was Nishina's sister-in-law, a widow of thirty-six called Saki Mitsuda. According to what she had told Nishina herself, she had been working in the fields at a farm inside the city when the bomb fell. She had been weeding a field full of taros, and was squatting on the ground at the time, with a cotton towel tied over her head. The broad leaves of the plants had served to screen her from the flash. She had not been killed outright, but probably had temporarily lost the ability to move.

For a while, she lay face down amongst the taros. The sky when she looked up was quite dark. Hakushima Nakamachi and Nishi-Nakamachi were a sea of flames. She told herself she must not stay where she was. She crawled towards the river bank. The water was a dark purplish color, and she felt frightened, as though the end of the world had come. The fire was spreading rapidly. But a widow has to be tough to keep going, and, gathering up all her courage, she jumped into the river and, grabbing hold of a bamboo raft, immersed herself in the water. (The raft was one of those that the city authorities had urged the inhabitants to have ready for use in getting away to safety in the event of an air raid.) The tide was in, and there was something over four feet of water in the river. Before long there was a shower and it got terribly cold. She clambered up onto the raft, and covering herself with a quilt that came floating down the river, used a piece of drifting plank as a paddle to take her downstream out of danger. She had burns on her left earlobe, her neck, and her shoulder.

She had arrived in search of her brother-in-law two nights previously. At that time, she had still had the strength to walk without aid, but the night before she had suddenly weakened, and had been groaning in constant pain until she had died a short while previously.

As the person in charge of the funeral of an outsider, I made a memorandum of all these details.

The farm in the city where she had been working had formerly been the Riverside Park. In spring the previous year, almost the whole of it had been put under cultivation, in line with the government's policy of making use of all available space, and eggplants, cucumbers, tomatoes, taros, and other vegetables were growing there. All the other people in the area at the time of the raid were said to have been wiped out, including the girls from the First Girls' High School and the Municipal Girls' High School who were doing war work there. In living until today, in fact, she had been cheating death of its due.

The manager was still preoccupied with his own obsession. "Shizuma," he said to me, "Make sure you go to bed early tonight after the service is over. We need you to go to the Clothing Depot again tomorrow to put in another application for coal. Your ideas about getting supplies on our own initiative sound fine, but if you ask me they're really a case of giving up too easily. It's a nuisance, I know, but you must try to be a bit more determined."

"It's no use," I said, rather put out. "The only thing we can do now is to get a letter of introduction from Captain Nozu of the Signal Corps and go direct to the Ube mine to negotiate with them there. We can hardly be expected to obey the control ordinances if the Coal Control Corporation has disappeared, can we?"

"It's all very well to say that, but Captain Nozu is away on official business. I looked in at the Signal Corps' temporary office upstairs five or six times today, and there was only one NCO there. When I asked where the Captain had gone, he said it was a military secret. He said the same thing when I asked when he'd be back. A while ago I went to the warehouse, and there's only two days' supply of coal left. What are we supposed to do?" He clasped his head in his hands in despair.

"In that case, I'll go early tomorrow morning," I said. "Even if it does no good."

I resigned myself to going to the Clothing Depot once more, though I knew it was quite pointless.

Returning to our temporary home after the service was over, I was greeted by an aroma of toasted rice cakes that penetrated to the outside even though the shutters, on account of the blackout, were all closed. I could tell that they were being dipped in soy and cooked over charcoal.

I went in through the back entrance. Our two visitors were awake now, and seated at the table with Yasuko and Shigeko. On the table (a splendid affair in ebony that our landlord had lent us), saucers and other receptacles contained the toasted rice cakes. The visitors must have brought them as a present from the country. Yasuko and Shigeko were eating ravenously.

"Why, here he is!" said Shigeko in a cheerful voice, noticing me standing there in the unfloored entrance. "We didn't wait for you, I'm afraid."

"Hello, uncle," said Yasuko. "I'm sorry we started first. The rice cakes were too much for us once we started toasting them. They brought us some parched rice, as well. And there are some rice balls left over too."

"It was very good of you to bother about us," I said to the visitors, then seated myself on the wooden step between the entrance and the room, arranging myself so that the burns on my left cheek didn't show. The two guests stared at me with red-rimmed, startled eyes like rabbits, and both of them started shedding great tears. (One of them, Masao Watanabe, was Shigeko's elder brother; the other, Yoshio Takamaru, was Yasuko's real father.)

Takamaru, who had been sitting cross-legged, had hastily redisposed himself more formally on his heels, and sat now with his hands tightly clasping his knees, gnawing at his mustache and sobbing. This set off both Shigeko and Yasuko, who suddenly screwed up their faces and stopped chewing at their rice cakes. Watanabe sat quite silent, alternately wiping his eyes and peering at my face. I steeled myself against tears, but emotion welled up unbidden in my breast and my nose started to drip onto my upper lip. I shifted my position so that I was sitting with my back turned to them.

"I'm so glad to see you all safe, so glad!" said Watanabe. "To see all of you safe and alive! We were sure we'd never see you again. The most we hoped was to find the spot where you had died."

"I'm so happy too, indeed I am," joined in Takamaru. "We'd given up Yasuko for lost. You've always taken such good care of her that we all thought she'd gone with you to the other side. The whole family, in Kobatake and in Hirose too, had given up hope for you."

I stayed seated where I was, sipping at the tea Yasuko had poured out for me. "You've had a lot of worry on our account," I said.

Bit by bit, Watanabe conveyed to us something of the shock the folk back home had received, with Takamaru joining in from time to time to supplement his account. Verbal reports of the bombing had begun to reach Kobatake village early on the evening of the sixth, they said. An extraordinarily high-powered bomb had been dropped on Hiroshima. One-third of the entire population, including troops and voluntary war workers, had been wiped out instantaneously. Another third were badly injured, and the remaining third had all without exception suffered some kind of injury. This, it was claimed, was not defeatist rumor but sober fact. Further reports followed on August 7 and 8. This time, they were still more alarming.

Now, people who had been injured in Hiroshima began to arrive back in the villages in a steady stream. Some died shortly after reaching home. Some suffered excruciating agonies. In Hirose there was a doctor, a specialist in children's diseases, who had fled to the country from Kobe. He came to look at the patients, but declared that the only diagnosis he could give was of an unknown disease, one for which there was no known treatment. He gave them ointment for their burns, and injected those who complained of violent pain with "Pantopon," but he had only been able to secure a dozen ampules of the latter, and there were so many patients that there was not enough medicine to go around after the first day.

There were two injured men who came back to Kobatake, both with burns and broken bones. Our visitors had been to ask them about the damage in the Senda-machi area of the city, but all they could say was that the houses had been burned down and that all the survivors were injured; there was not the slightest clue as to whether we were alive or not. If we had been injured, though, we should almost certainly have come back to the village by now, so our failure to arrive might well mean that we were dead. And either way, we obviously could not be living in a burned-out waste. It was agreed, in short, that we must have perished.

Yet even if we were dead, something ought to be done about it. Somebody must go to look for the remains, at least. Watanabe was debating in his own mind what to do about it when, at almost exactly the same time on the morning of the tenth, five relatives turned up at his place as if by preaccord. They conferred together, and decided that, as a first step, Watanabe and Takamaru should come to Hiroshima on everybody's behalf. So they set off, taking with them some rice cakes and parched rice—the most suitable things they had at hand in the way of offerings for the presumably deceased.

As they were leaving the village, they called to inform my old mother, and found my younger sister there with her two children. My mother, convinced that all three of us had either been blown to pieces or crushed beneath the house, had got our three photographs arranged on the home altar, with three cups of water placed before them, and some dahlias in a vase.

"If you're going to Hiroshima," she said to them, "I'll trouble you to take some incense, at least. And some water and fresh leaves from the village. You can burn the incense on the place where the house was, and sprinkle the water and scatter the leaves there for them. And while you're about it, take some *kemponashi* nuts for Shigematsu—he was always fond of the *kemponashi* trees."

She put some water from the well in an empty vinegar bottle, wrapped some incense sticks and some fresh green leaves in a piece of paper, and gave them all to Watanabe. Then she picked up two or three *kemponashi* nuts that had fallen while still green, and put them in the small pocket of his rucksack.

The village of Kobatake lies approximately 1,800 feet above sea level. On a tableland surrounded on three sides by mountains, it stands at the watershed of the Ashida river, which runs southward through the eastern part of Hiroshima Prefecture, and the Oda river, which waters Okayama Prefecture. In the old days, the area had belonged to the Nakatsu clan in Kyushu, and there had been a clan office there. Even now, what were once samurai mansions still stand in the village, but nowadays the village is in a steady decline, and lacks transport facilities. Watanabe and Takamaru had to walk for about two hours down the road that follows the Ashida down the valley, and had reached a place called Uokiri before an empty charcoal-driven truck came by and they got a lift. It was past ten at night when they arrived in the ruins of Fukuyama.

Fukuyama had been bombed on the eighth, and all but one section in the north of the town had been burned down. There was not a light in the place. Going along a road, straining their eyes to see in the dark, the two of them hit on the Sanyō line, and followed the tracks westward until they came to what seemed to be a station. They wanted to buy a ticket, but could not find a station official anywhere. They did, however, bump into a stranger in the pitch dark, and they stood talking with him for a while. Judging from his voice, he was a man of fifty or thereabouts, and he had what they took to be a Tokyo accent. He had come to Fukuyama a month previously to escape the raids, he told them, but had been burned out of his home.

He described the raid on Fukuyama for them. Around midnight, sixty B-29's had come and dropped large numbers of flares over the hills round the town, then had switched to the attack, sweeping in over the town in waves.

"Incendiary bombs make a kind of swishing noise as they fall," the man said. "Then, when they hit the ground, it's not a proper bang but a series of thuds. And they give off a terrific glare. I remember that with one of them there was a tinkling sound, like a pane of glass breaking."

According to the man, incendiary bombs came done up in a bundle inside some material like corrugated iron, which was fastened with a brass wire. As they fell, the brass melted, the corrugated iron—or whatever it was—opened up, and the bombs spread out in midair and fell separately, which was what made the swishing sound. The tinkling, he claimed, was the sound of the wire falling on the rockery in his garden.

Fukuyama Castle had been hit, too. An incendiary had gone through a third-floor window of the keep, and the whole five stories had gone up in a pillar of fire, then collapsed. The structure housing the Lady Yodogimi's bathroom, brought there from the celebrated Fushimi Castle in Kyoto, had been destroyed, together with the adjoining corridor and terrace, and the surface of the stone ramparts had been burned white and flaky. All that was left standing was a three-storied turret and a gateway known as the "Iron Gate."

"Actually," he said, "there are anti-aircraft emplacements at the castle and by the bridge over the Ashida, but even so our side didn't fire a single shell, not even when the whole sky was crawling with B-29's. However low the B-29's came, we didn't fire at them, not once. Dark and silent as the forest, that's how it was down here. The strong, silent mountains, and all that . . . After all, they do say that the wise hawk hides its claws, don't they?" It was hard to tell whether he was taking the army's part or being sarcastic.

A lot of people who had been burned out of their homes seemed to be sheltering in the station, but it was difficult to tell for sure in the pitch darkness. Walking out onto the tracks, they could see lights in the direction of a small village called Gōbun to the west, and at Akasaka Station—the lights, one might say, of a people too dispirited by now even to trouble about the blackout regulations. They decided they would try to buy tickets at Akasaka Station, and set off groping their way along the tracks.

To cross the railway bridge over the Ashida, they had to get down on all fours, feeling their way forward with their hands, one tie at a time. One of them used the up line and the other the down line, the idea being that one could give the other a hand to haul him to safety in the event of a train's coming. They called out again and again to reassure themselves as to each other's whereabouts as they crossed. The things that gave them most trouble were their rucksacks, which flopped down on top of their necks if they kept their heads down, and swung around under their arms, or by their sides, if they kept their backs horizontal. Every time one thing or the other happened, their bodies swayed perilously, and they would clutch at the rails in alarm. Time and time again they were in a cold sweat of fear, but eventually they succeeded in reaching Akasaka Station without mishap.

A middle-aged railway official at the station, hearing their story, sold them a ticket for Hiroshima, but could not tell them when a train would come. All they could do was to be patient and wait, so they set about eating their packed meals as slowly and deliberately as possible. They were still at it when a Tokyo-bound train arrived and about thirty people alighted onto the platform. About half of them were injured, the rest being people who had been to Hiroshima to look for friends and relatives. There were loud exchanges between the latter and about twenty people who had been waiting for the train to arrive: "No luck!" "Did you find them?" "What happened to the house?" "Did you meet anybody we know?" "I stuck a notice on the railing of the bridge . . ."

Not one of them seemed to have been successful in finding those he sought. Mingling with the people already waiting there, the arrivals, injured and the uninjured alike—a man with a child, a woman carrying an infant in her arms, a couple who looked like brother and sister—made their way along the platform, through the barrier, and disappeared into the darkness beyond.

"We won't be much luckier, by the look of things," one brother said to the other. "We may at least find their ashes in the ruins," said the other. "After all, we can hardly go back now, can we?"

They got a train at something after one in the morning, and arrived in Hiroshima at something after five. It was a little after seven when they finally found the ruins of our house in Sendamachi. I had not put up any notice saying where we had gone, but Watanabe, who had been to see us there two or three times, recognized the place by the remains of the pine tree and the pond. Once there, though, they were at a loss: it was no use calling our names when there was nowhere left for us to be, and they had no implements for digging in the ashes. The one thing they felt sure of was that we were dead, wherever it had happened. And wherever it had been, they agreed to settle for here. So they lit the sticks of incense and stuck them in the earth by the pond, then they set the vinegar bottle containing the water for the dead beside it, and scattered the fresh green leaves beneath the charred remains of the pine tree. The *kemponashi* nuts they set in front of the incense.

Just then, a stranger came up and hailed them: "Would you be looking for the Shizumas?" When they said they were, he introduced himself as a Mr. Nakao who was living in a shack that stood nearby. Mr. Shizuma and his wife and their adopted daughter Yasuko had all gone, he told them, to the firm at Furuichi. "Weren't any of them hurt?" they asked. "Mr. Shizuma burned his cheek a little," he said. "Just a slight burn."

Mr. Nakao gave them general directions for getting to Furuichi. He traced a map in the ashes with a piece of charcoal, and Watanabe copied it into a notebook. With its aid, and that of countless people whom they asked on the way, they walked as far as Yamamoto station, and came by train from there to Furuichi, where they were given our address at the works. This was just after half-past twelve, they said. Then why—it occurred to me to wonder—had Mr. Nakao not told me that someone had been inquiring after us? I could only conclude that living among the ruins had fuddled his brains temporarily.

Shigeko and Yasuko had indeed noticed some green leaves lying at the foot of the pine tree, they said. They had also seen a vinegar bottle standing by the pond; the label was a rather gaudy affair, with a picture of a country lass wearing a bright red sash. It had puzzled Shigeko very much to see the bottle standing there undamaged among the ruins, especially with the green *kemponashi* nuts on the ground near it. I myself had noticed nothing, but, hearing the story now, I was amazed by my mother's thoughtfulness. She had obviously meant the nuts as a special offering for the repose of my soul. As a child, I had always been impatient for the *kemponashi* nuts to fall. I used to throw stones at the branches to bring them down, for which my father would roundly scold me. Sometimes, a stone went too far, and would land on the roof of the bathroom. Mother, it seemed, had never forgotten.

According to our visitors, a steady stream of neighbors and other friends in the village were coming to my old home to ask after us. In theory, at least, it was to ask after us; but from the tone of what they said, it was plain that they had really come to offer condolences. Only one of them, the proprietor of the local sundries store, had differed from the rest. "You should know better than to put their photos on the altar," he told my mother. "It's asking for bad luck. Wait a bit and see—they'll come back safe and sound." And he left without even saying the usual polite things.

I excused myself, as I had to get up early the next morning, and I went to bed in the small room next door. But I could still hear them talking. People in Kobatake, like everywhere else, they were saying, were going out digging for pine tree roots. Even my old mother was tottering off to dig in the hills, and had given herself blisters on her hands. Oil was extracted from the roots by steaming, and was used—so a naval officer had come specially to the village to tell everybody—to oil the engines of the planes whose job it was to shoot down B-29's. Pine-root digging had been organized as a type of voluntary war work, and a hut for steaming the roots had been erected by the river in the valley. . . .

This morning, I got up early and started to write a letter for them to take to my mother, but so many emotions crowded in upon me that I gave up the attempt. Leaving our visitors still asleep, I left to catch the first train. The train, as before, stopped at Yamamoto, and from there I set off on foot in the direction of Yokogawa Bridge. A distance of about two miles.

The ruins were very much as they had been yesterday. The human figures searching for remains among the rubble looked like people seen searching for shellfish on the beach. Stooped and motionless with their backsides up in the air, they would quite suddenly straighten up from time to time, only to return to their original position almost immediately. As I crossed Yokogawa Bridge, I looked for the horse that had lain burned and quivering below the bridge on the sixth. There was little more than the skeleton left by now. Just downstream from the bridge, a pair who seemed to be father and child were scooping up water in pieces of tin bent into a funnel shape. Above the bridge, too, two middle-aged women were scooping up water in similar containers fashioned from tin; they scooped busily for a while, then leaned against the stone embankment as though tired. They had stuck pieces of bamboo and sticks of wood into the embankment between the stones, resting pieces of board, matting, and corrugated iron on top to form a kind of shelter. I saw a number of similar shanties much further up the river.

In Sorazaya-chō at the northern end of Aioi Bridge, I saw two women seated on the ground amidst piles of broken tiles, weeping silently. They were both about twenty, and looked like sisters.

The Industrial Exhibition Hall and Industrial Promotion Hall had their upper stories shattered and dangling by the framework. Aioi Bridge, which was made of reinforced concrete, had a great hump almost a yard high in the center. The concrete was cracked like crazy paving, with rifts an inch or an inch-and-a-half wide running all over it. A water pipe that crossed the river beside the bridge was snapped, and one could see deep down inside its gaping ends.

As I reached the southern end of Motokawa Bridge, it was low tide, and among the pools left on the river bed I saw several fish like mullet lying badly decomposed, with their backbones visible. Here and there, crabs lay dead where they had crawled out from the stones of the embankment. The weeds on the river bank, with the exception of the tall, ear-bearing grasses, were proliferating wildly. However much I thought about it, I couldn't see how light and sound could make weeds start growing so furiously.

The balustrade of every bridge I crossed bore messages written on pieces of paper stuck on the stone, or scrawled on the bridge with charcoal. The number was astonishing. Some of the pieces of paper were fluttering in the breeze. Large numbers of people were scanning them, like the crowd that gathers before the bulletin board outside a newspaper office. Very occasionally, somebody would stop, write something, and go off again in a great hurry. The messages were all simple in the extreme, yet they seemed to convey something of the feelings and circumstances of the people who had written them. I jotted down a few of the sentences from pieces of paper stuck on the balustrade of Motokawa Bridge:

To Kōnosuke: Come to your Aunt's home at Gion—Father.
Father and Mother: Let me know where you are now—Mayumi, c/o Mr. Abe, Sakurao, Hatsukaichi.
Papa: The boy is worrying where you are—Hasue, c/o Yaichi Shintaku, Happonmatsu.
Shinzō Watanabe is alive and well. Present address: c/o Shigeki Sehara, Midorii.
Worried about members of the class. Will come here every day at ten—Taizō Ogawa, Class IIA, Industrial High School.
Grandfather, Grandmother, and Emiko missing. To Shōji and Natsuyo: Come to Mr. Tokurō Ida's in Ōkawa-chō—Yasuoka.
To Mr. Ikuo Nishiguchi of Kamiya-chō: Please leave your present address and I will return the debt. Thank you. From your acquaintance in Nakahiro-chō.
To Yaeko: Stop in at Mihara on your way back to Fuchū—from your Father.

I set off again at a run, beating about me with my cotton towel to get rid of the flies trailing me, but was soon out of breath and had to slow down to a walk. Along this road, too, I could see, between the broken stone walls and the ornamental rocks where people's houses had been, wood sorrel and vetch drooping under the weight of new shoots that had sprouted too quickly for them to support. I wondered whether the shock of the raid could have affected the cell structure of plants in the same way as with human beings.

I recalled something that an agricultural expert visiting the village had once told us. If rice in a paddy field was grown in water that was too deep, the part of the stem in contact with the water was weakened structurally, and the plant tended to topple over later. This, he said, was accepted scientific fact. But I had never heard anyone say that a sudden shock from light or sound or heat could set plants growing unusually fast. The bomb seemed to have encouraged the growth of plants and flies at the same time that it put a stop to human life.

Insects and plants, indeed, were thriving as never before. Yesterday, I had seen a new shoot a foot and a half long on a plantain tree in what had been the back garden of a noodle shop. The original stem had been snapped off by the blast and had disappeared without a trace, but a new shoot, encased in a sheath like bamboo, was already growing in its place. Today, the shoot was a good two feet long. Familiar with trees as I was, after a childhood spent on a farm, I was astonished.

The noodle restaurant in question had been an old haunt of mine. In the days when I was working at the Army Provisions Depot, I had come there to have dinner every Sunday, and the proprietor used to call me "the boss." When food started to get scarce, I sometimes traded on our acquaintance to persuade him, on the quiet, to part with some of his official ration of noodles.

He had done a very nice dish of noodles with meat and vegetables, flavored with curry. Many such details came back to me now, as I stood estimating the length of the plantain shoot with my finger. Just then, I caught sight of the noodle shop terrier peering out at me from behind a stone. I called to it and whistled, but today it would neither come to me nor wag its tail. It simply stood and stared. It must have run off somewhere during the fire, then come back when the fires died down to look for its master. I wondered how it could have survived in the middle of this scorched desert, without a scrap of food. It was thin and scraggy, and its coat was a dark gray all over. I had a mind to give it a piece of my rice ball, but in the end left it to its fate, persuading myself that if I gave it food it would only tag along behind me.

About four or five sites past the noodle shop, I heard a metallic hammering, and saw a man attacking a large safe, now burnt a rusty brown, with a chisel. He was middle-aged and wore a topee, with khaki shorts and a short-sleeved shirt of the same color. Moved by idle curiosity, I went up to the man and spoke to him.

"You've got plenty of energy I must say, in this heat. Won't the door at the front of the safe open?"

He glanced sideways at me without ceasing his banging, "Can't get the damn key to budge," he said. "So I'm having to get in from the back."

"Why don't you smash in the lock with a hammer or something?"

"I wonder, now? I wonder if a hammer would do the job? If I leave the contents inside it, safebreakers will make off with it before long."

A vast swarm of flies was dancing about him, frustrated in their attempts to settle. The man did not look like a thief himself, so I said, "Sorry to have disturbed you at your work," and left him at it.

In the ruins of what had been the district's shopping center, there were rusty safes whenever I looked. We had no safe at Senda-machi; the only people possessing them in our neighborhood seemed to have been Mr. Nakao and Mr. Miyaji—not that I knew until I saw the safes in the ruins. In Miyaji's case, of course, it was only around the middle of July this year that he had bought one, when enemy planes first started flying over Hiroshima, across the central mountain range and on to the Japan Sea. There was a sudden increase in the number of people moving to the country, and one was able to pick up second-hand pianos, harmoniums, and safes for the merest song. From late July on, enemy raids became far more frequent; there were air raid warnings in Toku-yama, Iwakuni, and Kure, and mines began to be dropped in the Japan Sea, whereupon the pianos and the safes were joined by a flood of chests-of-drawers, ornamental pots, bamboo poles, miniature trees, checker boards, framed pictures, washing boards, wash-tubs, tennis rackets, and hanging scrolls, all at bargain prices.

Hiroshima was always said to be the army's city, whereas Kure was the navy's. Kure was raided on June 22, then on July 1 a great incendiary raid razed the flat, central area of the city to the ground. There was another raid on July 24. On this occasion, the enemy was met by anti-aircraft fire from a Japanese battleship anchored out of sight behind an island, where it was marooned for want of fuel oil. Not enough pine root oil was being produced to replace the normal fuel, and it had found itself in the peculiar situation of being able to fight but unable to move. On that day, enemy planes also dropped bombs on Ujina. The next attack was the raid on Hiroshima on August 6, when the mysterious bomb was dropped, reducing the city to ashes.

Not a word, not a rumor had led us to suspect the existence of such a bomb. It was the same with most people, I imagine. One can usually tell the way things are going by watching the children, who are more simple in their reactions than adults. The middle-school pupils doing war work, who were almost without exception wiped out by the bomb, were helping to pull down houses to make firebreaks almost every day right up to August 5. Not one of their faces betrayed the slightest desire to play truant or to hide away. The schoolgirls in the voluntary labor units wore white cloths round their foreheads, and armbands proudly labeled "School Volunteer Unit." On their way to the steel factory, and on their way home again, they marched together, singing in chorus as they went:

> *A rifle in your hand, a hammer in mine—*
> *But the road into battle is one, and no more.*
> *To die for our country's a mission divine*
> *For the boys and the girls of the volunteer corps!*

The girls were employed at the steel works, turning anti-aircraft shells on the lathes. They worked in two shifts, and the later shift would be turning shells until ten at night. None of them, I am sure, ever dreamed of the horror that was waiting to descend on them.

CHAPTER 14 🍃

The number of people searching for bodies or cremated remains among the ruins was considerably greater than yesterday. Along with the people walking about in tatters or half-naked, I noticed quite a number of men dressed like firemen, with armbands inscribed "Special Relief Squad." Some of them were carrying megaphones, or bamboo stretchers. They had come from the country to give aid to the victims.

At the Clothing Branch Depot, I got precisely the reception I had expected.

"Yes, I quite see, Mr. Shizuma," Lieutenant Sasatake began slowly when he had heard my petition through. "But for the moment, I'm afraid, you'll have to carry on somehow as things are. The thing we most want, you see, is for soldiers and civilians to act as one, using their imagination and resourcefulness in finding a way out of each difficulty as it occurs. In an extreme emergency of this kind, we want the public as a whole to have a feeling of working together for the sake of the cause."

The only thing I was interested in was getting a ration of coal; abstract phrases of this kind were no comfort at all.

"Then will you write a letter of introduction to the Ujina mine, Lieutenant?"

"I'm afraid I can't answer you there till I've mentioned it to my superiors and we've had a conference. Even so, though, something must be done, I do agree."

"Couldn't you perhaps release the coal reserves at Ujina?"

"That's quite out of the question, as I explained to you once already yesterday. It's outside our jurisdiction, you see."

In just the same way as yesterday, I was left with a feeling of helplessness. The only difference was that today the phrasing of the refusal was somewhat less rigid and the manner rather less pompous. I decided there was no point in pressing any further.

Leaving the Clothing Branch Depot, I made my way through the ruins of Fukuro-chō and was walking along the road with the streetcar tracks, in the direction of the Communications Bureau, when a soldier with an armband inscribed "Relief Squad" overtook me. As he walked, he was shouting "Hello, there! Is there anybody from the Kōjin Unit about?" I glanced at his profile, and at the same moment he turned round to look at me.

"Good Lord, Tamotsu!"

"Why, if it isn't Shigematsu!"

It was an extraordinary coincidence, indeed, for Tamotsu came from Kobatake. A few years previously he had joined the Himeji regiment, and sometime the year before last, people in the village had been saying that he had been made corporal of a sanitation platoon. Now, however, he was wearing a new sun-helmet, with a military sword at his side, and had a sergeant-major's badge on the collar of his shirt.

"My, Tamotsu—you've gone up in the world, haven't you?" I exclaimed in surprise. "Carrying a long saber like that!"

"Well," he said, "A while back, I was transferred to the Fukuyama regiment, then on August 7, I was transferred here again. I'm a sanitation NCO attached to the special relief squads clearing up the ruins." He looked thoroughly out of temper at the idea.

The two men he had with him were also familiar to me by sight. One of them, Rikuo, was a member of the Kobatake fire brigade, an extremely taciturn man, generally held to be a master of firefighting techniques. The other, Masaru, came from a different district of the village, and was also a fireman, rumored to be not a whit inferior to Rikuo in his job. Both had been called out by police order the day after the bomb fell on Hiroshima, and had come to the ruins, as members of a special relief squad, to look for the members of the Kōjin Unit who had been at work pulling down houses.

Rikuo had a megaphone attached to a cord slung round his neck, and he and Masaru were carrying a stretcher with handles of still-green bamboo.

"Those bamboo handles came from the grove at the Kannon temple back at Kobatake, I'll be bound," I said. "It makes me homesick just to see them."

"Don't be silly," said Masaru. "The police at Miyoshi gave them to us."

The members of the relief squad, I learned, had not come direct to Hiroshima from Kobatake. First they had assembled at the village hall in response to a summons from the headman of Kobatake, then they had gone to Yuki to report to the local office there (the order had simply said that they were to report in their firemen's uniforms). At Yuki, they joined forces with men from other villages in the district and were addressed by the mayor on the subject of "Boosting the Morale of the Public Behind the Lines." From there, the whole company had been dispatched to Shōge, where they joined more men from other villages and were addressed by the mayor, then sent on to Miyoshi. Here, they joined forces with still more men from neighboring villages and listened again to an exhortatory address by the mayor, who declared them to be brave heroes, sallying forth to the ruins of Hiroshima to do their duty at a time of national emergency.

From Kobatake on to Yuki and then to Shōge there was no train, and they had gone by charcoal-driven bus, but from Shōge as far as Yaga-machi they had been taken by train. Not one had either complained or dropped out on the way. Their work was not to give aid to ordinary victims of the bomb, but to seek out members of the Kōjin Unit from their own or neighboring villages who had been in Hiroshima when the bomb fell.

"We're all grateful to you," I said formally to Rikuo and Masaru, with a little bow. I bowed to Tamotsu too, and said, "thank you."

"But isn't it a coincidence, though?" said Tamotsu. "Quite an extraordinary coincidence—that I should happen to be assigned to the relief squad for Kobatake and Takafuta. We're just on our way to the Communications Hospital to look for survivors."

"We've only found five from Kobatake so far," said Masaru. "Rikuo's been shouting steadily through this megaphone here till he's made himself hoarse. So I'm going to take over soon."

I set off walking alongside them in the direction of the Communications Hospital. Somehow, it seemed the right thing to do. The curfew at the works did not apply to me, and I felt that today it was natural that I should join forces with them.

Rikuo walked with the megaphone to his lips, shouting "Hello there! Any Kōjin Unit members from Kobatake? Any Kōjin members from Takafuta? Hello there! Members of the Kōjin Unit. . . ." I gazed about me as I walked, looking for some response to his cries, but the only things that met my eyes were fragments of tile, crumbled brick walls, the skeletons of automobiles, electric wires hanging in festoons like nets hung out to dry, streetcar tracks, charred timbers, scorched safes, and blackened window frames.

Suddenly the sergeant-major stopped in his tracks. "Look— that may be an official notice," he exclaimed, straightening his sun-helmet as he spoke.

Looking where he pointed, I saw a number of sheets of paper stuck up on the burned-out iron frame of a streetcar. The sergeant-major started walking toward the wreck, and I followed, with considerable trepidation, in his wake. It was a bulletin made by cutting rectangular strips off a roll of paper and pasting them onto the iron. In Hiroshima at such a time, only a newspaper company would have used paper like that.

I copied down one of the notices into my notebook:

"Announcement from H.Q., West Japan Military District," it said. "At approximately 11:00 hours on August 9, two large enemy aircraft penetrated the skies over Nagasaki and dropped what appeared to be a bomb of the new type. Details of the damage are still under investigation, but it is expected to prove comparatively light."

Another sheet bore the following notice:

"August 10, from the commander in charge of the defense of Hiroshima to the citizens of Hiroshima: Should burns have been incurred, it is recommended as a temporary measure that the person affected bathe in a mixture of one part of sea water to one part of fresh water. This method will ensure adequate protection against the effects of this type of attack. Electric car tracks and major roads are now passable on foot."

The piece of paper adjoining this one declared:

"From Imperial Headquarters: (1) Yesterday, August 6, Hiroshima City suffered considerable damage as the result of an attack by a small number of enemy B-29 aircraft. (2) The enemy appears to have used a new type of bomb in this attack, but details are still under investigation."

On the blank space at the bottom of the paper somebody, an idle scribbler presumably, had written in charcoal, "August 10: Soviet Union enters the war." He seemed to have written on the paper when it was already fastened against the streetcar frame. I felt sure, from the crude writing and the use of charcoal—of which there was plenty immediately to hand—that it was not an official announcement, yet I also found it impossible to dismiss it as an unfounded rumor.

The news affected me with the feeling, not so much that the end of the road had at last been reached, as that it had been passed some while ago. For a moment, I feared that my legs were going to give way beneath me. The left side of my face, the side with the burn, was twitching uncontrollably. I could feel it myself, numb though the burned surface was. At the same time, I was puzzled; the bulletins must have been posted at various points in the ruins two or three days ago, and I wondered why I had not noticed them before.

The sergeant-major and his companions trudged on again in glum silence. For some time, all four of us walked straight ahead without speaking. We had reached the entrance to the Communications Hospital when Rikuo finally said, as though to himself, "A nice bath of one part of sea water to one part of fresh, eh?"

The hospital was no more than the shell of what had been a Western-style building, but it was apparent even from outside the entrance that it was full to capacity with victims. People in surgical smocks were walking busily along the corridor, and injured patients were tottering to and fro on unsteady legs. A woman who seemed to be out of her mind was standing by the stone steps shouting something unintelligible. Nearby, there stood a group of people come from the country to look for the missing. Telling me to wait at the entrance, Tamotsu, as the sergeant in charge, led the other two into a room that seemed to be serving as the reception office. After a while he came out and said, "We'll look through the wards. You'll have to stay here, as you're not a member of the relief squad. I think we shall find some victims from Kobatake here."

So saying, he went off down the corridor with Rikuo and Masaru. The woman who seemed to be out of her mind began shrieking after Rikuo and his companion as though calling down curses on them.

By the stone steps at the entrance, a couple of women were sitting, talking busily. Neither looked like victims. They were about forty, and both wore grubby blouses, with baggy cotton trousers and long rubber boots. Judging from what she said, one was the wife of a victim in the hospital, while the other was his younger sister. Both of them were talking excitedly.

A large unit of the Soviet army, they were saying, had breached the Manchukuo border and come pouring into the country in great waves. The Japanese army in Manchukuo had therefore decided to drop on them a bomb similar to the one the B-29 had dropped on Hiroshima. The army had also, it seemed, determined to drop the bomb on the Pacific islands occupied by American forces, by way of reprisal for the Hiroshima raid. The bombs were being manufactured secretly at this very moment, on an island off Takehara City. The thing was that the enemy must be made to realize that Japan had a formidable navy as well as an army. . . .

Their conversation, apart from confirming the Soviet Union's entry into the war, also gave me some information about the state of affairs in the hospital. At the time of the explosion, the hospital's director, Dr. Michihiko Hachiya, had been hit by flying glass and splinters in more than thirty different places all over his body. He had, almost literally, been cut to ribbons. Since then, unable to stand, he had been directing the hospital's emergency operations from a bed in the ward. The symptoms of the patients, and of the director himself, were all the same: loss of appetite, vomiting, and diarrhea, with bloody stools in many cases. The director had concluded from this that the bomb must have contained either poison gas or dysentery germs. He had accordingly directed the doctors in charge of internal medicine to take measures as for an infectious disease, and had told Dr. Koyama, the acting director, to have an isolation ward constructed with all speed.

It soon occurred to Dr. Koyama, who was a man of action and great resourcefulness, that the only people in the ruined city who were capable of building anything in practice were the army. So he had conferred with the officer in charge of the troops stationed in the Communications Bureau close by, and as a result it had been decided that soldiers should be set to work building an isolation ward to the south of the hospital proper. The work was proceeding apace. The only drawback was that vital military establishments such as the headquarters of the West Japan Army, the Second West Japan Unit, the Military Preparatory School, the divisional headquarters, and the engineers were all situated in the vicinity of the hospital. They had all been wiped out by the bomb, it was true, but the area was certain to become the focus of a battle for the whole district in the event of an enemy landing. For the same reason, many of the patients became alarmed and called "Airplane!" or "Take cover!" in panic every time there was an air raid warning. . . .

I sat waiting on the stone steps for nearly an hour. Eventually, I began to feel that something must be wrong, and stepped into the entrance hall to see if there was any sign of the others. Inside, my attention was caught at once by a dish that had been placed on a ledge inside a small window to serve as a lamp. It contained vegetable oil, with a piece of bandage for a wick, but the dish itself, which must surely have come from somebody's safe, was a magnificent piece of *san-ts'ai* ware.

"Shigematsu!" said a voice. "Sorry to keep you waiting."

I turned round. The man on the stretcher carried by Rikuo and Masaru was all but dead, with no strength left even to moan. Dark, blackish stains showed on the bandages around his hands. His face was unrecognizably swollen and empurpled. From the tattered remains of his shirt, to which it was fastened with a safety pin, dangled a name-card. On it was written by hand, "Chūzō Hata, member of the Kōjin Unit, Kobatake Village, Hiroshima Prefecture."

When I was a boy, this same Chūzō's father had taught me how to sniggle for eels. He had also initiated me—as an adjunct to the more serious art of fishing—into the delights of bamboo shoots dug from a nearby grove and baked over a fire kindled on the dried-up part of the river-bed. You baked them with the skin on, then peeled them and ate them steaming hot, basted with bean paste begged from the nearest house.

A peculiarly offensive, fishy stench came from Chūzō as he lay on the stretcher. It may have been caused by pus, or by the fever in the body; either way, it was indescribably unpleasant. I offered to take one end of the stretcher from Rikuo, but he refused. "Don't be silly," he said. "Leave the stretcher-carrying to the relief unit people."

From time to time Tamotsu the sergeant-major, who walked in front of the stretcher, would bellow through his megaphone: "Hello there! Is there anybody from the Kōjin Unit? Hello there! Anybody from Takafuta?" I walked by his side so as to stay to windward of the stretcher. The sky was horribly blue.

A doctor called Norioka, Tamotsu told me, had hunted out Chūzō for them from all the many patients in the ward of the Communications Hospital. There were so many injured that all could not be accommodated in the ward proper, and they spilled out into the corridor, so that people who had come to tend to the sick or look for the missing had to pick their way between them. What was worse, their fever was extraordinarily contagious. It sometimes happened, even, that a healthy person caring for a patient would die before the patient himself. Such things were happening all around all the time. Yet despite the indescribable chaos, Dr. Norioka had found Chūzō for them.

Dr. Norioka, said Tamotsu, was head of a relief squad sent from the Communications Hospital in Osaka, and had arrived at the hospital in charge of a party bearing rucksacks stuffed with relief materials the previous day. Two days earlier, on the eighth, troops had turned up from somewhere and made a clean sweep of the hospital's medicines and bandages, and the relief squad from Osaka had come—as one nurse had put it—as "Buddhas to hell."

By the time we arrived at the relief squad's temporary headquarters, Chūzō was dead on the stretcher.

"He's quite dead," said Tamotsu as the stretcher was lowered onto the veranda in the garden, and he saluted as a mark of respect for the deceased. Masaru brought a leaf from a spear-flower that grew by an ornamental stone basin, and placed it by the dead man's head, then he and Rikuo stood together and, pressing their palms together, bowed briefly in silent prayer.

I recited the "Sermon on Mortality." As soon as I had finished Rikuo spoke. "Shall we cremate him, then?" he said. "I feel kind of bad towards old Chūzō about it, but it can't be helped." And he and Masaru took up the stretcher once more. The crematorium for the people here was a piece of vacant ground near the railway.

The temporary headquarters of the relief squad was a private residence overlooking the East Parade Ground on the side towards the foot of Mt. Futaba. On weekdays the head of the family, a schoolteacher or something of the kind, left home in the early morning, while on Sundays he went off somewhere to do volunteer war work. Since he was never at home in the daytime, the relief people scarcely ever saw him. His son, a boy called Minoru, was a naval officer on a warship somewhere at sea. His wife was a well-bred, intelligent woman, and there were two attractive daughters of marriageable age. The whole family was extraordinarily kind-hearted, and on no occasion made the slightest objection either to the members of the relief squad or to the injured from the Kōjin Unit.

The relief squad had first noticed the house as they happened to be going past and—because it looked as though it had plenty of space—had promptly asked, without any introduction or other formality, for use of its rooms as a reception center for survivors from the Unit. The husband had been out at the time, and the wife and daughters alone, but the wife had immediately agreed, as though it was something they had been expecting all along. She was an unusually thoughtful woman, they said, with an extra-ordinary sense of service to others.

The squad was using four large rooms on the first floor. Together with the survivors of the Kōjin Unit they numbered, in all, some fifty persons. Some of these were dying of raw burns, others groaning and excreting blood, and the same, foul odor hung over them all. Even so, the wife and daughters insisted on sleeping downstairs, in the kitchen, as though they felt it would be wrong to sleep upstairs in the circumstances. The husband, Tamotsu said, might be sleeping upstairs alone for all he knew.

I sat on the veranda facing the garden and discussed tomorrow's plans with Tamotsu as I ate the food I had brought with me. We sat near the uncovered, projecting part of the veranda, by the ornamental stone basin, so that our voices should not disturb the injured, but the stench of sickness reached us even here. From where we were, we could hear two or three who were groaning incessantly, and, from time to time, a sudden cry of "Take cover!"

The lady of the house appeared with a pot of cold barley tea. "You've been working so hard," she said with unaffected courtesy. "I've brought you some tea. It's not very cold, I'm afraid, but do help yourselves." She bowed and disappeared again. Not liking to stare, I had only a glimpse of her face, but I had a good look at her from the rear, and her bearing was as well-bred as I had expected.

I promised Tamotsu that I would go to Ōnoura by noon tomorrow. Today, a message came from the reception center for victims at Ōnoura (in the hall of the Ōnoura National Elementary School) to inform emergency headquarters here that they were caring for two members of the Kōjin unit, a man called Torao from Kobatake and another called Chōjūrō from Takafuta. Both wanted to go home for treatment as soon as possible, but one was so badly hurt that it was very doubtful whether he could as much as turn over in bed. They had let us know at any rate—the message went—thinking it might help us in drawing up a list of survivors of the Kōjin Unit. Since this meant that someone from the emergency headquarters would have to go to Ōnoura, I took on the task myself.

CHAPTER 15 🍂

August 12. Light clouds in the morning. A spell of pain in my leg. Fine in the afternoon.

I left the temporary headquarters of the reception center in Nagao-chō at something after five yesterday, and on my way back home followed the railway tracks of the main Sanyō Line to a point near Yokogawa Station. On the way, a middle-aged woman who overtook me glanced round as she was passing, then suddenly stopped and put herself in my way.

"Surely it's Mr. Shizuma? Why yes—it's Mr. Shizuma!" she exclaimed. "Well! Whoever would have thought it, here like this! Is your family all safe?"

It was Teiko, an old childhood friend of mine. Her surname was Fujita, and we had been in the same class at primary school. On finishing higher elementary school, she had gone to work in a spinning factory at Kurashiki, then had married the son of a farmer whose home was near the Hosokawa Clinic in the village of Yuda, outside Fukuyama. She had saved up to buy her wedding kimono herself. But her husband had died shortly after, so she had transferred responsibility for the family to her husband's younger brother and his wife, and gone to work as a maid in an inn in Kurashiki. Around the time of the Manchurian Incident she had come back to Kobatake for a while, but had left again, and since then had been working as a resident maid at the Kagami Inn in Fukuyama. When I started working in Hiroshima, I had got into the habit of stopping off for a while at the Kagami Inn on my way home for the Bon and New Year holidays. I made use of Teiko for my own convenience, using the telephone at the inn, getting her to take messages for friends, leaving baggage in her care, and in many other ways.

Last New Year, I was suffering from a painful case of piles, and stayed the night at the inn. Teiko knew a doctor who could cure the most stubborn cases, and wrote me an introduction to the Hosokawa Clinic in Yuda village. She even telephoned personally to the head of the clinic and told him I was coming. I put in a long-distance call to the works, got permission from the manager to take some time off from work, and entered the clinic. It took more than two weeks before I was completely cured. I learned from Teiko yesterday that she had been to the Hosokawa Clinic to see how I was doing, but found I had left a few days earlier.

I felt guilty. "I'm so sorry," I said.

"No no," she said, "I was going to my brother-in-law's at any rate, to buy some black market rice . . . But fancy, though, meeting you today in a place like this!"

Like so many others, Teiko had come to search the ruins of Hiroshima for survivors. Her brother-in-law had been called into the reserve in spring this year, and had been working in the kitchen of the Second Army Hospital. Several days had passed since the bomb fell, but they had had no word from him. It looked as though he might well have been killed. His wife at home in Yuda was in bed—having sprained her ankle a few days previously on an expedition to dig up pine roots for the armed forces—and was good for nothing but lying and weeping all day long. Her brother-in-law's mother talked a lot but was too old to be any use outside the house. At a loss what to do, Teiko had eventually gone to consult the head of the Hosokawa Clinic.

Dr. Hosokawa had a brother-in-law called Iwatake who ten days previously had been called up for duty in the Second Army Hospital. Also a doctor of medicine, he had been drafted not as a cook but as a medical reservist, under the so-called "punitive draft." From this, Teiko deduced that he must have been in the same barracks as her brother-in-law, and she wondered what had happened to him in the raid. There was a nephew of Mr. Iwatake's, too, who had been attending the First Hiroshima Middle School; they must certainly be worried about the boy's safety. Teiko began to wonder what they were doing about it all at the Hosokawa Clinic, and in the end went to see the doctor, partly to inquire after the safety of his relatives and partly to consult with him about her own.

"I just don't know—it's terrible," he told her. "I've resigned myself to the thought that both my brother-in-law and his nephew are so much charcoal by now. It's a dreadful thing, but there's no help for it but to face facts. I've told my brother-in-law's wife to resign herself too, but it's not so easy, you know, with someone you're married to, or of your own flesh and blood. She went off to Hiroshima in tears. I saw her as far as Fukuyama Station myself. That was the morning of the ninth.

"Two days have gone by already, but I've not even had a tele-gram or letter. . . . Not that the mail or telegraph and telephone services are much of a reality nowadays for us civilians, of course. It's the same with the newspapers—one supposes they're being published every day, but whenever you go to the agents' to get them they haven't come yet. No papers at all for five or six days at a stretch—then on the seventh day, perhaps, you'll get a whole week's issues in a lump. One patient I saw yesterday was pining because he hadn't had so much as a postcard from anyone for over three weeks. He said the owner of the place where he lives goes fishing for dace on the quiet, to help out with an invalid diet, and *he* complains that even the bluebottle grubs he uses for bait are undernourished these days. One depressing thing after another, he said. . . . You know, they say the new type of bomb they dropped on Hiroshima can pack the power of several thousand ordinary fifty-kilogram bombs into the space of a matchbox. Some really frightful chemical must have been discovered. If they're going to go around using it to kill people with, I just don't know what things will come to. As for my brother-in-law, though, I've given him up: he's dead and burned by now."

The tears rolled down his cheeks. Nothing more could be got out of him, and Teiko was left still wondering whether she should go to look for her brother-in-law or not. But when she told him she had determined to go to Hiroshima, he gave her a small bottle of creosote tablets as a parting present.

Arriving in Hiroshima, she eventually found the site of the Second Army Hospital by asking the way of people clearing away the debris. A single tent stood in the ruins. She got hold of one of the soldiers in the tent and asked him what she wanted to know.

"I'm sorry," he said after leafing through three ledgers in turn, "but there's no entry here for the person you're seeking—no army cook, that is, who fits in with the particulars. I'm very sorry. However, the survivors from this unit have been sent to reception centers at Hesaka and Shōbara on the Geibi Line, and some to the center at Kabe on the Kabe Line. Hesaka is not much more than six miles from here. The Kabe Line isn't running between Yoko-gawa and Yamamoto stations, but you can get to Yamamoto Station by getting onto the tracks beyond the Communications Bureau and following them to the left. Let me just show you— Yamamoto Station lies roughly in that direction. . . ."

Could the absence of any name in the records mean that the body had not been found? Or had he made off quite unharmed, under his own steam? Could the records be incomplete? She was standing there at a loss what to do when a young man sitting next to the soldier spoke to her.

"I think I should warn you," he said, "that almost all the injured from this unit are so swollen in the face with burns that even their closest relatives can hardly tell who they are. Some of them can't even answer when called by name. So they have a label giving their name and home address attached to the belt_of their uniforms. You must take a tight grip on yourself, you see, and look for the label." His way of speaking was not like that of a soldier.

Teiko vacillated between going to Kabe and going to Hesaka, but before long she pulled herself together, told herself it was no time for wavering, and decided on Kabe. Thoughtlessly enough, though, she left the tent without remembering to ask about Dr. Hosokawa's younger brother. After that, she said, she had just walked on in the direction the soldier had pointed out to her, until she came across me on her way along the tracks.

As I walked along by her side, she told me all kinds of things about life under wartime conditions in the area around Fukuyama. She also gave me snippets of confidential information, things that guests at the inn had passed on to her privately. One had told her that the twenty-odd kilns that traditionally made Bizen ware in the town of Imbe were now making hand-grenades and water-flasks of the same ware, under army orders. Some days ago, a group of noncommissioned officers had turned up in Imbe from somewhere or other and tested the performance of the hand-grenades. They had proved every bit as powerful as orthodox grenades, blowing a hole in a half-inch piece of pine board and bringing all the fish to the surface in a nearby pond.

Another had told her about some American-made tanks that the British were using on the Burma front. When one of these fired at a Japanese tank, the shell went clean through, but when the Japanese tank fired, the shell did nothing more than take a little paint off the enemy tank. "It's awful," the man had said. "What would have happened to the Japanese army if the British had had even a couple of those tanks in Malaya?" True or not, such talk was rumor-mongering and defeatism of the most barefaced kind.

We had to wait at Yamamoto Station, and it was already quite dark when we finally got on a train. Teiko declined to stop by at our temporary home, and we parted company at Furuichi Station.

She had a rucksack on her back, and was wearing baggy trousers and a white shirt with a Red Cross armband, which Dr. Hosokawa's wife must have advised her to wear. Probably it was the armband that had made the soldier in the tent treat her so civilly.

Before going home, I went to the factory and reported to the manager, whom I found in the canteen, on the state of the coal situation. Whichever way one turned, I explained, one came up against a blank wall; there was simply nothing that we could do.

He gazed dejectedly up at the ceiling. "I see," he said. "So that's that, is it? We're caught whatever road we try, aren't we. Thanks all the same for trying, though."

I told him about the Kōjin Unit and got his permission to go to help at Ōnoura, then went home.

Shigeko and Yasuko had finished supper and put the mosquito net up, and were now sitting on the veranda enjoying the cool of the evening. My meal was laid out for me on a small individual table inside the mosquito net. The intention was probably to make things look cool and pleasant, but the only effect was to make me feel half suffocated. Our two visitors from the country, they told me, had gone home on a train sometime before noon.

This morning I was awakened by pain in the toes of both feet. The pain, which was excruciating even though there was no external injury, was not an intermittent throbbing but continuous, as though both sides were being twisted on some instrument of torture.

"They say moxibustion is good for people affected by the bomb," Shigeko said. "Why don't you try it? I'll go and find someone to let me have some moxa."

She went out without even putting on the regulation cotton breeches and air raid hood, but it was over two hours before she came back. She had tried here, there and everywhere, until in the end she had got some moxa in exchange for a new hand towel at a farm just outside the town. It was in a paper bag printed with a picture of the god of agriculture holding a leaf between his teeth.

They say that to stop pain in the feet one should burn moxa on the spot known as *sanri*. Even I, however—much less Shigeko and Yasuko—did not know exactly where the *sanri* was, so Shigeko went to ask the landlord's old father.

"The *sanri*," she announced on her return, "is the dent just below the kneecap on the outside. Here—" And having no work breeches on, she hitched up her skirt—unnecessarily high, I thought—in order to show me. I found her behavior rather improper. At the same time, this reaction reminded me of something I had heard at the reception center. Tamotsu and Rikuo had been saying that those injured by the bomb, even if only slightly hurt, had all lost interest in sex. My own "injuries" consisted of nothing more than a burn on the cheek; even so, I asked myself whether I had felt any sexual interest just now, and my conclusion gave me an uneasy feeling that I, too, might have been poisoned by the bomb.

I applied the moxa myself on the designated spot, then forced myself to stand up despite the pain in my toes. I groaned aloud, which relieved the pain somewhat. Going to the toilet was a major undertaking. When I was ready to go out, I ate my breakfast sitting on the edge of the raised section of the floor in the hall entrance. It was a late breakfast. By the time I got out, it was past ten.

Luckily enough, the pain in my toes had abated by the time I got to Ōnoura. It seemed better to stay either lying down or on my feet, one or the other.

At Ōnoura I found that the National Elementary School was being used as a reception center for army and civilian injured alike. On my way there from Ōnoura Station, I passed a handsome woman of around thirty, and at the same time detected a most offensive smell. It was the same smell as yesterday in the reception center at Nagao-chō, the smell of the victims of the bomb.

"Excuse me," I said, stopping her. "May I ask if you're from the center for victims of the bombing—a doctor, or a nurse perhaps?"

"No, I'm not," she replied with great composure. "I'm a member of the Women's National Defense Association at Ōnoura. I'm doing voluntary nursing for the victims. Somebody else I passed yesterday asked me the same question. I expect I smell bad, don't I?"

"Yes—if you don't mind my saying so, you stink to high heaven."

"You're going to look for someone among the injured, I expect," she went on. "Let me take you there. Stay a little way away from me if I smell."

There were still some decent people left in the world, I thought. I determined not to worry about the smell and walked beside her, asking her about the reception center as we went.

(*Note:* I found later that she was Tamiyo Ōshima, a member of the women's association who showed great kindness in nursing the bomb victims. Her husband, who was with the army in Manchuria, was taken prisoner in Siberia at the end of the war, but returned to Japan before very long. No doubt it was the thought of her own husband, far away on the battlefield, that kept her working so selflessly for the welfare of the victims. The young soldiers and civilians among the patients were all fond of her. Those who itched unbearably from maggots in the burns on their backs would even wheedle her into scratching for them. Those lonely on the verge of death would call for her, and several of them died with their heads cradled on her lap. Shortly after the war ended, she went all the way to Takafuta and Shōge, in Jinseki county, to take the remains of two members of the Kōjin Unit to their families. No buses went there at that time, so she came to Kobatake first of all, then got a man called Tomonari Torao to take her up the path through the hills to Takafuta and so on to Shōge. Torao was the only survivor of the local inhabitants who had been taken to Ōnoura. The two others, a man called Fukushima from Takafuta and one called Maebara from Shōge, came home from Ōnoura as two boxes of ashes clasped in Mrs. Ōshima's arms. To this day, Torao still refers to her as the "Ōnoura Nightingale.")

I learned from this beautiful but stinking companion that Ōnoura lay about eight miles from the center of the Hiroshima explosion.

When the bomb fell on August 6, she had been weeding in the paddy fields with her elder sister, and they did not realize what had happened. There had been a bang, and the leaves of the rice plants had stirred noticeably. They had thought it was an earthquake. On their way home after another couple of hours' weeding, they had noticed that there were tiles off the wall of the toilet belonging to the local dry goods store. A particularly large number had been stripped off on the east side at the top. In the sky to the east, they could see a spreading black cloud.

"I wonder what that is—a smoke screen for some maneuvers, do you think?" her sister had said. "If it's not, then it's something really big."

In the afternoon, a truck turned off the main road and went in the direction of the National Elementary School. Even so, another two or three hours passed without their realizing anything.

About four o'clock, a member of the women's association came around with an announcement: "To members of the Ōnoura Women's Association: You are all requested to come to the National Elementary School. Please come to help nurse the injured. Come to the National Elementary School as soon as possible."

Getting ready and setting out in great haste, they were overtaken on the road to the school by several trucks carrying the injured. They caught glimpses of blackened skin, of ashen-colored skin, of raw flesh, of people lolled against the side and rear frames as though dead, of people with paper or towels plastered over their faces with holes cut out for the nose and mouth and eyes, of soldiers in the seats by the drivers. Their legs went weak, and for some while they had stood quite still, rooted to the spot.

Mrs. Ōshima took me to the school and said: "Well, I'll introduce you to that army doctor over there. He's very helpful, and interested in his work." She took me to meet a Lieutenant Katō, who was standing at the entrance to the teachers' room. The impression I got from his amiable expression was that he would not be a man to fuss unduly over trifles. I judged him easy to deal with. However, he stopped me before I could tell him my business.

"For the moment," he said, "this reception center is not a national elementary school but a branch of an army hospital. Things being as they are, we are accommodating both army and civilian patients at the moment, but I'd be grateful if the locals wouldn't interfere where the movement of patients is concerned. This story that documents have been sent from this reception center to the center at Nagao-chō is probably—not that I'm doubt-ing you personally—a fabrication of the locals. In fact, I'm pretty sure it is, so let's forget all about it. I'd like to impress on you again that the reception center is under the jurisdiction of the army."

I couldn't help feeling that he was playing with words, but gave in without arguing and started to ask if I could at least see the patients from the Kōjin Unit. But again he interrupted me. It was dangerous to go near the seriously injured, he warned me, as they gave off heat with some kind of poisonous element in it. The hospital was constantly having cases in which a healthy person who'd come to look after the sick was affected by the poison and carried off before the original patients. The more active a person was, and the more he rushed around doing things, the sooner he was affected by the poison. They had even had a case in which somebody who had come to take a slightly injured civilian home had himself been taken sick and had to seek help on the way back. (I later heard that Lieutenant Katō himself died after going back to his home in Tottori Prefecture following the end of the war. The trouble, it was said, was the same—he had been in close contact with too many of the victims of the bomb.)

The lieutenant must have been in a particularly bad mood. Or perhaps he was unwilling for any ordinary civilian to know just how chaotic conditions could be in a military hospital.

Accepting that nothing I said would have any effect, I went back to Hiroshima and reported on what had happened at the tem-porary reception headquarters for the Kōjin Unit at Nagao-chō. It was a classic case of having taken a lot of trouble for nothing, but I was too pleased that the pain in my toes had disappeared to care.

On returning home, I applied moxa to my knee again. It was pure luck that the pain in my toes had got better when I went to Ōnoura, but at the reception center Rikuo and Masaru told me that they, too, had been using moxibustion since the previous day as a charm to ward off the bomb disease. Tamotsu, as the sanitation NCO, was rather doubtful over the idea of a squad member using moxibustion so indiscriminately. As he saw it, it would have been better if somebody had got an expert to teach them the proper way, so that the rest could imitate his example.

(I have learned since that the number of persons suffering from radiation sickness admitted to the Ōnoura National Elementary School between 5 p.m. on August 6, and September 2, a period of 47 days, was 1,246. They were accommodated in sixteen classrooms averaging 720 square feet each, a total of nearly 14,000 square feet, and their treatment was undertaken by four civilian and seven army doctors, with a daily average of 25 nurses and 70 voluntary workers in four shifts. The number of bodies cremated was approximately 250. Ashes unclaimed were sent to Hiroshima City. These figures come from the records of the Ōnoura local office. At that time, victims of the bomb were being accommodated at national elementary schools throughout the Hiroshima area, but whether every town and village office still preserves similar records or not, I do not know. I have heard, though, that several thousand were sent to the national elementary school at Hesaka, that they could not all be accommodated, and that the school yard and even the gardens of farmhouses in the village were used as emergency reception centers.)

What follows is another addition that I am making now to this diary. I want to make it in order to correct erroneous reports previously included as fact, and for one further reason that I shall explain later. The relief squad consisted of two groups, fire brigade members (sixteen men) called out by a police directive, and workers from the health office (twelve nurses), called out by the prefectural office. I learned this only recently.

At about ten o'clock on the evening of the sixth, the day the bomb had fallen, the entire fire brigade of Kobatake village assembled at the village office in response to a circular from the village headman. The headman addressed them in more or less the following terms:

"I am sorry to call you out without warning at night, but a police order has made this meeting necessary. The fact is that at about eight a.m. today Hiroshima was bombed, and suffered enormous damage. No details are known yet, but you are to proceed to Hiroshima together with members of the fire brigades of every town and village in the country. You will be doing war work, this means, in accordance with instructions from the authorities. At the same time, however, I look to you all to take proper care to avoid accidents in any demolition work you may do, and also to make particular efforts to help anyone from our village working with Unit No. 32060, Central Honshu—the Kōjin Unit. I wish you all good luck on the field!"

Properly speaking, an address by the head of the fire brigade should have followed. However, his home was a long way from the village office, and blackout regulations ruled out lanterns to light the way there, so he had not been contacted. A man called Kaneshige, treasurer and assistant chief of the brigade, took his place. "It seems," he said, "that the chief job for the brigade in its forthcoming expedition, quite apart from pulling down houses, will be to give some help to the people of the Kōjin Unit. So I hope you'll rescue just as many as possible, men from here in Kobatake in particular, and bring them back safe and sound so that we shall all be ready for the defense of the village when the day comes—for come it will, you can be sure. Seeing as no details are available, I hope you'll all set to with a will in whatever way seems fit when you get to Hiroshima."

The brigade was dressed in fire-fighting uniforms with rubber-soled, split-toed socks, and carried saws, ropes, axes, air raid hoods and overcoats to sleep in at night. Their transport was a so-called "charcoal-driven" truck, and they had to hurry and chop wood into small pieces for use as fuel. What with helping them and seeing them off, the whole village was in a turmoil. The truck's headlights were covered so as to throw light for a distance of only three or four yards, and the people being seen off and those seeing them off could not even distinguish each other's faces in the gloom. Husband and wife knew each other only by their voices as hands were stretched down from the truck, hands stretched up to clasp them from below. . . .

The truck stopped first at the Takafuta village office. Here they were piled with flour, rolled *sushi,* sugar and the like by local well-wishers, and the head of the local veterans' association spoke a few encouraging words. Then, together with the Takafuta fire brigade, they turned back again to pick up the firemen of Toyo-matsu, Yuki, Fukunaga and four other villages and towns, arriving in Shōge around dawn. They left there by the first train in the morning. They arrived in Yaga-machi, outside the city proper, around ten, then entered the town on foot and set about the task of rescuing survivors and burning the dead.

Since the whole place had been razed to the ground, the ropes and saws they had brought for pulling down houses were quite useless. They gathered together any kettles and empty bottles they came across in the debris, filled them with water, and went around rationing it out to the victims, who were suffering from raging thirst. Whenever they came across a badly burned person stagger-ing along the road or sitting on the ground, they made him open his mouth and poured the water in, carefully, so as not to spill it. Such tasks and the cremating of the dead kept them more than occupied.

The rescuing of survivors, on the other hand, did not go so smoothly. They discovered a number of the twenty-one members of the Kōjin Unit from Kobatake, but altogether nineteen of them, including those killed outright and those who died later of radiation sickness, never got home alive.

In the meantime, the Kobatake health center had had a telegram on the night of the sixth, addressed to its head and saying: "Heavy losses. Come at once." The head of the center, a Dr. Satake, set out at once (he was in Hiroshima for only two or three days, then went home, but died after the end of the war), and immediately sent an order to Mr. Kano, head of the center's medical section, to come to Hiroshima right away to help in the relief of survivors. He was to bring with him the welfare nurses from Jinseki county. Kano set out on foot with twelve county nurses on August 10, but floods made it impossible to get a train from Shōge Station, so they walked to Miyoshi and spent the night there. The next morning they went by train to Yaga-machi, then proceeded to the relief headquarters.

The relief headquarters, they found, had moved to part of a brick warehouse in the grounds of the army's branch clothing depot. The nurses' main responsibility was to look after the injured. The chief at the headquarters, who was called Kitajima and was head of the Prefectural Office Sanitation Department, had a triangular bandage wrapped round his face where the bomb had caught him.

Kano was told to take charge of the clerical work. Patients came pouring in, but neither the chief nor the other doctors knew how to treat the disease, with its symptoms of high fever and diarrhea. The one thing they could do—on the assumption that dietary supplements at least could do no harm—was to get the nurses Kano had brought with him to use the vitamins and glucose for injections which they had packed in their rucksacks when they left. Between the tenth and the fifteenth days, when it had all gone, they had orders from above to make way for nurses who had come with medicine from another county. Kano, too, was dismissed and went back to the village.

On returning home, some of the nurses had diarrhea and slight loss of hair in the same way as the victims of radiation sickness. But there was no known treatment and no medicine. There was a great deal of panic-stricken consultation among them, as a result of which each did what she thought best. Some soothed their nerves by resorting to moxibustion; some avoided going out into the sun, so as to keep up their white corpuscle count; others stuffed themselves with tomatoes. Some even ate the leaves of potted aloes. I, for one, can well understand this need to clutch at any straw.

The members of the relief squad who had walked about the ruins fared much worse than the nurses. Of twenty-one from Taka-futa, one died on the spot, and eleven died of radiation sickness after their return. That was the result of simply walking in the ruins. In the village of Kitami, fifteen out of sixteen died, leaving only one alive today. In Senyō, all died.

Having no need to keep silent any longer, I have described these things, right down to the nurses' superstitious resort to moxibustion, just as they occurred. In the same way, I have set down the exact statistics of deaths among those who wandered about the bombed city.

My reason is that the talks on my niece Yasuko's marriage, which were rapidly approaching an agreement, have quite suddenly been broken off by the Aonos—the young man's family. Yasuko has begun to show symptoms of radiation sickness. Everything has fallen through. By now, it is neither possible nor necessary to go on pretending. Yasuko, it seems, has sent the young man a despairing letter saying she has started having symptoms. I wonder whether it was love for him that made her decide on this honest course? Or did she do it in despair, on the impulse of a moment?

Her sight has deteriorated rapidly, and she complains of a constant ringing in her ears. When she first told me about it, in the living room, there was a moment when the living-room vanished and I saw a great, mushroom-shaped cloud rising into a blue sky. I saw it quite distinctly.

CHAPTER 16 🌿

The last entry in the "Journal of the Bombing" was dated August
15, the day the war ended. Only three more days' entries remained
to be copied, but Shigematsu was too worried over Yasuko's illness
to concern himself with such detailed paper-work. It had also become urgently necessary for him to help Shōkichi and Asajirō see
to the pond where they were trying to rear their carp; for some
time to come, his days would be occupied with visits to the pond
below the bank on which Shōkichi's house stood.

Yasuko's illness grew rapidly worse. The blame lay partly with
Shigematsu and his wife for not having kept a more careful eye on
her behavior, and partly on her own excessive reluctance to confide
in them. The trouble had started before the young man's family
rejected the marriage, just as the match seemed on the verge of
being settled. She had clearly ascribed her symptoms to some dis-

turbance of the feminine organism caused by a mixture of acute happiness and bashfulness, and she had been too shy, even, to have a woman-to-woman talk about it with her aunt. Nor did she privately consult a doctor. All this they found out later. By the time Shigeko took Yasuko to the general hospital in Kobatake for her first medical examination, the disease was already far advanced.

Over and over again, they lamented the fact that Yasuko had been so shy about talking to them. Even allowing for the fact that she was about to become engaged, she had carried modesty too far.

"It was so *silly*," said Shigeko to Shigematsu, who was out in the garden when they got back from the hospital. "Her keeping everything to herself like that."

"I'm sorry, uncle," said Yasuko. She went past with her head bowed, her eyes on the ground.

This was around three o'clock in the afternoon. Afterwards, Shigematsu fetched a torch and the packed meal that had been prepared for him, and set off for the carp-rearing pond to help Shōkichi and Asajirō in regulating the temperature of the spawning pool.

It was already July, and the ponds in this district would reach a temperature of between 64° and 68°, ideal for the carp to spawn, around the Eighty-Eighth Night. However, it was not good for the water to be too warm at the start. Nor was it good to keep the males and females together from the beginning. They must be kept apart by means of a wooden partition, and the temperature kept down to 48°–50° until they had settled down. Then, and only then, the males and females were released together in a pool containing fresh water at just the right temperature for spawning. This immediately stimulated them into action, and the time from eleven or half-past at night until dawn saw them setting about preparations for spawning.

This was the method of getting the fish to spawn that Shōkichi and Asajirō had learned at the Tsunekanemaru hatchery. It was the first time that they were applying it in practice, and where everything relating to this particular subject was concerned they were as enthusiastic as schoolboys. Asajirō declared that he was going to keep watch over the carp until dawn in case there was a raid by weasels, and Shōkichi echoed him. It was arranged that Shigematsu should come early the next morning, and around eleven o'clock, when the carp were just beginning to splash about in the water, he went home.

There was a thick mist, and the upper branches of the *kemponashi* tree in the garden seemed to be melting into the night sky. The shutters at the entrance and along the veranda of the main part of the house were all closed. He cleared his throat loudly two or three times, whereupon one of the shutters on the veranda opened slowly and portentously. Flashing his torch, he saw Shigeko standing there in a night kimono much too short for her.

"Just a moment," she murmured.

He promptly put out the light. She closed the shutter behind her and, crouching down on the edge of the veranda that projected into the garden, whispered in Shigematsu's ear.

"Yasuko may not be asleep yet for all we know. Let's have a quiet talk somewhere outside."

"All right, let's," murmured Shigematsu. "Has anything happened to Yasuko, though? Tell me, quick."

Shigeko stepped down onto the stone step below, slipped on a pair of sandals and, walking stealthily so as to make no noise, led Shigematsu beneath the *kemponashi* tree.

It was only after she had let go that he realized she had led him there by the hand. It was the very first time, even including the days before their marriage and those when his old mother, who had died last year, had still been with them, that the two of them had behaved like this, tiptoeing furtively about the garden like lovers.

The garden was surprisingly light considering how thick the mist was. "Shigematsu," Shigeko began, busily brushing stray hairs back from her forehead as she always did when she was agitated, "I've simply got to tell you what I've heard from Dr. Kajita today. Nobody else must hear about it."

"Alright then, tell me. Nobody can hear."

A while ago, sometime after nine when Yasuko had fallen into a light sleep, Shigeko had slipped out to Dr. Kajita's house and asked him what had happened when he first examined Yasuko. It appeared from what the doctor said that Yasuko had been surreptitiously looking in books on home medicine and trying to treat herself. If this story got about, Shigeko said, people would get the idea that Shigematsu and his wife had neglected to do anything about her radiation sickness until it was really serious, an idea that would be further encouraged by the popular notion that the disease was incurable at any rate. There had been a similar case in one of the neighboring villages only recently. Occasionally, Dr. Kajita had said, a young woman's sense of modesty would work with an extremely stubborn disposition to produce tragic results.

"First of all, she got a temperature," Shigeko whispered, "so she looked it up in the home doctor and took some aspirin. But it didn't go down, so she looked it up again and took Santonin."

"But that's for worms, isn't it?"

"Yes, well then she had diarrhea, and her temperature went down after a few days. But then she got a painful abcess on her buttock. She was too ashamed to go to the doctor, and put some antibiotic ointment on it, thinking it was some nasty disease."

"Come to think of it now, she didn't use the bath for quite a while, did she? She must have been afraid of giving it to other people."

"Well, then the boil burst and she felt a bit better, but her temperature went up and her hair started coming out. Then it dawned on her with a shock that it was radiation sickness, and she ate three or four aloe leaves. It was after that she broke down and told you all about it. All this I heard from Dr. Kajita."

"Now that you mention it, I noticed that the roots of the aloe were sticking up as though someone had been pulling at it. The leaves are supposed to be good for anemia, aren't they? She must have thought it would increase the corpuscles in her blood, poor girl."

"Poor girl, yes—but more than that, it's the sheer silliness of it that gets me. Why ever should she get so complicated about a mere boil? Why couldn't she have told us earlier? I'm perfectly sure she'd no reason to suspect anything more unpleasant. . . ." Her voice failed her, and she drew in a deep breath.

Shigematsu heaved a sigh too. As things were now, there was no help for it but to see that Yasuko got plenty of nourishment and to keep her quiet in order to give luck and the doctor a chance.

The next day there was a heavy shower, and a thunderbolt struck the great pine tree on the site of the old magistrate's office. When the rain cleared, Dr. Kajita from the hospital came to see Yasuko, and it was arranged that he should come to examine her every three days. For the sickroom, the doctor selected a room in the separate wing where Shigematsu's mother had lived. Shigeko was to do the nursing, and they decided, without telling Yasuko, that Shigeko should keep a daily record of the progress of the disease.

Where food was concerned, they would do just as the doctor said and make her eat the same things as Shigematsu, who had a mild case of radiation sickness himself. Yasuko was to lie down when she felt like it, and to go for a walk when she wished—but three meals a day, the doctor said flatly, were absolutely imperative. In the alcove of the sickroom, Shigeko hung a landscape allegedly by the famous painter Chikuden Tanomura. The scroll had been left with them about five months after the end of the war, on the day of the year's first snow, by a textile dealer from Shin-ichi. He had come to Kobatake, apparently at the end of his tether, to try to buy food, and had bartered the scroll with Shigematsu for three *shō* of rice and five devil's tongue roots.

Shigematsu decided to show himself in the sickroom as little as possible, so as not to depress the invalid. He had been the first to fall prey to radiation sickness, but now their positions were reversed; Yasuko's symptoms were far worse by now than his, and it could hardly be pleasant for her to be constantly reminded of it. In fact, Shigeko said, she seemed to be shying away from him—though not, she added, wanting to go back to her parents' home. On the second day after she had moved into the separate wing, Shigematsu, going in to put an early-blooming pink in the vase in the alcove, was shocked to see how rapidly she had weakened. Catching him staring at her, she shut her eyes. In the past few days her color had deteriorated badly; the white, transparent-looking skin of her face was a clear sign of anemia.

Shigeko described each of the symptoms to him in detail, and showed him the record of the disease that she wrote down every night before going to bed. She wrote it not as a professional nurse would, but as an ordinary diary, with occasional descriptions and personal impressions mixed in with it. Even so, they were soon to find that it was well worth the trouble. Shigematsu, at a loss for further ideas on the illness, decided in desperation to go and consult the head of the Hosokawa Clinic, where he himself had been operated on, and to take the record with him as the best account available of the progress of the disease.

"Why don't you send this to ABCC in Hiroshima?" said the doctor after glancing at a page or two. "It seems to me it gives a good picture of a typical group of three—a hospital doctor, an atomic disease patient under his care, and the person doing the nursing. A trio of people, with the victim at the center, all worn out from not knowing what to do. A trio of victims, you might say.... That's clear from this at a glance. The ABCC in Hiroshima keeps records of all data on the victims of the atomic bomb, and from time to time publishes accounts of what is happening to sufferers from radiation sickness."

Shigematsu had not known of the existence of ABCC. Now he learned that an occupation army survey team had come to Hiroshima, together with doctors from Tokyo University, in the autumn of the year the war had ended. As the team went about its duties, it gradually developed into the Atomic Bomb Casualty Commission, an organization set up to carry out studies and gather statistics on the victims of the atomic bomb, and inspired by the highest ideals. Nonetheless, although it investigated the way the disease occurred in the victims, it did nothing to treat them.

Shigematsu was more concerned about Yasuko than about ideals. "The thing is, doctor," he said, changing the subject, "I know how busy you are but—" He said what he had hesitated to say before. "Doctor—if you've any spare time, I wonder if you'd read that diary? If you do I'm sure you'll realize why I'm looking to you for help. You see, as you'll learn from the diary, it's one of our family who's down with radiation sickness."

"You mean, that I should. . . . Radiation sickness?" said the doctor, looking extremely doubtful. "I'm a hemorrhoids doctor, you know. Any kind of piles, I'll treat. But radiation sickness is —well, we can say it's a kind of freak disease. My young brother-in-law had it, and I did everything I could, but it was as good as useless. But I'll have a look at the diary if you like—tonight, if I can. So I'll keep it for the moment."

The doctor having agreed so readily, Shigematsu left with a promise to come back in a few days' time.

The diary covered a period of seven days, beginning on the first day that Dr. Kajita had come from the hospital to see Yasuko. Shigeko had written it in an untidy scrawl, so he copied it out neatly onto ruled paper, altering the style to suit his own taste wherever he felt like it:

DIARY OF THE ILLNESS OF YASUKO TAKAMARU
July 25.   Thundery rain. Festival of the Tenjin Shrine.
    10:30 Attack of violent pain and retching, Yasuko suffers pitifully. The pain subsides after ten minutes or so. Temperature 100°. A little hair falls out.
    About 2:30, heavy rain. Two or three great claps of thunder.
    3.30 p.m. The rain clears and Dr. Kajita comes to see the patient. Temperature 102°.
    The abcess on the buttock has broken, he says, and another has formed somewhere else. I do not watch, for Yasuko's sake. Finally, he says he has finished and it's all right now. I place a wash basin and hot and cold water on the veranda outside, and go in.
    As soon as he goes out on the veranda, Yasuko covers her face with a towel. "That thunder a while back was enough to make one jump wasn't it?" says the doctor, and gives a laugh, then he takes Yasuko's pulse again and says to himself: "Better inject. . . . a hundred thousand units of penicillin." He gives the injection with a practiced hand.
    I see the doctor to the gate and am told: "She seems more listless than yesterday. It's the effect of the fever, I imagine."

For supper, stewed dace, egg, tangle, shallots, one bowl of rice, tomatoes. The doctor said before he would come every three days, but after talking with my husband and with Yasuko, I go to Dr. Kajita's house to ask him to come every day. He agrees.

The patient goes to bed at eight.

July 26. Fine. A cool breeze.

In the morning a temperature of 100°, feels chilly. Bean paste soup, dried seaweed, shallots, pickles, egg, half a bowl of rice.

Noon, 97°. No appetite, so just tomato and lettuce for lunch.

3 p.m. Dr. Kajita comes. He says, "Let's check the stool just to be on the safe side, shall we?" and Yasuko very reluctantly agrees. The second abcess has burst and a third formed. He treats it. He gives us ointment and powders.

Supper: Soup, fish sausage, dried mackerel, cucumber salad, two bowls of rice.

She is reading Sōun Yada's *Life of Hideyoshi.* Bed around nine-thirty.

July 27. Great rain clouds.

Morning, 99°. Feeling better. For breakfast, bean paste soup with eggplant, french beans, egg, two bowls of rice.

Smiles for the first time in ages.

Reading Sōun Yada's *Life of Hideyoshi,* which she started yesterday.

Noon, 99°. Pickled cucumber, burdock root cooked in oil with soy, stewed dace, omelet, one bowl of rice.

A letter from a friend who used to work with her in Furuichi; writes a long reply and goes to post it herself.

Lies down until around three when Dr. Kajita comes.

Temperature normal, 98.6°. No sign of hookworm or round-worm, stethoscopy normal, the doctor says.

After treating the abcess the doctor is just leaving when he says: "I had a call from my home in Ishimi this morning to say that my father has had a stroke, so I'm leaving early tomorrow morning. Dr. Moriya has agreed to take over from me, so please don't worry." Cannot help feeling rather taken aback. Recall a long-standing rumor that Dr. Moriya used get to along badly with Dr. Kajita.

"But surely, doctor, you won't be going back to Ishimi for good, will you?" I say.

"Oh no, I shan't do that. They say the stroke was a light one. Well, look after the invalid."

"Oh dear, Doctor, I can't help feeling let down somehow. . . ."

Just then, my husband comes back from the fish pond and we both see the doctor to the top of the hill. He sails off down the hill on his motorcycle and out of sight.

Evening, 99.5°. New shallots pickled in brine, lettuce, stewed dace, meat croquettes, two bowls of rice, tomato.

The evening is hot and sticky, so we all, Yasuko included, put out benches on the stumps of the *kemponashi* trees and enjoy the cool outside air. We help ourselves to salted soybeans and chat of this and that.

Old Takizō from Shōkichi's place, who is eighty-nine, brings three eels for Yasuko; the day after tomorrow, he says, is the fiercest of the dog days, when everyone is supposed to eat eels to keep his strength up. We sit with him on the benches and indulge in idle conversation. He is tactful and avoids all talk of sickness. Instead, he recalls old local traditions and tells various fantastic tales. He talks very solemnly and importantly, and Yasuko laughs a great deal. The old man remains perfectly serious, which makes it doubly funny.

"Long ago," he says, "when my grandfather was only a lad, they were there on a bench, sitting under that very *kemponashi* tree, when what should happen but along comes a wily old badger to eat the scraps the human beings had dropped, and pokes his face out at them from under the seat. Ah, those were the days, all right."

"Long, long ago," he says, "when my grandfather was but a lad, there was a man called Yoichi over at Ogata in Kobatake, and he was very good to his parents. In fact, he was known in all the neighboring villages for his filial piety, and travelers knew of him too, and even the adders that bite human beings had heard of him, and had a proper respect for him. Those adders were particularly fond of biting travelers, so it came about that when a traveler saw an adder he would say 'My name is Yoichi of Ogata!' 'I'm Yoichi of Ogata!' he would say, and by the time he'd recited it three times the adder would bow its head and slither off smartly out of the way. So they all lived safely ever after!"

"When my old grandfather was just a lad, long long ago," he says, "a huntsman caught a deer, and was on his way home when a monk-wolf started following him, slinking along after him in its wolf shape. When the hunter turned round to look behind him, it leapt and sank its fangs in him. But the hunter was too smart for it. He had some salt hidden in a bag he carried on him, and you know how unclean spirits detest salt. So he sprinkled the salt about him, and thanks to that, he arrived home safe and sound after all. Ah, those were the days, those were. . . ."

July 28. Fine and sunny. A shower around noon, then sunny again.

As soon as he gets up, my husband goes to Dr. Kajita's home to pay for the medicine and take a parting gift. When he comes back, he says it looks as though the doctor has decided not to return to Kobatake any more. I suspected as much at once, from Shigematsu's pale face and the heavy way he was breathing.

The patient feels well, her temperature 98.6°. For breakfast, bean paste soup with taro in it, shallots, egg, pickles, and two bowls of rice.

The third abcess breaks. She applies ointment herself.

All three of us discuss which doctor she should go to, but reach no conclusion. At his wits' end, my husband even produces, amongst other things, a book on divination, but gets no further than turning the pages. We decide in the end to let Yasuko herself choose, and after lunch she says she feels well and her temperature is normal, so she goes off to find a doctor.

I want to go with her, but do not insist when she says she doesn't need to be accompanied everywhere she goes.

My husband leaves to see to the fish pond under the bank. I envy the way he can go off so cheerfully. The first mating of the carp was a failure, he said. The second time they succeeded, using the males and females they'd kept in reserve.

I fillet one of the eels and broil it plain.

Before that, I put Yasuko's quilts out to air.

About four o'clock, the old man from the general store comes hurrying over to our house.

"We've just had a telephone call from the young lady," he says. "She asked us to give you a message. She's decided it would be best to go into a hospital, the Kuishiki Hospital in the next village. But there's nothing particularly serious, and you're not to worry, she said."

"Are you sure it was her?"

"It was Miss Yasuko."

A bolt from the blue that leaves me stunned. I pull myself together and send a telegram to her parents asking for someone to go to the hospital right away. Then I go to the fish pond under the bank to tell my husband. He goes straight off to the Kuishiki Hospital.

At dusk, the old man from the general store comes running over once more.

"Telephone from your husband. He's talked it over with Yasuko's father, and they've decided to let her stay in the hospital as she wants. He said to tell you he might be late this evening."

"How is she?"

"He didn't say. Oh, but I'm sure she's all right."

I remember now that this morning my heart started pounding strangely, as though something dreadful was going to happen.

July 29. Fine.

My husband got back late last night. The diagnosis at the Kuishiki Hospital was rather different from Dr. Kajita's. The fever, they say, is due to the abcesses. The abcesses are not due to a single germ, but to a combined infection by a mixture of different germs. In short, they have diagnosed other complications on top of a mild case of radiation sickness, and gave her a tuberculin injection.

This morning on my way to the hospital, I drop in at the general store to thank them for coming over last night. The old man remarks that he saw Yasuko coming out of the Kuroda Clinic yesterday afternoon. At this, Mrs. Yoshimura, who happens to be in the shop at the time, says, "Now you mention it, I saw her too. Had a yellow parasol, didn't she? I saw her going into the Ōmura Clinic."

The only girl in the village with a yellow parasol is Yasuko. Mrs. Yoshimura saw the parasol about half-past two, and the general store man saw her around one. She must have gone to the Kuroda Clinic first, then to the Ōmura Clinic, and then to Kuishiki Hospital. It's true what they say—that sickness makes the mind lose its bearings. One drifts this way and that from moment to moment, doubting and fretting, clutching at one straw after another, any straw. . . .

The Kuishiki Hospital is built of mortar on a wooden frame so that it looks like a Western-style building, and the room, though rather cramped, is light and well ventilated. The bed is half screened by a curtain. As soon as she sees me, Yasuko starts weeping. She doesn't sit up. "I'm sorry to be so selfish," she says, and buries her face in the pillow. I make no comment, just talk about the broiled eel I've brought, then go on to give her what little information I've picked up about the rearing of carp. I might have saved my breath for all it does to bring her out of herself.

About ten o'clock the director of the hospital comes on his round. Tuberculin reaction negative, temperature 100°. I go out until he has finished attending to the abcess. I stand watching the carp in the ornamental pool for a while, then go back. I meet Dr. Kuishiki in the corridor and stop talking to him for a while.

He tells me that in the middle of last night a nurse on her

rounds found Yasuko kneeling on the wooden floor, leaning against the bed and sobbing. Asked what was the matter, she said the place where the abcesses were itched so badly she couldn't endure it. The nurse told her to lift her night kimono and, peering with her torch, saw a wriggling mass of seat worms. A type of small worm that lives as a parasite in the human body, they crawl out of the anus during the night to lay their eggs. It seems likely that they had laid their eggs in the putrefying tissue of the abcess. Anyway, the doctor would like to take a piece of the tissue for examination under the microscope, then perform surgery to remove it completely. Just now, he has found another abcess developing right beside the anus.

"If you remove the bad tissue as you say, what will happen to the place afterwards?"

"The flesh will gradually fill in."

"There'll be some scarring of the skin, won't there? Won't it be little hard on her?"

"Well, now," he replies, "I suppose there might be a certain tendency for that to happen. . . ." The doctor is about fifty years old.

Yasuko seems tired, and the lunch bell rings, so I take it as a signal to leave.

I pass them bringing lunch in the corridor: dried mackerel, french beans in sesame oil, egg, pickles, a round lacquered container holding the rice.

July 30. Fine.

In the afternoon my husband goes to the Kuishiki Hospital.

Yasuko's temperature was 98.6°, he tells me when he gets back. She had violent pains in the night. She had a sulfadiazine tablet at noon today, and is to have more every four-and-a-half hours. When he cut up a peach he had brought and gave it to her, she tried to bite it with her side teeth instead of the front ones. He asked why, and she said that two of her front teeth were getting rather loose, and seemed to move when she ran her tongue round them.

Telling the doctor that Yasuko complained of lack of appetite, my husband was informed that whatever she ate or didn't eat, she must at least take the sulfadiazine regularly at the prescribed time, as the most urgent thing of all was to put a stop to the abcesses. New ones are forming and old ones breaking all the time. I wonder what it can really be? "Whatever can it all mean?" I say to my husband. "I don't know," he says, "but there doesn't seem to be *anything* right with her, what with her teeth loose, and pain in the buttocks, and a temperature, and violent pains every day."

A sudden, squally wind this afternoon. The wife of the man at the watermill drops in saying she happened to be passing and wondered if we'd been all right in the wind. Then she starts talking about the atomic disease. She tells me what happened at Dr. Hosokawa's place in Yuda village. The doctor's younger brother, himself a doctor of medicine, was at the army hospital in Hiroshima when the bomb fell. He got maggots in the places where his cheeks and ear-lobes had festered from the burns, and they ate away the lobe of his right ear. His hand was so terribly burned that the fingers coagulated and it looked like one big palm without fingers. His body wasted away to skin and bone. Even with three or four thick quilts under him he still complained that the hardness of the tatami made him ache unbearably. Once he even stopped breathing, and seemed to be dead. But Dr. Hosokawa went on looking after him, and in the end restored his health remarkably.

No sooner has the woman from the water mill gone than Yasuko's father arrives. He's thinking of paying all Yasuko's medical expenses out of her marriage portion, he says. My husband looks outraged but says nothing, sitting with folded arms, gazing at the floor. One might call him taken aback.

CHAPTER 17 🍂

Shigeko had begun to suffer dizzy spells from the strain of tending to Yasuko, so a nurse was hired to stay with her, and it was arranged that Shigematsu should go to see her on the odd days of the month; on the even days, Yasuko's father was to go. Shigeko, it was found, had strained her heart.

The middle of August brought a spell of weather unusually hot for the upland area where Kobatake lay, and it became obvious, even to the ordinary onlooker, that Yasuko's condition was becoming almost hopeless. She complained of ringing in the ears, she had no appetite, a lot of hair fell out whenever she combed it, and the puffy red patches on her gums became more pronounced. Dr. Kuishiki diagnosed a probable case of peridontitis. He tested her Mantoux reaction, took blood samples, and gave her another day's supply of sulfadiazine. The tablets were similar to those she had had on her second day in hospital, and she was to take one every four-and-a-half hours.

"Do I really have to take this medicine again?" she asked, looking doubtful. "Yes, you must," Shigematsu said.

The nurse told them that the patient invariably had an attack of violent pain once a day. During these attacks, she suffered unbearably, writhing and tossing in agony, her whole body filled with pain. They came chiefly late at night.

She grew pitifully emaciated; her dry, flaky lips were the same color as her skin, and her nails a dull, muddy color.

One day, Shigematsu asked to see inside her mouth. He found then for the first time that her upper front teeth were missing, although the roots were still there. Until a few days previously, the looseness had affected the whole tooth, root and all, yet now they had broken clean off at the base, above the root. Her gums were swollen and constantly stained with fresh blood. Rinsing the mouth with a solution of boric acid was not enough to stop the bleeding. If she kept her mouth closed for a while, a thin thread of red would gradually form along the line where her lips met.

Two new abcesses had formed on her buttocks, and being close to each other were beginning to spread and run together like creeping plants in a garden. The old ones had all been excised, but the places would not heal. The flesh remained red and puffed up like a split water melon. The skin around them was a dark, bluish-green, putrid color. Shigematsu, of course, did not see this himself, but the nurse, who came with him to the bottom of the stairs as he was leaving, told him.

Wherever he turned, no ray of hope offered itself. Running into the hospital director, he began to question him, but could get no straightforward answers.

"The sedimentation rate is not good, I must admit," said the doctor. "There's something up with the blood. There are a lot of unidentifiable shadows on the slide, and the red corpuscles are less than half what they should be."

This was tantamount to saying that he had thrown in the sponge. The "unidentifiable shadows," he said, might possibly be abnormally shaped white corpuscles, but if they were, then there were far too many of them. Abruptly, Shigematsu's mind revolted against all these vaguely menacing medical terms that only aggravated the sense of guilt he felt towards Yasuko. The cause of her radiation sickness was almost certainly not only the black rain, but also the way they had wandered through the still-hot ashes of the ruined city. He remembered, too, how she had grazed her left elbow on the way from Aioi Bridge to Sakan-chō, when they had crawled beneath the dangling power wires. That graze could hardly have failed to offer an opening to the deadly radioactive ash. He had been wrong—though recriminations were pointless at this stage—to drag them all the way from the Japan Transport branch at Ujina to the works at Furuichi. If he had only asked Mr. Sugimura, the branch manager, he would surely have put Yasuko up for two or three days. Shigematsu felt very much to blame on this score. And it was he, he could not forget, who had brought Yasuko to Hiroshima in the first place.

One day, a letter with an enclosure came from the Hosokawa Clinic in Yuda village. Dr. Hosokawa was an elderly man, and the letter had an old-fashioned formality:

My Dear Sir:

May I thank you once again for the gift of dried sweetfish which you were so kind as to bring us on your recent visit? Since that time, I have given the most careful consideration to the matter you mentioned, and am writing now to present you with my conclusions.

I should state first of all that my brother-in-law's recovery was due to the most remarkable good fortune. The whole sum of my "treatment" was a few injections of Ringer's solution together with blood transfusions. For the rest, I stood by with folded arms, as it were, helpless to do anything but watch. In the hope that you will appreciate this fact, I have had my brother-in-law send me the notes which he made on his experiences, and am sending them to you under separate cover. One of my reasons for doing this is to escape the charge, as a doctor, of having refused to treat a patient. Another is the hope that you will perceive how essential for the patient is the determination to fight his sickness. It also shows, I might add, that one should never despair of a miraculous recovery even in the most gravely ill.

I should be grateful if, after perusal, you could return the manuscript to me. And may I offer my earnest prayers for the patient's comfort and well being?

The account was entitled "Notes on the Bombing of Hiroshima, by Hiroshi Iwatake, Medical Reserve." Quite probably Dr. Hosokawa, not knowing what to do in the face of Shigematsu's request for the impossible, had telephoned Tokyo especially to ask Iwatake to send it.

Shigematsu read it seated by Shigeko's bedside, exclaiming "A miracle," "Yes, a miracle" over and over again as his reading progressed. "We must let Yasuko read it too," said Shigeko. It was all there, just as the woman from the water mill had said. Iwatake had been far more seriously hurt than Shigematsu. His body had shrunk to a mass of skin and bones, his fingers had fused together, and maggots had eaten away one of his earlobes. Yet he had come through. Plastic surgery had even restored his fingers to normal. Today, he was working as a general practitioner at a place called Suzaki-chō in Mukōjima, Tokyo.

The notes began in the following fashion:

My draft card, summoning me to the Second Hiroshima Unit barracks, arrived on July 1, 1945. I hastily set my affairs in order and boarded a westbound train from Tokyo. Nagoya and Osaka were badly damaged by the raids. At Okayama, the station as we went through was still burning from a raid the night before. It had begun to drizzle, and I saw a group of bombed-out people walking along beside the tracks half-naked, holding cushions over their heads to keep off the rain.

I got off at Fukuyama and went to see my wife and children, who had been evacuated to Yuda village out of the way of the raids, and changed into the regulation garb for the new recruit. I went to the barber's and got him to take off my mustache and shave my head. Then I donned a field service cap and puttees, shouldered my rucksack, and boarded a Fukuen Line train, my wife and brother-in-law coming to the station to see me off. The age limit for the latest draft is said to be forty-five. I was a C-grade recruit called to the colors on the verge of my forty-fifth birthday. I could not bring myself to follow the usual custom and have my photograph taken in case I got killed in battle.

I stayed the night with relatives in Hiroshima. At eight a.m. on August 1, I passed through the portals of a military barracks for the first time in my life. I was one of over fifty recruits who assembled in the yard outside the barracks' medical office. Everybody was from Hiroshima Prefecture or Okayama Prefecture. They say that people like us from Yamaguchi Prefecture went into the Yamaguchi regiment, while the doctors from Shimane Prefecture went into the Hamada regiment. We were told we should be sent, first of all, not to the army medical training center but to an infantry unit. We were kept waiting for more than an hour in the yard under the blazing sun, then were sent to sit in a wooden-floored room about 25 feet square. Eventually a Lieutenant-Colonel Washio, commander of the First Army Hospital, a great brute of a man fully six feet tall, came in with two other army doctors and took his place in front of us. A quick muster was called, then without preliminary he launched into a violent harangue.

"I'm Lieutenant-Colonel Washio," he said. "What d'you think you're up to, hanging back without volunteering at a time like this, when the nation's fighting for its very life? You're little better than a pack of traitors, if you ask me. That's why the authorities have rounded you up, every man-jack of you, just to let you know what's what! From now on, your lives are in *my* hands. So far, you've had it pretty soft, and I expect you've got yourselves into some pretty cushy positions. But nothing you know will get you anywhere in the army. As far as we're concerned, your heads are stuffed with a lot of crap, and you've got about as much of the proper military spirit as a flea's turd. From now on, the emphasis is going to be on instilling the right military outlook into you, so you'd better keep that in mind!"

Next, each one of us was made to stand out before the lieutenant-colonel, report his name and past career, and submit to cross-questioning as to why he hadn't volunteered for the reserve. As proof that I had in fact volunteered, I produced a document out of my rucksack which I had already sent to the First Division and the Hiroshima Regimental District in January last year. This had the effect of cutting the questioning rather short. And in fact, those who came before me, and after me too, had all sent in their applications. Many had actually been drafted both this year and the year before, but had been sent home again on the same day because of physical defects.

Sure enough, when the physical check-up began, there was scarcely one whose physique anyone would have envied. There was one man who'd brought a corset with him because of spinal tuberculosis, another who wore a bandage round his neck for inflammation of the cervical glands, another who had a hollow where he had been operated on for caries of the ribs, and another with one leg that would not bend properly at the knee because he had broken it at a sports meet in his school days. Lieutenant-Colonel Washio, new to the command, had not been told the facts by his colleagues—or possibly the documents showing who had volunteered and who had not had been lost. Either way, his blustering began to seem peculiarly pointless, and he was just beginning to look a trifle foolish when one doctor from Hiroshima City was rash enough to smile mockingly and give a great yawn. The commander walked straight up to him and hit him full across the face with his open palm, then, as he reeled from the blow, swept his hand back to hit the other cheek. This was repeated two or three times. The brutality of the action gave me a depressing presentiment of what was in store for us.

As a result of the X-rays and sputum tests, a number of the new recruits were sent home the same day. Others were sent back because their absence would have left their hospitals without a doctor. I envied them as they shouldered their rucksacks and went off with pious expressions on their faces, barely able to restrain their glee. . . .

In due course, Iwatake was posted to an infantry unit, where for fifteen days he received basic infantry training. The main aim seemed to be to master the technique of throwing themselves, holding bombs, in front of enemy tank units in the event of an enemy invasion of Japan proper. Dozens of times a day, they practiced charging dummy tanks made of wood, flinging beneath them bomb-shaped pieces of timber attached to ropes, then throwing themselves flat as rapidly as possible. He discovered later, after he had been posted to the training center, that it was planned to post the "punitive draft" unit to the coastal defense forces, where each would be considered to have done his duty if he disposed of one enemy tank at the cost of his own life.

On July 14, an order came for them to transfer from the infantry unit to the Second Army Hospital training center, and they moved to a two-story barracks beside the Ōta River in Hiroshima. They found about eighty recruits from the Yamaguchi and Hamada groups already arrived there, so that in all they totaled more than one hundred and thirty men.

Lieutenant Yoshikawa, the education officer, was only twenty-three, an army doctor who had done an abbreviated course at Pyongyang Medical College. In content if not in manner, his address was still more virulent than Lieutenant-Colonel Washio's.

"These barracks are well known," he said. " 'The Devil's Barracks,' they call them. Now you're coming in here, you'll have to change your thinking. Soft stuff with the likes of you, and you begin to get above yourselves. We've got orders from above to put you through the hoop, so you'd better be ready for it. In the first place, you (the next fifty words or so were omitted)." The people who gave such addresses referred to them as "pep-talks," but the only effect in practice was to plunge their hearers into the heaviest gloom.

When this talk was over, they were summoned to the unit commander's office, three at a time, and questioned about their families and family finances, doubtless for later reference in deciding which men to post to dangerous areas.

The next day, the really intensive training began. "It was more like a forced labor camp than a training unit," Iwatake wrote. "Often in the mornings, partly for the fun of it, they would give us what they called an 'emergency call,' which meant running two or three miles through the morning mist at the crack of dawn. We went through the Gokoku Shrine, over Aioi Bridge, then around behind the Honganji branch temple to the north, past Aioi Bridge again to the Nigitsu Shrine, and so back to barracks. It goes without saying that a lot dropped out on the way. The number of men with persistent slight fever or diarrhea increased, and some had to report sick. The thing that really soaked your uniform with sweat, so that you could almost wring it out, was the crawling course. If you stuck up too much at the rear you got a heavy boot on your backside; if your rifle was pointing too low you got jabbed in the shoulder with a parade sword. Your elbows got scraped till the blood began to run. There was one reserve man called Nakamura who had a maternity home back in Tokuyama. A middle-aged man weighing 190 pounds, with a big protruding belly, suffering from an enlarged heart, he had been sent straight back home the year before, but taken into the army this year. To work his way forward on his belly holding a rifle in his hand was more than he could manage, and Lieutenant Yoshikawa kicked him several times in the backside as he lay squirming, far to the rear of all the others. Nakamura shed tears of mortification; he even considered killing himself, he declared later." It was as though a man were to be kicked by his own offspring, somehow transformed into an unmanageable ruffian. As Iwatake himself put it, "His face displayed unconcealed perplexity and disappointment, like a father being bullied by his own son."

There was an air raid warning about six-thirty on the morning of August 6, and two or three B-29's came and flew off to the south again without dropping a single bomb. They saw nothing unusual in this; it had often happened before. The warning was lifted at something past seven, then at 7:50, while an alert was still in force, the whole unit—commander, doctors, sanitation orderlies, and reserves—fell in in the yard, bowed towards the east, where the Imperial Palace lay, and listened to a ceremonial reading of the Imperial Rescript to the Army to mark the anniversary of its promulgation.

The senior medical officers and medical orderlies were in the front rank, next came the medical reserves drafted from Yamaguchi and Shimane prefectures, in their best uniforms, then, at the very rear, the medical reserves from Hiroshima, whose uniforms were the poorest. The army had not given those responsible sufficient warning before the Hiroshima people had arrived, and they were still in what were little better than fatigues, with no stars on their collars or other trimmings.

The ceremony over, the second-in-command began his address, but it was now that a B-29 dropped the atomic bomb. What follows is Iwatake's own account of what happened.

The ceremony was over in about twenty minutes. It happened just before we were to be dismissed, as we were getting a talking-to from the second-in-command for not being snappy enough in following the required procedure during an air raid. There came the familiar drone of a B-29. It came from the south, and when it seemed to be directly above I involuntarily glanced up at the sky. For a moment, I had a glimpse of something that looked like a captive balloon drifting lazily downwards in the sky beyond the barracks roof. The next moment, there was a white flash like lightning, or the light from a great mass of magnesium ignited all at once. I felt a wave of searing heat. At the same time, there was a terrifying roar, and that was all I knew. What happened after that, or how much time passed, I do not know. Struck down by the blast, I may actually have lost consciousness.

Someone else stirring and planting an army boot on my neck and head in the effort to get up, restored me to consciousness. I was somewhere pitch dark, wedged tight beneath a piece of timber. Gradually recovering my senses in that small space where it was impossible to move, I found I could make out a source of dim light in the darkness and, exerting all my strength, started to crawl towards it. I realized that I was beneath a wooden roof minus all its tiles.

It seemed to me to take a considerable time, but eventually I found myself standing on open ground. Looking back now, I believe I was in the space between the general affairs office and the kitchens. Even allowing for the distance I had crawled, I must have been blown quite a long way. The two-story buildings of the infirmary and the education unit no longer rose against the sky. Everything had been flattened and scattered in disorder. All about was silence, with no sign of life anywhere. It was dark, as though dusk was drawing in, and black smoke was rising from the direction of the kitchens and the infirmary.

The right half of my uniform was smoldering and smoking, and the wallet that had been in my right breast pocket, the watch on my left wrist, and my spectacles had all vanished. After a while I succeeded in rubbing out the fire in my uniform. The skin on the back of my right hand had peeled off and hung down a grayish-white color, and the raw flesh beneath was coated with black soil. My whole face felt on fire, and the back and fingers of my left hand, though not skinned, had turned white as though cauterized. Below the waist I felt no pain even when I walked, but my back must have been hit by a piece of timber or something, for it hurt excessively. For want of something better to do, I made my way to the wash-place, where the pillars were still standing. I tried turning a tap and, to my surprise, water came out. I first washed the dirt off the back of my hand, then bound it with a loincloth that someone had left behind in the drying room. I am very shortsighted. Without my spectacles, everything seems dim, and distant objects are indistinct.

There was nobody about. Getting my bearings from the position of the washplace, I succeeded in reaching the bank of the Ōta River. Here I found two or three soldiers I knew by sight, and another lying half-naked on the ground.

A pile of blankets, taken out of the barracks at the time of the air raid, was lying in the open, so I helped myself to one and flopped down on it on the ground. Tension temporarily left me, and I felt empty and exhausted. Our number increased to five or six, but none of us could give any convincing account of what had happened. The only feeling was one of shock in the face of the result. The destructive power was fantastic. I had thought at first that the barracks had been destroyed by a near miss, but as I calmed down I realized that this was not so, for the houses on the opposite bank had also gone.

Red flames rising from the direction of Mitaki Bridge and around the Honganji branch temple on the opposite bank showed where fires had started. It might be that both explosive and incendiary bombs had been dropped at the same time, but it was almost unthinkable that this could have happened when there was no air raid warning in force. Three or four of my fellow reserves turned up, Miyoshi and Itō among them. All were men who had been with me in the rear rank. All of them seemed to be past speech. Many of those who had been in the front ranks must have been still trapped under the buildings, but it was hopeless to think of getting them out from under ruins from which the flames were already rising, when one was injured oneself, and with no implements save one's bare hands.

Miyoshi and Itō somehow agreed that it was dangerous where we were, and that we should take refuge at the Mitaki branch hospital. I decided I would go along with the rest. I knew from experience that the flames from a fire tended to sweep over the surface of rivers. On the night of March 9 in Tokyo, when the Asakusa, Honjo, Mukōjima and other districts bordering the Sumida River were burned in the raids, the whole area had become a sea of flames, and I myself saw people who had been burned to death as they floated in the water.

We started to move upstream. Every road worthy of the name was blocked by fallen buildings, and for a while we were obliged to follow a path trodden out along the river bank. Several times I tripped on holes in the ground, and finally lost one of my shoes. I looked for it, but in vain, and Itō called out to me not to lag behind. I seemed to hear someone groaning in a patch of briars nearby, but I was fleeing in a kind of daze, and was incapable of doing anything to save him. The fires were closing in. My face was gradually swelling up, and the pain growing steadily worse. I had difficulty in walking. I reproached myself as a doctor for leaving another human being to his fate, but the situation was too desperate to leave room for anything but flight.

I do not know what time it was, but to make our way past the Nigitsu Shrine and reach the river bank again must have taken at least two hours. Around the time that we arrived, a weak sun was trying to break through the cloudy sky. From what I learned later, I imagine it was then that the dark mushroom cloud was at last beginning to disperse. . . .

The barracks where Iwatake was stationed were close to the center of the explosion, which suggests that his flight kept him on a course where he was in a position to see the mushroom cloud from directly underneath. This would explain his reference to a "cloudy sky." It is extraordinary that he should have got to safety with such serious burns and then lived on to tell the tale. He was one of the only three survivors from among the more than one hundred and thirty men in the unit.

When he got to the road by the side of the Nigitsu Shrine with his two colleagues, someone told them not to go any farther because of the danger of explosions near the Heavy Artillery headquarters, and they were instructed to ford the river to the center shoals. So they put the blankets on their heads to keep them dry, and waded up to their chests in the water as far as the dry sand at the center of the river. At this point, they noticed flames gleaming amidst the smoke billowing up towards Mitaki. Mitaki had had it too, it seemed. So they changed their plans and went ashore on the bank farther upstream. By now, Iwatake felt neither hunger nor pain; all he wanted was a place where he could lie down and be left undisturbed.

Numbers of army trucks were driving hurriedly in the direction of the city. The driver of one, seeing them lying out flat, shouted to them as he passed:

"Hey there! You soldiers? There's a place called Hesaka on the north side of this hill. They're getting a reception center ready there, so keep going. They say there's plenty of medical supplies there. Just over on the north side of this hill."

"Hesaka, Hesaka," the three of them repeated to each other, and started off to the north. Iwatake, with his one bare foot, followed limping in the others' wake. They had been told it was just over the hill, but it seemed an awfully long way. In fact, it was about six miles. The road there, with its procession of frantically fleeing wounded, was a gruesome sight.

At Hesaka, the National Elementary School had been taken over as a reception center to accommodate the injured; there was no medical relief center as such. There were just two single-story school buildings, with two tents erected as emergency accommodation in the tiny playground. Both buildings and tents were besieged by the injured, who stood awaiting their turn in long lines even though the sun was already setting. In the corridors were people lying groaning on the floor where they had collapsed, and others who lay with pieces of cloth over their faces, having struggled all the way there only to breathe their last. Parents were calling the names of their children, and children were calling for their mothers. The only people giving treatment were some applying mercurochrome and others applying a mixture of flour and oil as a substitute dressing for burns. There seemed to be nothing to make bandages with, and no medicine for injections.

Iwatake's face swelled up more and more until it was as round as a watermelon and his eyes closed up almost completely. Miyoshi had a great blister on his cheek and all the skin off his hands. Itō had a burn on his cheek and a lump on his forehead caused by a blow. Miyoshi was a doctor of medicine, a specialist in obstetrics. He always carried a photograph of his baby daughter concealed in an inside pocket. Itō was a general practitioner in the town of Miyoshi, and an expert on pharmacology.

Iwatake and his two companions got themselves painted with

mercurochrome, then, finding a vacant space in the corridor near the entrance, wrapped themselves up in the blankets they had brought and spent the night there. Perhaps because they were too agitated, they experienced no hunger, although they had had nothing to eat or drink since breakfast. They did feel thirsty, but refrained from drinking any water for fear of contagious diseases. None of them spoke much, no longer having the energy for it.

The next day, soldiers and civilians were sorted out and the soldiers installed in the classrooms of the school buildings. Iwatake's face was swollen up to about twice its normal size, and he could not see unless he pried open his eyelids with his finger, so he was put on a stretcher and carried to the classroom at the east end of the building, where the seriously injured were accommodated. He never saw Miyoshi again. He was also separated from Itō, but discovered later that the latter was shortly afterwards reunited with his wife, whose loving care saved his life. He is alive and well today, practicing medicine in Miyoshi.

The following is Iwatake's own account of conditions that day:

There was nobody else from the medical reserve in the classroom into which I was taken, all the other patients being ordinary soldiers, all of them young men and seriously injured. I had an unbearable thirst. My bones felt as though there was no connection between them. I was intensely cold, and developed a fever. It must have been over 104°. My eyelids were so swollen that I could not see, and to lie still was the only thing I could do. On August 7, I was given one bowl of gruel. I passed water only once in two days.

I was not supposed to drink water, but in the end I could not hold out any longer, and, opening one eye with my fingers, stole out to the artesian well and drank. The water tasted metallic, but it gave me a new lease of life. The number of tents in the school playground had increased to six, but they were still overflowing with patients. The bodies were laid out in a heap at one end of the sports ground. With nightfall, the moans became still more anguished. One patient with brain fever leapt out of the window without warning and started walking through the paddy fields outside. In the course of the night, nearly one-third of the men in our room quieted down. As each corpse grew cold, it was unobtrusively carried away on a stretcher.

I cheered myself up by telling myself that I should never die from the degree of burning that I had suffered. Yet I was still baffled by the question of what could have produced so many casualties all at once. A nurse came round taking the name, rank, unit and home address of each patient and noting it in a book. I asked her to let my family know that I was in the Hesaka reception center, but she refused. There was no sign of any military doctor coming to examine us. . . .

CHAPTER 18 🐦

On the morning of August 8, there was a sudden announcement. The number of patients had become too great for the temporary reception center to handle, and some were to be transferred to the army branch hospital at Shōbara, to the north in the same district. Any man, therefore, who felt himself capable of going on a train unaided was to speak up.

The number of new bomb victims being brought in was, indeed, far greater than the number removed by death. No sooner was a corpse got out of the way than more injured arrived to take its place. The classrooms and the tents on the school playground were all jammed tight. Even the storerooms and woodsheds of the neighboring farms were full, and victims were lying outside in the gardens. The national elementary schools in towns and villages in the Hiroshima area had all been converted into emergency centers in the same way as the Hesaka school, and all, it seemed, were full to overflowing. It was necessary therefore to disperse the victims more widely and to more distant areas. Otherwise, there would not be enough doctors to go round, and a certain percentage of patients would have to be left out in the open air.

"Attention! Urgent announcement!" repeated the voice of a sanitation orderly. "Did you all get it? Those who want to go to the Shōbara center are to let us know. Any who can manage to get to Shōbara by train without help, raise your hands. It's three hours from Hesaka to Shōbara by train."

"Is there anybody who wants to go to Shōbara?" came the milder, feminine tones of a member of the Women's Defense Association. "Those of you who feel up to going by train, please raise your hands. It takes three hours from Hesaka to Shōbara by train."

At the mention of Shōbara, Iwatake, who was lying on his back, opened his eyelids with his fingers and looked at the ceiling. He could distinguish the grain of the wooden boards quite clearly. It gave him the feeling that he could manage the walk to the station at Hesaka. So he shut his eye again, summoned up all his energy, and raised a hand. He could not get much strength into his arm, and the hand dangled limply from the wrist.

The other patients seemed to be in two minds. "I'd like to, but can't," Iwatake heard one soldier call, though he could not see what kind of man he was or what his injuries were, "stop your kidding, will you?" "Those who want to, let 'em go!" muttered another, equally unidentifiable soldier almost defiantly. "I'm going!" bellowed yet another.

Iwatake determined to stay alive long enough to get to Shōbara at least. Even if the worst happened in the end, he had no fancy for breathing his last on the train. For one thing, Shōbara was his home, the place where he had been born. Moreover, the commander of the Hiroshima First Army Branch Hospital at Shōbara was Dr. Fujitaka Shigeaki, who was from the same village as himself, had graduated before him from the same university, and had been drafted into the army as a medical officer. As a doctor, he was strict but kind. Dr. Fujitaka, Iwatake told himself, would at least put some oil on his burns for him. It was a heaven-sent opportunity. It was such a remarkable piece of luck, in fact, that he would have raised both hands if only he could. As it was, his raised right hand soon got so tired that he had to change to the left.

"Alright! lower your hand!" came a voice close by. 'I'll issue a confirmation tag." Iwatake lowered his arm and, prying open the lids of one eye, perceived a sanitation corporal, who came and attached a luggage label to the belt of his military uniform. Iwatake half raised himself to a sitting position, and discovered that he was labeled "For Shōbara," in black ink.

"When do we leave?" he asked the orderly.

"As soon as we've made sure of the number. We'll be assembling in the school yard before long."

Lunchtime came, and a kind of cross between gruel and dumpling soup appeared, but Iwatake had no appetite. All he could get down was a cup of tea. It must be the fever, he told himself.

The order to assemble came at three in the afternoon. They gathered in the school yard, their nostrils assailed by the smell from the piles of bodies there, then set off walking in single file, a good six hundred of them, along the paths between the paddy fields leading in the direction of the station. Iwatake held open the lids of his eyes, first the right, then the left, as he walked. None of the party was in anything like presentable shape. It was a sad, shambling procession of ghosts.

As they went up the hill leading to the station, his throat became so painful from thirst that he called to an old woman standing in the entrance of a farmhouse on the righthand side of the road: "Excuse me, but could I have some water, please?" She went inside with no sign of repugnance at his swollen face and raw-burned lips, muttering and nodding to herself as she went. Poor man!" he heard her say, "How thirsty he must be! Yes, of course . . ." From the unfloored area inside, she brought a large cup on a tray. It was not water, but cold strong tea.

The events following his boarding the train at Hesaka Station were described in his account as follows:

With great difficulty, I got a seat in the rearmost car of the special troop train. It was a train of the same Geibi line that ran through my home in the country, and I had traveled back and forth on it a number of times during my middle school days. The sound of its whistle cheered me immensely. Somehow, I felt I could not possibly die now that I had heard that well-remembered sound from the past. The emotion that flooded me at the prospect of a time free from the sleeplessness, strain, and apprehension of the past three days made the three-hour journey seem excessively long and the train excessively tardy. My body felt on fire with fever. Tension tends to let up suddenly, yielding to the feeling of sliding irresistibly downward, down into the depths. My consciousness grew vague. At each station, the train jerked violently, as though encouraging me to pull myself together. At every one, middle-aged or elderly women wearing the sashes of the Women's Defense Association doled out tea and pickled sour plums. Even though my lips and the inside of my mouth were so swollen, the plums tasted good. The women were unrestrained in their expressions of sympathy. "How dreadful!" said one. "How awful for you," exclaimed another. Some of the younger ones were in tears. All of them, I am sure, had sons or husbands on active service. One old woman, even, burst into helpless sobbing. It was my first contact with feminine emotion since joining up, and it reminded me of a poem by the Chinese poet Li Po that I had learned thirty years earlier at middle school. For the first time, I realized that it was not just a piece of skillful description, but a work of intense emotion. In our car alone, two soldiers were already still and cold. I was worrying about my wife and children. As for my nephew, I felt I must resign myself to the worst.

We stopped at the station for Miyoshi, where I had gone to middle school. I was practicing opening my left eye without using my fingers when the sight of a girl I knew, standing on the platform, made me catch my breath in surprise. She had been a ward of an aunt of mine at Shōbara ever since she was small. Since she could hardly be expected to recognize me in my present sadly altered state, I called to attract her attention. She had left school by now, I found, and was doing war work at the station. I told her, in briefest outline, how she came to see me as a soldier in such a pitiful plight. Right away, she contacted Shōbara Station over the station telephone, and got permission from the Shōbara and Miyoshi stationmasters to come with me on the train.

All this had been possible because the train had stopped so long at the station. However one looked at it, it was the most extraordinary coincidence. Thanks to the meeting, I should soon be able to contact my relatives and friends. The thought cheered me inestimably. The tension gripping me must have relaxed without my realizing it, for, strange to say, my condition suddenly took a turn for the worse and I began to shake violently from head to foot.

At Shōbara Station, the girl from my relatives went off to contact my aunt. From there, they would certainly contact my own home, which lay some way outside the town. The place to which we broken-down soldiers were taken in the meantime, riding in a charcoal-driven bus through the evening twilight, proved to be not a hospital, but a classroom on the floor of an elementary school—no different, in fact, from the national elementary school at Hesaka. By the time I had found a space in the crush and lain down, I was barely aware of where I was, and was in the grip of a violent chill and shivering fit. By dark, my fever had grown worse and I had lost the power of speech. If I tried to talk, nothing came out.

I remember dimly that there was one air raid warning that night. . . . In all, I have lost consciousness three times in my life. Once was when I blacked out immediately after the bomb fell. The second time was that evening when, after long jolting in the train, I arrived at the Shōbara national elementary school. The third time was a period of a few days in early September, when I hovered between life and death following the onset of the radiation sickness. An invalid on the brink of death, I was unaware, in my half-conscious state, of what was going on about me, and very frequently could not even take note of my own symptoms at all clearly.

On the morning of August 9, the fever that had persisted all night abated somewhat and I noticed the signs of returning interest in things about me. The fever was the type that accompanies septicemia—a suppurative fever, one might call it. That day, a medical officer came round to see us and gave instructions on our treatment to an orderly. It was the first time that a medical officer had examined us since the bomb fell. Yet he did not even use his stethoscope.

My injuries consisted almost entirely of burns, on my head, face, neck, wrists, fingers, and even the lobes of my ears. The skin was peeling off my wrists; my back, they told me, was like a piece of raw beef, with the ribs all but poking through. The cause, as I learned later, was exposure to a momentary radiation of several thousand degrees. The bomb, indeed, had been of a power beyond the mind of man to conceive.

The orderly applied a liquid resembling picric acid to my burns, and covered the part that touched the floor when I lay down with a piece of antiseptic gauze one foot square. That was the sum of his treatment, and he promptly went on to deal with the next patient. Since they were dealing with a whole trainload of patients, some hundreds in number, one could hardly afford to complain if the treatment was rather rough-and-ready.

The next day, August 10, when the orderly stripped the gauze from my back, I could not help crying out. The heat and weight of my body, and its secretions, had made it stick fast to the burns all over. He stripped it off from below, in an upward direction, and as he did so the pain made me unconsciously lift my body with it. But even seated on my heels, with my hands resting on the floor at my sides, I could only raise myself so far. When the limit had been reached, my body sank down, to rest on my buttocks once more. Then the gauze came off, willy-nilly.

Ignoring the blood that came spattering down, the orderly brushed my back with the medicine, covered it with gauze, applied more of the liquid to my head, face, neck, and upper arms, to the backs of my hands, my wrists, and my fingers, then passed on immediately to the next patient. Even I, who pride myself on being able to endure a lot, was appalled at the treatment we received. As at Hesaka, the patients were dying off and being carried out in steady succession. Here too, members of the Women's Defense Association had come to help, attending to bedpans and such matters, but the penetrating odor seemed to be getting them down rather.

In the afternoon, I was aroused by a voice calling, "Attention there! Is Iwatake of the medical reserve here? Iwatake?" It was followed by another voice, shrill, a woman's voice: "Hiroshi! Are you here, Hiroshi? Hiroshi?" It was my wife. I tried to answer, but my lips were too swollen for me to get anything out. I managed, painfully, to raise my left arm a fraction. . . .

She had been to the ruins of the army hospital in Hiroshima to look for me: hearing I had gone to Hesaka, she had gone to the national elementary school there, then, learning that I had been transferred to Shōbara, she had come on after me. When she finally found me, my face was so altered that even she did not recognize it. . . .

Along with this account came a record of Mrs. Iwatake's recollections of the same period. Somebody had obviously gone to question her about Iwatake's miraculous recovery, and had taken her replies down in shorthand. It promised to be useful for reference in treating Yasuko.

"I was living in the country away from the raids at the time," (the account ran) "and was staying at the Hosokawa Clinic in Yuda, outside Fukuyama. Hiroshi my husband was serving in the medical reserve with the Second Hiroshima Unit, and our nephew, who was in my husband's charge, was attending the First Middle School in Hiroshima. Dr. Hosokawa in Yuda is my elder brother.

"August 7 was the night of the air raid on Fukushima. From the next morning on, the Fukuen and Igasa lines connecting with Fukuyama were both out of action, so early on the morning of the ninth my brother took me from Yuda to Fukuyama on the back of his bicycle. From there on, I went on foot to Kusado. From Kusado I went to Tomonotsu, then from Tomonotsu by bus to Matsunaga, this side of Onomichi, where I got a train, arriving in Hiroshima after dusk. It's strange I should have followed that particular route—Kusado, Tomonotsu, Matsunaga, Onomichi, and on to Hiroshima—a historic route, the one that some of the defeated Taira clan, and later on Ashikaga Takauji, are supposed to have taken in the old days when they were fleeing overland to reach the western sea.

"There were tents up in front of Hiroshima Station, and I went into one to wait till the morning. There was a soldier on guard, and a lot of people who seemed to have been caught without anywhere to spend the night. Before I left Yuda, my brother had tried to stop me from going—it was useless, he said—but I couldn't get rid of the feeling that my husband was still alive. So I filled a medicine bottle with saké—my husband likes a drink—and put it in my rucksack. Then I borrowed a Red Cross armband from my brother, to make it look as though I was an army nurse or something, and set off. Without an armband, no woman was allowed into Hiroshima. I was wearing cotton breeches, with sandals on my feet.

"I don't know my way about Hiroshima at all. I asked a soldier the way to the Second Army Hospital, but he said it was a waste of time to go, as everything in that area was in ruins. Then I asked about the First Hiroshima Middle School. The pupils had all been wiped out, he said, and the place reduced to ashes. It seemed almost certain that our nephew had been killed. So I lay down in the tent to sleep. There was a child there, an orphan who was pining for his parents and wouldn't go to sleep however much the soldiers fussed at him. I lay beside him and got him off to sleep at last. Around four in the morning I slipped out and made my way to the Second Army Hospital to look for my husband.

"It was a burnt-out waste—no barracks, nothing, only tents.

An officer—I don't remember his name, but he was from the Tokyo area—told me they wouldn't know anything for a while yet. I was to go home and stay there till I was notified by the army. He found some crystal sugar and some tea for me. I asked about the First Middle School again, to make sure. Yes, it was in ruins, he said. He kept telling me to go home, so I decided to look around for myself. I set off walking upstream along a river that ran nearby. On the banks, I saw some lean-tos made of corrugated iron and straw mats, but all the people inside had black faces, with only their teeth and the edges of their eyes showing white, and they were in rags, like the destitute people you see in old picture-scrolls. Farther on, I came across a group of people lying on the ground groaning, so I called out in a loud voice, 'Hiroshi, are you here?' but there was no answer. I listened hard, but all I could hear was groans; they might have been the voices of ghosts. . . .

"What a terrible bomb it must have been, I thought. A passer-by I spoke to said yes, it was a 'special new-type bomb' that had been dropped. He knew the reception center where soldiers from the army hospital who'd been injured by the bomb had been accommodated, so I asked him to tell me, as I was determined to try anywhere at all likely. There were three reception centers, he said, but I was in such a state that only one of the names stuck in my head. Hesaka. What a coincidence that was! I decided I couldn't visit them all at once at any rate. I'd go and look at Hesaka first, then keep my ears open to help me find the others. So I only memorized the one name. It's about six miles from Hiroshima. By the time I arrived in the village after walking there, there was only an hour to noon. I kept to the embankment all the way. As I went, I kept wondering about the officer I had met in the tent in the ruins of the Army Hospital —why hadn't he told me where the reception centers were?

"At Hesaka, I went round all the farmers' houses one by one. By the time I reached the national elementary school, where the temporary reception center headquarters was, it was about four p.m. The tents in the school yard, the classrooms, and the corridors as well, were full of injured, but they told me that no list of patients had been made yet. I went round corridors and classrooms and tents calling 'Hiroshi! Are you here, Hiroshi?' but there was no answer. Then someone told me that those who weren't so badly hurt were being accommodated in nearby farmhouses, so I set off again on the round of the farms.

"In the end, I was completely done in. Past shame or caring, I called out to the people in one of the farmhouses to allow me to rest there, and laid myself down on the soothingly cool boards of the veranda. This was about five in the afternoon. I must have slept a good two or three hours, then I went back to the national elementary school. This time, I found the list of people there was ready, and they told me Hiroshi had been transferred to the national elementary school at Shōbara the day before. I was greatly relieved to hear that only the lightly injured had been sent, but my relief didn't last more than a moment, for somebody else who'd seen them told me they'd looked as though they were on their last legs.

"It was odd, but I felt just as pressed for time whether I thought my husband was only slightly hurt or seriously hurt. On my way to Hesaka Station, for instance, I walked just as fast as I could. The train was just leaving when I got there, but it was full and so slow that when we came at last to change at Shiomachi we found the last Shōbara train had already gone through. There was no help for it, so I spread a newspaper on the platform and sat on it to wait for the morning.

"The man next to me, who came from Fuchū, talked a lot, and it came out in the course of conversation that he knew the Fuchū branch of the Hosokawa Clinic. So I scribbled a note to my brother, telling him that I was on my way to Shōbara and asking him to bring whatever was necessary, and gave it to the man to deliver to the branch clinic. Here was *something* to be thankful for, at least. It was all most convenient, as the man was taking a Fuchū-bound train, on the Fukuen line, (the Fukuen line was running except for the area around Fukuyama), while I was getting on the Geibi line. Shiomachi is the junction.

"Thanks to this, the Hosokawas were successfully contacted, and my brother, a nurse, and our daughter, who had been evacuated to the Hosokawas with us, arrived at my aunt's house in Shōbara in the early evening of that day, August 11. My aunt herself was out. Thanks to the call from the girl my husband had met, she knew that he had been transferred to Shōbara, and had gone to his home to let them know. I myself had arrived, though, and was resting and tidying myself up a bit. I went straight to the hospital. Actually, it was the national elementary school building, and when a sergeant or sergeant-major who seemed to be acting as an orderly took us into the classrooms we found that every inch of floor to be seen was covered with injured, just as at Hesaka. I had no idea where my husband was. The soldier who looked like an orderly called 'Medical Reservist Iwatake! Where are you?' so I called out too: 'Hiroshi! Are you here, Hiroshi?'

"Something seemed to grip my chest so that it was difficult to breathe. There was no reply. Then I saw a hand raised feebly, and it dawned on me that it was him. His face was swollen to twice its normal size, and the whole of his right ear was covered with gauze held in place with sticking plaster. He was in pain in his ear. One thing that struck me as strange was that when one patient groaned all the others would start groaning at the same time. It was an uncanny sound—perhaps I shouldn't say it, but it was for all the world like a chorus of frogs starting up in a paddy field.

"Officially, I suppose, this reception center in the school building would have been called the 'Temporary Reception Center, Hiroshima First Army Hospital Branch.' The medical treatment and the facilities were inadequate, of course—you could hardly complain in an emergency like that—but the regulations were as strict as in the army. Since the members of the Women's Defense Association were there to help, there was a ban on the relatives of patients doing anything to look after them. Even so, I could hardly go home and leave my husband there at death's door, could I? So I tried one of the phrases everybody used during the war—the only important thing, I said, was to get just as many of them better as possible, 'so that they could be of use to their country.' It was very forward of me, I thought. But the medical orderly, or whatever he was, didn't so much as smile. I was in a terrible fret, so I went to see the commander, who had been to the same college as my husband, and persuaded him to have Hiroshi transferred, at his personal order, to a room with only two people in it. This meant that he was receiving the same treatment as a medical officer. Strictly speaking, even though he was in the medical reserve, he was only a second-class private, supposedly still learning. In practice, this 'promotion' only lasted an hour or two. A colonel, commander of an infantry unit, who was already in the room he was taken to had encephalitis and was out of his mind, and he passed away before the night was out.

"The next place he was moved to was a tiny room for three patients. The two men there before him were a doctor of medicine from Okayama Prefecture, who had been drafted and was now Second Class Private Nagashima of the Medical Reserve, and a young corporal, a volunteer from Kasaoka in Okayama Prefecture. Nagashima had burns on his face and hands, and was suffering from diarrhea. The young corporal was not burned, but had a great wound in his head.

"The attitude of army people towards civilians was always very precise, but it had its extremely mystifying side as well. This may not have been true of all of them, of course, but I certainly noticed it in some. After my husband was transferred to this room for three, my brother Dr. Hosokawa arrived with a nurse, bringing as much as they could carry in the way of gauze, bandages, Ringer's solution and glucose for injections, oil for dressing burns, and so on—all of them worth their weight in gold among civilians at the time—and suggested to Lieutenant Hanaki, the army doctor in charge, that they should be allowed to be of some use. The lieutenant looked very sour and gave them a sharp talking-to. The army had its own way of doing things, he said, and he didn't want civilians bringing in their own stuff. Yet it was this same lieutenant, mark you, who directed the nurse to paint my husband's burns with some transparent liquid of unidentified origin. One day, after they had put the stuff on, Hiroshi found a cucumber seed sticking to him. The next day, he asked the nurse what the medicine was, and mentioned the seed he'd found on him. 'What?' she exclaimed. 'Was there a seed left? After all the trouble we took straining it!' That gave the game away, of course: they'd been using cucumber juice as a dressing. My husband couldn't help smiling, even though his lips were all swollen. In the old days, cucumber juice may quite possibly have been used for burns—as an old wives' remedy, that is. But anyone with burns on more than one-third of his body dies, they say, unless you keep replacing the liquids in him with Ringer's solution, glucose, salt solution or something similar.

"One other incident—it was the thirteenth of August, I remember, and my husband began to suffer really unbearable earache in his right ear. The next afternoon, a draft lieutenant called Kutsubara—an ear, nose, and throat doctor from the Red Cross Hospital at Shōbara—came along. He had an extremely arrogant manner and overbearing way of talking, and examined Hiroshi's ear in a very ungentle way. When he took the gauze off the ear lobe and removed the cotton wool, a thick, oily liquid came oozing out of the earhole, and the area from the scab up to the entrance to the ear could be seen crawling with maggots—about two hundred, each a millimeter or so long. At the lieutenant's instruction, I washed the maggots on the lobe off into a basin. Then the lieutenant himself got out the maggots inside the ear.

"Thanks to this treatment, the source of the irritation to the eardrum disappeared, and the earache stopped. The fever, too, began to show signs of going down, and I poured a drop or two of the saké I'd brought for Hiroshi into his mouth. He's lost the lobe of his ear for good, eaten away by the maggots, and he still complains of ringing in his ears, but even so, he was so grateful to Lieutenant Kutsubara for getting rid of the maggots that he told me to take a bottle of saké to the lieutenant, as a token of his gratitude. I got my aunt in Shōbara to spare a bottle somehow, and took it wrapped in a wrapping cloth. When I gave it to him, though, he just put the bottle away in a closet, and flung the cloth down on the floor. 'Here, I don't want this,' he said, 'take it away with you.' When I got back, I told Hiroshi what had happened. He put it down to the war. That was the kind of thing war did, he said—produce that kind of person; what was quite sure was that it never did anybody any *good*.

"While I was in Shōbara, I slept at my aunt's and went to the reception center in the daytime. My brother Dr. Hosokawa stayed only one night at my aunt's, then took the nurse and our daughter back to Yuda. On August 15, the day the war ended, my husband suddenly got a high fever and nearly died, but the next day his temperature began to go down gradually. But he was terribly debilitated, and the treatment was very poor, so we decided to take him to the Hosokawas'. So on the twentieth we hired a charcoal-driven truck at the black market rate to take him there (by this time it was permitted for patients to go anywhere they liked). He and I got in the front, and we drove to Fuchū sitting by the driver, who had a pad over his mouth and nose to keep out the smell that the bomb victims gave off. My husband stood up to the journey better than me—*I* was all in!

"The day after he entered the clinic at Fuchū, Hiroshi showed signs of atomic disease. If he'd stayed only one day more at Shōbara, he'd probably never have left there alive. It wasn't a question of his relaxing now that he was home, or having kept going on will-power up to then. It seems there's a certain time after exposure to the bomb when the sickness catches up with you, and his time had come. Mr. Nagashima in the same room at Shōbara, for example, was far less badly hurt than Hiroshi, but he passed away on the very day we arrived in Fuchū.

"We were only at the Fuchū branch clinic for a couple of days and nights, then went on to my brother's home at Yuda, but even so the room at the clinic where my husband had been smelled so bad that they had to leave it open for more than ten days.

"In Yuda village there's a peach orchard growing a particularly famous local variety. We bought two lots of 80 pounds each from them, and my husband ate the lot, 160 pounds in all. His lips and gums were all burned, and the whole of his mouth inside was inflamed, so that he could only take liquid foods. I'd grate the peaches on a horseradish grater, fill a bowl with them, break two or three eggs into the mixture, and more or less pour the result into his mouth. It was remarkable—he would finish the bowl to the last drop; it couldn't have taken a month for him to get through the whole lot.

"We got back to Yuda on the twenty-second, and the radiation sickness set in in earnest on the twenty-third. The worst time of all, the time when he seemed to stop breathing and I broke down in tears, sure that it was all over, came around the twenty-third of September. It was at that time, in a barely audible voice, that he made his will. The dying can talk all right when it comes to their wills, and they take notice of what you say to them, too. I said to him: 'I'll do as you wish if, in exchange, you'll agree to us treating you as we think fit from now on, so that we don't have any regrets afterwards.'

"He agreed, but when we gave him blood transfusions and Ringer's solution he developed a terrible fever and suffered a great deal. He asked us to stop, but I insisted for once. 'Let us try just this, and if it doesn't work we'll give up,' I said. And we went on with the Ringer's solution and the transfusions. Whether that did the trick or not I don't know, but he gradually began to pull through. Even then, his left leg developed an infection. He insisted it was not the fault of the Ringer's solution, but probably a kind of septicemia. He wouldn't let anybody else operate on him, either, but cut the place open with a scalpel by himself, while my brother was away at the branch clinic in Fuchū. He's awfully stubborn, and won't let anybody else do surgical operations. He still has the scar to this day.

"At that time he was just like a mummy, all skin and bone and nothing else. There was a dummy skeleton standing in my brother's place, and Hiroshi was just like that. It was still hot, so we kept the mosquito net up to keep off any flies that might cause maggots, and when you looked at him through the white gauze he and the skeleton were as alike as two peas in a pod. It made my sister-in-law so uncomfortable that she shut the skeleton away in a closet or somewhere.

"At this period, my husband didn't have a single day free from pain. His muscles had all wasted away, leaving only skin and bone, and he complained that he could feel the hardness of the tatami on his bones, right through the quilts. We piled the quilts up high, as high as a bed, and put two feather mattresses on top. We thought that was sure to make things easier for him, but still he could tell whether or not there was a joint in the tatami underneath the quilts. You'd hardly credit it, would you? Later, we found that the tatami underneath were rotting.

"The only doctor he would see was my brother, Dr. Hosokawa. After all, it was my brother who had given him Ringer's solution and blood transfusions when other doctors had thrown in the sponge and everybody had written him off. His blood type is 'O', and in our family the children are 'O' too.

"We were comparatively well off for food. When we asked some neighbors if they could get us some liver, for example, they brought a whole cow's liver—as if anybody could get through all that much! The mainstay of his diet, even so, was peaches and eggs, which were what he seemed to take best. I was afraid we wouldn't be able to get them once the season was over, so I got two big lots and stored them at the bottom of a deep well. Yuda is a traditional peach-growing district, and its white peaches are famous for their flavor. In those days, though, the growers didn't like to be paid in money, so I had to take along my kimonos and things. I sacrificed two wicker trunks full of kimonos in that way.

"It was generally accepted at the time that you could tell whether a victim of radiation disease was going to die or not by whether his hair fell out. My husband's hair did in fact come out, the whole lot, but I expect the symptoms varied very much from patient to patient. I can't talk from experience of anybody except my husband, but I do know that his appetite went down sharply from the time the radiation sickness set in. On top of the disease itself, the patient won't take proper nourishment, so it's impossible to make up for the wasting, and he begins to look like someone with cancer. The white corpuscle count goes down steadily too, but in my husband's case it stopped at a little under two thousand.

"Another symptom was that he was constipated for about ten days after the bomb fell. And he could only pass water a few drops at a time. It really must have been a terrible bomb—to have taken all the skin clean off his wrists like that, for one thing. 'Penetrating rays' they call them, apparently. It seems they affect the internal organs as well as the outside of the body. In my husband's case, the membrane lining the bladder came clean away and stopped up the urethra, so that he couldn't pass water. You know the kind of filmy white stuff you find inside when you split open a piece of dry bamboo? Well, the stuff that came off the inside of the bladder was just like that. The rays from the atomic bomb make mucous membranes peel off, you see. This was after we went to my brother's, so I'd say it was about three weeks after the bomb fell. All the same, he could make himself pass water by straining downwards and then, when the urine went into the urethra, pressing down on the sphincter muscle. You press with both hands on the lower part of the abdomen. Each time he went he'd pass it into a cup and examine it, then he'd show me how much of the stuff like bamboo film had come out. There was always quite a lot.

"No—I don't imagine it's only the bladder. The stomach and the intestines and the liver—all the organs—are affected to some extent, I suppose. The surface between the teeth and the gums is affected in the same way, I believe. That's why the teeth come loose, isn't it? Some people I heard of had bloody stools, and others got diarrhea. With my husband, it was constipation. The bladder trouble clears up once you've finished passing all the membrane. A new membrane forms in its place, I imagine.

"Our nephew was in his first year at Hiroshima First Middle

School at the time. It was to find what had happened to him, as well as my husband, that I went to Hiroshima, but when I got to the city and asked the soldier in the tent in front of the station, I was told that all the pupils at the school had been wiped out. I felt as though my chest would burst—it was so cruel. When I found my husband, I didn't tell him for the time being. I wonder now if it wasn't the shock of losing our nephew, working on my nerves, that helped drive me all the way to Hesaka, and then on to Shōbara, looking for my husband. But what a horrible end for the poor boy, though. . . .

"The special relief squad that went to Hiroshima the day after the raid on the city cleared away the ruins of the Hiroshima First Middle School. They came to the Hosokawas afterwards to report on what they found. The remains of our nephew, who was in Hiroshima doing war work, were found in a classroom, where he was burned to death at his desk. He must have been killed by the rays. Every middle school pupil in those days wore an identification tag, and somebody brought his back; it was the only thing of his left, they said. It was made of tin, with nothing but the name on it, and it was hard to make out even that."

These reminiscences of Iwatake's wife, taken together with Iwatake's own account of his experiences, suggested that no proper treatment for radiation sickness had been discovered yet. The only measures taken in Iwatake's case were blood transfusions and large quantities of vitamin C, with a diet of peaches and raw egg. With him, that seemed to have done the trick—that, and an enormous will to beat the disease. Such, at least, was Shigematsu's conclusion after finishing his perusal of the document.

CHAPTER 19 🦋

The most important thing of all was to prevent Yasuko from losing her determination to survive. She must be given confidence that she would live. In fact, to keep her going on food and willpower was the only course open to them, since she was growing weaker every day, and there was no known treatment.

According to Shigeko, Yasuko had been to see two doctors in Kobatake on the morning of the day she entered the Kuishiki Hospital. Both, of course, had given her medicine to take, but she had thrown both lots away in a ditch, without so much as touching them. The woman from the sundries store at the bottom of the hill had seen the names and date on the packets. She had had a look inside, too, and there was no doubt, she told Shigeko, that Yasuko had thrown them away without taking a single dose. It showed what a despairing frame of mind she had been in. She must be provided with a good example in Mr. Iwatake's determination to conquer his disease.

Iwatake himself related the events around the time he left the Army Branch Hospital as follows:

Perhaps because of the removal of the maggots in my ear, the earache and the fever got better, but I became more and more debilitated every day. However, I didn't want to die just then, in that hospital; I'd decided that I'd rather die somewhere else, of some proper disease that I could account for.

On August 23, permission to go home was given for those who felt they were up to it, provided it was not too far off. I didn't feel up to it, but my one idea was to get home all the same, and with Dr. Fujita's permission I got a certificate of emergency discharge. I gathered my strength for the journey, not as far as Tokyo, which was impossible—but at least to the Hosokawa Clinic in Yuda—and we contracted with a charcoal-driven truck normally used for carrying charcoal to take us the thirty miles or so to the outskirts of Fukuyama.

They dressed me in my white hospital smock, with my army cap on my head. Thus attired, scarcely knowing who I was or what I was doing, I somehow got to the Hosokawa branch clinic in Fuchū. The route took us over an appallingly bumpy road. Nobody who went over it could have failed to get the implications of such a terrible state of neglect. Several times, in that stiflingly hot cab beside the driver, I drifted off into a state of delirium. Even my wife, who sat in attendance on me, fainted twice with fatigue. The three hours of the journey seemed like a year.

I was precisely at that crucial juncture where the merest hairsbreadth separates life and death. The next day, the twenty-fourth, I developed radiation sickness. If I had stayed one day— half a day, perhaps—longer, my call to eternity would have come, beyond all doubt, at Shōbara.

I was still only half-conscious when I was shifted from the Fuchū branch clinic to the Hosokawa Clinic at Yuda. Blood transfusions, injections, injections, and still more injections . . . that much, at least, I remember. Gradually, I became a little more aware of my surroundings.

Every day I had a temperature of 104°. My white corpuscle count was two thousand, and the flesh steadily fell from me till I was a very skeleton, a living mummy. The burns on my back were inordinately painful—not to speak of those on my wrists and ears. Even when one is only skin and bone, one still feels pain. My wife told me that the place where my back had been burned was dark and hard like a beef steak, and the "steak" came off in chunks till the ribs were almost showing. Medically speaking, it's the state that precedes nephrosis and gangrene. At the time of the explosion and flash, the rays had struck me at an angle, but even so, this was the result. I expect it's related in some ways to bedsores. As likely as not, the circulation was bad too, which would have encouraged the phenomenon still further.

The debility reached an extreme pitch; time and time again I lost consciousness. At times my heartbeat was inaudible and my respiration seemed to have stopped: a great sore developed on my back, and the membrane of the bladder came away, leading to anuria. Neither my brother-in-law nor any other doctor gave me any chance. The doctors who stood in at the examinations gave me up for lost. The hair of my head came out in handfuls, with scabs attached at the roots and looking like pieces of a wig.

Making up my mind that this was the end, I told my wife my dying wishes. But I didn't die. It was my wife's cry of anguish at my bedside that brought me back. She was sure my heart had that moment stopped, she told me later. The skin of my face twitched, my eyes turned up, and I showed signs of the death throes, with cyanosis symptoms. Yet all the while I myself felt as though I was floating somewhere bright and spacious, with no particular pain. People talk of the death agony, but the person most concerned is surprisingly free of suffering. To every-one else, even so, I must have seemed to be in mortal agony.

During the two weeks following the onset of radiation sickness, I survived largely on the juice from a full 80 pounds of peaches. The injections of vitamin C and the transfusions may have helped, too. From then on, over a period of a year and a half, my ulcers, which resembled X-ray burns, gradually healed. While I was sick in bed, I was the merest framework of a human being—but it was like the iron framework of a building under construction, for later, when I got new muscles and flesh, I acquired, more or less literally, a new body. Today, I have one earlobe missing, and when I take a drink the scars on my cheek and wrists turn red, but apart from a stubborn ringing in my ear I have no after-effects at all. The one thing that troubles me is the ringing; it persists in my ear day and night, like the tolling of a distant temple bell, warning man of the folly of the bomb. . . .

When Shigeko went to the Kuishiki hospital to see Yasuko, she took the account with her so that the head of the hospital could make use of it in treating Yasuko.

If one is depressed, it actually helps to keep oneself occupied. Left alone, Shigematsu hastily shut up the house and went off to Shōkichi's to see how the baby carp were coming along. It so happened that Shōkichi and Asajirō were by the pond. Asajirō's bald pate was bent over a mortar, in which he was pounding cabbage. Shōkichi, of the lame leg, was scooping fry out of the hatching pond with a net, then sorting them and transferring them to the pond nearby.

"Hot, isn't it?" said Shigematsu. "Hello there! Hot, isn't it!" the others replied. This was the stock greeting in the village on a fine summer's day. In the evening, it would change to "Tiring day, wasn't it!" If it happened to be wet, both sides would greet each other with "Nice drop of rain!"

Shigematsu helped Asajirō with the mortar. They finished pounding all the cabbage, then put in some liver and pounded that, mixed in some chrysalis powder and flour, and rolled the result into small balls which they dropped into the hatching pond.

"This is just like preparing bait for fishing," Shigematsu said.

"They say that nowadays bait has salted fishguts in it. I wonder what would happen if you put fishguts in this?"

"No good at all," said Asajirō. "They say the fry get all worked up if you put anything salty in. You have to bring 'em along gentle, like."

Today, Asajirō wore yellow-tinted spectacles against eye strain, which might, he considered, give the radiation sickness a chance.

Approximately eighty percent of the fry hatched from the two lots of spawn they had gathered had perished. That left—assuming that one spawning produced about twenty-five thousand fry—some ten thousand in the hatching pond. They were about the same size as killifish. At this stage, they were called *kego*. About two months after hatching, their backs would begin to turn bluish and they would reach a length of from one to two-and-a-half inches. At this stage they were called *aoko*, and were released into the main pond. Those that were a year or more old were called *shinko*, and those that were big enough to eat were called *kirigoi*.

The three ponds into which the *aoko* were to be released had been ready for more than twenty days now. They had first been completely drained, then fish entrails, kitchen waste, and the like had been put in along with silage and other stuff, and the whole lot left to decompose in the heat of the sun. Only then had water been run in. Both Asajirō and Shōkichi agreed that the water had turned cloudy to just the right degree. It was not transparent like spring water, they explained, but had nourishment in it, producing vegetable plankton and water fleas. The water came from the stream nearby, and the pond was so arranged that it flowed gently through for five or six hours every day.

It was Asajirō's and Shōkichi's private ambition to rear the carp to from one-and-a-half to two-and-a-half ounces during the autumn, then the next year to fatten them up to two or three pounds or more, ready for eating. Then they would release some in the big pond at the foot of Agiyama, too. Thus they would have provided the carp in the big pond themselves, and the woman from Ikemoto's wouldn't be able to complain if they went fishing there. The only problem was what percentage of the ten thousand *kego* would actually grow into *aoko*. They were both sure that in a running-water pond even an amateur could count on fifty percent surviving. They had started with the hatching a little late in the season, admittedly, but so long as you regulated the water temperature and provided food, taking care to adjust from the old calendar to the new, it wasn't too late, they said.

When he arrived home, Shigematsu got out an almanac—Daigaku Katō's "Treasure Almanac," it called itself—and studied it carefully. It was the seventeenth of the sixth month by the old lunar calendar—the "seventeen-day old moon," when it was appropriate, according to the almanac, to sow certain varieties of giant radish, kidney beans, and a particular kind of Chinese cabbage on the soil where one's carrots, marrows, and the like had been. A good piece of advice that, thought Shigematsu—it was obviously based on the farmers' experience in taking advantage of the Indian summer that regularly occurred in September. On the same principle, carp fry should do nicely, too. It also occurred to him that there were only three days to go to the anniversary of the Hiroshima bomb, which occurred on the sixth and was followed on the ninth by the anniversary of the Nagasaki bomb.

"I'd forgotten," he said to himself. "Only three days to go. I must get on with copying the journal." He ate his lonely supper, then fell to transcribing his "Journal of the Bombing," and was still at it when Shigeko arrived home off the last bus.

"You're late," he said. "You brought Mr. Iwatake's journal back, I hope?"

She deposited the bundle containing the journal on the edge of the table, then went and fetched a cotton towel.

"The hospital director read the journal while I was there," she said, dabbing inside her blouse to dry the sweat as she spoke. "It was interesting to watch the changes in his expression as he was reading."

"Did he say anything about the treatment? That's the important thing."

"Twice while he was reading he said 'Now this *is* useful.' After he'd finished, he told me that he himself had gone into the Second

Hiroshima Unit under the punitive medical draft. He joined the same unit as Mr. Iwatake, on the very same day."

"But he's alive, isn't he?"

"It seems he was sent straight home the same day as a result of the physical examination. He had a plaster cast round his middle at the time, because of caries of the ribs. It's funny what a difference such details can make, isn't it? He was frowning all the time he was reading, and once he swallowed rather hard."

"I'm not at all surprised," Shigematsu said. "I shouldn't wonder if he wasn't fighting back the tears."

Shigeko gave him a detailed account of Yasuko's condition. Two hours or so after the evening meal, the head of the hospital had given her a blood transfusion and a Ringer's injection, and she had gone off peacefully to sleep.

Shigematsu postponed transcribing the remainder of his journal of the bombing until the next day.

August 13. Fine, slight clouds in the afternoon.
I woke up at five the next morning, and immediately started to worry about the coal again. The works canteen wasn't open yet, so I got the cook to pour hot water on some cold cooked barley mixed with bran, and ate it. For my midday meal, he gave me some rusks that he'd found in the bottom of an empty box in the warehouse. I'd no prospect of getting any coal, and no particular destination; in the body, I was simply drifting, yet mentally I still felt the same sense of urgency. I decided, at any rate, to get on the train for Hiroshima, and to do my thinking on the way.

It was still early morning, with no breeze at all, and smoke from the funeral pyres was rising in neat columns at the foot of the hills and from the river bed. The columns grew fewer as we drew nearer to the city area; the reason was plain: the badly hurt who had fled from the city as far as the outskirts had died off quickly, while victims who had fled from the outskirts into the surrounding country had been dying off yesterday evening.

The middle-aged man who sat next to me on the train was full of hot news. Item: the Soviet army had not only breached the

Soviet-Manchurian border, but had rolled on in a great wave southwards and crossed the border between Manchuria and Korea too. Item: the Soviet Union might have a bomb similar to the Hiroshima one. Item: if the American forces occupied Japan, all Japanese men would probably be castrated. Item: the reason why healthy people who came to Hiroshima after the bomb were dying was there had been poison gas in the bomb. One parachute, in fact, had been equipped with poison gas, the other with the bomb. Item: of the one hundred and ninety doctors who had been in Hiroshima before the bomb, more than one hundred and twenty had died. . . .

He was a perfectly ordinary-looking man in worn, dark blue breeches, but he had an answer for everything I cared to ask about. (It transpired afterwards, though, that his information was full of errors.)

Among the ruins, the reflection of the sun on the pieces of broken glass on the road was so strong that it was difficult to hold your head up as you walked. The smell of death was a little fainter than the day before, but the places where houses had collapsed into tile-covered heaps stank vilely and were covered with great, black swarms of flies. The relief squads clearing the ruins seemed to have been joined by reinforcements, since I saw some men whose clothes, though bleached with frequent washing, were not soiled with sweat and grime as yet.

Walking on aimlessly, I came to the ruins of the Coal Control Company. There were seventeen or eighteen messages posted on the site, every one asking the whereabouts of the company's "temporary office." Nothing afforded the slightest clue as to the answer. Nothing was possible, yet I must do *something*. Racking my brains for some idea, I suddenly recalled seeing coal piled up by the side of the Hesaka road. It was at a place called Oda, about halfway between Hesaka and Yaguchi stations. I had been to and fro along the Hesaka road three times in spring and early summer that year, and each time I had noticed it—a great pile of good quality coal.

As raw material for the clothing it made, our firm used hemp, which had to be boiled and dried before use, and the Raw Materials Section always kept enough in stock for a week or ten days' work. There was plenty of hemp, therefore, to keep going until past the twentieth of the month, but coal stocks had all but hit rock bottom. It was too late in the day to rush about trying to find what had happened to the head of the control company, so I decided to find the owner of the coal by the Hesaka road, and to try to make a deal with him.

The village of Oda lies on the mainstream of the Ōta river, on the opposite side from Furuichi, where our firm is. It would take me rather out of my way, but I could follow the Geibi line through the cool areas at the foot of the hills, then cross the river at a point directly opposite the company in Furuichi. So deciding, I got onto the railway tracks and started walking.

It dawned on me that I had left the bundle containing my meal lying on a foundation stone at the Control Company, but I couldn't be bothered to go back. By the side of the tracks, beneath trees, on vacant lots and in the corners of fields as I walked, I could see temporary shacks that had been put up by the refugees. Every kind of material that could be scraped together had been used: old boards, scorched corrugated iron, old straw mats, old sacks, straw, rushes—even green grass. Clothing and washing were hanging on the living branches of trees, and in some cases the tree itself had been called into service as a pillar.

One shack had a cooking place made of piled-up stones, with a piece of corrugated iron twisted into a cone standing on it to serve as a pan. Another had a tall pile of dead branches beside it. At one shack—less a shack, really, than an arbor of branches—I saw something wrapped in a white cloth lying on top of a pile of stones, with some flowers arranged in an old can beside it. There was an old woman in this rude shelter, lying on her back on a bed of green rushes.

One thing common to all the shacks was the stock of fresh grass and fallen cryptomeria or cedar needles that stood by the entrance. This was obviously for use in warding off the mosquitoes. It is a method in use on farms, I believe, the same method that they use to make ash for fertilizer. They set fire to the dead needles, then pile fresh grass on them before they burn up completely, and leave them to smolder all night. I saw two or three shacks with injured people lying in them. One family was busily making smoke, even though it was broad daylight, with few mosquitoes about. It seemed to be a rather eccentric household altogether. They had dug a hole by the side of the house, lined it with a large piece of waterproof paper, and filled it with water, and a young woman was fishing stones out of the bonfire and dropping them one at a time into the water. I've heard the "mountain folk" use this method for making baths, but whether these people were really mountain folk or not I don't know. If the aim was just to get themselves clean, the river nearby would have done perfectly well. Perhaps they were making a bath for the person who was hurt?

At Hesaka Station, there was a crowd of people waiting for a train. I left the tracks and, skirting the front of the station, got back onto them on the farther side. But the coal I had pinned such hopes on was gone, and the place where it had been showed signs of having been covered over. I asked at a neighboring farm, and the old man there told me that the coal had all disappeared in the course of a single night.

"When?" I asked. "The night after the raid on Hiroshima," he said. I asked him who the coal had belonged to. At first, he said, it was supposed to have been an open-air store of the army's, but actually nobody knew whose it was. One had only to spread word that something was an army store, and people hesitated to lay hands on it, which was very convenient. Probably somebody had been laying in a stock of black market coal, I thought to myself. When I suggested as much, though, the old man gave me a suspicious look. "But then, coal's a vital commodity, isn't it?" I said, and made off without further ado.

I walked on as fast as I could until I was directly opposite Furuichi. I made my way down to the dry river bed, thinking to ford the shallows of the river, and found a dying man on the ground where he had collapsed. He had fallen face upward. His eyes were turned up sharply showing the whites, his mouth was open, and his belly, covered only by a pair of pants, was rising and falling ever so faintly. A great rock to one side of this barely living creature threw shade over half his body; on the other side of the rock were two corpses, their heads badly burned.

I tried to walk softly as I passed, but I could not stop my shoes crunching loudly on the loose stones of the river bed. Since the bomb, I had seen my fill of dead bodies, but they still frightened me. The setting sun, reflected off the water of the river, got in my eyes unpleasantly.

The stones of the river bed gradually gave way to sand, then to running water with a slowly shelving bed. As I took my clothes off, I murmured to myself the "Sermon on Mortality" "Sooner or later, on this day or the morrow, to me or to my neighbor. . . . So shall the rosy cheeks of morning yield to the skull of eventide. One breath from the wind of change, and the bright eyes shall be closed. . . ."

I undid my puttees, and took off my boots and trousers. I rolled them up in my undershirt, and tied them with my belt for ease in carrying as I crossed.

We had had a long spell of hot, sunny weather, and even at the deepest place the water only came up to my thighs, but more than once I slipped on a stone and sat down in the water.

In contrast to the left bank of the river, the right bank was dotted with countless makeshift crematoria. I could see them both upstream and downstream from where I was, any number of them, still smoldering and sending their smoke drifting towards the water of the river. I hurried straight across the sand, scaled the embankment, and clambered down beside a paddy full of rice plants, amidst the hot, heavy smell of summer grasses. My underpants were wet, so I left my other clothes off as I walked along the path between the fields, crossed the Furuichi road, and made my way back to our temporary home. It was still light, but nobody I passed showed any sign of surprise at my nakedness. There had been plenty of others like me, refugees who had fled with next to nothing on.

"I'm back," I called, "I came across the river. The current's surprisingly strong when you actually get in it. Shigeko! I'm starving!" I didn't tell Shigeko that I had left my lunch behind among the ruins; that would only have doubled the sense of loss.

When I am hungry my voice tends to get hoarse, but louder than usual. As I washed myself in the stream at the back of the house, I recounted to Shigeko, in a loud voice, my walk back along the Geibi line. I told her, too, about the people making a bath in waterproof paper, like mountain folk.

I was still there when she appeared from the house carrying a pair of underpants, a cotton kimono, and a sash. "The manager's here to see you," she said with an air of importance.

My first guess was that he had come to press me to do something about supplementary coal supplies. That must be it, I thought—it was only to be expected. Hastily, I donned the kimono and went back into the house, where I found Mr. Fujita sitting on the step in the entrance. He was dressed, most unusually for him, in Japanese clothes, and beside him stood a square wooden box of the kind fitted with shelves inside and used for carrying meals.

"Nice to see you, Mr. Fujita!" I said. "I was coming to see you after supper. Though I didn't have any luck with the coal again today."

"Look, Shizuma," he began, ignoring my remarks. "Your wife told me this morning that she and your niece are going home to the country. They've been bombed out, so naturally there's no difficulty about getting permission. But I thought the least I could do was to bring along your meal for this evening, and mine with it. Thought we could all have it here together. It's the canteen stuff, of course, so it's pretty meager fare. . . ."

I got the point at once. Yasuko and I, who worked for the firm, ate our meals in the canteen. But Yasuko—and I too—felt awkward at taking Shigeko to the canteen with us. On the other hand, though, commodities were so scarce that it was hopeless for anyone without such connections to get hold of food. There was no telling how long the war would last, either; in fact, there had been a lot of talk lately about carrying the war onto Japanese soil, and "last-ditch stands." So Shigeko had decided to go back to our home in the country for a while, taking Yasuko with her, and had said that she would suggest as much to the manager sometime today. I had agreed, of course. To me, therefore, the food box and the manager's formal kimono meant only one thing: Yasuko was being granted an honorable discharge from the firm.

I showed the manager in, and thanked him formally for all he had done for Yasuko. Shigeko, and Yasuko herself also, thanked him in their turn.

The food box was of the outsize variety they used in the canteen. When Shigeko removed the lid, there stood revealed, in addition to the canteen meal, a one-and-a-half pint saké bottle and a can of corned beef—gifts for us, it seemed. There were two rather aged tomatoes, too. I judged the contents of the bottle to be *shōchū*. It was many a day since I had seen such a luxury.

"I really don't know how to thank you," said Shigeko, giving her deepest bow and speaking in Tokyo dialect out of deference to the manager.

"Thank you very much indeed," said Yasuko, bowing in the same fashion.

I was itching to get down to the meal. I'd never seen the manager in Japanese dress before. He was sitting formally, on his heels, and I could see a white patch about two inches square where his kimono had been mended at the knee. That pint-and-a-half bottle must have meant an enormous sacrifice for him. Every time I looked at the patch on his knee I felt unutterably selfish at accepting it. My fondness for a drink was well known to him, and he himself shared the same taste.

"What's in the bottle, Mr. Fujita?" I asked.

"Alcohol, of course!" he said. "Made from gentian bitters. There's medicinal syrup in it, too."

In the Japanese pharmacopoeia, he explained, what was called "simple syrup" was a solution of something over three parts of white sugar in something over six parts of distilled water. Doctors used it to make medicine more palatable. "Gentian bitters" was made by putting powdered gentian root, orange peel, and other ingredients in medicinal alcohol and filtering the mixture under pressure. Nowadays, the drugstores in the towns refused to sell either gentian bitters or syrup, but at country stores they'd sometimes sell it to you, at a negotiable price. The manager had been to his home in the country the previous Sunday, and had got a drugstore friend of his to distill some bitters for him. He had bought some syrup too, which he was keeping as a sugar substitute.

"It's really precious stuff, with all the trouble you've taken to get it," said Shigeko. "But I'd better get some water if it's alcohol, hadn't I?" She went out into the kitchen.

"Gentian bitters is awfully bitter unless you distill it," the manager said, shifting to the informal, cross-legged position. "But if you don't mind that, and wash it down with water, you only need a third of a pint or so to get quite happy. This New Year I drank two-thirds of a pint of the stuff undistilled. I got happy all right, but the next day I had diarrhea—odd, considering it's supposed to be good for the stomach and intestines."

One at a time, Yasuko took the dishes out of the box and set them on the table. The meal that the works canteen had conjured up today consisted of five mulberry leaves made into tempura, bean paste and salt, two slices of pickles, and a bowl of boiled barley mixed with bran. This was repeated four times, for four people. The idea of the mulberry leaves had been hit on by someone working in the kitchen. They had got them from the mulberry orchard next door to the works. The farmers had stopped rearing silkworms because of the war; they had pruned back the branches of the mulberry trees, and were growing vegetables on the ground in between. Around this time of year the mulberries sprouted late buds from the sawn-off stumps of their branches, and by now were bearing young leaves just right for eating.

The tomatoes were carried off to the kitchen by Yasuko, who brought them back cut in half, one half on each of four dishes. The can of corned beef she shared out on the four plates she had brought for the purpose.

The four of us sat down to our meal. Under the manager's watchful eye, Shigeko poured water and alcohol into glasses, seven parts of one to three of the other. The movements of her hands were somehow deferential, as though she was handling something of great value. The manager stirred the liquid in his glass with the wooden chopsticks, so I followed his example.

"I'll bring spoons," said Shigeko, starting to get up. "We've got some we use for curry, if they'll do."

"No, no, Mrs. Shizuma—" the manager said, "I never use anything but fragrant wooden chopsticks for stirring drink. I'm strict about these things. In mixing water with alcohol, too, I'm a firm subscriber to the 'seven parts to three parts' theory. But as you see," he added cheerfully, pouring a little more of the drink into his own glass, "theory and practice don't always go hand in hand!"

"Here goes then, Mr. Fujita," I said, taking up my glass. "But first, to your health!"

"To our health," he said, clinking his glass against mine.

The faint bitterness in the drink may have been my imagination. The aroma was certainly good—the alcohol was the pure stuff, after all—and the syrup in it seemed to give just the right amount of sweetness.

Neither Shigeko nor Yasuko drank, so the manager persuaded them to start eating before us. A thirty percent proportion of alcohol was too strong for me, but instead of pouring in more water I drank it in very small sips. I'd never had mulberry leaf *tempura* before, but I found that, dipped in salt, the leaves went very well with the drink. I've had similar *tempura* made of chrysanthemum leaves or young persimmon leaves on a number of occasions since the war.

The manager had provided what was intended, one might say, to be a cosy little dinner for our family. But it turned out to be a farewell party, devoted for the most part to working over and over the same, depressing topics. The manager himself, I found, had also been to the site of the Coal Control Company in Hiroshima. Then he had gone to see Lieutenant Sasatake at the Clothing Depot, but he had found himself frustrated at every turn. He had gone to call on Dr. Koyama, an acquaintance of his at the Communications Hospital. However, finding that the doctor was rushed off his feet attending to the patients in the hospital, he had not insisted on meeting him personally, and had been lighting a cigarette at the exit to the hospital when a conversation he overheard between two nurses taught him, for the first time, the correct name for the thing that had caused the monstrous flash-and-bang over the city.

"An 'atomic bomb,' " he said, his face pale from the effect of the drink. "That's the name for it, apparently. It gives off a terrific radiation. I myself saw some bricks in the ruins that were all burnt away, with bubbles raised on the surface. The tiles, too, had gone a kind of flame color. A terrible thing they've produced. They say nothing'll grow in Hiroshima or Nagasaki for another seventy-five years."

The name of the bomb had already undergone a number of changes, from the initial "new weapon" through "new-type bomb," "secret weapon," "special new-type bomb," to "special high-capacity bomb." That day, I learned for the first time to call it an "atomic bomb." But I couldn't believe that nothing would grow there for seventy-five years. Hadn't I seen weeds running riot all over the ruins?

"Now that you mention it," said the manager when I told him, "I saw them, too. I saw a plantain drooping over at the top because it had grown so tall."

I remember reading an essay by the novelist Hakuchō Masamune. It appeared in the *Yomiuri Shimbun*, I believe, around the time that Germany, Italy and Japan formed the Axis, and in it the author remarked that a film of Hitler addressing the Hitler Youth had reminded him of nothing so much as the roaring of a dangerous tiger. It was very unusual at that time for anybody to say anything unfavorable about Hitler in public. Some members of the Hitler Youth had paid a visit to Japan, and the governor of one prefecture had even organized his own youth corps in exact imitation of them. The article made a very strong impression on me; I found it refreshing that somebody should write like that at a time when everybody else was jumping on the bandwagon. Going to work in a factory producing military supplies, and preoccupied every day with increasing production, I slipped into the habit of hoping, for our sake, that Hitler would win. But from the time the bomb was dropped, my ideas had suffered an abrupt about-face, and I began to feel that what I had been believing was a lot of nonsense.

On the surface, even so, I went along with the same official line as before, and I myself had made a copy of an appeal to the inhabitants of Hiroshima Prefecture issued on August 7 by Governor Kōno, and had posted it at the entrance to the works.

"The latest disaster," it read, "is part of an enemy plot to destroy the fighting spirit of our nation by means of air raids of appalling savagery. Citizens of Hiroshima—the losses may be great, but this is war! Undeterred by any eventuality, we are already devising relief and reconstruction measures, and the Army is providing us incalculable aid. Go back to work without delay—not a day must be lost in waging the struggle!"

It was August 9 when I put this notice up on the board—not long before the moment, between 10:50 and 11:00 in the morning, when the second bomb fell on Nagasaki. I only realized this after I had seen a bulletin about the Nagasaki bombing and had heard a detailed report. By then, someone in an idle moment had penciled a ring around the word "incalculable" in the sentence "the Army is providing incalculable aid." The next day, the notice had gone, torn down by unknown hands. On the painted board where it had been, someone had penciled in large letters: "You can't wage war on an empty stomach!"

(The manager must have noticed the writing too, but he said nothing. Nor did I rub it out. It stayed there until August 15, then, after the imperial message ending the war, I found it had gone—rubbed out with a cloth, as far as I could tell. The penciled ring, the writing, and the way the same writing had been erased all seemed to me to epitomize the feelings of the factory workers during the war.)

I drank three glasses of alcohol with water and ate my fried mulberry leaves. It was the first drink I had had in ages, and I got slightly drunk. Yet somehow I couldn't get into the right mood. The manager drank three times as much as me. The more he drank, the paler he got, and the more savagely he attacked Lieutenant Sasatake at the Clothing Depot and all his ways. We had both had the bitter experience of being forced to grovel before the people at the Clothing Depot in order to keep the factory running smoothly. One hated oneself for the way it brought out the meaner human qualities. To them, we must have seemed like so many funny little wooden puppets, moving at their bidding.

The manager emptied his bowl of boiled barley quite clean, then started to take his leave. As he was going, he suddenly announced with a kind of grim abandon that he was going to sell his best national uniform on the black market tomorrow. Then, plumping himself down on the step in the entrance, he observed, with the cheerful inconsequence of the blind drunk, that it was exactly the same as the uniform the members of some new religious organization had been wearing for years. In the garden of the religious organization's headquarters, he announced next, he had seen a bunting's nest, with the parent birds busily bringing grubs for their young.

"Say—" he demanded abruptly in a loud voice, rolling up the sleeves of his kimono like a workman. "D'you know what the bunting says when he sings? I'll tell you—he says *Just a line or two*, that's what." He turned to Yasuko. "Now, young lady, when you get home, be sure to write me a letter like that—*Just a line or two*."

"I certainly will, Mr. Fujita" said Yasuko. "But the buntings where *I* come from sing *Bring a cup, big boy, let's have some vinegar*."

"Come off it, now—that's far too long."

"When I was a *little* girl, though, they used to go *Cheep, cheep, twenty-eight days*."

"Good! That's much shorter!" He got unsteadily to his feet, and took his leave.

When I was a child, too, the buntings had always said, *Cheep, cheep, twenty-eight days*. The children used to imitate it. They'd repeat the phrase over and over again, and at the end they'd chant: *Carrots and burdock are fit for a pig, Fried bean curd twists but it's better big*. To this day, I have no idea what it meant.

CHAPTER 20 ✒

August 14. Cloudy, later fine.
Shigeko and Yasuko set off for our home in Jinseki county at a
little after five in the morning, leaving me with a letter for our
landlord. I made them take some parched rice to eat on the way,
together with a little salt and a flask of water. There was absolutely
nothing else in the way of food or drink in the house. According
to regulations, they should have got a certificate from the head of
the neighborhood association, showing that they had been bombed
out, but they went without as they were taking the train north via
Kabe and Shiomachi without passing through Hiroshima. No
restrictions were being placed on people traveling away from the
ruined city.

I went back to sleep after seeing them off, but dreamed that a
one-legged man in a kimono too long for him came hopping after

me with a long spoon over his shoulder, and woke up. I was sweating slightly. Taking off my nightwear in order to dress for going to work, I found I was wearing my wife's red belt and her bathrobe. After the manager had gone home the night before, I had cleared the table and gone straight to bed, but finding that Shigeko and Yasuko had taken my undershirt and night kimono to wash in the stream at the back, I must have put on whatever came to hand.

The one-and-a-half pint bottle was still one-third full. Should I drink it or not? I took out the cork, smelt it, put the cork back again, went to the kitchen, and was looking for a glass when an air raid alert sounded.

A few days previously, the West Japan Army authorities had issued a warning that the entrances to air raid shelters should be covered and exposure of the body avoided, since the enemy bomb depended for its main effect on blast and a wave of intense heat. They also said that one should take cover even when there were only one or two enemy planes. Unfortunately, our landlord's shelter was a simple hole dug in the ground. I went outside, but could see no sign of a plane, either in the sky between the hills in the Kabe direction or in the direction of Hiroshima. I locked up, and set off in the direction of the works. Now, though, the air raid warning sounded, and I heard a number of explosions like bombs falling. The ground shook. "Iwakuni!" I heard someone shout in a house by the roadside. I walked past the workers' dormitory and into the office building. Not a soul was there yet. At a loss for something to do, I put a cigarette butt into a small-bowled pipe, and was smoking it when two or three of the factory girls came rushing along. "Good morning, Mr. Shizuma," they said, all out of breath. "What's up?"

"Nothing special," I said. "Why—is something wrong?"

"The dormitory superintendent told us to come and ask what's happened. He said something *must* have happened, as you had arrived at work in such a hurry, and we were to come and ask you."

As they were talking, another three or four factory hands came up with uneasy looks. "Good morning, sir," they said. "Has something serious happened?" One of them went on, "The noise during the raid a while ago was ordinary bombs, I think. Everybody's saying it was Iwakuni, actually. . . ."

I felt awkward. "Nothing unusual's happened," I said. "I'm going to Kai Station to negotiate for some coal today. I came to get something to take for my lunch." It was the first thing that came into my head, but I decided privately that I really would try going to Kai Station.

They were right, I reflected: it was unnaturally early for me to come to work. I should have known better than to behave so irregularly. Before, when I was commuting from Hiroshima, I had arrived at the works between twelve and twelve-thirty on as many as twenty-seven or twenty-eight days in a month. Why did I have to arrive in the early morning today of all days? Small wonder it had made the workers nervy. Ever since the Hiroshima bomb, no one had known just when the enemy might land, or the whole nation be called to lay down its life, and at heart the factory workers must be just as frightened as I was. The trouble was that all of us, spiritually, were bound hand and foot, and fiercely suppressed every urge to express anxiety, let alone dissatisfaction. Such was the power of the state.

Breakfast consisted of boiled barley with bran, and bean paste soup with chopped parsley; the lunch I was given to take with me consisted of cakes of the same boiled barley, together with some shellfish boiled in soy. Normally, one didn't eat parsley after April because of the leech eggs and grubs that stuck to it. An elderly worker called Tanaka, sitting next to me, said to the woman who brought the food:

"Did you boil this soup well?"

"Yes, twice as long as usual," she said.

"What's the shellfish in my lunch?" I put in, "Clams?"

"No, they're *shiofuki*. The black market woman brought some boiled in seawater, so the cook did them down in soy. Everybody's getting them for lunch."

In the fishing towns along the Miyajima line—so Tanaka told me—they'd taken to cooking *shiofuki* in seawater, or pounding them into a paste and making round cakes of them, for sale on the black market. They used seawater because their official salt ration also went on the black market. Salt was growing more precious every day. If you went too many days without salt—according to Tanaka—a fly could settle on your right hand and your left hand would be too weak to swat it.

I set off for Kai. As on the previous morning, the columns of smoke from the funeral pyres grew steadily fewer as we passed from Furuichi, through Gion and Yamamoto, and on to the ruined city. Again, the only way of getting from Yamamoto to Yokogawa was on foot. It is only one stop from Yokogawa to Kai-machi, so I walked along the tracks. I had no definite knowledge of any coal train on the sidings at Kai Station, but such was my sense of urgency that I felt I was chasing after my own shadow, which fell faintly on the ties ahead of me.

Glancing back for no particular reason, I suddenly saw a white rainbow, stretching across the morning sun that gleamed dully in the thinly clouded sky. A rarity of rarities. I clearly remembered marveling, as a child, at a silver rainbow seen late one night stretching into the sky from the near side of the hills, but this was the first time I had seen one in the daytime.

At Kai Station, the stationmaster and his assistants were holding an emergency conference. I decided to wait until they were through. The walls of the waiting room were plastered with inquiries for missing persons, and a member of the military police was going round inspecting each of them in turn. There was something self-important about his appearance that irritated me.

Every bench without exception was occupied by raid victims. On the one nearest the ticket barrier, two children were sprawled on their backs completely naked, with not so much as a pair of underpants between them. An old man and woman, their eyes closed, were squatting beside them. The old man's face was turned towards the children, and occasionally he would half open his eyes. The old couple, I suspected, had been left with their grandchildren, with no resources and no one to turn to.

The stationmaster's conference ended before long, and an "up" train passed through carrying a formidable load of passengers. No coal wagons were attached to it. I secured an interview with the stationmaster and asked him about coal trains, but he told me that not one had arrived since August 6, nor had there been any word about the next arrival. Since the sixth of the month, it had been all they could do to transport passengers; freight trains were out of the question for the time being.

The only thing I could do was to explain how things were with our firm and beg the stationmaster and his assistant, as eloquently as I knew how, to make inquiries over the railway phone as to when the next shipment might be expected. As I was talking, the military policeman came into the room without a word, and clumped around the room scrutinizing each of the notices on the walls. Finally he went out again, still without saying anything. In all probability he had been sent from some unit in another district to inquire into the state of public morale in Hiroshima. He wore a sergeant's badge.

"Quite human, for a military policeman, wasn't he?" said one of the assistants. The stationmaster said nothing. The policeman had, in fact, been comparatively mild for one of his kind. It struck me that, ever since the bomb, the military had been uncertain whether they could throw their weight around as much as they had done before.

The stationmaster agreed in general terms to my request and I took my leave, promising to come back in a day or two's time to find what had happened.

Here too, the houses still standing in the streets were "standing," but that was all. Bricks had been blown away, eaves were tilting, and not a single pane of glass was left in the windows. Even the window frames were askew and looked as though they would not open. Some families had had to remove the sliding doors facing the street so that they could get in and out.

I walked back along the main road that skirted the higher, residential districts. On the way, near the road, I noticed a house of painted board. From its modern, Western-style entrance ten or more bomb victims were spilling out onto the road. All were injured, with congealed blood on their wounds; some had faces swollen like balloons, other had scorched hair, others only the barest indications of human features. There was no noticeboard outside, but I took it to be a doctor's residence. The office, I realized, was full, and these people were awaiting their turn. They were people who had failed to get into a reception center, or who lacked the strength or the will to get themselves herded in with all the rest.

I hurried past. I saw several more injured in the entrance of another building that looked like a warehouse. They were all lying flat out on the ground, but among them was a child holding its hand up in the air. Again, I hurried past as quickly as I could.

The cloth I was using to wipe myself with was black with sweat and grime. Thinking to wash my face, I walked along a road next to some paddy fields, but none of them had any water left. The irrigation canals had dried up too, and the dead loach that lay piled up in hollows in the muddy beds were almost all reduced to bones by now. I saw a sparrow lying dead by the canal. Part of its wings were burned, and it gave off the familiar stench of corruption. It was lying with its body half plunged into the mud, at an angle, with a trail behind it as though it had slid some seven or eight inches. Unlike the pigeon I had caught by the lotus pond, it had not escaped, it seemed, but had been slammed down into the mud at the instant of the blast.

I ate my lunch as I walked through the paddy fields. I was near the hills now, and I could see the smoke rising from the crematoria.

Back at the works, I found the manager drinking cold barley tea in the canteen with several of the factory hands. Everybody had an unusually pensive air.

I reported to him, avoiding any mention of the previous night's party in front of the men. "I asked the stationmaster at Kai to contact them about the coal," I said. "They'll know something, for better or for worse, by tomorrow or the day after. At least, I'm fairly sure they will."

"Thank you," the manager said glumly. "Incidentally, Shizuma, how do people in Hiroshima interpret it?"

"I didn't go into Hiroshima today," I said. "But what do you mean—interpret what?"

"The important broadcast tomorrow, of course. The radio said there'd be an important broadcast beginning at noon tomorrow. We were just wondering what it could be about."

I felt a faint tingling at the tip of my tongue. I had no idea what the "important broadcast" was, but most likely it meant either peace talks, or surrender, or an armistice. Calls for last-ditch stands on Japanese soil were too familiar by now to warrant a special broadcast.

The workers tended to stay silent, but occasionally one of them would suddenly start speaking as though something had just occurred to him. Someone would answer, then another would chime in, and another respond in turn. The result was disconnected, but the general drift was as follows.

Another squadron of enemy planes had flown over that day unmolested, but they had dropped no bombs, and none of our guns had fired at them either. Nor had our guns fired at them yesterday. With the exception of the raid on Iwakuni today, things had been different during the past two or three days. It probably meant that the powers-that-be had already come to some kind of terms with the enemy, and were going to make them public at noon tomorrow. Even so, neither a peace conference nor an armistice seemed very probable, considering the way enemy planes were flying about as though they owned the place. The only possibility, therefore, was surrender, which would probably mean that the enemy—just as the Japanese Army had done in places it occupied overseas—would land in Japan, occupy the harbors, and disarm all Japan's armed forces. . . . Or could it be that the important broadcast was going to be a declaration of war on the Soviet Union? If so, it was tantamount to Japan's taking on most of the world singlehanded. What was going to happen to Japanese forces serving overseas? To civilians at home? So far, it had seemed that no life could be worse than that of the moment, but if it was a question of the whole nation being wiped out, a man was ready to do his bit. (Just what that bit was, though, no one was quite sure.) The enemy had military might on his side. In all likelihood, every single Japanese male would be castrated. . . . Wouldn't it have been possible to surrender before the bomb had been dropped? No—it was because the bomb was dropped that Japan was surrendering. Even so, the enemy must have known that Japan was beaten already; it was hardly necessary to drop the bomb. Either way, those responsible for setting up the organization that had started this war. . . .

At this point, the conversation threatened to stray into forbidden territory, and conjecture went no farther.

ᵧI recounted to the manager again my dealings at Kai Station.

"Well," he said, "Perhaps you'd get the documents for submission to the Kai stationmaster ready by noon tomorrow, would you? There's this important broadcast coming, and I want everything down in writing so that things are all cut-and-dried, whoever cares to investigate later on. We don't want any misunderstandings such as we had before, do we? That's an order from the manager, by the way." He spoke very clearly, so that the workers nearby could hear too.

The "misunderstanding" we'd had before had occurred in the spring, when a carload of coal had been sent to another firm by mistake and we'd been suspected of letting them have coal on the quiet. Later, it was proved to have been a mere mistake, but for a while the Coal Control Company had tried to find a scapegoat at our works.

I told the manager and the factory hands about the white rainbow I'd seen on my way to Kai. "Well—so you've seen one too!" exclaimed the manager, giving the table a great thump. "I saw one too when I was in Tokyo, on the day before the Feburary 6 Incident. A white rainbow, mark you."

His rainbow, like mine, had crossed the sun horizontally. He'd been walking near the Imperial Palace at about eleven in the morning on the day before the incident, and he'd told himself the sea must be rough that day, as hundreds of gulls were gathered on the palace moat. It was late February, and there was a flock of wild ducks on the embankment too, but the number of gulls was quite extraordinary—it might have been hundreds, or even thousands. He was thinking how strange this was when—stranger still —he had seen the white rainbow in the sky, cutting across the middle of the sun.

"It's an omen, you see," the manager said in all seriousness, "an omen of something unpleasant. The very next day, the February 6 Incident occurred, so the omen obviously appears the day before it happens. When I told one of the high-ups at a government office that I'd just seen a white rainbow, he was shocked. A 'white rainbow that pierces the sun'—it was a sign from heaven that armed disturbance was imminent, he said. It's apparently a quotation from the life of somebody or other in the Chinese *Book of History*. I told myself it was a lot of nonsense, but at dawn next day the trouble started."

"The one I saw was narrow," I said, "and it kind of skewered the sun."

"That's right—it's not very wide, but it's very streamlined, and white. I'm not being superstitious, but a white rainbow bodes nobody any good. There's no doubt about it, it appears to me."

I'd been walking all day, and was tired. I decided to do the documents about the coal trains the next morning, and had supper in the canteen with the manager and the factory hands.

"There's some of last night's alcohol left," I informed the manager privately. "Fine!" he said. "That's real news! I may be along tomorrow evening, depending on how the important broadcast turns out."

August 15. Fine.
My tiredness the night before must have made me sleep particularly soundly, for I woke up early. It seemed that the time for me to set off for the works canteen would never come. As usual, I drank some water in the attempt to deceive my stomach. Even when I was ready it was still too early, so I sat myself down in the entrance hall to wait. I was still there when the old gentleman who owned the house appeared.

"What would this 'important broadcast' be, now?" he asked,

handing me something wrapped in a piece of newspaper. It was some coffee beans from Brazil, he explained. His nephew, who had gone to work in Brazil twenty years ago, had sent them a few years back. He hadn't known how you ate them, so he'd been keeping them in a paper bag tucked away in a closet. I myself had never seen real coffee beans before, and had no idea how to roast or grind them, but I accepted them gratefully, and, calling up something the manager had once told me, said, "I wonder if these are the mocha or a Brazilian variety? They say the most common kind being cultivated in Brazil these days is a hybrid of the two strains, don't they?"

The old man had not come to see me under any impression that I was well versed in the progress of the war. He was simply disturbed about the important broadcast, and wanted someone to talk to. I was strictly noncommittal in expressing my views.

He told me that fish were still dying in the Temma River in Hiroshima. They weakened and floated to the surface, belly uppermost, and if you took them in your hand the scales came off and the dorsal fins fell out. Most of the carp in the lake at Asano had been killed outright in the raid, but now some of those that had survived were losing their scales and beginning to swim groggily. He'd also heard that people who'd walked about the ruins without having been in the bombing itself were getting blotches on their skin, or losing their hair, or finding their teeth coming loose.

As for myself, there was no telling what the future would bring, but at the moment I could tug at my hair without it coming out, and there were no blotches on my skin. Nor was there anything wrong with my teeth. (Two years after the raid, though, when I'd begun to think I was safe, two of my teeth began to wobble, and I found that I could pull them out without any trouble. Next, four others began to move, and I took them out myself, without the slightest pain, simply by holding them in my fingers and tugging. Today, I have a complete set of false teeth in my upper jaw. If I tire myself with manual work, I get eruptions the size of beans on my scalp. Shōkichi, who had started the carp farming with us, had all his teeth fall out, quite painlessly, in a space of two months the year after the bomb, and now has nothing but false teeth in both his lower and his upper jaws. Shōkichi's upper gum is so low that it's almost flush with the roof of his mouth, and the dentist made the plate of his false teeth as high as was technically feasible, so as to improve the appearance of his lips. Even so, the upper lip still looked as though it was turning inward, into his mouth, so he grew a mustache, which he still has. It's a fine, bushy, manly mustache. Sometimes the villagers, who ought to know the story behind it perfectly well, forget and say that Shōkichi has a mustache above his station. As far as Shōkichi is concerned, though, social vanity plays no part in it at all. He is the most humble and worthy of men, and I hereby speak up on his behalf.)

When the old man had gone, I set off for the works, had breakfast with everybody else in the canteen, then set about drawing up the required papers—the documents to be submitted, at the manager's orders, to the stationmaster at Kai. A great deal of thought was required, since, besides setting down the amount of coal the firm needed for one week and our production figures for clothing, I also had to give a minute account of our recent negotiations at the Hiroshima Branch Clothing Depot, as well as the state of nonexistence affecting the Coal Control Company. It would not do for me to say that the officer in charge of coal rations at the Clothing Depot was irresponsible. On the other hand, if I said he had cooperated with us, our appeal would lose all its effect. It took me much labor to produce the necessary periphrases and evasion. I decided to intersperse the text with a few purple patches, too; "in such a grave emergency"—went one of my better efforts —"a lump of coal is the equivalent of a drop of blood." With the Control Company gone, personnel and all, and a system of controls still in effect, to write like that was probably the only policy that offered any hope.

I had finished the papers and was reading over what I had written when the sound of the factory machinery suddenly stopped dead. It was five minutes to twelve, time for the important broadcast. I put the documents in a drawer, and went out into the corridor. I ran down the stairs, then, on a sudden impulse, turned out through the emergency exit into the courtyard at the back. The works radio was in the canteen, but I shrank from the important events that the words emerging from it would initiate. The feeling was just the reverse of the common compulsion to look at something one is afraid of. Everybody seemed to be walking along the corridors in the direction of the canteen, and the dull murmur of their footsteps came to me where I stood.

The courtyard was silent and deserted. Three sides were enclosed by company buildings, while the other faced the slope of a hill where oak trees grew. An irrigation canal some six feet wide flowed from among the oaks into the courtyard and out again via the gap between the office building and the building housing the engineering section, bringing a cool breeze with it. The damp soil on this side of the canal had thick-growing clumps of moss and liverwort, and beyond the canal I could see a cluster of tall plants with small, pink flowers. Here and there, there were tall white flowers with large yellow pistils.

I peered into the office from outside, but there was nobody there. I considered going to the canteen, but changed my mind. I looked into the factory hands' room: nobody. Putting my nose in at the back door of the improvised kitchen next to the office, I saw a large kettle boiling on a stove, its lid leaping merrily. The clerks who brought their own lunches had obviously put it on to boil, then gone off to listen to the radio, leaving it untended.

The broadcast had begun, but all I could hear from the courtyard was fragments of speech in a low voice. I made no effort to follow the sense, but walked up and down by the canal, occasionally stopping and standing still for a moment. The canal had solid stone banks about six feet deep, and the bed was flat and paved all over with stones. The water was shallow, but absolutely clear, and the effect was immensely refreshing.

How had I never realized there was such an attractive stream so near at hand? In the water, I could see a procession of baby eels swimming blithely upstream against the current. It was remarkable to watch them: a myriad of tiny eels, still at the larval stage, none of them more than three or four inches in length.

"On you go, on up the stream!" I said to them encouragingly. "You can smell fresh water, I'll be bound!" Still they came on unendingly, battling their way upstream in countless numbers. They must have swum all the way up from the lower reaches of the river at Hiroshima. Newborn eels usually swim into the rivers from the sea in mid-May. Within the first mile from the estuary they are still flat and transparent, like willow leaves, and the fishermen of the bays around Hiroshima call them "sardine eels," because of their likeness to sardine fry. By the time they reached here, though, they looked like real eels, about as big as a large loach but far slenderer and more graceful in their movements. I wondered where they had been swimming on August 6, when Hiroshima had been bombed. I squatted down by the edge of the canal and compared their backs, but all I saw was different shades of gray. None of them showed any signs of harm.

I wondered if one could fish for them, and if so what kind of bait they'd take. I walked away, and was making my way back towards the emergency exit when a factory hand emerged from the door and came jogging past me.

"What's up?" I called. He swung round, but glanced at me unseeingly and started running towards the kitchen. Everything about him—the way he clutched his working cap in his hand, the stiff, awkward way he broke into a run—told me that something was very wrong.

I walked along the corridor towards the canteen. A stream of workers passed me, their expressions grimmer than I had ever seen them before. Some of the male hands were crying. Some of the girls had covered their faces with their work hats. One of a group of several factory girls making their way back to their dormitory had her arm around her companion's shoulder and was saying soothingly, "Don't cry, dear! There won't be any more raids now, will there?"

Tears started into my own eyes. Ashamed to be seen weeping, I stopped to wash my hands at the stone washbasin by the entrance to the canteen. A middle-aged kitchen helper who had just finished setting the table came up to me. "Oh Mr. Shizuma," she began, bowing formally in the manner of one who offers condolences, "I really don't know what to say at a time like this. You know, I may not be much—I'm only a poor old woman—but I feel so sad, and so angry. . . . I don't want. . . ." Her voice faltered. "Oh dear. . . ."

For all that, she was not crying. My own tears had dried up, too. If the truth be told, I suspect they had not been tears genuinely shed for that moment—that moment, shortly after noon, on a particular day of a particular month—but for something quite different. They reminded me of the time when I was very small, and used to go out to play around our house. At those times I was often tormented by a village lout, almost a half-wit, called Yōichi, but I would never let myself weep in front of him. No—I would run home instead, and badger my mother into baring her breast for me; and it was only then, at the sight of that familiar haven, that I burst into tears at last. Even now, I can still remember the salty taste of her milk. The tears I shed were tears of relief, and I believe that my tears this day were of the same kind.

In the canteen, a bare twenty or so people were at the table, including the manager and staff members. All were getting on in years, and they sat still and silent, like rows of stone Buddhas. A young kitchen helper was standing with a cloth in her hand, beneath the short curtain that hung over the entrance to the kitchen, looking as though she had just been reprimanded.

"Mr. Fujita—I got those papers done at last," I said, lowering myself into a seat opposite him. "It seems it's surrender, doesn't it?"

"It looks like it," he replied with unexpected crispness. "The Emperor just broadcast a message. The radio's not working properly, though. One of the hands tried to adjust it, but the more he tinkered with it the worse it got, and we couldn't hear very well. But it seems like surrender, all right."

The bowls of boiled barley with bran were all dry on top, and the flies were gathering on them. There were some shellfish stewed in soy, and they were collecting flies, too. Nobody moved to shoo the flies away.

"Well, everybody," said the manager with forced heartiness.

"Let's cheer up and eat, shall we? Hey, miss—bring us some pickled plums, will you? Count them before you bring them so that there's enough for three each all around. By tomorrow, the enemy forces may be in charge of the works, and then I shan't have any say in these matters."

Nobody said anything, but the manager picked up his chopsticks, so we all followed suit. We each got three pickled plums. Following the manager's example, I put my three on top of the boiled barley, poured tea over the lot, and stirred it well with my chopsticks before eating. Halfway through, as I was pouring in more tea, I saw there was only one plum in the bottom of the bowl. The other two had disappeared. I had no recollection of spitting out the stones, and I couldn't have eaten them without at least some faint recollection of doing so. In short, I must have swallowed them whole with the barley. I ran my hand over my throat, but there was no sign of anything stuck. They were on the large side, too. . . .

After the meal, a factory hand called Yoda suddenly claimed that the Imperial broadcast had been an exhortation to the nation to fight still harder. Everyone looked tense for a while, and neither the manager nor the staff members made any move to leave the table. Then, abruptly, somebody shouted, "Irresponsible rumor!" Encouraged by this, an official from the works section called Nakanishi declared that he had heard His Majesty say quite distinctly, "Should hostilities continue any further, the final result. . . ."

"Me too," said the manager. "I'm not absolutely sure, but I must say that's how it sounded to me."

Two or three of the others confirmed that that was what His Majesty had said. If they were right, no amount of imagination could turn it into a call to fight harder. Finally, everybody agreed that Japan had really been defeated. The defeat was confirmed over the radio at five that afternoon. (A printed copy of the Imperial message that I saw later said:

"The enemy is using a new and savage bomb to kill and maim innocent victims and inflict incalculable damage. Moreover, should hostilities continue any further, the final result would be to bring about not only the annihilation of the Japanese race, but the destruction of human civilization as a whole. . . .")

I fetched the papers from the office to the canteen and had the manager stamp them with his seal. In fact, now that we had lost the war, a factory making clothing for the military had no reason left for existence. Nor was there any point in my going to Kai Station.

"Where shall I keep these documents?" I asked the manager. "I'll take them and put them in the safe," he said. "Remember I've got them, now." He took them from me, and left the table.

I too left the canteen and, passing through the emergency exit, went into the back courtyard to take one more look at the baby eels on their way upstream. This time, I approached the canal particularly carefully, treading gently so as to make no noise. But now not a single baby eel was in sight, and the waters of the stream ran clear and empty.

The transcription of the "Journal of the Bombing" was finished. Nothing remained but to read it over and give it a cardboard cover.

The following afternoon, Shigematsu went to inspect the hatchery ponds. The *aiko* were coming along well, and in a shallow corner of the larger pond some water weed was growing. Shōkichi had probably planted it there; he must have got it from the Benten pond at Shiroyama. Its oval, shiny green leaves dotted the surface of the water, and from their midst rose a slender stalk on which a small, dark purple flower was in bloom.

Shigematsu looked up. "If a rainbow appears over those hills now, a miracle will happen," he prophesied to himself. "Let a rainbow appear—not a white one, but one of many hues—and Yasuko will be cured."

So he told himself, with his eyes on the nearby hills, though he knew all the while it could never come true.

Japan's Modern Writers

SUN AND STEEL

Yukio Mishima
Translated by John Bester

Part autobiography and part reflection. "His literary testament."
—*The Times Literary Supplement*

PB, ISBN 0-87011-425-5, 108 pages

A WILD SHEEP CHASE   A Novel

Haruki Murakami
Translated by Alfred Birnbaum

"Haruki Murakami is a mythmaker for the millennium, a wiseacre wise man." —*The New York Times Book Review*

PB, ISBN 4-7700-1706-5, 312 pages

ALMOST TRANSPARENT BLUE

Ryu Murakami
Translated by Nancy Andrew

"A Japanese mix of *A Clockwork Orange* and *L'Etranger*."
—*Newsweek*

PB, ISBN 0-87011-469-7, 128 pages

H   A Hiroshima Novel

Makoto Oda
Translated by D.H. Whittaker

A surreal universe of people of varying racial and ethnic backgrounds struggle against the desecration of society and the environment symbolized by the first atomic bomb.

PB, ISBN 4-7700-1947-5, 218 pages

THE SILENT CRY

Kenzaburo Oe
Translated by John Bester

Awarded the 1994 Nobel Prize
"A major feat of the imagination." —*The Times*

PB, ISBN 0-87011-466-2, 288 pages

Japan's Women Writers

THE DOCTOR'S WIFE

Sawako Ariyoshi
Translated by Wakako Hironaka and Ann Siller Kostant

Japan's leading woman writer focuses on the role of women in Japanese society. "An excellent story."—*Choice*

PB, ISBN 0-87011-465-4, 184 pages

THE RIVER KI

Sawako Ariyoshi
Translated by Mildred Tahara

"A powerful novel written with convincing realism."—*Japan Quarterly*

PB, ISBN 0-87011-514-6, 248 pages

THE TWILIGHT YEARS

Sawako Ariyoshi
Translated by Mildred Tahara

"Linger[s] in the mind long after the story has ended." —*The New York Times*

PB, ISBN 0-87011-852-8, 216 pages

THE WAITING YEARS

Fumiko Enchi
Translated by John Bester

"Absorbing, sensitive, and utterly heartrending." —Charles Beardsley

PB, ISBN 0-87011-424-7, 208 pages

REQUIEM A Novel

Shizuko Go
Translated by Geraldine Harcourt

A bestseller in Japanese, this moving requiem for the war victims voiced the feelings of a generation of women. "Unforgettable and devastating." —Susan Griffin

PB, ISBN 4-7700-1618-2, 132 pages

THE PHOENIX TREE AND OTHER STORIES

Satoko Kizaki
Translated by Carol A. Flath

Women in search of home and a sense of self — caught between tradition and a need to define themselves in the modern world.

PB, ISBN 4-7700-1790-1, 242 pages

Social Sciences and History

THE ANATOMY OF DEPENDENCE

Takeo Doi, M.D.
Translated by John Bester

A definitive analysis of *amae*, the indulging, passive love which supports an individual within a group, a key concept in Japanese psychology.

PB, ISBN 0-87011-494-8, 184 pages

THE ANATOMY OF SELF

The Individual Versus Society

Takeo Doi, M.D.
Translated by Mark A. Harbison

A fascinating exploration into the role of the individual in Japan, and Japanese concepts of self-awareness, communication, and relationships.

PB, ISBN 0-87011-902-8, 176 pages

BEYOND NATIONAL BORDERS

Kenichi Ohmae

"[Ohmae is] Japan's only management guru." — *Financial Times*

PB, ISBN 4-7700-1385-X , 144 pages
Available only in Japan.

THE BOOK OF TEA

Kakuzo Okakura
Foreword and Afterword by Soshitsu Sen XV

The seminal text on the meaning and practice of tea, illustrated with eight historic photographs.

PB, ISBN 4-7700-1542-9, 160 pages

THE COMPACT CULTURE

The Japanese Tradition of "Smaller is Better"

O-Young Lee
Translated by Robert N. Huey

A provocative study of Japan's tendency to make the most out of miniaturization, that reveals the essence of Japanese character.

PB, ISBN 4-7700-1543-3, 196 pages